Kerrigan's Copenhagen

A Love Story

also by

Thomas E. Kennedy

Novels

Crossing Borders (1990)
A Weather of the Eye (1996)
The Book of Angels (1997)

Short Story Collections

Unreal City (1996)
Drive, Dive Dance & Fight (1997)

Essay Collections

Realism and Other Illusions: Essays on the Craft of Fiction (2002)

Literary Criticism

Andre Dubus: A Study of the Short Fiction (1988)
Robert Coover: A Study of the Short Fiction (1992)
An Index to American Award Stories (1993)

Anthologies

New Danish Fiction (1995)
Small Gifts of Knowing: Contemporary Irish Writing (1997)
Stories and Sources (1998)
Poetry and Sources (2000)

Kerrigan's Copenhagen

A Love Story

Thomas E. Kennedy

Wynkin deWorde

2 0 0 2

Published in 2002
by

Wynkin
deWorde

Wynkin deWorde

PO Box 257, Tuam Road, Galway, Ireland
derhamroger@hotmail.com

A CIP catalogue record for this book is available from the British Library

ISBN: 0-9542607-1-6

Typeset by Patricia Hope, Skerries, Co. Dublin, Ireland.
Illustrations by Roger Derham (cover: an adaption of a Thomas E Kennedy photograph of Andreas Kolberg's Copenhagen statue, *The Drunken Faun.*)
Jacket Design by Design Direct, Galway, Ireland
Printed by Betaprint, Dublin, Ireland

Kerrigan's Copenhagen – A love Story

'He stands on his head, he stands on his belly
he stands on the table, glides up
in the air with his whole mighty body
as if he were the earth, as if he were the cork
in these bottles . . .'

– Jens August Schade, *The Painter Dances*

'Drunk I was, I was more than drunk
on the best kind of ale-drinking
when afterwards,
every man gets his mind back again.'

– Odin, *Sayings of the High One*

'And then, when I have swallowed down my dreams
In thirty, forty mugs of beer, I turn
to satisfy a need I can't ignore . . .
I piss into the skies, a soaring stream
that consecrates a patch of flowering fern.'

– Arthur Rimbaud, *Evening Prayer*

Acknowledgements

My deep and sincere thanks for their inspiration, encouragement and sustaining friendship to Duff Brenna, Walter Cummins, Greg Herriges, Susan Schwartz Senstad, Bob Stewart, David Applefield, Mike Lee, Rick Mulkey and Susan Tekulve.
And to Roger Derham and Valerie Shortland for their belief in this book, which has made all the difference.

Dedication

This could only be for Alice
But also for my brothers
George, Jerry, Jack
and always for Daniel and Isabel

and of course for Copenhagen, with love;
city of the ever-changing light.

“ ‘Are you an absolute libertine, then, sir?’
the judge enquired sternly. ‘Do you *never*
entertain the word *no*?’
‘Your eminence,’ replied Justin. ‘I have taken
upon myself an important and arduous vocation.
Let others say no. I have dedicated my life
as an assault against that ugly little word.’ ”

– T F Thondy, *The Life of Terrence Justin*

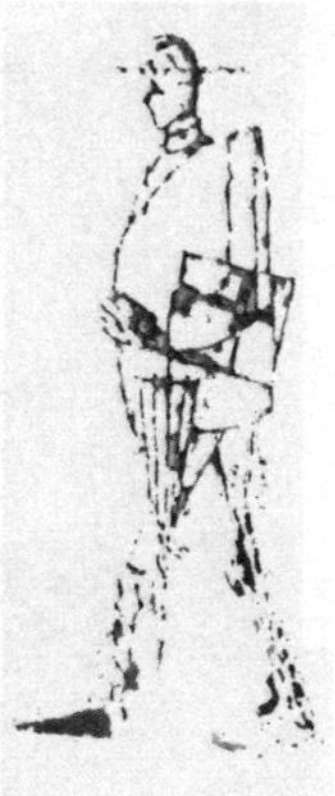

CONTENTS

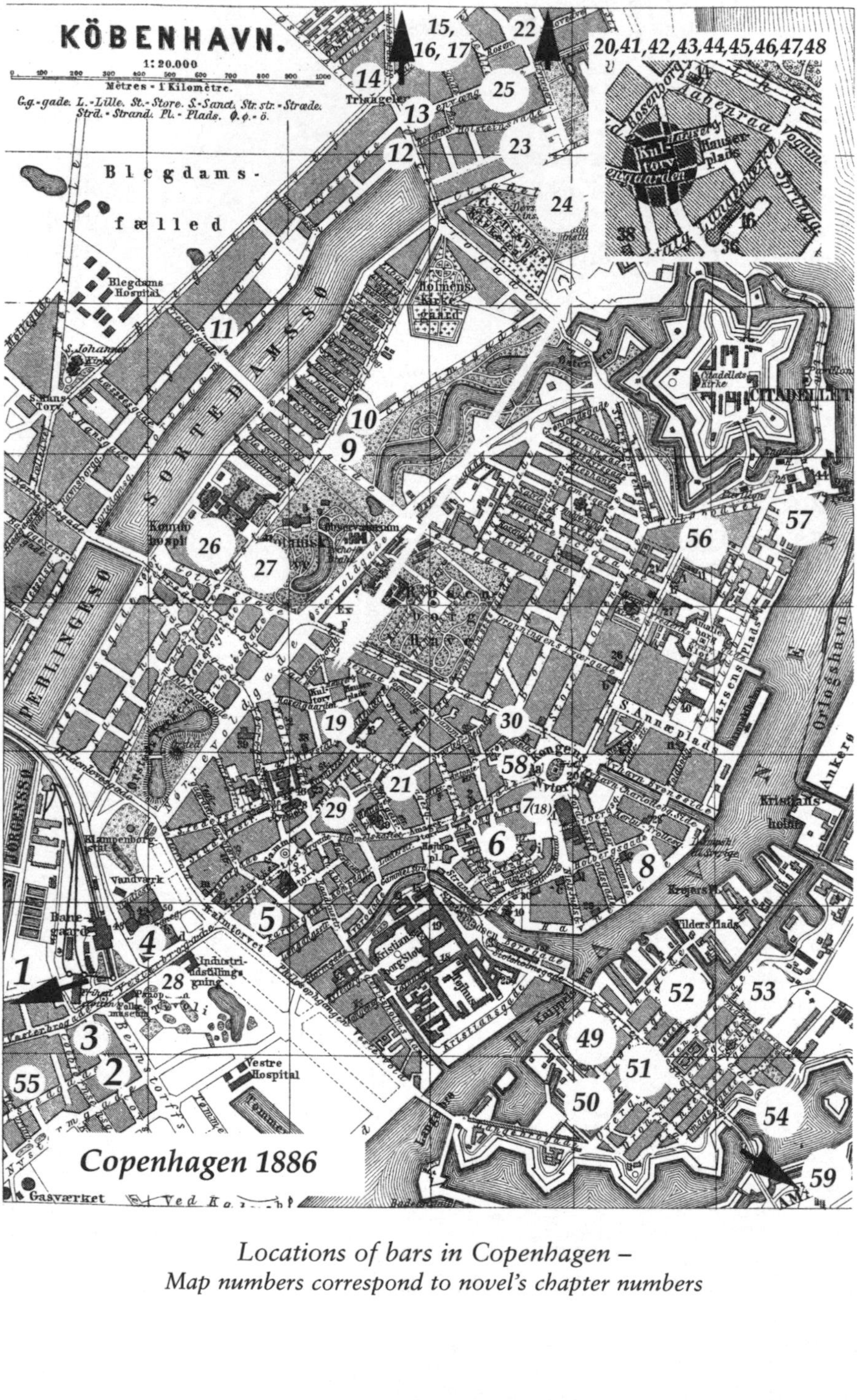

Locations of bars in Copenhagen –
Map numbers correspond to novel's chapter numbers

Kerrigan's Copenhagen – A Love Story

FOREPLAY

Terrence Einhorn Kerrigan is in love.

When his wife and children, after all those years, were taken from him, he told himself he would never love a woman again, and he never did, not in that way, which requires a surrender of the sovereign spirit. But a man must love nonetheless, and thus a love affair begins this story – a love affair with a city.

Here he has made his home, in a city whose moods are unpredictable, unfathomable, unimpeachable as a woman's, often still and dark, perfidious as its April weather – now light and sweet as the touch of a summer girl who fancies you, now cold as snow, false as ice, merciless as the howling, beating wind, now quietly enigmatic as the stirring of the great chestnut trees which line the banks of the lake beneath his windows.

The city is Copenhagen, the city of the Danish smile and blue eye, the Danish national character that one of its great unknown sons, Tom Kristensen, described in his great unknown 1930 novel *Hærværk*, made into the great unknown 1977 film *Havoc*, as 'false blue eyes and blond treachery'.

It is the city of Peter Boyesen who greets all happy boys from the wall of the city jail, and greets all happy girls when he is out. The city of a hundred vices and fifteen hundred serving houses, bars, cafés – more of them than one will ever come to know in a lifetime without a very major effort. Kerrigan has decided to make an effort. He came to Copenhagen, like Gilgamesh, driven by death to seek the land of eternal life, and like Gilgamesh, he kept meeting instead an Alewife who filled his glass and said,

> 'Kerrigan Kerrigan
> Wither rovest thou?
> The life you seek you will not find.
> When the gods created mankind
> Death for mankind they set aside.
> Thou, Kerrigan, let full be your belly.
> Make you merry by day and night.
> Of each day make thou a feast of rejoicing.
> Day and night dance and play!
> Let your garments be sparkling fresh,
> Your head be washed; bathe you in water!
> Pay heed to the little one that holds to your hand.
> Let your woman delight in your bosom.
> For this is the task of mankind!'

Kerrigan agrees, even if there are no little ones anymore, no woman. Gone. All, all gone. And that is how all stories end. Yet he knows no better city in which to follow the Alewife's bidding. He does not know precisely how many bars there are in Copenhagen. He has not yet decided how many of them he will visit over what time scale or how many of them he will include in his book. He has no idea what might happen in each of the places he visits, what adventures he might encounter, what dark nights of the soul he might descend to, what radiant bodies he might win with a flattering tongue.
And this is good, he decides.

DAY ONE

Across the street from paradise

'Terence, this is stupid stuff
You eat your victuals fast enough
But nothing much amiss tis clear
To see the rate you drink your beer
And oh good lord the verse you make
It gives a chap the bellyache . . .
Ale, man, ale's the stuff to drink
For fellows whom it hurts to think.'

– A E Housman

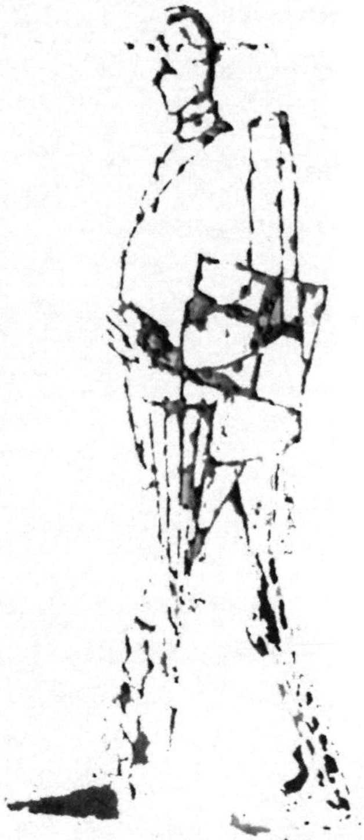

1

Wine Room 90 *(Vinstuen 90'eren)*

Vinstuen 90'eren
Gammel Kongevej *(Old King's Road)* **90**
2000 Frederiksberg
København

The front window of this noble wine room tells us it was established in 1916 – the middle year of the first great war, World War I, in which Denmark declined to participate as a nation, although 30,000 of her men chose to – on which side is another matter. Lettered on the plate window is a promise of 'Well poured draft beer'.

The promise is in the process of being kept.

Kerrigan sits there on the edge of the turning millennium with his back to the red wall, glancing obliquely through the obverse lettering on the window, waiting for the completion of the lengthy tapping process of his first pint of the day. To pass the time, he lights a small Sumatra, stirs his tongue around the parched sourness of his mouth. A narrow shelf along the wall supports a slender white vase from whose mouth projects the face of a wilted rose, blackened petals – dry as his palate.

Beside the vase is propped his leather zip-satchel containing notes, a dog-eared copy of Joyce's *Finnegans Wake* which he once again has been trying to read, reassured somewhat by Seamus

Deane's assurance that the book truly *is* unreadable and boring. Already, however, it has led him to discover Giambattista Vico (1668-1744), who greatly inspired Joyce. Vico held that while a philosophical system divorced from reality could be perfectly apprehended, the reality of life could only be imperfectly so, yet he chose the latter and the study of the universal principles underlying the history of nations. Joyce put this into practice in his novel about a sleeping man dreaming the history of the world, the fall from prelingual Grace into imperfect language, from world to word, between which is an 'L' of a difference. The sin, it seemed, occurred in the Eden of Phoenix Park, inside the main, eastern gate of which stands a tall obelisk erected in 1817 in honor of the Dublin-born Brit, Arthur Wellesby, Duke of Wellington, who in 1807 brutally bombarded Copenhagen with much death and destruction, and where in Joyce's *Finnegans Wake*, a father and a daughter exposed to one another the physical difference between them.

Or as Louis Simpson put it:

> 'We huddled in the corners of the stair,
> And then we climbed it. What had we to lose?
> What could we gain? The best way to compare
> And quickest, was by taking off our clothes.
> O, we loved long and happily, God knows!'

However, Kerrigan is baffled by the seeming current rash of incest and child abuse. Could it be true? Has it always been so, only covered over? Why has Nabokov's *Lolita* such enduring interest? As someone once said, 'When a great book is also a popular book, the popularity is invariably based on a misunderstanding.'

Yet paradise is quite another matter. The paradise of man and woman naked to one another's sight could hardly be a sin.

Kerrigan draws meditatively on his agreeably bitter Sumatra, thinking about paradise. If in Dublin it was Phoenix Park where might it be in Copenhagen? *Ørstedsparken*, Ørsted Park? Gay.

No differences to expose. *Fælledparken*, the Commons? Perhaps Christiania, the Free State, squatter -inhabited military complex? Perhaps.

Then he thinks of the lakes where he lives and recalls his first visit to Copenhagen two decades before when, strolling round the city lakes, he saw a purely blond, purely naked young woman sunning herself on the sloped bank of *Sortedamsø*, Black Dam Lake, the sunlight golden in the redgold hair arranged around her shoulders like a fan, patched at her rounded belly, like a fleece. He never told his wife. He only knew he would be back.

The lakes, then! Let it be the lakes. He remembers then flying over India in a jet once, and seeing the shadow of his plane moving along the yellow earth beside the silver thread of the Ganges. How quaint is a river in the age of a jet. How deep the stagnant lake where 'full fathom five' my father lies about it all.

Across from him sits his Research Associate, a handsome woman of seven and fifty years who in her youth was a beauty. A little rack of advertising postcards beside the door displays a naked dwarf, a copy of a shop sign that says *Yes, we are open*, a print of Magritte's perfectly rendered, realistic pipe entitled, *Ceci n'est pas un pipe*. No, it's not; it's a picture. Or is it about the relationship between word and picture? Both? No, it is about the fact that art and life are two different things. A picture of a pipe, no matter how realistic and recognizable, is not a pipe but an arrangement of pigments and a character in a fiction is not a person but an arrangement of words.

It takes ten minutes to smoke a small cigar, thinks Kerrigan. It takes fifteen minutes to draft a pint of Tuborg, twenty minutes to drink it, fifteen to drink a glass of wine, twenty-five a double whiskey. The minutes haunt him with their mocking brevity. All bottles are essentially empty, defining an empty space. Every clock wears the face of a pompously indifferent sadist.

Why is a young girl so pretty and why does it last so short a time? The question is Søren Kierkegaard's.

Why do I see in the face of the winter-fevered rose the silken visage of a time that is no more? That question is Kerrigan's.

Kerrigan feels he should have been a poet, wishes that he had tried harder, agrees with Ole Jastrau in Tom Kristensen's 1930 novel *Hærværk*, *Havoc*, that intoxication is a poem that cannot find its form.

His Research Associate removes from her large leather bag a 5 by 8 notebook whose cover is printed with pale, sand-colored images of starfish and sea anenomes. She runs her slender, chiselled finger down the handwritten contents page, taps with a red, pointed fingernail the line she was seeking and flips halfway through the book.

She smiles and reads aloud from the notes she has researched for him. 'The pictures on the walls here were painted by Jens Julius Emanuel Madsen Visnek . . .'

'How many people is that?' Kerrigan enquires testily, still thinking about his failure as a poet.

'One.' She smiles again. 'He was a scenographer. He painted these to pay off his bar tab.'

Kerrigan nods, glances back at the bar where the silver-bearded, white-aproned bartender uses a spatula to work foam from two half-full pints.'Why is the beer taking so long?'

'I have that right here,' she says. 'They tap it very slowly so the acid foams off, giving it a soft and stomach-friendly taste. Incidentally, the street outside was part of the sixteenth century, dusty, thirsty highway to *Roskilde* where the wrecks of three viking ships were fished up out of the fjord in . . .'

'What else have you got there?'

'It was one of Simon Spies's favorite bars. You know Spies – the Danish travel agent magnate with his long, grey beard. He was always surrounded by beautiful young women, whores mostly. You may have heard of the so-called "Spies sandwich" or "*tvangbolle*" – mandatory sandwich – he invented it when he opened a package shop to sell late-night beer. Everybody wanted to be able to buy beer late at night, but the law said you couldn't sell alcoholic beverages unless you also sold food. So he put an enormous basket of tiny sandwiches wrapped in plastic foil – a tiny roll with a tiny slice of cheese on it – and everyone who bought a sixpack to go had to take a sandwich to fulfill the law. They were included in the price of the sixpack. The word *tvangbolle* also has a double entendre in Danish – like "mandatory sex".'

'He still around?'

'He died years ago, heirless . . .'

'*Hairless*?'

'*Heir*less. When he knew he was going to die, he married and left all his millions to a 22-year-old woman, who worked as a piccolo in his firm – Janni; she is one of the social elite now, remarried to a very wealthy man. She sold Spies's empire a few years ago.'

'Mmmm.'

'This was also one of my father's favorite bars. We lived just a few streets over,' she adds, just as the waiter places the two radiant amber schooners of beer on their table. Kerrigan's mood lifts as he lifts the chill glass, salutes his Associate with it in the Danish manner. Their eyes meet, they nod, say, '*Skål*,' drink, present the glass once more, set it down.

'You know the origin of the word *skål*?' she asks. 'The Vikings used to cut off the tops of their enemies skulls and use them as drinking cups.'

'That's a fallacy,' says Kerrigan.'Based on a mistranslation. *Skål* just means bowl. They drank out of bowls. In fact, they used to pass a communal bowl that each person drank from.'

'Always nice to be lectured about your own language by a foreigner with a heavy accent,' she says.

'Maybe I have an Icelandic accent,' snaps Kerrigan.

'And maybe you do not.'

He laughs, drinks again.'My mother was Icelandic,' he tells her, but remembers then things he does not wish to be questioned about and quickly changes the subject. 'We were talking about your father.'

Her smile is warm, slightly naughty for she can see, he sees, what he is thinking. This is not the first time she has assisted him with research; last time they worked together they were close to getting involved, sat up late one night over wine, sharing confidences. For some reason it never went further than that, and he would not mind taking up now where they left off then.

Kerrigan drinks another taste of the soft, golden, brilliantly tapped Tuborg, looks at his Associate whose cornblue eyes watch him with amusement.

'Your father,' he says again, hoping to recreate the interrupted moment.

Her lips cooperate with a subtly provocative smile.

She had a complicated relationship with her father, which she told Kerrigan about in her cups that evening some time ago.

What she had told him was how once, years before, when she was fourteen years old, on a lazy weekend morning, she sat at her mother's vanity table in her parent's bedroom. Her father was still in bed, and she was trying out the various potions in the jars lining her mother's vanity. Then she began to pin her long blond hair up on top of her head, ostensibly watching herself in the mirror, but in fact she watched the reflection of her father who lay beneath the eiderdown with a dreamy smile on his face. The eiderdown was hopping at its center. She watched the movement with interest, felt complicated sensations rising within her just as her mother looked in the door.

'Harald!' the mother snapped. 'Stop that swinery while the girl-child is present!'

The girl's eyes focused from the mirror like two darts, like snake eyes, on the face of her mother, and the words of her thoughts flew like unvoiced daggers: *Go away, mother! Go away!*

The story ended there, an anecdote really, but Kerrigan values it. It is one of his favorite stories, which he wrote down in his journal for future use. It and the other story she told him that night of the time when their apartment building was being refurbished and a huge piece of floor planking had been torn up so that there was an open gap in her floor and in the ceiling of the downstairs neighbour boy's bedroom, just below hers. She used to lie at night in her bed while he played a melody on his flute down below in his own bed. They never spoke through the gap, never acknowledged it was there, but she lay there and listened and he lay there, 15 feet below, and played the block flute, a Danish psalm written by N F S Grundtvig in the mid-nineteenth century:

> 'How sad for those whose ways do part
> Who fondly wish to walk as one . . .'

And listening to the lovely, plaintive notes of the melody lifting through the hole in her floor, she embraced herself and experienced for the first time in her life a sensation for which she had no name.

In her starfish book, she also had a note on N F S Grundtvig (1783-1872), a Danish poet, historian, bishop, and educationalist, the founder of the so-called 'Danish Folk High School' movement. He is primarily known outside of Denmark for his educational innovations but was in fact a prolific writer, translator, and researcher in Nordic mythology at a time when it had been forgotten in favor of Greek myths. Among his translations to Danish are *Beowulf* from the Anglo-Saxon and Snorri's *Heimskringla* from old Icelandic. His own poetry, especially his sacred poetry and psalms, have made him a leading figure in Danish literature.

His hymns were not of sin and damnation but of hope and resurrection and the beauty of life, and his anti-authoritarian, democratic approach to religion and society has made a deep impression on the Danish national character.

There is a sculpture of Grundtvig standing outside the Marble Church, *Marmorkirken,* in Copenhagen, alongside a dozen other psalmists and theologians. There is another of Grundtvig as a prophet, kneeling in the courtyard of the Church of Vartov, sculpted by Niels Skovgaard in 1932.

Kerrigan contemplates these matters now, watching his Associate, picturing her listening to the music of the flute through the open floor as she lay in her young bed. The level in their pints of beer descends, leaving lovely froth patterns on the sparkling walls of their glasses.

Before coming here they stopped just diagonally across the street at Old King's Road 95, at an establishment Kerrigan had off-handedly, perhaps perversely or provocatively (he had to admit), told her he wished to include in his book. It is known as *Paradis* – Paradise in English. There they browsed among the shelves of leather and plastic and metal wares. Toys and straps and implements, piquant undergarments with strategic openings, video films, electronic devices to stimulate and shock, shackles and molded bits of latex as well as an array of adult furniture: an internal examination bench, an X-formed wooden cross with wrist and ankle straps, stocks, pillories, even a dental chair.

He was curious about her reaction, but she took it all in with sublime cool. 'Did you mean to try any of these?' she asked, picking up a metal and leather contraption in a blister pack with a label that said, *The Seven Gates of Hell Penis Cage*.

'I think not,' he said and thought.

Her cheeks flushed slightly and he felt his own do the same, but they continued smiling. 'None of this can match the images behind the eye,' he said.

'No?' Her smile was sphinx-like.

Now, however, the air is still somewhat charged where they sit in Wine Room 90, waiting for the waiter to prepare fresh pints of draft.

'One should order the second as soon as the first is delivered,' muses Kerrigan.

'I did not know you had such thirst.'

He grumbles, lights another small Sumatra and watches his Research Associate's cornblue eyes. He wets his tongue with half of what remains in his glass, draws on the cigar, blows smoke rings.

She has removed her cornblue coat and leans slightly forward across the table, leaving him to wonder if it is her wish for him to see there what he sees in her décolletage – what the Danes call the 'Cavalier Passage', and in English has the harsh and uncharming title of 'cleavage'. Always a mystery! Devilish strategy. How lovely, he thinks, is the process of the grain in the blood, and he chances a quote from *The Tain*: 'I see a sweet country,' he says. 'I could rest my weapon there.'

She returns the sentiment with a word from Odin's wisdom familiar to both of them from the ancient *Sayings of the High One*: 'Remember always to praise the woman's radiant body for he who flatters, gets.' The undertone is ironic, though irony, he knows, in Danish, is often a mask of affection. As the popular poet Piet Hein, born in 1905 says, 'He who takes the serious only seriously and the humorous only with humor has misunderstood the nature of both.'

2

The Railway Café *(Jernbane Cafeen)*

Jernbane Cafeen
Reventlowsgade 16
1651 København V

Heard melodies are sweet,' he says quietly to her in the taxi. 'Those unheard sweeter yet.' They sit close, their knees almost touching. But she is relentless. '*Den tid, den sorg*,' she says. 'That time, that sorrow – Old Danish proverb.' The cab rolls to a stop at the curb. 'Are you aware how many places we must to visit?' she demands as they climb out to stand on the sidewalk outside the Railway Café.

'No!' Kerrigan yelps. The sign outside the bar says *Øl* in red neon and *Bier* in flat blue. A sidewalk placard gives the English translation, *Beer*. International, he thinks. He eyes the life-sized golden Tuborg girl in an aquamarine frame alongside the door, pinches his eyelids and sees a little dog nipping the hem of her skirt so it tears. She doesn't seem to mind, even as the neckline of her blouse slips down over her breasts.

'This von is a must,' his Associate says.

'Why?'

'Because I have to pee.'

Kerrigan laughs and thumps the fatty lumps of his lower back. Kidneys of steel!'

She pokes his tum. ' Not to speak of the abs that are not there!'

'How would you know?'

'Always nice to know new experiences might await me.'

Kerrigan follows her. Inside there is no tap, so he orders two bottles of green Tuborg while his Associate finds the loo. He sits at the bar and surveys the art on the walls: paintings of locomotives, street scenes of old Copenhagen, a faithful dog, a splashy seascape, photos of trains and a long glass case of HO-gauge model trains.

'Nice-looking pictures,' he says to the nice-looking, plump, blond, fortyish barmaid.

'Yeah,' says she. 'Some of them.'

'When was this place established?'

With one eye closed she puffs her cigarette, and it wobbles between her lips as she speaks.'Long time. Three generations in any case.'

An elderly man at the bar hollers, 'Confounded deuce it! I got to walk the devil dog again,' and heads for the gents to the chortling of a table of regulars behind him.

Kerrigan notices there is a functioning transom over the entry door, tilted open. 'Don't see many of them around anymore.'

'You're right enough there,' the barmaid says without looking at him and trims her cigarette on the edge of a heaped-full, black, plastic ashtray.

Half a dozen men sit at a long table raffling for drinks with a leather cup of dice. As Kerrigan sips his green, the old guy returns to the bar, while a short, broad, crewcutted woman barges through the front door, and stands in the middle of the floor; Good day!' she shouts and looks at the barmaid.'My god, you do look sexy today, sweetheart!'

'I usually do,' says the barmaid quietly, and the crewcutted woman moves to the bar.'Damn, give me a beer, my wife's been breaking my balls!' Then she turns to the older man beside her, reaches and rearranges the material around his flies, saying,'If you had that cut a little different, it might look like you really had something there, old fellow.'

'Sweetheart!' the man grumbles in his gravelly voice, 'My nuts have been hanging there just like that since before you were born!'

They both laugh, and she turns to Kerrigan and says, 'I got to catch a train back to Sorø so my wife can start breaking my balls again. So if you were thinking of buying me a bitter, you'll have to be fast. I don't have much time.'

'Sorø!' says Kerrigan. 'That's a terrific place. The old Sorø Academy. The Oxford of Denmark. The great Ludvig Holberg is buried there in the chapel. I was there once.'

'*Once*?' she says.'Try and *live* there.' She makes mouths of both hands and has them gossip rapidly at each other. 'Bla bla bla bla bla . . .'

Kerrigan's Research Associate emerges from the loo and takes a place at the bar on the other side of Kerrigan.

'Sorry, honey,' says the crewcutted woman. 'I saw him first.'

'You're velcome to him,' she says.

'Well, wait, hel-lo!' says the woman, 'Where have you been all my life, sweetheart?'

'Growing up,' says the Associate, and the woman laughs heartily, says, 'Don't go away now, I just have to water my herring.'

'So what do you have in your starfish book about this joint?' Kerrigan asks, and his Associate digs it out of her bag, pages through. 'Nothing,' she says. 'Only that the street was named for Christian Ditlev Frederik Reventlow, 1748-1827, early in this century. He led the way to the end of adscription.'

'What the fuck is "adscription"?'

'The idea that the peasants were serfs, bound to the land and whoever owned it. It's strange really, the whole idea of someone *owning* land. But this street used to be called *Tømmerpladsvej*, Lumber Place Way, before that, because it ran down to the harbor where lumber – *tømmer* – was shipped in, but that closed down in 1885.'

'So now it only has to do with *tømmermænd*, ey?' *Tømmermænd* is the Danish word for a hangover, carpenters – little men in your head hammering and sawing.

His Associate winces.

The crewcutted woman swaggers back toward the bar. *Sotto voce*, Kerrigan suggests, 'Shall we drink up?' He orders a bitter for the crewcutted woman, to keep her occupied at the bar when they leave in hopes it will keep her from following them.

3

The Stick *(Restaurant Pinden)*

Restaurant Pinden
Reventlowsgade 4
1651 København V

Kerrigan can't help but think that the Stick has a typical feature of many Copenhagen serving houses. From across the street it looks positively uninviting, particularly with the grafitti on its side door. Approached from the same side of the street, however, as they stroll up *Reventlows* Street from the Railway Café, it is a little more welcoming, with a cut-out of a kindly-looking waiter bearing a tray of beer steins by the door.

And inside, when they go to hang their coats, the painted wardrobe window is even better.

They sit at the bar, bracketted three steps up against the wall, and are greeted by a pleasant, dark-haired woman who asks what they would like. Again, no draft! He orders a bottle of green Tuborg and his Associate asks for a bottle of sweet red, reading her notes to him while they wait.

'This place opened in 1907 and was acquired a dozen years later by Betty Nansen. You know, the actress – the theater in *Frederiksberg* near where we were at Wine Room 90, the Betty Nansen Theater?'

'I think I saw the play *Vidunderlige Kælling* there – *Gorgeous Bitches* – in the 70s. You know, the one where all the famous actors and actresses danced naked.'

'That was at the Falkoner Theater, not the Betty Nansen. They're both in *Frederiksberg*, near Wine Room 90.'

'No, wait, I was involved in a literary festival at the Betty Nansen in the 80s. We had William Burroughs and Ken Kesey there. And the Fugs.'

'The *Fugs*?'

'A satirical folk group from the 60s. They did that famous hit number, " I Feel Like a Great Big Bowl of Homemade Shit." '

'How delicious,' says his Associate, lips tart.

'No shit! That's true. That was the title of the song.'

'In any event, some of the objects on the walls here are from the theater apparently, the Betty Nansen.' She leans closer and lowers her voice. Only women are allowed to serve in this bar.'

'Alewives.'

'*Kun en pige*,' she says.

'What's that?'

'A book. By Lise Nørgaard. You know, the woman who wrote *Matador*, the television play that ran in about 50 parts telling the whole story of Danish social changes from about 1920 to maybe the 60s? *Kun en Pige* means *Only a Girl*. It's Nørgaard's memoir of her life in the 1920s and '30s. Her father was a real, what the Japanese call, *Plick*.'

He laughs, pours his green Tuborg along the inner side of his glass.

'In any event,' she continues, 'It has had various names. The Gentel Bar and the Regina Bar. Then, in 1950, it merged with another much older bar called the Stick. The name came from a game of chance they played with matchsticks.' She turns a page. 'Do you know the Danish actors Dirch Passer and Jørgen Ry? They used to come in here regularly.'

'Dirch Passer is buried in Assistens Churchyard on the northside,' says Kerrigan. 'Where Hans Christian Andersen is buried. Andersen's half sister was buried there, too, but in an unmarked grave. I saw Dirch Passer's stone. All it says on it is *Dirch*. Nothing else. No dates, no last name, nothing. Pretty short-sighted if you ask me. In 20 or 30 years no one will have the foggiest who's buried there. Jørgen Ry was funny, though. I saw some film with him where he did that bit about the dust mites in your eyelashes? Very creepy! He winds up screaming "Mite king!" out the door of a laundromat. Gave me the chills. Like the human body, like a statement on the human body as a fraud, King of the Mites, but all the little invisible organisms live on us like we live on the earth. Like *Lord of the Flies*. You know, the devil. Like Charles Simic: "I'm not just any black flea on your ass! I shouted to every god and devil I could think of!" '

She watches him steadily, blinks. 'How do you come to know so much about that?'

He shrugs. 'I don't know. It gave me the creeps.'

She studies him a moment longer, looks back to her notes. 'This also used to be a regular spot for the people who worked in the central station. The station used to be on the other side of *Vesterbrogade*, West Boulevard, you know. Now it's been on this side since 1911. They have music, too. Four nights a week. A piano player.'

A man in his 40s takes the seat beside Kerrigan at the bar, and the barmaid smiles. 'Hi, Ole, how do you have it today?'

'*Tømmermænd*,' he says. Carpenters hammering and sawing in the head.

Her smile brightens. 'Maybe you should just admit to the fact that you can't drink so much.'

Kerrigan glances at the man from the corner of his eye. His face is pale. 'Was I that bad?' His voice breaks.

'Nooo,' she says, pursing her lips. 'Not so bad. Of course, you did try to kiss me about half a dozen times. Sloppy ones.'

'Oh yeah! Well I also spent a fortune on goddamned drinks, too!'

'Ha! In a pig's nose. You won most of your drinks raffling.'

Clearly she is having a ball. So is Kerrigan. But Ole doesn't look so happy. Kerrigan is gazing at the rows of bottles behind the bar and the theatrical pictures mounted above them, neo-Victorian showgirls and dancing minstrels and such.

Then he remembers something his Associate said before. 'Isn't that like against the law or something?' he asks her.

'What?'

'Only to hire women for the bar?'

She comments with an inhalation, which is not the usual inhalated Scandinavian affirmative, but a subtly bitter expression of irony. He puzzles over it for a moment, then excuses himself to find the gent's. A sign with an arrow points the way past another painted window, this one displaying a black cat.

Upstairs it takes him a moment to distinguish between the doors of the *Herretoilet* and the *Dametoilet*. Cautiously he peeks into the first door; the fixtures inform him he has chosen correctly. As he stands before the porcelain looking down at himself, he understands suddenly the meaning of her inhalated irony, remembering another story she told him last time they were together. Originally it was her wish in life to be a journalist, but she was not allowed to.

'Why not?' he asked.

'Well,' she said mildly. 'Let's say it was because I have a cunt.'

She was a good student, judged '*egnet*' – 'suitable' – to proceed from primary school to secondary school in the academic line. There are three categories – suitable, unsuitable, possibly suitable. When a Danish child is thirteen or fourteen, one of these words is stamped upon him or her. The novelist Peter Høeg, best known for his *Smilla's Sense of Snow* (1992), also wrote a novel entitled *De Måske Egnede* – literally *The Possibly Suitable*, although it was published under the translated title *Borderliners*, which does not quite convey the harshness of it. Høeg himself had been judged 'possibly suitable' when he was a boy.

But Kerrigan's assistant was suitable and went on to gymnasium – the Danish secondary school for those judged suitable to go on to university, which she was. Her father, himself a journalist, pulled strings to get her a job as a secretary in the editorial offices of Copenhagen's oldest, most conservative daily newspaper, *Berlingske*

Tidende. She worked there for a year waiting for the head of personnel to do what her father had told her he would, begin to try her out on small journalistic assignments, obituaries, social notices. Finally, when nothing happened, she approached him about it, and he expressed surprise. He told her there was never any connection between the administrative and editorial or journalistic functions at the paper, that it was never his idea that she should do anything more than simple secretarial work. '*Du* er *kun en pige*,' he said with a smile. 'You *are* just a girl.'

'He really said that to you?' Kerrigan asked.

'It's a conservative paper. And he was a very conservative guy.'

'What year was this?'

''59.'

Kerrigan blushes now as he zips, washes his hands, remembering the book she mentioned before. *Kun En Pige*. Only a girl. The autobiography of the writer with the chauvinist father.

His Associate confronted her father about it, and he denied ever having promised anything. She should be happy to work for that fine newspaper. It was a good solid job. She didn't have to keep those terrible hours journalists did, participate in the rat watch. It was a good job for a young woman who was not yet married, and she wouldn't turn hard, the way journalists do.

Kerrigan returns to the bar, gazes at her. 'I'm sorry,' he says. 'I just remembered what you'd told me. About your father and all. Just a girl.'

'I was stupid,' she tells him now. 'By then I was used to the money. I didn't know how to fight. Maybe I was afraid to. I met a handsome young lawyer from the newspaper's legal department. He was seven years older than me and I was . . .'

'You were a knock-out. I've seen pictures of you. Remember?'

Whether she does or not she does not say; instead she says, 'I had a cunt instead of a prick. So here I am now, nearly 40 years, four husbands, three daughters, and five grandsons later. I work as a research secretary. On the weekends I go barefoot around my little east-side apartment in leotards and play at being an artist.'

'You've sold pictures.'

'Big deal. I know it's no excuse,' she says. 'But you know what really galls me. Years later, many years later, my father gave me a copy of that book for Christmas. *Just a Girl*. He got Lise Nørgaard to sign it for me. He knew her. I just don't understand what he was thinking. Maybe he wasn't thinking at all. Maybe he just took it for granted. Because I have a cunt.'

'I certainly hope you don't hate your cunt.'

'I really like my cunt,' she says. 'It just has been something of a handicap at times.'

' "The Speed of Darkness," ' Kerrigan says.

Her cornblue eyes hang a question toward him, and he recites,

> 'Whoever despises the clitoris despises the penis.
> Whoever despises the penis despises the cunt.
> Whoever despises the cunt despises the life of the child.'

The tilt of her head and of her mouth expresses skepticism.

'That's Muriel Rukeyser,' he says. 'Wonderful American poet. She died almost twenty years ago.' He continues,

> 'My night awake
> staring at the broad rough jewel
> the copper roof across the way
> thinking of the poet
> yet unborn in this dark
> who will be the throat of these hours.
> No. Of those hours.
> Who will speak these days,
> if not I,
> if not you?'

She nods now in affirmation, but says, 'What has that got to do with this place? The Stick?'

'The cunt,' says Kerrigan, 'is a beautiful strong word. I think it is the strongest word in the English language. What is the Danish word?'

'*Fisse*,' she says.

'I thought that meant "fart." '

'One less "s".'

'*Fisse*,' he says, trying the sound on his tongue.

'There's also *fisselette*,' she says.'A little cunt. A tight one. As my first ex always said, "Little cunt, big joy; big cunt, little joy." And then there's also *lille kone dag* – little wife day – which was Wednesday, the traditional one day a week that Danish men fucked their wives – other than Saturday of course.'

'Once a week's better than once a month,' says Kerrigan, and she laughs brightly. 'Oh, I almost forgot, there's also *kusse*, another word for it.'

'*Kusse*. I like it. Sounds like kiss.'

'You're just trying to win cheap points!' she says and sticks her tongue between her teeth.

'You know you remind me of the Wife of Bath,' Kerrigan says, pouring the last drops of green Tuborg into his glass. He swallows them.'You're kind of a Bohemian. And it really is incredible to think that in my lifetime, only three or so decades ago, women were mocked, cheated of their rights, even had to use titles that revealed whether or not they were married for Christ's sake!'

'I got a daytime job,' she says.'I'm doin' alright. Don't forget your little satchel now.'

The thick novel bulges in the satchel. She asks what he is reading, and he finds himself telling her a little about Joyce, Dublin, as they step out into *Reventlowsgade*.

'There are many connections between Dublin and Scandinavia,' he says. 'Dublin was settled by Vikings, especially the Danes. Joyce believed he had Danish blood in him. Dublin, you know, is from *Dubh Linn*, the black pool, and I can't help but think of the lake where I live when I think of that – *Sortedam Sø*, Black Dam Lake.'

'How is the book?' she asks.

'A rough trudge. But it has its merry moments.'

4

Axelborg Bodega

Axelborg Bodega
Axeltorv ***(Axel Square)*** **1**
1609 København V

Across *Reventlowsgade*, his Associate points at the back of the Astoria Hotel. She has her starfish notebook opened in her hands. 'When that was built in 1935, they nicknamed it *Penalhuset* – the Penal House. For obvious reasons.'

'Good illustration for Kafka's "Penal Colony," ' says Kerrigan. 'That's where Lance and Andi Olsen stayed when they visited Copenhagen in '94.'

'Who're they?'

'Lance is a novelist, small publishers. He writes hip sci-fi and cyberpunk. Read his novel *Burnt*. Very funny. Got another coming out titled *Nietzsche's Kisses*. Published by a little press, Wordcraft, in LaGrande, Oregon, run by a poet and fiction writer named David Memmott. Very dedicated man. Andi is Lance's wife, an artist. She's done some of Lance's covers, but her sculptures are fantastic. She works with animal bones, among other things. Bird cages, baby carriages, you name it.'

'Sounds cozy.'

'Do you like art?'

'Some,' she says, and he tries without success to read her face – angry, bitter, hurt.

Passing the Central Station, he glances down at the tracks below the pavement. He can feel his beer. They cross *Vesterbrogade*, West Bridge Street, past *Fridhedsstøtten*, the Liberty Pillar, erected between 1792 and 1797 to commemorate the liberation of the serfs with the repeal of adscription (1733-1788) by which the peasants had been virtually the property of the person who owned the land they worked. The pillar is mentioned repeatedly in Tom Kristensen's *Havoc*.

'You know Ole 'Jazz' Jastrau in *Havoc* lived just around the corner from the Railway Café where we just were,' she says. 'He walks past this monument numerous times in the novel.'

'Symbolic.'

'Funny, as far as I can remember, Tivoli is never mentioned in the novel,' she says as they pass it on the other side of the street. 'Look at the trees!'

They pause to gaze across *Vesterbrogade* at the front of the Tivoli Park. 'The Park is more than 150 years old now,' she tells him. 'And the trees are just that shade of green only once a year. So feast your happy eyes.'

He looks at her, reminded of something, looks at the blue shadows of her eyes in the fading afternoon light, and what he feels at once attracts and repels him.

'Can hardly see it at all in this light,' he says.

'Well look harder,' she snaps and without waiting for him to follow leads the way to *Axeltorv*, Axel Square, bounded by the broad front of the Scala Building, the Circus Building across the other end, the many colors of the Palace Theater which looks like a birthday cake standing across the square.

She says, 'That theater was painted by the fellow who overturned the idea that hospital's have to be sterile white by decorating the interior of Herlev Hospital in the north of Copenhagen in every shade of the rainbow – a most cheerful hospital to be sick in if you have to be sick.'

'I took my kids to hear Little Richard in the Circus Building when they were little,' he says without thinking. 'So many years ago.' He shakes his head. 'Little Richard. I danced to him when I was thirteen, and the kids loved him, too. He was 60 and just as loud and wild as ever. He played nonstop for four hours, though he sat at the keyboard more than he used to . . .'

'How old are your kids now,' she asks, and he feels his face harden, remembering. 'Forget it,' he mutters. To chase the memory, he focuses up the street on the lovely long hair of a young woman pushing a bike with a case of Carlsberg beer balanced on the carrier.

They stand over the sheer vast pool of the shimmering fountain, so full it seems convex, always about to spill over, but it never does. He is battling memories: how his kids, when they were walking the streets of a strange city, used to each lay a hand on one of his shoulders, as if they were blind and trusted him to lead them. Someday, he thinks, he might be able to savor that memory, someday far off in time when he has travelled so long his heart has grown immune to caring. But not now.

When he says nothing more, she turns a page in her starfish book, says, 'This square was built in 1863 when the old Central Station was opened,' and he eagerly welcomes the lilting soothing feminine music of her voice. 'It used to be there where the Palace Theater is now, but was relocated across *Vesterbrogade* in 1911. The Scala there is Copenhagen's attempt to have a mall, but it used to house a hall where couples came to dance during the war. The square itself is named for Bishop Absalon, who founded Copenhagen in 1167, although it is now believed the city is actually older than that, from the last half of the year 1000. You can see Absalon's statue on horseback wielding an axe down on *Højbro Plads*, just off the *Strøget*, Walking Street.'

'A Bishop wielding an axe? Interesting.'

'The Danish literary critic Georg Brandes spoke at the unveiling of the statue in 1902 and pointed out that the axe was not only a weapon of battle, but also a tool of civilization – to chop trees and firewood. Absalon, by the way, is the Hebrew version of the Danish name Axel. Here's Axelborg Bodega – the Danish national radio had its studio here from 1929 to 1941, and this place was hot stuff then.'

She leads him in, and they take a table facing the *Tuborg Øl Depot* sign – Tuborg Beer Depot, and he orders a pint of Tuborg and sits unspeaking, from time to time lifting his glass to his mouth. He does not toast and she respects his silence, which does not fail to escape his attention – he feels her watching him and wishes she would stop, but at the same time thinks of her question about his kids and hopes she does not pursue the subject; it could mean the end of their association if she does. Then he remembers asking her if she liked art and further that she had already told him she paints herself, that it is her passion. The lapse makes him feel egocentric, semi-autistic.

'I hope I can see your pictures sometime,' he says, hoping she will ignore his previous comment, and she replies, 'If you're ever hungry and low on funds, they serve an excellent *Skipperlabsskovs* here – lobscouse, sailor's stew, a huge portion of potatoes and boiled beef in a pale gravy made with beer; it's served with dark rye bread and pickled beets. For a pittance.'

The place is nearly empty, and Kerrigan slowly relaxes, absently watches a man who sits alone at an adjoining table. The man is about his own age, drinking a bottle of Tuborg *Påske Bryg*, Easter Brew, strong beer brewed around the Easter season for a few weeks every year. The day it hits the streets, the young people in Copenhagen go on a rampage with it.

The man glances at them a couple of times – wistfully, Kerrigan thinks.

'What does your little book have about Danish beer?' he asks, and her delicate fingers rattle pages.

'It's been brewed in Denmark since around 4000 BC – 6,000 years ago. They've found a preserved body of a bronze age girl – the Egtved Girl – in Jutland at a gravesite with a pail of beer between her legs. She was in her mid-twenties, and the beer was made from malt wheat, cranberries, pollen and instead of hops, bog myrtle for a bitter spice, also known as "sweet gale".'

'Sweet gale. I like that. Beer was known as "mead," right?'

'Wrong. Mead is fermented honey. A kind of wine. Beer is made from grain water, yeast and seasoning. Hops didn't reach Denmark until about the year 1000. Until then they used sweet gale to give it the bitter taste. The Vikings used to drink to Freja, their goddess of fertility.' She turns a page. 'But it wasn't until the nineteenth century that the Danish beer really began to excel. Thanks to the German yeast culture provided by Emil Christian Hansen to I C Jacobsen – the brewer of Carlsberg. The alcohol content of the various Danish beers – and there are more than 150 types brewed by fifteen breweries – ranges from under 1 per cent to nearly 10 per cent. Pilsener is 4.6, gold beer 5.8, Easter and Christmas beer are 7.9, and superpremiums up to 9.7. There is another that is 10 or 11 per cent, but it escapes my memory just now. The stronger beer is better with richer, heavier, or spicier food. And the Easter or Christmas beers are best after dinner – a nice substitute for a sticky dessert wine.'

'How about snaps?'

'Much younger than beer. Only about 600 years old. Actually it was originally known as *brændevin*, brandywine, and the best of it was called *aquavite*, water of life in Latin, which is also the origin of whiskey – from the Irish *uisce beatha* or Scots Gællic *uisge beatha*, also literally the "water of life".' She turns another page. 'At the end of the 1700s, the German word *snaps* was adopted to replace brandywine. It means *dram* or *mouthful* but also is from *snappen* – to snap – which is when you take the snaps down in one shot. It was around that time the snaps glass was introduced, too. They used otherwise to drink from the bottle. Or from a pocket flask. Which in Danish is called a *lommelærke*, a pocket lark, because it "chirps" when you drink from it. Snaps was *very* central to Danish life up until 1917. In 1880, statistics show a snaps consumption equal to 70 liters a year for every adult male, but it was also used for toothache, sluggishness, bad stomach, arhthritis, all sorts of pain, and as a sleeping medicine for children. It was 47.5 per cent alcohol then, much stronger than now. Then in 1917, the tax was raised so the price of a bottle of snaps quintupled, which achieved the goal of reducing consumption. Before that most men were drinking the better part of 2 liters a week.'

'Let's have one,' says Kerrigan and signals the waiter by tipping an imaginary snaps glass to his lips. The waiter comes with a bottle of Jubilaeum and two glasses.

'Doubles, please,' says Kerrigan.

'Adult size,' says the barman and fills the glasses to the lip.

They raise them by the stems carefully, nod, snap them dry.

The man with the *påskebryg* looks over again, still wistful, and his wistfulness invades Kerrigan's spirit. To break the mood, he faces her and says impulsively, 'We are no more responsible for the thoughts in our minds than for the beasts in the forest.'

She nods. 'And what thought is it that you wish to evade?'

He chuckles. 'Bright girl. Jung said that.'

Again she nods. 'Had enough for today?'

'Ri-dic-ulous! We haven't even danced yet! When there's music to be danced to, play, gypsies, play!'

5

Palace Hotel Bar

Palace Hotel
Rådhuspladsen *(Town Hall Square)*
1785 København K

They cross H C Andersens Boulevard to the Town Hall Square, pausing to glance at the statue of Hans Christian Andersen seated in bronze, gazing up toward Tivoli Park. She is into her starfish book again.

'This was done by Henry Luckhow Nillson in the 50s. There's a duplicate of it in Tokyo where the Japanese have replicated the Tivoli Gardens. Luckhow Nillson's daughter, Jane, negotiated the rights to use the cast of this.'

'I know her,' says Kerrigan. 'She's an artist herself. I have a couple of her pictures.'

'My goodness,' says his Associate dryly. 'May I touch you?'

They stand gazing at Hans Christian in his bronze chair.

'There's one of him in Central Park in Manhattan, too,' says Kerrigan. 'In New York City. Put up in 1956.'

'There's also another, much older one in *Kongens Have*, the King's Garden,' she tells him. 'You see it in the film *Nattevagten – Night Watch* – from the late 90s. Two young men are drinking beer in the King's Gardens at night, and they vow never to refuse a dare made to one of them by the other. They close the deal by smashing their beer bottles against Andersen's face. The Erotic Museum on *Købmagergade* also has a big poster of that Andersen sculpture with a naked woman seated on his knee. How Andersen would have blushed. That sculpture was made during his lifetime. There was a competition for his seventieth birthday, and the first couple of entries Andersen looked at showed him reading to children – which had been stipulated in the competition guidelines. He didn't like it. "Madonna with child," he hissed. The one that won he picked himself – himself all alone, telling a story to an imaginary audience he didn't have to share his stone with. He was a vain man in his old age. All his life actually. Poor H C,' she says, pronouncing the 'h' as 'ho' in the Danish fashion. 'Poor Ho C. Such success and so unhappy. All the women he adored, to no avail, poor man. First there was Riborg Voigt in his home town of Odense who he really had a chance with, but he blew it. Then Louise Collin, Sofie Ørsted, and Jenny Lind who he didn't have a chance in hell with. Louise Collin was the daughter of one of his many benefactors, the Collin family, what he called his "home of homes", over on *Bredgade*, Broad Street, number 4.' She pronounces the name Danish fashion: Co-lean, stress on the second syllable. 'The other Collin siblings teased him unmercifully at dinner – or maybe only affectionately – because he was so odd and cried so easily. He would run weeping from the table. Louise, who was younger than he, used to go after him and comfort him. But then he grew ardent . . .'

'And that was not what she meant at all, ey? Not what she meant at all.'

'Right. She made sure there was always a chaperone present. Andersen "got his money back," though, as he used to refer to writing about his sorrows – whether it was a toothache or a heartache. He put Louise Collin in his tale, "The Swineherd" as the haughty princess and in "The Little Mermaid" as the prince. Hans Christian himself was the mermaid by the way.'

Kerrigan laughs. He lights a small cigar and sits on a bench just back from the statue. She joins him at the opposite end of the bench. He glances at her face, her lips, charmed by her great knowledge, her enthusiasm, her wit and irony. He wants to kiss her mouth, considers taking a bold course and doing just that, but he doesn't dare run the risk of scaring her off. He says, 'Hard to picture that sweet little bronze lady on her rock in the water off Langelinje as a transvestite. Andersen in scaly drag.'

'Not everyone shares your view of her as sweet.' She digs a packet of Prince from her bag, lights one, chin tipped up as smoke issues from her pursed lips.

'Yeah,' he says, 'I hear someone cut her head off.'

'Twice. The statue was sculpted by Edvard Eriksen and had sat there peacefully since 1913. It was donated by Carl Jacobsen, the founder of Carlsberg Breweries, who donated a great many sculptures to Copenhagen – 60 or more. Then one night in 1964, someone climbed out to her rock with a metal saw and cut her head off. Many believe it was done by the artist Jørgen Nash who has been referred to as the "Mermaid Killer". He is nearly 80 years now and scarcely as avant garde as he was then, but I like his pictures very much. The mermaid's head was recast and replaced, but someone did it again about 25 years later. The theory is that the first time Nash did it because as an artist he was furious that such a sentimental statue based on such a sentimental tale should come to be a symbol of Copenhagen. The second time, however, it was said to be a journalist trying to make news and a name for himself.'

'It's not Andersen's best tale I suppose.'

'The way it ends! Her soaring to the heavens to sail off on a rose-red cloud. My goodness.'

'Speaking of mermaids,' he says, 'I once went Zodiac rafting out among the rock formations along the west coast of Vancouver Island looking for sea lions. I found a rookery of stellars. You could hear them blowing before you saw them, laid out on the rocks sunning themselves. The bulls are huge, one to a rookery. They look like bears but spend their time lolling about, massive heads pillowed on two or three females. But the shes are something else again. This has to be where the mermaid myth started. They're small and sensuous and delicate and very curious. The bulls were completely indifferent to my presence, but suddenly the raft was surrounded by half a dozen shes, just beyond arm's reach, dancing up and down in the water, looking and looking at me, their round black eyes shining, their tender sweet faces and glistening flanks. Suddenly I could understand all the superstitious lore and tales of the sea. I was entranced. The water turned rough without my noticing and I lost control of the raft. I was being thrown toward the rocks, but those half a dozen mermaids were unphased, just bobbing there, watching with their big black eyes.'

He notes with secret pleasure his Associate's concern and interest. 'What happened?' she asks.

'Well, I capsized, but managed to right the thing again and get back to shore. I survived. Obviously.'

'You went rafting in those conditions all alone?'

'Yeah. Well. Nothing much mattered to me in those days.'

She watches him. 'Why?'

'It's not interesting.' He reaches over to touch the bronze book on Andersen's bronze knee. 'So who else did the old boy have the hots for?'

'Sophie Ørsted – the daughter of H C Ørsted . . .' She consults her book. '1777 to 1851. He discovered electro magnetism in 1820 – you know they still call the unit of magnetic strength after him – an oersted.'

'Isn't there also a park named for him here in Copenhagen? Ørsted Park?'

'Yes,' she says. 'It is among other things where lonely men go at night looking for each other, though it is a very charming place to sit and have a beer on a sunny day or just to meditate. There is a very fine collection of sculpture. They have also named a street, an institute and an electrical plant for Ørsted. Anyway, Sophie's father was one of Andersen's friends – one of the first to recognize that Andersen's true greatness was not in his plays or novels or travel books, of which he wrote many, but in his tales. Most of the critics of the time thought the tales trivial and offensive. They were non-academic, even anti-academic, because they were written in colloquial language. Andersen became an international success in 1835 with his novel *The Improvisatore*, the same year that he published his first book of *Fairy Tales, Told for Children*. Ørsted, who was not a literary man, had a better sense than the critics of the time. He told Andersen, "The novel may have made you famous, but the tales will make you immortal." Andersen always believed he would be famous. He came to Copenhagen at the age of fourteen as a pauper and threw himself at the mercy of society. "First you go through a cruel time and then you become famous," he explained, and by the time he was 30 had proven that was true. But in terms of his love life, it was always a cruel time.

'Next after Sofie Ørsted was Jenny Lind, the Swedish opera singer who he wrote one of his finest tales about, "The Nightingale". She, in fact, had the popular nickname "The Swedish Nightingale". Do you remember the tale?'

'Not completely.'

'It's about a Chinese royal court seduced by the song of a mechanical nightingale, by the fixed and unchanging sound of its song. It can sing it exactly the same 37 times in a row. So the real nightingale is banished because its song is so unpleasantly unpredictable. But then of course something in the mechanical nightingale goes *snap!* And then the Emperor falls into a fatal illness until the real nightingale comes back , and its song is more powerful than death. Jenny Lind was like the real nightingale, with a natural song, as compared to the more prominent trained voices of her day. And the nightingale is also, of course, Andersen himself with his anti-academic, natural language.'

'Jenny Lind,' Kerrigan says. 'I just remembered. I was in Pablo Neruda's house once. *Isla Negra*. South of Valparaiso in Chile. He has a wooden masthead sculpture of Jenny Lind in one of the main rooms, looking out over the sea.'

'She was the last one Andersen broke his heart over. She liked him "but not that way". He was 40 then. After that you can read his sex life in his journals. For every day that he sets an X he practised onanism.'

'Honeymoon of the hand, ey? What cafés did he frequent in Copenhagen?'

'I don't know that he did at all. He was a homebody, as I said, although he had no real home himself. He was always dining at the homes of others. I know that Søren Kierkegaard visited a couple of Konditoris where the literati gathered, including one that was just across the street where the Dubliners Pub is today, on *Amagertorv*.'

'Right – spent many a good afternoon there with good old Paul Casey.'

'But the only café I know of where Andersen went regularly was the Caffé Greco in the Via Condotti in Rome where the artistic crowd gathered around Bertel Thorvaldsen, the famous sculptor who lived from 1770 to 1844, residing in Rome for 41 of his years and only returning to Denmark in 1838. You can see his statue in Ørsted Park also. And his work in the Thorvaldsen Museum and in the cathedral here, *Vorfrue Kirke*, Our Lady's Church, over alongside the old university between *Fiolstræde*, Violin Street and *Nørregade*, North Street. There is a particularly beautiful statue of Jesus by the altar, very simple, elegant. And a magnificent frieze over the entry. Thorvaldsen's art is in many other places as well, including busts of Walter Scott and Byron in Edinburgh. He did the twelve apostles at Our Lady Cathedral here also as well as the David and Moses flanking the entry. That Cathedral was originally built in 1191 and destroyed by the British bombing in 1807, then rebuilt and reconsecrated with Thorvaldsen's sculptures in 1829.'

'He was a religious artist?' Kerrigan asks.

'He said that he didn't believe in the Greek or Roman gods either, but had no trouble sculpting them. He became famous in 1803 for his sculpture of Jason and the Golden Fleece. Antonio Canova . . .' She looks at her book. '. . . 1757-1822 . . . called Thorvaldsen's *Jason*,"*uno stilo nuovo e grandioso*" – a new and magnificent style. Canova's word was enough to elevate him to fame. Thorvaldsen might be considered a Danish Golden Age sculptor but his themes are classical, not involved with the Nordic themes of the Danish Golden Age. He was a strikingly handsome man, too, and tall for those days. 1m70.'

'My height,' says Kerrigan.

'Tall for those days. He was a gambler, too, and nicknamed

"Thor" for his lusty appetites and energy, though he seemed to have more passion than love in him. He never married. "Name me one women who would not make a cuckold of me," he is quoted as saying, and when he ran from Rome home to Denmark for a spell, it was to escape a romantic tangle involving three different women – his Italian mistress, a young German beauty, and a Scottish lady he was manipulated into proposing to. She was very thin. "How I shudder at the thought of those spiky frames," he said. "Give me flesh on the bones." '

Kerrigan laughs.

'Caffé Greco was the haunt of everyone in Rome,' she continues. 'Casanova, Goethe, Gogol, Byron, Liszt. Andersen used to go there in 1833 when he was in Rome for the first time. He was 28. Just before he got famous. But Thorvaldsen recognized him. The story is that one of the first days that Andersen was wandering the streets of Copenhagen when he was fourteen, Thorvaldsen was home on a visit and he passed Andersen on the street and both stopped to look back at one another. I guess Thorvaldsen turned back because Andersen was such a tall, gangling boy mostly, but he said to him, "I suspect we shall be seeing more of each other." Intuition.'

'Let's see,' Kerrigan says. 'In 1833, Kierkegaard would have been twenty, right?'

'Yes. And writing in his journals, "Oh, the sins of passion and of the heart – how much nearer to salvation than the sins of reason!" '

'Sounds a little bit like Andersen.'

'To Kierkgaard, Andersen was "a sniveller", the word he used in a review of Andersen's third novel. Kierkegaard was one of his sternest critics.'

'How did Andersen take to criticism?'

'Generally he would weep. I read somewhere that Mrs Collin once found him prostrate in her garden weeping into the grass over a bad review. And when he visited Charles Dickens in England, Dickens found Andersen once lying face down on the lawn of Gad's Hill place, Dickens home, weeping. Another bad review.

Dickens cheered him up, told him reviews are like mud on your boot, forgotten in a week, while the work itself lives on. Andersen stood on the bank of *Peblinge Sø*, Peblinge Lake – just a few blocks from here – and wept. But he always got his revenge, always got his "money back". He inscribed a copy of his *New Fairy Tales* for Kierkegaard like this, "Dear Mr Kierkegaard, *Either* (whether) you like my little ones *Or* you do not like them. They come without *Fear and Trembling*, and that at any rate is something." Word plays on titles of Kierkegaard's most famous works, *Either/Or* and *Fear and Trembling*.'

'The phrase "And that at any rate is something" also features prominently in a climactic scene of Camus's *The Stranger* which was heavily influenced by Kierkegaard. A coincidence maybe. We'd have to compare the original language versions.'

'Andersen didn't take his ultimate revenge on Kierkegaard until 25 years after the philosopher's attack on him – and six years after Kierkegaard's death – when he wrote the tale "The Snail and The Rose Bush" in 1861. Kierkegaard is the snail, spitting at the world and retiring into his shell, while the rose . . .'

'Andersen.'

'Naturally. . . keeps on blooming because it can do nothing else.

Kerrigan laughs loudly again, then nods. 'Kierkegaard was a great writer, far greater than Andersen.'

'Not everyone would agree,' she says and meets his gaze. 'But the critic who for all purposes *discovered* Kierkegaard, so to speak, twenty years after his death, started the process of his international fame and also took a poke at a couple of Andersen's most revered fairy tales. Georg Brandes – 1842 to 1927. He pointed out that business about the rose-red clouds at the end of "The Little Mermaid". And also that in "The Ugly Duckling" the swan that emerges is a domesticated one, not a wild swan.

'Another of Andersen's critics,' she continues, consulting her starfish book, 'was Johan Ludvig Heiberg – 1791 to 1860. Heiberg was a playwright and manager of the Copenhagen Royal Theater. He wrote vaudevilles and was wildly popular. His most famous and most lasting work is *The Elfin Hill* – *Elverhøj* – from 1828.

You know, the myths of the strange creatures in nature – ghosts, elves – these are unlike fairy tales where after all the woes and troubles the character's experience, they tend to end happily, in one way or another.'

'Like Andersen's cruel period followed by fame.'

'Yes, even if his love life did not follow the pattern. But in the folktales in Denmark, in the ballads and so forth, we're dealing with some wildness in nature and in our soul and fate. Anyway, Heiberg's most famous play was about the elves, just as many of the old Danish folk ballads were about the elfin women who lure men so they become elfin-struck, elfin-wild, making them dance in the woods and lay with them.'

'Like Keats's "La Belle Dame Sans Merci". But tell me, were there no elfin *men* luring *women*?'

'Yes. And there were also elfin women who stood glittering at the edge of the road through the woods waving to lonely travellers to come and dance with them, but if a traveller left the road to go to her, he was led in deeper and deeper as the elfin woman backed away. Finally, when he reached her she would turn and he would see she had no back, and he would disappear into the back that was not there, never to be seen again.'

'Are you trying to tell me something?'

'Yes. About Heiberg. His wife, Johanne Luise Heiberg – 1812 to 1890 – starred in Andersen's play, *The Mulatto*, which was a great success in the theater in 1840. Andersen greatly "admired" her as well – you can see her portrait on the new 200-kroner notes. But Heiberg damned Andersen as "an improviser," a play on the title of Andersen's successful novel. The implication was of shallowness. In one of Heiberg's own plays the damned in hell have to endure the double torment of witnessing two of Andersen's plays.'

Kerrigan shifts on the bench, chuckling. He wonders that she is able to sit so still and straight with her cigarette while producing such a wealth of facts. 'I guess Ho C watered Mrs Collin's grass again over that one with his tears,' he says.

'No doubt. But two years later he wrote a piece in which he himself descends into hell and finds it is true that the damned must witness his two plays, but only as a warm-up for the ultimate torment to come, a play by Heiberg! In another piece, *Galoshes of Fortune*, he represents Heiberg as a parrot.'

'Got his money back again,' Kerrigan says. 'And in the end, who really remembers Heiberg – outside of Denmark anyway? Are you turning in your grave, Johan? Many are called, few chosen, most forgotten.' He studies the face of the bronze sculpture seated so high above him. The thick lips curving out over protruding teeth, the Hebraic nose, the narrow eyes. 'He couldn't have been a very easy person to get on with.'

'To say it mildly. Truly neurotic. He travelled with a length of rope in his luggage in case the hotel caught fire, so he could lower himself from the window. He was even said to leave a note by his bedside every night: "I only seem dead". In case he should slip into a coma while sleeping.'

Kerrigan laughs. 'Did he have any friends at all?'

'Well, he had many fans and royal champions. He knew Mendelssohn, Heinrich Heine, the Grimm brothers, Liszt, Victor Hugo, Alexander Dumas. Charles Dickens presented him with a twelve-volume illustrated edition of his works, every volume of which was inscribed with the words, "To Hans Christian Andersen from his friend and admirer Charles Dickens". In fact, one of Andersen's tales, "The Dung Beetle", was written on a public challenge by Dickens to write a story about such a creature. Andersen dedicated the first English edition of his tales to Dickens. He was also Dickens' houseguest in 1857, but he overstayed his welcome by about three weeks – ignoring the visdom of the old Danish proverb that a fish and a guest begin to stink after three days. After that, Dickens stopped answering his letters, even stopped acknowledging the books and photographs Andersen sent him. Andersen wrote sadly about the end of the friendship in his journals: "All, all over," he wrote. "And that is the way of every story". Which are the closing words of his own tale, "The Fir Tree". Funny, when he first met Dickens years before, he wrote in his journal that his eyes filled with tears of joy, and the friendship ended in his tears as well. Dickens is said to have put a sign up over the bed when he finally left, which proclaimed that H C Andersen slept here for five weeks that seemed like eternity.'

Now Kerrigan finds himself watching not the statue of Andersen but the face of his Associate, her eyes like blue lamps flickering to blue shadow. The sureness with which she spoke, the volume of information, faltering only occasionally to consult her starfish book.

He drops his cigar and steps on it, looks at her again. 'You are a very learned person,' he says softly.

She gazes at him with a mild blankness. 'I am an autodidact,' she says. 'A good research secretary.'

'I know. You go barefoot on the weekends. I rather find that a charming picture. I would dearly love to see your naked little trotters. Do you paint your toenails?'

'Would you not like to know.' She stubs out her cigarette against the iron foundation of the bench and tosses it into the gutter. 'Shall we push onward to the Palace?'

The Palace Bar is just across the Town Hall Square. Kerrigan looks with distaste at the Burger King and 7-Eleven shops on either prime corner of the Square leading into *Strøget*, Walking Street and the Kentucky Fried Chicken joint a few doors away.

'This whole square,' she says as they cross it, 'used to be crisscrossed with trolly tracks. Tom Kristensen describes it in *Hærværk* as a kind of desert that he crosses each evening from his job there in the newspaper.' She points to the east, diagonally across the square to a sign on the second floor showing that the newspaper *Politiken* has its offices there.

'*Hærværk* is a great novel,' says Kerrigan. '*Havoc.* I know the Danish title literally means "vandalism", but "havoc" is the right translation I think.'

'A great unknown novel written in 1930 by a great unknown Danish writer that was made into a great unknown Danish film in 1977 by Ole Roos who also wrote the script, along with Klaus Rifbjerg, who is something like a Danish John Updike, and Ole

Ernst plays the main character beautifully. All unknown. Outside Denmark anyway. And maybe a few other countries.'

'Why do you suppose it *is* so unknown?'

'I think simply because it was not written in English, French, German, or Spanish, but in Danish.'

'Well it *was* translated. Kristensen always reminded me a little bit of the American writer Nathaniel West – he lived 1904-1940, and *Havoc* reminds me a little bit of West's *Day of the Locust* from '39, and maybe even more of *Miss Lonelyhearts* from '33, which was also a newspaper novel. And maybe even John Fante's *Ask the Dust*, also published in '39, though it was virtually unknown until it was reprinted 40 years later on the recommendation of Charles Bukowski. But *Havoc* came first. It really deserves to be read more.'

They stand at the door to the Palace Hotel, but they can see from the street that the bar is not open. She says, 'This hotel was used in the film version of *Havoc*. The main character, Ole 'Jazz' Jastrau, wakes up in one of the rooms here after a mammoth intoxication and looks out of that window up there at this statue of the Lyre Blowers . . .' She checks her book. '. . . sculpted by Siegfried Wagner and Anton Rosen and erected in 1914. Rosen also designed the Palace Hotel here. And the sculpture was a gift to the city from Carlsberg to commemorate the hundredth anniversary of the birth of J C Jacobsen – 1811-1887 – whose initials are engraved on the pillar. He was the father of Carl Jacobsen – 1842-1914 – and named the beer he brewed for his son – Carl and *berg* for the hill on which the brewery was built. They were a second and third generation of brewers and did much for Copenhagen with their cultural funds – not to mention what they did for the Danish beer. Carl, the son, opened *Glyptoteket*, the New Carlsberg museum, in 1897. Incidentally, it is said the horns of the lyre blowers only sound if a virgin over the age of eighteen walks past and that, in fact, they've never been heard.' Kerrigan laughs. 'Where is the Bar des Artistes?' he asks. 'Where 'Jazz' Jastrau in *Havoc* raised his Lindbom cocktail – one part gin, four parts absinthe – and whispered, "Now we begin – very quietly, very slowly – to go to the dogs." '

'I've never been quite certain if it's this bar or the Queen's Pub in the Hotel Kong Frederik, just on the other side of the Walking Street, a 100m or so from *Politiken*'s offices. Either of them could match the description of the bar in *Havoc*, but especially the Palace and the Queen's because you can enter the bar from the hotel lobby in both, so no one on the street can know for sure if you are entering the bar or the hotel or the restaurant.'

Kerrigan is thinking about the character of Ole 'Jazz' Jastrau, a failed poet turned literary critic, going to the dogs. 'It was a religious book really,' he says. 'Very spiritual. A man revolting against the lies of a "profession", of employment. Remember he says he thinks he could never forget Jesus among the whores, and the more he squandered and drank, the closer Jesus came to him, rising amidst the havoc of his heart.'

'My mouth is dry from all this talk,' she says as only a Danish woman can say it. 'Let us get a drink.'

6

Café Nick

Café Nick
Nikolajgade ***(Nicholas Street)*** **20**
1068 København K

They cross past the looming dark structure of St Nicholas Church, no longer a church at all, but a restaurant, among other things, with a green metal pissoir on the street outside it, a stone's throw from *Højbro Plads*, known in the Golden Age of Copenhagen (1800 1850) as 'thief's square', where stolen property could be had, and un-had. Theft was severely dealt with in the Golden Age, she tells him, and embezzlement, corruption and fraud were also rampant in the civil service.

Hans Christian Andersen's 1829 novel *O.T.* deals with social and political conditions in Denmark. Even the two magnificent golden horns – emblem of Denmark's Viking past, found by country people in the fields in 1639 and 1734, were stolen in 1802 by a goldsmith who melted them into 1,200 rigsdollars of counterfeit gold coins for which he was sentenced to life imprisonment until released in 1837 for being a model prisoner.

In the Café Nick across the street from St Nicholas Church, Kerrigan asks, 'What did Hans Christian Andersen drink?'

'He liked porter.'

'Let's drink a porter then,' says Kerrigan as they sit beneath a 20s painting of a woman in a lilac shirt smoking a cigarette, no doubt a racy matter at the time, and the waiter brings them bottles of Carlsberg black stuff.

They toast the dead tale-teller with a *skål.*

'How wonderful if there are really ghosts,' says Kerrigan. 'If Andersen's spirit were here right now, witnessing our toast.'

Then they sit in silence among the paintings and darkness of the Nick. Kerrigan is a little tight and wonders if she is really as sober as she looks. He glances at her starfish book on the table, wondering how such a slender pad can contain so much information; she dutifully opens it, though he thinks he sees some hesitation pull at the corner of her comely mouth.

'There used to be an expression, Nikolaj Bohemians. It applied to the customers of all the small bars and cafés that were around this square, around the church, Sankt Nikolaj. You know what trade Sankt Nikolaj was the patron saint of – aside from being Santa Claus?'

He shakes his head.

'He was the patron saint of sailors! There's been a church here for over seven hundred years, but the original burnt down in the great fire of 1795. The one there now was rebuilt in 1917. This café opened in 1904. It was the main café frequented by artists, but they called the whole area the "Mine Field" because there were so many places to go in and explode your consciousness with drink. The story goes that this place doesn't have its name from the church, but from a sailor named Nikolaj Christensen who was served a lukewarm snaps here in 1914, complained, got into an argument with the waiter, and bought the place just so he could fire him. There used to be only artists and writers here, but now,' – she nods towards a pair of men in suits sitting a few tables away, 'it is mixed.'

'I know something about this place,' he says. 'A poem. Want to hear?'

'If I say yes I can preserve the illusion of free will.'

He laughs, says, 'Smart-ass,' drinks some porter. 'Now you'll have to beg me.'

Her blue eyes look up beseechingly at him. 'Please?' she says softly, and his blood jumps. He clears his throat, recites:

> 'The painter dances singing in a beer bass
> about all the great earth – at Café Nick
> in Copenhagen – and gaily fly the wild
> angels forth who love his lovely trick.
>
> He stands on his head, he stands on his belly
> he stands on the table, glides up
> in the air with his whole mighty body
> as if he were the earth, as if he were the cork
>
> in these bottles – he sinks again
> to the floor down in the great peace
> in glorystreams that everyone
> glimpsed until he gently slid
>
> down from the chair and under the table,
> where he lies and leads the meeting:
> "Dance, dance in a sky-blue
> roar of tones" – then the painter stopped.'

Her eyes lighten as she watches him recite, and her excited reaction excites him.

'Who is that?' she asks.

'Ah-hah! So your little junior woodchuck's manual doesn't contain *every*thing after all! That's "The Dancing Painter" by Jens August Schade, who Poul Borum called "the greatest Danish poet of the 20s and the liveliest force in modern Danish literature". Schade was born in 1903, died in '78. He was considered a pornographer for years because he wrote about all the things dearest to our hearts – sex and love and drink. Borum compares him to D H Lawrence, e e cummings, Henry Miller and the Frenchman, Eluard, but Schade is in some ways better than any of them because he combines all their qualities and transcends all their weaknesses. His first book of poetry, *The Living Violin*, came out in 1926 and was subtitled *spiritual and sensual songs* and that is his force, the lack of dualism between body and soul. Borum really hits it when he calls him a happy Baudelaire, although his last book, a novel, *I'm Mad About You*, explored eros as psychosis. There Borum points something out – how close the name Schade is to Sade.'

'And Borum is dead now, too,' she says.

'Dark dark dark,' says Kerrigan. 'They all go into the dark. You know he once invited me to collaborate with him on a translation of the poems of Pia Tafdrup. Borum, I mean.'

Her gaze flickers. 'You *knew* him?'

'Never met the man. The offer came from a third party. I declined.'

'Why in the hell did you do that?'

'Because I was stupid. I was afraid. I guess I was afraid I couldn't measure up, that Borum, that Denmark maybe, would swallow me alive.'

'Are you still afraid of that?'

'No. Now I know myself a little better. I *know* I can't measure up so there's nothing to be afraid of.'

'Do you know Pia Tafdrup?'

'A little. She is a fine poet. Powerful and delicate at the same time. I've translated a few of her poems, but it's such an impossible task, translating, so frustrating. I don't even try anymore.'

'Why?'

'Because a good translator – as a friend of mine who is a good translator told me, Stacey Knecht, who translated Marcel Möring from the Dutch, she told me this just as she had decided to quit translating and go over to writing her own stuff – a good translator has to put himself second. And that has always been too difficult for me.'

He lights a Sumatra, sees her watching him, extends the box, and to his surprise she takes one. He strikes a match, holds it across the table, and she lightly guides his hand with her fingertips. The touch runs across the surface of his flesh, and he thinks of Schade in the Copenhagen bars and serving houses and *drikkesteder* (drinking places – the Danes believe in calling a spade a spade, just as the

Danish word for brassière is literally "breast holder") surrounded by the women he loved so – his muses, he called them – drunk on red wine and desire, writing his poetry even under the table. He feels the water in his eyes, thinking of the man, thinking he might have met him once before he died in 1978 had he only stirred himself to action. He thinks of all the things he could experience still if only he could stir himself to do so, overcome his ego.

'Here's another,' he says, 'In the Café,' and recites:

'A good song
A crazy little miracle
Comes out of the jukebox
While I keep still,
And to everyone's surprise
I move the chair away beneath me
And keep sitting on the air

Before me sits a girl
With ugly teeth
And fleeting eyes.
She is still
– we each know
What is going on inside the other,
And strong as lions our souls kiss.

She rises in the air
And I with her
We find each other
There over the tables.
And to boom and applause
At the song's miracle
We wrap ourselves around each other
And roundabout out the café.'

She flicks a crumb of tobacco off her pink tongue, asks, 'What is your education?'

'My education? I have a doctorate. A Ph.D.'

'Oh! Can I touch you?'

He laughs, remembering the Norwegian-Danish Aksel Sandemose's novel about the so-called *Janteloven*, The Law of Jante, the first commandment of which was, *Thou shalt not think thou art something*. 'It's just a piece of paper,' he says, 'right?'

'Meaning,' she says, 'wrong, *right*? That it is something *more* than just a piece of paper, *right*?'

He shrugs, smiles, caught out in his self-pity and sentiment and seduction and pride. He doesn't mind. He glimpses a mild gentleness lurking beneath her caution and mockery.

'What was your subject?'

'Literature. Specifically, verisimilitude. Want to know more?'

'I think you're going to tell me.'

'No. Only if you want.'

'Please.'

'How writers of fiction seem to create reality. *Veris similis* in Latin. *Vrai semblance* in French. The appearance of reality. The way a writer creates a credible illusion to get the reader to suspend disbelief long enough to listen and experience what the writer wants to transmit. Beneath the illusion, if the writer is serious, lies the stuff of truth, of a deeper reality, that has nothing to do with the trappings of everyday life that were used to build the illusion – unless those very trappings are what he is writing about. But the reality beneath that illusion can help us understand something about human existence. Fiction, even the most seeming realistic fiction, is not existence, but *about* existence. For example, Kafka uses sensory images to make us believe, or at least accept, the preposterous notion that Gregor Samso has turned into a beetle or a cockroach or a bug, depending on the translation, and because we believe that for a little while, we experience some deep mystery of existence.'

'What is the word again?'

'Verisimilitude. It took me half a year just to learn to pronounce it.'

She trims her cigar on the edge of the ashtray. 'And now you are writing a book about bars.'

'What could be more existentially essential? Reason is an unreasonable faculty. It will strangle us if we take it too seriously. It needs damping, and that is why we come to these places, *n'est-ce pas*?'

She smiles wanly, and they sit in silence for a time, listening to music from a radio behind the bar. Bob Dylan is singing the end of 'When I Paint My Masterpiece'. There is a pause and then he begins, 'I Threw It All Away', and Kerrigan finds himself remembering an afternoon perhaps fifteen years earlier when he was on the board of a literary festival, a three-day festival assembling people like William Burroughs, Ken Kesey, Michael McClure, the Fugs, and a dozen or more fine Danish poets. Kerrigan got involved through an American he knew who owned a bookshop and who was the driving force in the whole event which was to take place at the Betty Nansen Theater. The Danish Ministry of Culture gave him 25,000 crowns as a seed fund, no small amount, particularly then, and Kerrigan's friend, in a fit of altruism, appointed a down-and-out Vietnam vet he knew as treasurer. It wasn't completely altruistic – the vet's mother was secretary to another arts fund. But it was also altruistic. He and Kerrigan had to come into Nick's one afternoon looking for the vet who had absconded with the funds and had been seen in various bars around town, ordering full bottles of whiskey – which at Danish bar prices is unpayable. They found him here at a table beneath this very painting, an Inuit woman on either side of him, helping him polish off a liter of Dewar's. Ghost of Schade in him perhaps.

They got the money back, most of it, thanks to the guy's mother, and the festival was held, and Kerrigan remembers afterwards winding up at the end of the first night in a bar on *Frederiksberg Allé* in hot embrace with a Swedish mystery writer ten years his senior. He still can recall the feel of her lips on his. Such beautiful kisses. Where did she ever learn to kiss like that? All, all gone, he thinks now. His American friend, his beautiful artist wife who took her own life. And somehow thinking of himself at that time, looking back upon himself, he sees a man in his 30s who was young and brash and so very full of himself that he threw all the greatest potential for joy right out the window.

How he wishes he could go back and adjust himself somehow, wonders if he is a better person now or if his character is still and always will be muddied with such overweening egotism.

And then of course, there is the other thing which makes him wish to enter a dissociative fugue. What his mother did. His wife. His little ones. All, all gone.

He tips his stout bottle over the edge of his empty glass, but not a drop slips out. He wills himself from the gloom, glances at her handsome face, lost in its own distance, its own music. Such a lovely face, he thinks and realizes suddenly that she recognizes that she herself must also bear some blame for the fact that she did not get the education she wished for, and his awareness of her awareness of this touches him with a sense of kinship with her.

We have both been foolish. We both have regrets, and here we sit in our 50s in an old café over empty glasses, empty bottles.

He touches the back of her hand. She smiles and removes it to reach for her cigar in the ashtray.

7

Hviids Wine Room *(Hviids Vinstue)*

Hviids Vinstue
Kongens Nytorv *(The King's New Square)* **19**
1050 København K

He can feel the drink in his legs as they walk down *Vingårdstræde*, Wine Yard Street, where years before someone had attempted, in vain, to cultivate grapes for wine. Not suited to the Danish climate. Somewhere he seems to remember reading of a Roman expedition to Scandinavia – was it in Tacitus? – in which the leader explained his withdrawal by saying: The land is uninhabitable. There are no olive trees.

They come out behind *Kongens Nytorv*, the King's New Square, and she points east. 'That's the National Bank there,' she says, and he responds, 'Nine hundred and ninetynine million pound sterling in the blueblack bowels of the bank of Ulster.'

'Sorry?'

'Joyce,' he explains and pats his leather satchel. '*Finnegan.*' When she does not respond, he continues, 'You know Joyce visited Copenhagen. In September 1936. He was convinced he had Viking blood in him. Dublin and Cork owe their origins to Danish Vikings – but he also once told his brother Georgio that he wanted to go to Denmark because the Danes massacred so many of his ancestors. He had taught himself Danish in order to read Ibsen –

at that time Norway was under Denmark. In fact, Joyce's first publication, at the age of seventeen, was a long article about Ibsen's last play, *When We Dead Awaken*. The review was published on April Fool's Day, 1900. Joyce professed to believe that Ibsen was the greatest dramatist of all time, even greater than Shakespeare. But he also admired Andersen greatly. When he was here he even bought a toy as a reminder of Andersen for his five-year-old grandson. He called Andersen, Denmark's greatest writer. He was also full of praise for Carlsberg beer, and his wife was full of praise for the Danish light, its continuous changes, which is one of the things that caused me to fall in love with Denmark, too. Joyce also had a high opinion of Brandes and even had a picture of him drawn by Ivan Opfer, also a Dane, who drew Joyce as well, though Joyce did not at all like that picture. Brandes apparently didn't like *his* either. So either this Opfer was maladroit or sharp as a knife. By the way Tom Kristensen met Joyce when he was here.'

She listens carefully to what Kerrigan is telling her, then stops walking finally and says, 'Tell me something. You know so much about Copenhagen already. Are you toying with me? Why do you need my help? I hope you don't have something else in mind.'

Kerrigan hopes the darkness hides his blush. 'I only know a little,' he says. 'And very little about the bars. You know much more than I do.'

They are standing outside the Royal Theater. 'Do you know who those two are?' she asks, pointing to the great seated statues flanking the ornate entry.

'Heiberg and Oehlenschläger, right?'

'*Holberg* and Oehlenschläger. Ludvig Holberg was born a century before Heiberg, in 1684, and if you are interested in drunks you ought to read his *Jeppe På Bjerget*, Jeppe of the Hill. It is about a drunken peasant who ends up in the bed of the baron. Holberg is our Molière and our Voltaire.'

He hears resentment and distrust in her tone. 'Right,' he says. 'I always mix up those names, Heiberg and Holberg. Heiberg is the guy who wrote the vaudevilles and *The Elfin Hill* and made snide remarks about Andersen. What about Oehlenschläger?'

'He introduced romanticism to Denmark. He wrote a poem about the golden horns that had been found in the Danish field in the fifth century by a young girl and a farmer. Children of nature, you see. Not academics.'

They are crossing the King's New Square toward the wine room. 'Do you resent me?' he asks. 'Because of my education?'

'Certainly not. Oehlenschläger's point is that pagan and Christian ideals stem from the same roots. Those are the same horns that were stolen and melted down for the gold. The thief thought the gold was worth more than the art and the history.'

He feels heavy as they enter the labyrinthine cave-like dimness of Hviids Vinstue, established in 1723, the same year as the Duke in Dublin, older than any bar in the US – older than the US for that matter. They move past the bar to one of the snugs to the side. There are many pictures on the walls, photographs, cut-out articles, caricatures. She has her starfish book out again, and he has to concentrate on her words. 'Upstairs here,' she tells him, 'used to be the Grand Café, and these two together were the outer rim of the Mine Field around Nikolaj Church I told you about before. From the 1950s to the 60s.'

The bartender comes to take their orders, and Kerrigan asks for a pint of Carlsberg. 'In honor of Joyce.'

'I can't drink any more beer,' she says, and Kerrigan ignores the fact that he can see two tips of her nose. 'Why not have a campari?' he says.

She nods. 'Good idea.'

As the waiter crosses back to the bar, Kerrigan says, 'He looks like a pug.'

'That's Jørgen Gammel Hansen,' she says. ' "Old Hansen", they call him. He used to be middleweight boxing champion of Europe about twenty years ago.'

'I walked right into that,' he says, and as their drinks are set before them and the bartender leaves again, Kerrigan looks at her glass and says, 'Campari, red as breathless kisses.'

Her eyes meet his. He can't read them, but he goes on nonetheless. 'Jens August Schade again. "In Hviids Wine Room". 1963.'

'Can you say it for me?'

He nods, recites:

> That time that time –
> it took so many years
> when I came down to earth to see
> all the crazy people at "Hviid"
>
> We drank Absinth – as light green
> as the woods and like frogs,
> Campari red as breathless
> kisses and red panties
>
> Blessed was the golden beer . . .'

He stares up at the ceiling. 'I've lost the rest.'

'How drunk are you?' she asks, her eyes friendly.

'Just a wee twisted,' he says. 'But not on beer alone.'

'Meaning?'

'Did anyone ever tell you your eyes are like blue lamps?'

'Frequently,' she says, but the subtext he thinks he hears is, *Never, I like it, say it again, but not just yet.* Then she writes something in her starfish book and says, 'I really must read Schade. I've heard of him but never actually read him.' She closes the book and slips it into her black leather bag, and he recites:

> 'The starfish crawl upon the wall
> upon the floor and through the door
> the starfish with their many legs
> and not so many eyes
> the starfish that can hug and crush
> never seeing why.'

She sips her red Campari. 'You must spend a great deal of time memorizing verses.'

'Hey, that was my own! I just wrote it right now this minute.' In his own ears, his voice is hoarse from beer and cigars.

'*Sludder*,' she says, which means *nonsense* in Danish, but somehow more effectively, with the double soft 'd' sound of garbage, slush.

'Not *sludder*. There is no drunkeness like mine. I have been guzzling wine. Sometimes when I get to a certain point, words start leaking out. Like Tom Kristensen said, intoxication is just a poem that hasn't got a form. Here . . .:

> Where are the Cruzes of yesteryear
> whose cheek was a dimple of cheer
> who wore a blue bra
> and laughed hardy har
> as I dance on the floor, no more, no more.'

'Who are the Cruzes?'

'Evelyn Cruz. The first girl I ever kissed. I was fourteen. She was wearing a blue bra. I could see its lacey edge in the V of her blouse, and I said, "I see you're wearing a blue one today" – very daring words for a lad in those innocent days – and she smiled the sweetest dimply smile, and she let me kiss her.'

'Did you really just make up that rhyme? I'm impressed.'

'I hoped you would be, even if it's not very good.'

'Why? Did you hope?'

'Because your eyes. Like blue lamps. My Associate's eyes shine like lamps of blue / She drinks campari from a glass so red and true . . .' He pauses, knows he's lost it, entered the stage that comes after the facile rhymes: Dark dark dark,' he says.'They all go into the dark. Even T S Eliot. I'm stuck. I always start mouthing Eliot fragments when I'm stuck. Like the test patterns on a TV. Let's you know it's still in function, even if there's no show.'

'Recite that Schade for me again. That last one. The one with the campari.'

And Kerrigan thinks how happy he would be if she were wearing red ones. And let him see.

8

Café Malmø

Café Malmø
Havnegade *(Harbor Street)* **35**
1058 København K

He realizes too late, crossing the King's New Square toward *Nyhavn*, New Harbor, that it was a mistake to suggest one more stop. Had they simply ordered a taxi from Hviids to his place – or hers – perhaps things would have gone differently. Of course, she had only asked for the poem, but he did not fail to see the glint in her eyes over the line about the red panties, which did not fail to set him to puerile speculation over what color hers were: How foolish he felt at his age to wonder breathlessly whether she were wearing red ones. Foolishly happy. Happily foolish. And at what age might that be? Late youth. Advanced late youth.

He tries to save the moment by reciting another, composed on the spot, that he feels is true in his lungs:

'Has anyone seen that friend of mine
Who said with a smile, "This is wine.
Have a glass. See what you think.
Sit down. Relax. Drink." '

But his anticipated pleasure of its hedonistic resononance sours. He feels suddenly like nothing so much as a drunk, thick-tongued, with slurred vision.

Now they walk along the quiet side of *Nyhavn*, past the *Sorte Ravn*, the Black Raven Restaurant, along the canal where the old boats sit lashed between impassable low bridges – drawbridges actually – toward the harbor and the Malmø boats, hovercraft that take you across to the once-Danish now Swedish city in half an hour or so – a city that will soon be reachable by the bridge scheduled for completion later that year at which time the hovercraft to Malmø will disappear. Everything forever vanishing. *Ubi ubi sunt*? He asks her to point out the different places where Hans Christian Andersen lived here.

She shows him *Nyhavn* 20, the narrow tall house where Andersen stayed in 1835 when he started writing fairy tales, and *Nyhavn* 18, his last home before he moved in with a friend to be nursed as he died of liver cancer in 1875. And she gestures down *Lille Strandstræde*, saying, 'He lived there in number 67 from 1847 to 1865.' But Kerrigan hears the chill of professionalism has returned to her tone, and he regrets having suggested they stop into Café Malmø to see the world's largest collection of beer openers, as reported in *The Guiness Book of Records*.

They turn down *Havnegade*, Harbour Street and he tells her about someone he knows who lives there, an affluent physician named Hugo Berning who with the late consultant, Jørgen Steen Olsen, co-authored a book entitled *Time's Arrow* aimed to disprove the third law of thermodynamics and the postulation that the universe will end in the heat death. He mentioned this once at a cocktail party to the scientific attaché at the American Embassy who said, 'Well I hope they don't succeed. Otherwise my car won't start when I turn the key tomorrow.'

'Entropy,' Kerrigan says and regrets it even more when they climb down the steps into the basement pub, and the first he sees across the bar section are two men passed out at a little table as Paul McCartny sings from a sound system, 'I'm So Sorry, Uncle Albert'. One of them is wearing a Napoleon's hat fashioned from a sheet of newspaper. On the wall above their slumped heads a sign offers beer and tequila shooters at a cut rate.

As they sit and wait to order, she reads to him from her starfish book that the café was opened in 1870, has its name from Copenhagen's twin city, Malmø, just across the sound in Sweden. It is an old sailor's bar, but many international guests come to see the beer opener collection.

The beer openers are everywhere, framed on the walls, hanging in thick clusters like stalagtites from the ceiling. Kerrigan tries to imagine tourists streaming in from near and far to study these thousands of basically pretty boring openers. He wonders if there are doubles. 'So Sorry Uncle Albert' is still playing – the part where the music sounds like a 20s dance hall.

Then the barmaid is there – young and punk-haired – admiring the blue lapus lazuli cross that Kerrigan has not even noticed all day at his Associate's throat, although he does see now that it is the same blue as her eyes, and he says, 'It really is, really is *beauful*,' and his own ear catches the loss of the syllable. 'Beauti-ful,' he enunciates to demonstrate that he is at least not that far gone, but he says the word too loudly, and the man with the newspaper hat lifts his head. He is leaning against the wall where Kerrigan notices yet another sign: *Table Whores Club*. A man of desolated face, eyelids flicking low and the smile of *Sheelanagig*, unforgiven unforgiving unrepentant dissoluted idiocy on his wet mouth which opens and says, 'Ha! Ha! On the bottom of the sky the shewolf lies!' Then he once more wraps his dreams about his heart and slips away through the wall fallen falling forever, pig without arse ahmen!

In the course of these movements, his elbow overturns a glass whose stale-looking content spills into the lap of the other sleeping man who jolts upright and croaks, 'That was juice-*sizzle*-me *smart*!'

'Well you're not so *cancer*-eat-me clever yourself, you clown.'

'Fok,' the first says and lays his head down once again, and Kerrigan begins to realize he is watching these events through closed eyes himself as his thought wanders into a variation of an abbreviation he intuits as FOQ – Frequently Oinked Questions from the snouts of horny swine.

'Mr Kerrigan!' his Associate snaps.

'Yes, we are open,' says Kerrigan, remembering some sign he saw on some shop door. 'Shoulden we dans?'

'You'll be doing it alone, sir,' she says.

'It is a lonely dance,' he says. 'Upon *monsieur*'s sword.' And notices that hanging just above the cross is a steel shield-like ornament half the size of a cigarette pack. 'Whas'at?' he asks.

'In fact,' she tells him, 'it is a North African chastity belt.'

He misses a beat. 'You puttin' me on?'

'No,' she enunciates, demonstrating for him how utterly nil the word's message can be.

Disgrace multiplies as he stumbles, climbing up out of the basement pub and, again, stepping into the idling cab outside, that his Associate has called.

'*Nu går det hurtigt*,' he says to her in Danish. 'It's going fast now.' A Danish saying. By which he means to disassociate himself from the involuntary acceleration of his intoxication. 'Intoxication,' he says, 'is a poem which has not found its form. That's Ole Jastrau, 'Jazz' to his friends and colleagues.' Written by the man who wrote a poem about a barfight of flying billiard balls . . .'

'I read the book,' she says. She is chill but not so chill as to provoke him, he observes through the fog. 'A drunken man understand more than you think,' he mutters. And, 'You have experience at this. Handling sssslightly intoxicated gentlemen.'

'My father gave me some practice.'

He leans closer, smells her perfume and feels the ache of loneliness in his heart. He wants so badly to touch her, for her to touch him. He wants to recite Joyce to her:

> 'Touch me. Soft eyes. Soft soft soft hand.
> I am lonely here. O, touch me soon now.
> I am quiet here alone. Sad too.
> Touch touch me.'

Or even to jocularize with a word of Molly's: Give us a touch, Poldy. I'm dying for it.'

But he would feel a self-pitying fool for it and wills discretion upon himself. 'Listen,' he says quietly. 'I'm not that bad. Just didn't eat enough. Cup of forkee fix me right up in case, just in case, you might like for example to sleep in my arms after I brush my teeth and shower. I promise you: no uninvited monkey business.'

'Is your self-control so certain?'

Rhetorical question? 'Absolutely,' he assures her. 'Of course it would be hard. I mean, I mean, *difficult*, but . . .'

She smiles. 'Not this time, Mr Kerrigan,' she says as the cab pulls in along the curb at his apartment on *Øster Søgade*, East Lake Street.

'What a lovely view,' she says, admiring the lake across the road.

'Nicer from the apartment inside,' he says.

She shakes her head, opens the door for him. 'Can you get your key in the lock or will you need help?'

'Cour*sh* I can,' he says, manages not to lunge at her for a kiss, gives her his hand instead, which he feels she takes warmly with a gentle embrace of her fingers. *Touch touch me*. 'Deep down you *are* a gentleman,' she says.

'Cour*sh* I am.'

He stands swaying on the street outside his building as the cab rolls off. He sees her fingers twinkle at him from behind the dark glass, then the whispered roar of the engine is moving off, the rump of the car disappearing.

We followed the rump of a misguiding woman, said Fergus.

He is standing just outside the white picket fence of the building beside his own, finds himself staring at a forsythia bush – at first blankly, then, slowly, perceiving that it is in bloom, an explosion of yellow leaves. Dimly he remembers something she said earlier about the green of the trees at the Tivoli gate and is suddenly aware of the fact that the forsythia is in fact already beginning to fade. It bloomed probably a week or more ago, and he has not even noticed until this moment when it only has perhaps another week left before the dazzling yellow leaves fade to the green of any other bush. Yellow as the curls that frame her face.

His eyes fix upon it, fighting the blur of his intoxication, and he begins to consider his age, how many springs remain for him, how many more times he will have the pleasure of seeing the yellow forsythia or the green of the Tivoli trees.

Slowly he climbs his dusty, shadowy staircase toward the little stone angel beside the door to his apartment. And he remembers then from whence these thoughts originate. His father's favorite poet, A E Housman:

> 'Loveliest of trees, the cherry now
> Is hung with bloom along the bough . . .
> And since to look at things in bloom
> Fifty springs is little room,
> About the woodland I will go
> To see the cherry hung with snow.'

Fifty springs? Hardly. Not half. Or half that.

Upstairs at his desk he peers blearily across the lake to a row of night-shadowed buildings; they remind him of the sense of mystery he left behind with his youth. Then he believed such buildings across such bodies of water at such a dusky hour contained wondrous secrets. Now he sees they are only more buildings, containing more people. The mystery is much more pedestrian, much closer to home, the mystery of his own fingers holding this pen, writing these words.

He rises, puts on a Rautavaara CD: Einojuhani Rautavaara (b.1928), Finnish composer of mysterious bombastic modern classical music – greater to Kerrigan's mind than Sibelius, greater certainly than the Danish Carl Nielsen, whose face is carried on the new Danish hundred-crown notes, greater than Mahler (1860-1911), who is said to have been Thomas Mann's model for the main character of *Death in Venice*.

In his armchair he watches the flashing red and green neon sign of the Jyske Bank ripple across the water, disappear, reappear, as the strains of the Helsinki Philharmonic doing *Angels and Visitations* fill the darkness of his room; the composition is from 1978, the first of Rautavaara's Angel series (*Angel of Dusk*, 1980, *Playgrounds for Angels* and *Angels of Light*, 1994).

In Rautavaara's words, 'These angels did not stem from fairytales or religious kitsch, but from the conviction that other realities exist beyond those we are normally aware of, entirely different forms of consciousness. From this alien reality, creatures rise up which could be called angels. They may bear some resemblance to the visions of William Blake, and are certainly related to Rainer Maria Rilke's awe-inspiring figures of holy dread: " . . . every angel is terrible . . ." '

Rautavaara tells how the first impetus for *Angels and Visitations* came from Rilke: ' . . . should one suddenly press me to his heart, I would perish by his more powerful presence . . .' This caused Rautavaara to recollect a childhood dream of an enormous, grey, powerful, silent creature who would approach and clasp him in his arms. 'I struggled for dear life – as one is supposed to wrestle with an angel – until I awoke. The figure came back night after night, and I spent the days fearing its return. Finally, after dozens of those battles, I learned to surrender, to throw myself into the creature . . . This was a visitation.'

At the climax of the symphony, when the visiting angel's embrace is finally accepted, a man's deep surrendering scream is heard amidst the exquisitely high encompassment of the violins and harps and celesta.

But before that moment arrives this night Kerrigan has staggered into the bedroom, shed his clothes and crawled beneath the covers of his bed. The scream enters the darkness of the next room, fades into silence.

DAY TWO

Around the lakes, the Seducer

'Most men enjoy a young girl as they do
a glass of champagne,
in a single frothing moment.'

– Søren Kierkegaard, *The Seducer's Diary*

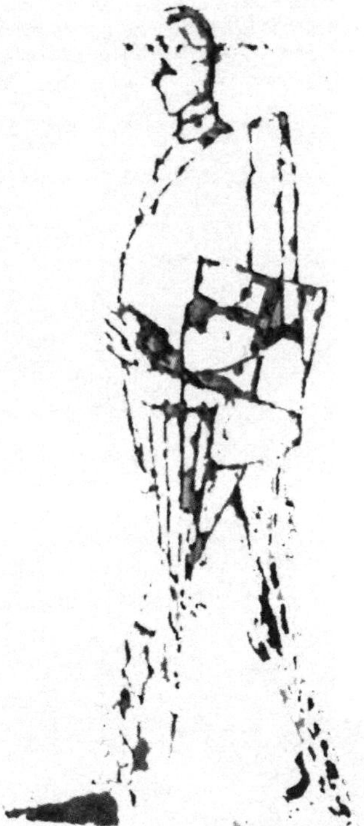

9

Preben's Sausage Wagon *(Preben's Pølsevogn)*

Preben's Pølsevogn
Sølvtorv *(Silver Square)*
2100 København Ø

TCHIK! TCHOK! TCHEK!

A harsh ratchetting sound cuts at the semi-conscious semi-paradise of sleep. Groggily he recognizes it to be the song of the magpie nesting in the tree outside his bedroom window. He regrets having scared a yellow cat out of that tree recently, regrets not having leaned out to poke down the nest with a broomstick.

Song?! Non-song. The song of a ratchet making quarter turns. He lies there trying to think of the word, the combination of letters that would describe the ugly sound, this noise. Thinks lazily of the speech of the cat in *Ulysses*.

-*Mrkgnao!* it said as Mr Bloom promised milk for the pussens, and somewhere in S J Perlman a cat walks into a room and says, "Mrkgnao!" and someone observes that it is a very intelligent cat, for it can quote James Joyce.

Then, as he puzzles again over the words of the magpie, he is startled to realize it is rather like the sound of his own initials – *Tchek!* And *Tcheklechklechekclecheklechek! Tchek!!* – and falls abruptly awake, but slides part-way back down again into that cozy paradise. This is not the dream but the recollection of a dream he realizes as he labors semi-consciously to translate perfect dream images into imperfect words. As one dreamy part of his mind examines the verbalized image of himself and 'the woman' standing at a private window draped in two tongues of curtain one falls away as he touches it and they flee not to be caught looking in by the policeman who watches and a red-jacketted postman delivers the letter, another less dreamy part understands why when he tells a dream, even if occasionally some of the words he chooses illuminate its meaning – no not *meaning*, *power* perhaps, *scope*, *perfection* – other words alter it hopelessly, disturbing the cooperation of a hundred nuances and successfully evading the perfect core.

He realizes now he is staring at the ceiling even as his eyes droop again back into semi-contented semi-paradise, his hand beneath the eiderdown *showmemineI'llshowyouyours*-stiff as a stickloving phantom in the gallery of lost cunts cornblue eyes the mirror happy hopping hopalong eiderdown honeypie furrypie drive me crazy sweet and ***TCHEK! TCHEK! TCHEK!***
– the motherfucking fuck ugly magpie rips away his sleep.

Now his eyes are irreparably open. The ceiling floats with shadow and light and he is gazing upon the molded plaster borders, considering that they are a good selling point if he wants to move out. The ceiling is white and shadow drifts slowly there in an agreeable manner. He is heavy but not unhappy, not at all, for his now wakeful mind harbors an image of the twinkling eyes of his Associate.

He pictures her face, her full lips, delicate hands with red nails, the fullness of her breasts and shadowed line between them beneath the black neckline of her blouse, how she looks from behind, narrow dark slacks on her trim hips. Dreamy again, his eyes float with the shadows on the ceiling, fragments of memory, light on her smiling white teeth, pointed red nail tapping the page, her sculpted fingers he would kiss. His breath is deep and slow, the images behind his eyes a mix of pleasure and longing.

Dreamily he recalls the orgasmic cry of the man embraced by

the angel in Rautavaara's symphony and remembers then the Finnish girl he met some time ago at the bar in Hotel Këmp in Helsinki, teaching him the word *Multatuli*. In Finnish it means 'earth and fire' but also means, as she explained in her slow ponderous English, 'I haf just hod an orgasm.'

' "I came" you mean,' he said, and her icy blue eyes and warm mouth regarded him. She also taught him to say *Perkele*:

> *Perkele*! she taught me to say,
> The Finnish girl with ice blue eyes.
> No, *louder*! she said. *Stronger*!
> Fist the table, let it fly:
> *Perkele!*
> It means Satan, she said,
> The most evil you can speak.
> And the ice glittered in her eyes,
> her teeth, her warm hands.

His hand slides beneath the cover as he thinks of her, of his Associate, of Perkele and Multatuli which was also, he knows, a pseudonym for the Dutch writer Eduard Douwes Dekker (1820-1887), a controversial anti-colonial Dutch writer whose masterpiece was the novel *Max Havelaar* from 1860, translated into English by R Edwards in 1967 and made into a film in the 1980s. However, the word *multatuli*, as used by the Dutchman, is from the Latin and means literally, 'I have suffered much', which it occurs to Kerrigan is perhaps a variation of the old saw, After orgasm all animals are sad, the little death, *la petite mort*, the gentle killing. However, Kerrigan notes, he is *not* sad after his orgasm. He is sated and happy and meditating his Associate.

Then abruptly his contented meditations stop flowing smack against the awareness that he does not remember how the night ended. He remembers New Harbor, Andersen's residences, sky the deep blue of Danish April night. He remembers her pointing to a door, can remember no words. That in itself is like a dream: a woman points to a door. The woman points to the door.

Sweat is hot on his forehead now. Desire leaves him. He takes his hand from beneath the covers. Then he remembers the Café Malmø. McCartney's 'Uncle Albert'. A conversation. Was there dancing? Did he dance? Did he reach for her? Pucker up sloppily for a kiss she did not want, denied him. *That is not it at all, that is not what I meant at all.* With the edge of the sheet, he wipes sweat from his brow. *Asshole.*

He gropes to his nightstand for his glasses, touches also a book, Hemingway's *In Our Time*. He opens it at random, begins to read 'Big Two-Hearted River' and burns out by the second paragraph. Pills. Strong drink-headache pills with codeine – Codymagnyl. Mega codeine you can purchase over the counter in this country.

And as he rises from his bed he feels true pain invade his skull. He stands in the center of the bedroom, temples throbbing evilly, the blank patches of memory filled with humliating possibilities. His eyes cling to a shelf of books against the wall – Poe, Dostoyevski, London, Aristophanes, Appolonius Rhodius, Voltaire, Kipling, Saki, Turgenev, Augustine, Dante, Gibbons, St Jerome, Conrad.

The horror! The horror!

Or as Stanley Elkin put it, "Ah! The horror, the horror".

Nausée. Mr Kerrigan – he dead. We are the hollow men, a penny for the old guy, we are the stuffed men.

He reaches for the Danté and opens it to a double-page reproduction of the William Blake illustration for the sphere of the lustful, coils of naked embracing bodies swirling away. Must it be bad to lust? To desire? Even if it *is* an illusion, it is a lovely one. What is wrong with illusions anyway? Especially if, in the end, everything is one?

The throbbing in his head slows, and he reaches to the bureau top for the jar of pills, pops two, dry. He turns from the wall, eyes sweeping past a framed Asger Jorn print from 1966. *Dead Drunk Danes*, oil on canvas, a colorful swirl of molten faces painted seven years before Jorn died at 59. (That would leave me four to go.) Cobra School painter – Copenhagen, Brussels, Amsterdam. Brother of Jørgen Nash, the mermaid killer.

Oh, my mind is full of cobras and dead mermaids. No, scorpions. The end is near but golf goes on. Her buttocks were so lovely. *Those girls those girls those lovely seaside girls.* Why *do* I so wish to plunge my fingers between them? *We followed the rump of a misguiding woman*, said Fergus. Unworthy thoughts. Dualist pig! Carpe diem!

A poem for my Associate:

> My mind then sold for but a rump?
> By those hips parenthesized?
> Up from the chair two comely lumps,
> Over the shoulder, her fetch-me smile.

A spasm of his colon drives him to an act less elegantly literary than Leopold Bloom's 95 fictional years before, and no church bell tolls as Kerrigan sits hurriedly to void with a groan and waits, elbows on hairy knees, for more.

What do I learn, sitting here, watching what is around me? Surely there is a lesson here, perhaps a key to all of life, of my life, a life, but what? I must see clearly. The world around me must not be some vague blur, although the word for 'vague' in Italian, he recalls, has a completely different value than the English word. In Italian the word is '*vago*' and the same word means not only vague, but also lovely, attractive.

Italo Calvino (1923-1985) speaks of this in his essay on 'Exactitude'; how the word carries an idea of movement, uncertainty, indefinite gracefulness and pleasure, but to do so, he tells us with reference to the Italian poet Giacomo Leopardi (1798-1837) requires 'a highly exact and meticulous attention to the composition of each image . . . to a minute definition of detail, to the choice of objects, to the lighting and the atmosphere, all in order to attain the desired degree of vagueness'. The subtlest sensations must be grasped with eye, ear, nose and hand.

What do I learn then as I sit here, awaiting a possible further spasm? I learn perhaps what a marvel is the common moment, the fact of light, the height of sky glimpsed through the unclosed WC door, out the front window, aroil with cloud, the sheer mystery of this small enclosure, the blue-grey linoleum between my feet with its vague yet irrefutable suggestion of faces in its pattern – there, eyes, a nose, a stern mouth, there a sharp profile, undeniable as if ghosts were imprinted there, and in that yellow corner between the blue drainpipe and the standing plunger, the threads of a web on which waits a spindly-legged spider with a tiny yellow button of a carcass; hidden universe.

This roll of white paper a clue to the times in which I live, the chain I pull that drops liters of water upon my odiferous waste. Trousers to raise, metal teeth of a zipper, brass buckle of a belt, hands and a bar of fragrant soap beneath a chrome spout of water. Marvel of modern plumbing! Gleaming white, clean, sanitary.

And through the window I see a pony-tailed man in a leather vest who pauses to place the palms of his hands on his kidneys as *he* observes something which has caught *his* attention – what? A bird it seems, a sparrow, simple as that, yet what a marvel that commonplace! Lifts with a shiver of wing into the air and flies up to a chestnut tree and there stands the tree, wiser than a man perhaps, even senseless amidst all this.

Kerrigan stands over the guest sofa upon which he has spread out research materials, the coffee table where there is more, the dining table which he has converted to a desk for this book. His zip-satchel there surprises him – wonder he didn't lose it.

His mind is atremble, his body ashiver, but to demonstrate to himself that his will is stronger than his pain, he sits and takes up his pen, puts its nib to the white-lined pad before him and begins to write.

He writes: 'Just slap anything on when you see a blank page staring at you like some imbecile. You don't know how paralyzing that is, that stare of a blank page which says to the writer you can't do a thing. The page has an idiotic stare and mesmerizes some writers so much, that they turn into idiots themselves. Many writers are afraid in front of the blank page, but the blank page is afraid of the real, passionate writer who dares and who has broken the spell of "you can't" once and for all.'

The words please him, even if they are not his own; are cribbed from a letter from Vincent Van Gogh to his brother Theo from October 1884, six years before his death in 1890 at the age of 37. (I would already have been dead eighteen years ago. But Vincent put a bullet in his heart. My bullets are soft and consoling.)

The Van Gogh words – Kerrigan has only changed 'canvas' to 'page' and 'painter' to 'writer' – kickstart him. The words are slow and clogged at first, but he keeps the pen in motion, and a space clears in the milchy surface of his mind. Words begin to flow, and it is as if he has found the words necessary for him to know he is alive and to start the day.

He pauses, looks up from the pad and sees the window alongside his writing table. Through the window panes, framed in shadow, the tin silhouette of the little angel, given to him years ago by a woman named Alice, holds a star up to the dazzling yellow blossoms of a chestnut tree.

The day smiles to him. He opens the window to see the whole tree, the lake behind it. A man in black cycles away on a red bike. He leans out to see the tree even more fully, in its fullness, fills his senses with its scent, its color, the gentlest rustling of its leaves beneath the cloudless blue sky. Light sparkles on the surface of the lake, and he thinks of the elfin women, thinks of his Associate whom he will not see again until Monday. Three days. He wonders what she is doing, pictures her barefoot, painting, and the wonder turns to a dryness at the back of his throat, thirst. He looks at his watch. Too early, much too early, but he has to move, remembering in John Cheever's diary where he records that his days have turned into a struggle to keep from taking the first gin before noon, a fight he more often than not loses, and the bitter remarks of some asshole reviewer deriding the failing wonderful storyteller for gazing so honestly upon himself.

The bathing of the head and breast in water, brushing of teeth, scraping clean of jowels, the annointment with stinging scented fluids, and donning of clear fresh raiment – his expensive Italian jeans, a tie of plum-colored French silk, a jacket of fine hand-woven Irish tweed – console and heal the spirit of torment as he heeds the advice of the Divine Alewife to Gilgamesh: *Let thy garments be sparkling fresh, thy head be washed . . .*

Then he is jogging down the stairs, out upon the street, and stares over the lake, inhales profoundly.

A brisk walk he needs but first he must tend to the demands of a growling belly, a hungering mouth, a brain that calls for fried fats. It is the hunter in us, he thinks, that craves fat, to sustain us over the long chase and through the long winter. He ducks on quick-moving legs across the streets of the Potato Rows, *Kartoffelrækkerne*, where he lives – workers' housing erected in the last quarter of the last century and which now houses artists, writers, young professionals, politicians, architects, a contessa or two now reduced to office labor, and any number of self-loving curmudgeons, row after row of little brick rowhouses, a dozen short streets of them, each named for a Danish 'Golden Age' (1800-1850) painter or other notable, written about in the fiction of Herman Bang (1857-1912), specifically in the novel *Stuk* (1887) – *Stucco* – a story about Copenhagen itself, growing beyond its original walls.

He crosses *Webersgade* where, in the so-called Blue House at number 30, lives the novelist Lotte Inuk who supplements her writing income by reading Tarot Cards at the Unknown Bookshop near Grey Friars Square. At Silver Square, *Sølvtorvet*, diagonally across from where the K Brun electrical installation shop used to be, currently housing a house of Chinese medicine, he visits Preben's Sausage Wagon, a tiny sausage restaurant on wheels, one of the so-called Cold Foot Cafés. The first such wagons were set up on the streets of Copenhagen in the 20s by a prosperous butcher. They caught on and soon there were many hundreds throughout the city, but with the advent of international fastfood joints like MacDonald's and Burger King, their numbers dwindled again to a hundred and a half or so at present. A few years back, one enterprising sausage man dubbed his wagon 'MacErik's' and the entire great corporation of MacDonald's dragged this one little man running one little wagon to court for violation of trademark. Happily, MacDonald's lost, but not before they had evoked the ire of the Danish *Autonomes*, part of an international movement of anarchists, to attack and reduce to splinters a MacDonald's on northside Copenhagen. Kerrigan did not agree with their methods, but understood their rage against the MacOccupiers who pander to weaknesses insidiously undermining the quality of European civilization.

From within Preben's wagon a tape recorder issues Billie Holiday singing 'Gee Baby Ain't I Good to You' against the sweet tenor strains of Ben Webster. Preben sits within, big-bellied, gazing across the variety of sausages sizzling on his grill.

'Got a hole to fill?' he asks.

'*En ristet med brød, tak*,' says Kerrigan. A fried red hot with bread, thanks. And is given a piece of waxed paper with a dollop of mustard and ketchup on it, flat on the counter, a fried sausage, and a little heated bun. He asks for some chopped raw onion as well, stands thinking about the fee for service principle as he waits for the steaming meat to cool. Fee for sausage. Instead of an hourly wage, you get a fee for each and every item. A few kroner for the sausage, a couple for the bun, a few øre for the condiments, for something to wash it down, all day, everyday, mouths, hands, the exchange of coins, bills. A nickle here, a dime there, enough makes one a millionaire. Fee for sausage.

The water now runs in his mouth in anticipation. He nips a sheet of napkin from the dispenser, wraps it around the end of the sausage. The sausage is hot. He likes hot sausage. He dips the sausage into the mustard and then into the ketchup, turns it in the little pile of chopped onion so that onion flakes cling to the ketchup and mustard, then raises it to his mouth.

The sweet smell of sausage grease touches his nostrils. He likes the smell of sausage grease. He bites the sausage and feels the hot juices burst upon his tongue. His tongue is very sensitive, and the sausage is a little too hot still. Steam rises from inside it. But he relishes the sensation, the taste. He chews the sausage and all that exists for him is the taste, the fullness of his mouth, the ascent of the fats to his brain. Fat, the hunter's food. Fuel for the fight, the chase, the fishing.

He dips the end of the bun into the ketchup and into the mustard and bites off an end so that the bread mixes in his mouth with the sausage. Happily he chews the two things togther, smiling as he munches. He feels good. He likes this sausage wagon. It is a good sausage wagon. He likes Preben. He pops the last bit of sausage and bun into his mouth, chews, swallows, polishes off the last of the club soda.

Two park attendants lean on the side counter ledge of the sausage wagon, taking a beer break from their work at *Øster Anlæg*, East Park, the green area that stretches out along Stockholm Street, which ends just beside where he stands.

The one attendant says, 'Maybe we ought to get back to work,' and the other says to the sausage man, Preben, 'This gentleman cannot relax for even two seconds.'

'He doesn't dare,' says Preben the sausage man. 'Otherwise he'll find out he can't afford to relax.'

They laugh, and Kerrigan joins their laughter as he belches discretely behind his fist, says, '*Tak*,' and Preben the sausage man says, '*Selv tak*.' Thanks yourself.

'*Hej hej*,' he says, which is pronounced Hi Hi.

'*Hej, hej nu*,' says Preben the sausage man. '*Kan du ha' det*?' – Bye bye now. Can you have it good?

Danes say goodbye by doubling the word Americans use for hello. And sometimes they add, '*Kan du ha' det*', which means 'Can you have it good?' a rhetorical question with the last word ellipted – 'Can you have it?' – meaning basically, have a good day.

It tickles Kerrigan to double hello to mean goodbye, just as it tickles him to literally translate what Danes sometimes say when they receive a very beautiful present: '*Hold kæft er du ikke rigtig klog*?' Literally, 'Shut up, are you not rather unclever?'

He enjoys Danish wisdom. *Summen af laster er konstant* or 'The sum of the vices is constant', the truth of which he learned years ago when he quit smoking cigarettes and began to inhale his wine. Or what Danes say when they go to a dinner party where the food is good, but you are not urged to take more: 'The pressing was not so good.' And Danish curses: *Kraft edemig* – Cancer eat me; *Fanden bank mig* – The devil hammer me; *Fanden tag mig* – The devil take me; or simply *For satan!* or *For helvede!* – so innocent-sounding in English, The devil! Hell! – but serious matters in Danish. Even the Danish for 'innocent' he prefers to the English for it, in contrast to the English 'unknowing', means 'not guilty' – *uskyldig*. He loves the low Danish – *Øl, fisse og hornmusik* (Beer, pussy and horn music) – and the elegant irony and understatement of the Danes, manners left from the day when Denmark was a world power, now also fallen on hard times. The year Søren Kierkegaard was born, 1813, the Danish state – which had been a world power for centuries – went bankrupt, following the British bombardments, the loss of her fleet and of Norway following the Napoleonic Wars and later, the war over South Jutland, finally reduced her to a small country, but never took away her tongue or her culture, her eye for beauty and for harmonious surroundings – all perhaps inspired by her magnificent light, and her joy of the senses.

10

Café Under the Clock *(Café Under Uret)*

Café Under Uret
Øster Farimagsgade *(East Farimags Street)* **4**
2100 København Ø

Turning from the sausage wagon, he realizes he has to relieve himself, considers stepping down into the *Café Under Uret*, Café Under the Clock, an old establishment he has long meant to visit just at the corner of Silver Square where *Øster Farimagsgade* meets *Stockholmsgade*. It was established in 1883, the year Franz Kafka was born, originally as Café Roskilde, but a watchmaker moved in to the rooms above the café in 1906 and hung a large illuminated clock in the corner window above where the two streets meet. When the watchmaker died, the owners of the café left the clock in place and changed the name of the café in its honor.

Kerrigan has heard they sell herring (*sild*) and warm Danish meatballs (*frikadeller*), cold draft beer and iced aquavit snaps of a half dozen or more varieties and knows he will be tempted even though it is only quarter past one and despite the lovely sausage nestled so pleasantly in his food sac, so instead of the café facilities, he makes use of the green metal pissoir just across Stockholmsgade, facing across to the National Museum of Art in the square named for Georg Brandes (1842-1927), commemorated there by a bust sculpted by Max Klinger in 1902. Brandes was the influential Danish literary critic who raised the work of Søren Kierkegaard out of international obscurity some 20 plus years after the philosopher's death and made it possible for the remainder of Europe to know his writings and for Frenchmen like Sartre and Camus to fashion, of its basic tenets, braided with that of others such as Nietzsche, modern existentialism.

Kerrigan stands over the zinc trough, eyes closed with pleasure, his water sizzling on the residue of leaves there, pleasantly redolent of Boy Scout outings in New Jersey of years gone by, as he thinks about the effect Brandes had on European culture. Had he never introduced Kierkegaard's writing to the Germans when he was visiting there, Sartre might never have learned about it when he studied in Berlin and Freiborg half a century later, and Kierkegaard might never have fathered existentialism with the Frenchmen, and Camus might never have written *The Stranger* in 1942, a year before Kerrigan was born, the novel which saved Kerrigan's sanity, such as it is, when he read it in 1960 as a soldier stationed in the now defunct Fort Benjamin Harrison in Indianapolis, undergoing a security investigation for a top secret clearance where the investigators became acutely interested in the fact that he replied honestly to the question of whether he had ever had normal sexual relations with a woman and expended many hours involving polygraph machines and officers of fieldgrade rank to explore the reasons for his virginity. Finally they were satisfied with the obvious explanation: He was seventeen years old, had been educated by Irish Christian Brothers at all-boys schools for twelve years, and was shy. But in the meantime, Kerrigan had learned to identify intensely with the fate of M Meursault in Algiers.

Two scenes from *The Stranger* continue to resonate in him more than 35 years later. The one is straight out of Kierkegaard: Meursault sits in his prison cell considering all the things that might happen to him, one by one, all the way through to the possibility that they might come in that very day and execute him, and once he has run through the whole list of terrifying possibilities, he wins for himself an hour's peace and thinks, 'And that anyhow was something'. A clear reflection of Kierkegaard's 'Leap of Faith', by which one runs through all the arguments for and against the existence of God, reaches the end-point of final utter ignorance, then chooses the only way forward – the leap across the gap of that ignorance to the embrace of faith – be it a faith in God or the pleasure of sensual existence or the simple assertion that although one dies and is unhappy, one insists on living and being happy. The other scene Kerrigan remembers with relish is where M Meursault is visited in his cell by a priest who wishes to have him take upon himself the consolations of religion; Meursault grabs the cleric by his collar and shouts, 'All your certainties are not worth one strand of hair from a woman's head.'

He shakes and zips with a nod of thanks toward Brandes Place, decides to leave his visit to the Café Under the Clock to another time, walks up *Stockholmsgade* – Stockholm Street – to number 20, the Hirschsprung Collection, named for the Danish cigar manufacturer, Heinrich Hirschsprung, whose trademark was a leaping deer, the meaning of his name in German. He gazes up at the statue there of an equestrian barbarian sculpted by Carl Johan Bonnesen in 1890.

Kerrigan ponders the short muscular helmeted figure, armed with knife and scimitar, mounted upon a short strong steed, two decapitated human heads dangling from his saddle. Odd motif, thinks Kerrigan, just across the trees from the civilized Brandes, a mere bronze head in comparison to the muscular body of this armed man and powerful horse with the severed head trophies.

He thinks of the Greek poet C P Cavafy (1863-1933), and his poem, 'Waiting for the Barbarians':

> ' . . . night has fallen and the barbarians have not come.
> And some who have just returned from the border say
> there are no barbarians any longer.
> And now what's going to happen to us without
> barbarians?
> They were, those people, a kind of solution.'

Yes, someone to chop off our heads, stop thought.

He turns again, back along Stockholm Street past a green bench painted with the words *Blood and Honour*, thinking of the skinheads, white supremacists, neo-nazi groups throughout Europe again. Xenophobic parties like Jörg Haider's in Austria or the Danish Centre Party and *Dansk Folke Parti* right here, the *Front National* in France and very extreme groups like the Free German Worker Party, the Swedish White Aryan Resistance, the Austrian VAPO. Bombings and burnings, marches to honor the memory of Rudolf Hess, *Hang Nelson Mandella* tee-shirts, hate mail and grafitti.

Kerrigan has been affiliated here as a translator with the Rehabilitation Center for Torture Victims founded by the Danish physician Inge Genefke who has been short-listed several times for the Nobel Peace Prize. He copy-edited their manual for therapists working with torture survivors which gave him a glimpse into a world so ugly it put even his very worst memories in perspective.

One of the survivors told his therapist that while he was being held in a filthy basement cell, beaten several times daily, subjected to procedures referred to with ugly euphemisms – *the Submarine*, where his head was forced into a barrel of water afloat with faeces while he was beaten; *Roast Chicken*, where he was hung upside down over a fire; *Flying Lessons*, where he was suspended by the arms and swung back and forth while being beaten. After months of this treatment, he began to lose the will to live. He lay on the damp filthy floor of his windowless cell and apathy seeped through him.

Then two angels appeared to transport him from the prison out beyond the walls within which he was imprisoned to a beautiful field where he could see the grass and the trees, smell the fresh clean air, see the blue sky, feel the gentle sunshine on his face and arms and hear the song of birds. The angels apologized to him that they could not keep him out of the prison. They had to take him back in just a few moments, but they could promise him he would be free one day and would be part of the beautiful world again. They asked him to remember these few moments in freedom as proof of their promise to him. Then they took him back to his cell.

The man told his therapist, 'You might have some kind of

psychological term to explain that phenomenon, but I can tell you what it really was. It was two angels. They were there, and they took me out of the jail and made a promise that saved my life from those *animali*.'

Kerrigan was so moved by this that he wrote a story about it which he launched in Copenhagen with a public reading at a café on *Gothersgade*. A couple of dozen members of the American Women's Club attended. One of their husbands, the Public Information Attaché at the Embassy, was also there as were a number of shadowy figures who sat in a cluster at the dark far end of the café bar. When Kerrigan got to the part in his reading where the torture victim talks about the angels having saved him from the animals who tortured him, the men at the end of the bar began to make loud animal noises. Kerrigan read louder, and they grunted and snorted and brayed all the louder.

At the end of the reading, a young Latin American woman approached him and asked if his story had a title. 'If not,' she said, 'I think you *e*should call it *gringo* because that is what it makes me think.'

'Are you with those people at the bar?' Kerrigan asked. 'I'd like to talk to them.'

'I would not advice you to *e*speak to them,' she said. 'You could get hurt.' And she returned to her comrades.

Kerrigan turned to the U S Information Attaché who was putting on his topcoat. 'Did you hear that?' Kerrigan asked.

The man smiled quizzically. 'Hear what? Did something happen?' as he and his wife hastened toward the door.

Kerrigan went to the bar and ordered a beer, watching the group at the end. The barman was from India; he said in Danish, 'That was a stupid story. You understand nothing. You live in a country where if someone opens his mouth to complain they shove a piece of cake into it. Other countries must take other measures. Someday perhaps people like you will understand this.'

'You think treating human beings in that way can ever be justified?'

'You are so naive,' said the barman with a friendly sneer.

Kerrigan could not make out the faces in the shadows at the end of the bar, but thought they were Latin Americans, and it occurred to him that at least some of the exiles who had taken refuge in Denmark were not necessarily people a democracy would want to collect.

A short time later he received an e-mail Christmas greeting from one of the secretaries he knew at the Rehabilitation Center. There was a short friendly note from her and an attachment captioned '*Feliz Navidad*' – Merry Christmas in Spanish. When he opened it, his computer froze and a number of his files were destroyed before he shut the computer down. He phoned the secretary, who advised him someone had stolen her e-mail file and was sending those messages out in her name.

Blood and Honour, Kerrigan thinks, and crosses back through the Potato Row houses to *Øster Søgade*, East Lake Street, and stands on the bridge that bisects Black Dam Lake – called the Peace Bridge, *Fredensbro*. Across the lake stands a tall monolithic sculpture titled *Fredens Port*, the Peace Gate, erected in 1982, by Stig Brøgger, Hein Hansen and Mogens Møller. It rises at a tilt from the grass of tiny Peace Park: like modern society, the monument seems locked in a constant fall that never concludes.

To his right, framed between two chestnut trees, behind the buildings on the opposite bank of the lake, the top of the state hospital looms up like a huge marble grave toward a white ceiling of cloud.

This building was the setting of the horror spoof *Riget*, or *The Kingdom*, filmed by the brilliant contemporary Danish film maker Lars von Trier, the 'von', a noble European title, assumed by Trier in honor of von Stroheim. Von Trier has also filmed *Dancer in the Dark* (2000), *The Idiots* (1998), *Breaking the Waves* (1996), *Europa* (1991), *Epidemic* (1987) and *The Element of Crime* (1984). In many ways his first film, *The Element of Crime*, to Kerrigan's mind, is the best of von Trier's so far. It captures images so deep in the soul, a near perfect replica of a dream, replete with inexplicable perfect things the eye of the sleeping mind conjures – a horse being lifted on a crane from a bay, water everywhere, people moving on rafts through shallow water covering the floors of their modern dwellings.

Von Trier was also one of the prime movers of the Dogma School, a pact made by a group of younger directors to film only outside of studios, using only natural lighting and no background music unless it is intregal to the scene at hand. One of the great films made in this manner was the debut film of Thomas Vinterberg entitled *Celebration* (*Festen*, 1998). There is a sequence in this film which awes Kerrigan: a young man attends his father's sixtieth birthday party, a great event in the life of a Dane which must be celebrated with due ceremony and speeches. The party is in the father's great home out in the country, and many guests arrive. One son, the oldest sibling, strikes his glass for attention during the banquet and rises to hold a speech about the father – a Danish custom on such occasions. He speaks mildly, with seeming affection, but suddenly he is telling about how when he and his twin sister, who has recently committed suicide, were very young, their father would occasionally take them into the bathroom with him, lock the door and rape them.

The other guests demand that he sit down and be silent, but as soon as the uproar dies down, he rises again and continues, so they seize him and eject him from the house, but he comes back in and continues his speech. This time they throw him out and lock the front door, but he finds his way in the back and resumes his speech, so a contingent of the male guests take him out into the woods and bind him to a tree and leave him there, so great is their fear of his great determination to tell the truth instead of simply honoring ceremony.

Kerrigan thinks with admiration of the film, pleased that it has won such recognition internationally, including a rave review in the *New York Times* and European film festival prizes. Ever since a best foreign film Oscar was awarded to the movie of Karen Blixen's short story *Babette's Feast*, and Bille August the following year won one for *Pelle, the Conqueror*, based on the outstanding proletarian social realist novel published in 1910 by Martin Andersen Nexø (1869-1954), Danish film has been emergent. Bille

August went on to direct the film versions of Isabel Allende's *House of the Spirits* and Peter Høeg's international bestseller *Smilla's Sense of Snow*, also published in England as *Miss Smilla's Feeling for Snow*, a title which the author preferred to the former translation by Tiina Nunnally, which resulted in her removing her name from the English version of the book – the translator mentioned there is claimed to be a fictional name.

Celebration and Søren Kragh Jacobsen's *Mifune's Last Song* (1999) also gathered prizes at the Cannes and Berlin festivals, as did von Trier's *Dancer in the Dark* which won the golden palm and an Oscar nomination in 2000, and the first great promise of Danish film has emerged since Carl Theodor Dreyer (1889-1968) whose work includes the acclaimed *The Passion of Joan of Arc* (1928), *Vampire* (1932), *The Word* (1954) and *Gertrud* (1964).

There are other distinguished Danish film-makers too – notably Henning Carlsen, whose films versions of Knut Hamsun's *Hunger* in the 1960s and *Pan* in the 1990s are memorable, powerful movies. Hamsun (1859-1952) is the Norwegian novelist who won the Nobel Prize in 1920 but in his 80s became a pawn of Hitler during the Nazi occupation of his country and was fined for collaboration in 1948 – all of which was explored in a three-volume work entitled *The Trial of Knut Hamsun* by Thorkild Hansen, published after massive research in 1978, and in the film *Hamsun* made in the late 1980s by the Swedish director, Bo Widerberg, whose film *The Baby Carriage* in the early 60s has become a permanent part of the furnishings of Kerrigan's mind.

It is interesting to compare the Danish and American versions of Ole Bornedal's film *Nattevagt/Night Watch*. Basically a thriller, the Danish version also touched upon a number of religious and philosophical moments that were excised from the American version which dealt only with the horror elements. Apparently the American film makers were offended or perhaps just bored by the suggestion of spiritual significance – or else they found it simply unprofitable. The American film, despite Nick Nolte, was poor.

Kerrigan wonders if Danish directors like von Trier and Winterberg will live up to their promise of producing works that measure up to the films of their Swedish neighbor, Ingmar Bergman, happily contemplating the works of art that may come forth from them, hoping they are not swallowed up by global commercialism.

He stands now at the mouth of the Peace Bridge, *Fredens Bro*, across the lake, and belching into his fist remembers the fried sausage he has just eaten. It occurs to him that the two sides of the lake are like kidneys on either side of the spine of the bridge. He realizes this is far-fetched, but it makes him chuckle nonetheless as he sees a filthy fish nip a fly from the filthy surface of the water. Big two-kidneyed lake, he thinks, remembering how vindictive Hemingway could be when ridiculed, physically attacking the author of a review of *Death in the Afternoon*, titled 'Bull in the Afternoon', when he met him in Max Perkins's office one afternoon; Hemingway wound up on his butt, spectacles askew, though to his credit, according to the report by A Scott Berg, he came up chuckling at himself.

Those were the days, thinks Kerrigan, when an American man defended his honor with his fists, as though power and honor are synonymous or fists can do anything but silence the opposing view. He recalls Hemingway's ludicrous statement about his progress as a writer:

> 'I started out very quiet and I beat Mr Turgenev. Then I trained hard and I beat Mr de Maupassant. I've fought two draws with Mr Stendahl, and I think I had an edge in the last one. But nobody's going to get me in any ring with Mr Tolstoy unless I'm crazy or I keep getting better.'

True bull in the afternoon. As bad as the ridiculous practice of fighting duels over one's honor – which killed Pushkin, Alexander Hamilton . . . Blood and Honor.

Kerrigan chuckles aloud and realizes he is still slightly intoxicated from the evening before. Hemingway, he realizes, would soon have been 100 years old, had he not blown out his brains – so they spattered on the wall, as Robert Coover suggests, in a pattern that said, 'It is important to begin when everything is over.'

11

The Bridge Bodega *(Broens Bodega)*

Broens Bodega
Fredensgade and Sortedamsdossering
(The Peace Street and Black Dam Bank)
2200 København N

Across the bridge and on the other side of the street, he gazes over at *Broens Bodega*, the Bridge Bodega, with its reproduction of the famous *Thirsty Man* advertisement for Carlsberg, painted in 1900 by Erik Henningsen, mounted on one of the side doors, a corpulent man pausing on a dusty road to lean back against a fence and mop perspiration from his brow. The picture reminds Kerrigan of his own thirst, but as he surveys the broad front of the bar, cornered between Fredensgade, Peace Street, and Sortedamsdossering, Black Lake Bank, he knows he will not go in there. The front window advertises billiards and opening hours from midnight to 5pm. A house of all-night and all-day drinkers. And he remembers early one morning standing at the bus stop just across from that bodega seeing three young people emerge from the darkness inside the bar. It was eight in the morning, which could only mean they had been in there drinking the night away.

Kerrigan, who had been staring across at the bar, turned his eyes away quickly not to provoke attention, but they had already seen him. They started across the road toward him. Occasionally, the Danish press carries a story about some young disenfranchised man or men who drink enormous quantities of beer, snaps, and vodka and then go out in a state of pure id and beat and kick some innocent bystander into a wheelchair for life.

Kerrigan feared this moment could be right to hand for him. Fate on a random morning. The horseman stopping. To make himself invisible, he turned his back and studied the bus schedule posted on the bus-stop pole. He was in fact waiting for the bus to take him to Gentofte Hospital where the son of a close friend had just undergone a spinal operation.

When the three youngsters – two men and a woman, perhaps twenty years old – stood immediately behind him at the bus sign, he felt certain nothing good would come of it. Then the young woman leaned up against him, so that he could feel her breasts against his back and her breath at his ear.

'What bus are you looking for?' she asked in Danish, and without turning he said, 'The 184.' He wondered if he should offer them money to continue their drinking with, wondered if she was in the process of trying to sell herself to him, whether they hoped to lure him away and roll him. It was a bright mild summer morning, and he had an intense experience of the absurdity of the moment, the utter random coinciding of paths, as he stood there with this young woman leaning against his back, two young men standing behind her. Butch Cassidy and the Sundance Kid with Etta Chance, and Kerrigan with the fat bankroll, a train to rob, Woodcock the trainman.

She shifted her weight back from him, and he seized the moment to circle the pole and get it between them while pretending to read the schedule on that side. The bridge and the banks of the lake and the streets were empty, a sleepy, summer Saturday morning. He noted a mallard paddling slowly across the green water.

'Why do you want the 184,' the one young man asked neutrally, blond, baby-faced, thick-shouldered in a white tee-shirt, and Kerrigan told him. 'I'm going out to the hospital to visit the son of a friend whose spine was just operated on.'

The young man visibly gathered himself and literally bowed his head in the Danish manner of formal respect, a quick curt snap forward of the brow. 'I am very sorry to hear that,' he said with obvious sincerity, and as if by prearrangement, the three walked off along the lake, leaving Kerrigan in peace on the Peace Bridge, waiting for the 184 in the shadow of the Peace Port across the street from the Bridge Bodega.

Now, for a moment, he is tempted to go in, sit at the bar with whatever bleary persons might be seated there in the early afternoon of a late April Saturday, playing billiards, smoking cigarettes, drinking beer and bitters, to gather material for his book, but he decides to remain on this side of the bridge, to take a brisk walk around the entire circumference of this lake and the next, Peblinge Lake. In days gone by he might have sailed on the lake ferry, the whole length from the eastern edge of *Sortedamsø* at *Østerbrogade* to the Sea Pavillion at the west end of *Pebblingesø*, in boats sponsored by Otto Mönsted, the margarine magnate who lived in a margarine-colored mansion on Kristianiagade, which now houses the Russian Embassy. Painted on the sides of the boats were, 'Otto Mönsteds Svane-Margarine is Firm and Long Lasting', and the company logo – a swan – sat as a figurehead at the prows. The ferries were in function from 1894, but discontinued in the 1920s because they were loud and polluted air and water on the lakes.

Better to walk it, get his blood pumping and his lungs working.

As he trudges past an old disused bomb shelter on the bank, his thoughts drift back in time to the year of his birth, 1943, the year after Camus wrote *The Stranger*, the third year of the German occupation of this city, this country, and yet another century back again to 1843, the year Søren Kierkegaard wrote *Either/Or*, the first of his most important works, all written in a mere three years, between 1843 and 1846.

Either/Or is a book that particularly fascinates Kerrigan, it is such a mix of things. On the one hand, it makes him think of Pascal's *Pensées*, written nearly 200 years before, but *Either/Or* is even fuller. Subtitled *A Fragment of Life*, it is a gathering of aphorisms, essays, a sermon, and lodged within it all, a novel in the form of a diary, *The Seducer's Diary*.

The concept of 'either/or' was Kierkegaard's response to the Hegelian concept of mediation – the negotiation of contradictory ideas, 'thesis' and 'antithesis', into 'synthesis', which is meant to include and reconcile them both. *Either/Or* was Kierkegaard's refutation of this 'both/and' approach to thought.

But it is the seducer's diary within the book that captures Kerrigan for in it the first-person narrator, Johannes, walks the banks of this lake Kerrigan now walks, beneath the six windows of Kerrigan's apartment, dreaming of the object of his desire, Cordelia, who unlike Lear's third daughter *does* carry her heart as a kiss on her full pretty lips.

It is fascinating to Kerrigan that here on the banks of these lakes where he now pauses to watch a swan glide along the stippled glittering water, Hans Christian Andersen stood weeping real salt tears one day over his mistreatment by the world while Kierkegaard's fictional Johannes the Seducer stalked his beautiful young Cordelia in the pages of the fictional diary set like a substantial gem in a book of philosophy and meditation.

To Kerrigan's mind, the fictional Johannes is as real, realer perhaps in a very real sense, than the figures of history who walked here. For though he knows that Andersen and Kierkegaard were men of flesh and blood, the very intimate record available of them is still mostly indirect, while in Johannes we have a mind and a soul laid open for study in detail throughout the course of an extreme action.

Yet equally fascinating are the real life events that precede *Either/Or*, an irresistible literary illusion suggested by it, and a real life person who – as depicted in a novel by Henrik Stangerup in 1988 – was Søren Kierkegaard's literary enemy and upon whom Kierkegaard is said to have based the character of Johannes.

Kerrigan pauses, turns back to gaze the length of Black Dam Lake to the twin copper towers between which now lies Willemoes Street, *Willemoesgade*, but where once stood the house into which Kierkegaard moved in 1850, from the windows of which he could gaze out upon the waters of these lakes. The foot of either tower now houses, respectively, a supermarket and a discount appliance store with a gaudy yellow sign so unworthy of the elegant green of the copper spires above. He wonders what Kierkegaard would think if he could have been transported a century and a half forward in time to see this world now. Then he wonders what this very place might resemble 150 years from *now*, the year 2149. The changes from 1850 to 1999 were in truth great, but some of the basic background of the place is still there, and he realizes that this lies at the core of his love for Copenhagen, this constancy, slow growth, this possibility of a culture to move forward slowly in time, retaining the structure of the past, allowing things to disintegrate or disappear at a natural pace or by sudden catastrophe – the great fires of 1728, 1794 and 1795, the British attack of 1801 and bombardment of 1807, the German occupation of 1940-1945 – as opposed to the plunderous commercial demolition and raking away of structures that define a people, a society, a time, along with the international infiltration of low quality sameness, the disease of the plastic junk-food emporiums, MacDonald's, KFC, Burger King, 7-Eleven . . .

Kierkegaard might still recognize some of this, might find his way, even if the buildings have multiplied, their density having thickened, just as Goethe, had he not died in 1832, but lived another dozen years, might have seen in Kierkegaard's Johannes the Seducer some ironic reflection of the Young Werther whose sorrows made him so suddenly famous in 1774, two years before the American War of Independence, 69 years before Kierkegaard's Johannes walked the banks of this lake, the romantic bumbling Werther's cynical contriving counterpart articulating visions of a femininity that could only have been meant to reveal the sadistic mechanations of seduction:

> 'It can be explained why when God created Eve,
> He let a deep sleep fall over Adam; for woman
> is the dream of man . . . She awakes first at the
> touch of love; before that time she is a dream.
> Yet in her dream life we can distinguish two
> stages: in the first, love dreams about her; in the
> second, she dreams about love.'

A few days ago, Kerrigan read in a Danish newspaper an interview by a Danish journalist, Thomas Treo, with the American bluesman John Lee Hooker in which Hooker is quoted, in his 70s, as saying, 'The blues began with Adam and Eve, and one thing never changes. I will love woman until the day I die. I'm a man, what can I do?'

And he remembers Johannes the Seducer's speculation: 'Woman will always offer an inexhaustible fund of material for my reflection, an eternal abudance for my observation', as in the opening of the diary when he envies the coachman and footman's access to a view of the ankle of his lovely as she climbs into the coach.

Kerrigan stands now on the bank of the lake watching the swans and the ducks, watching the continuous infinitessimal changes of the Danish light, feeling this great long history of a culture around him, this talk of women and of love. He thinks of his Research Associate's cornblue eyes, her father's hopping eiderdown, and he thinks of his mother who was taken from Iceland by his Irish father via Dublin, New York and Brooklyn to the loneliness of the northwestern Palouse where she would one day fulfill her destiny of murdering all but one of her children and their spouses and all of her grandchildren.

The thought strikes him with a force that is physical. He literally staggers, as he steps down through the tunnel between the two segments of Black Dam Lake, its walls festooned with ornate grafitti scrawled over with obscenities, *Superfucked* and *Fuck Spaghettis* answered by *Fuk Racism* and *Blood and Honour* and *Fuk You Nigga* and again *Fuk Racism*. And he looks ahead to the light at the far end and tells himself that when he comes out into the daylight again he will dismiss this memory.

As he climbs the inclined path back up into the day, he sees the *Kaffesalonen*, the Coffee Salon, off to his right and further on down the long narrow street the spire of the church in which he, himself, was married, *Sankt Johannes Kirke*, the Church of St John, further still an oval frieze of a praying figure beneath which sit two doves, further again a sculpted bird on a brick wall, and he keeps walking, blanking out his mind with the movement of his legs, his feet striking the dusty path, the swinging of his arms, the breath in his lungs, the sweat in his armpits and on his back, filling his eyes with saving details, past the fairytale-like white structure of the *Søpavillion*, the Lake Pavillion, and around the foot of Peblinge Lake and Jarmers Plads and the ruins of Jarmers Tower from 1525, part of the old fortification, now but a stubble of brick preserved in a grassy enclosure. Circling round the other side of it, a green bronze sculpture of a lion and lionness fighting for the corpse of a wild boar, sculpted by an artist named Cain in 1878.

And that name can not but remind him of Milton's Adam and Eve in 1674 leaving Eden with wandering steps and slow, hand in hand – the work with which Milton set out to justify God's ways with man, and Housman two and a half centuries later telling Kerrigan's namesake, Terrence, over the edge of the grave, read by Kerrigan at a time when he was desperate for justification,

> 'Terrence, this is stupid stuff . . .
> Malt does more than Milton can
> To justify God's ways with man . . .
> Ale, man, ale's the stuff to drink
> For fellows whom it hurts to think.'

How fitting then that just across Gyldenløves Street near the bank of *Sankt Jørgens Sø*, St John's Lake, stands Andreas Kolberg's sculpture *A Drunken Faun* (1857) – a smiling boyish satyr drinking wine from a horn held high over his head so the wine runs down his face. He has feet rather than hooves and drags a half-empty wine sack along the ground behind him. His stick is discarded at his feet and his lion skin has slipped back, exposing his sex. Carl Jacobsen, the Carlsberg brewer, gave the faun to Copenhagen – a laughing, happily drunken lad and, this being Copenhagen, there is no moral intent beyond the moral pleasure of joy.

Yet as he crosses the little park on the bank, he stops to consider a sculpture cut from the stump of a dying elm tree, infected by the epidemic which hit Copenhagen's elms in the 1990s. This sculpture is by Ole Barslund Nielsen – a naked woman rises from the center of the broken double-trunked stump, a child to one side and below, a seated figure in a hollowed arch in the trunk itself. It is entitled *In the Beginning was the Word.*

He loops across Gyldenløves Street to *Ørstedsparken,* can see from the street the statue of the great man himself: H C Ørsted (1777-1851), discoverer in 1821 of electromagnetism as well as of aluminum, comforter of Hans Christian Andersen. Kerrigan enters the park for a closer look. Ørsted stands on the remains of the old northside rampart, *Nørrevold.* Sculpted by Jens Adolph Jerichou in 1876, the statue shows Ørsted on a pedestal, as if lecturing, connecting two wires on an electro battery; at the base of the pedestal sit the three Nordic goddesses of fate: Urd (the past), Verdande (the present), and Skuld (the future).

Kerrigan's feet carry him further along the paths of the park, beneath the willows and beeches, to yet another sculpture, another satyr – Louis Hasselriis's *Wine Sucking Satyr* (1888). Cleft-footed, goat-legged, the satyr boy sucks wine from a bronze urn more than half his own height.

Kerrigan ponders the lad's face, its youth. No grisly goatman this, no sardonic seducer, but a boy conceived in the mind of Hasselriis, 125 years before. The Danish culture is a lusty one. Little room here for the haters of the flesh, the shunners of the grape. Only in Jutland does the *Indremissionsk* sect thrive – the Inner Mission Christians who dress in black and disavow all vices – drink, dancing, tobacco, allow themselves only coffee and Christian song for pleasure.

Yet Jutland is also the home of *den lille sorte* – the little black, a drink concocted thus: You place a coin in a cup, then pour in coffee until you can no longer see the coin, after which you pour in aquavite, the clear Danish snaps, until you can see the coin again.

Kerrigan remembers the fact that the aquavite of his mother's homeland, Iceland, is called *den sorte død,* the black death. And she was a teetotaler.

It occurs to him that Louis Hasselriis also did the sculpture of Søren Kirkegaard that sits in the garden of the Royal Library:

plume in hand, distant look, mess of books beneath his chair. Sculpted three years after this satyr boy. Another Kierkegaard stands with pot belly outside *Marmorkirken*, the Marble Church, on *Store Kongensgade*, Great King Street, sculpted in 1972 – the pot-bellied philosopher outside his church.

'Lead us into temptation,' murmurs Kerrigan and walking in through the park comes upon *The Dying Gaul*, a bronze made from a 2,000-year-old Roman cast. The Gaul is wounded, naked, dying, balanced on hip and hand, head lowered, mouth in pain, eyes meeting death, his sword discarded on the bronze earth alongside his bronze hand, the warrior's gold braid about his neck. What, Kerrigan wonders, is meant by the quiet agony of that face? And the response is from Chaucer, the dying White Knight's song:

'What is this life
What asketh man to have
Now with his love
Now in his cold grave.'

He turns back toward the lake.

Kerrigan is exhausted. His wet shirt sticks to his back, as he reaches *Peblinge Sø*, the lake bank where Hans Christian Andersen wept. He sits on a bench, closes his eyes and remembers the lake two winters before when he moved into his apartment here, skaters and strollers on the frozen water before the Lake Pavillion on a freezing sunny winter Sunday.

There is a poem he once translated by a very minor Icelandic painter and poet, an adventurer who went by many names – Karl Einarsson, the Duke of St Kilda, Charles E Dungannon. The Icelandic Nobel laureate, Halldor Laxness wrote about Einarsson in his book *Seven Magicians*, and he was later celebrated in a radio play by the contemporary Icelandic writer Sveinn Einarsson (no relation), but what Kerrigan remembers most about the man is that he loved Denmark and wrote a concrete poem dedicated to Danish beer which Kerrigan translated and which he thinks about now with longing:

> 'Lupulin of fine hops
> barley corns and pressed yeast
> gush forth liquid which will slake
> the parched complexion with a golden
> lake of foaming brew pouring
> in our mouths. Cheers for the AleWife
> who spills the brew with which
> our mouths we fill
> feeding body, heart and mind
> turning us completely blind
> to all the so-called goods we seek.
> Fate sometimes is closer
> than an open eye presumes.
> Let children jump the rope
> and Our Father's heavenly loaf
> be damned before the honest man's
> pleasured gulp of beer.
> Chug-a-lug the pitcher dry
> and lie to sleep
> all wrapped about in dreams.'

But he must not, he will not allow himself to escape memory in that way. Not yet. Instead he turns his thought back to Kierkegaard and Johannes the Seducer, Goethe's *Sorrows of Young Werther*, and Henrik Stangerup's *The Seducer, It is Hard to Die in Dieppe*, translated into English in 1990 by the Irish translator Sean Martin.

They are all dead, Goethe, Kierkegaard, even Stangerup, three men from three centuries, writing about the same thing from different angles. Two Danes and a German.

The Sorrows of Young Werther inaugurated a life of fame for Goethe at the age of 25. It is the story of a young upper-middle-class man of foolish sentiments, quick and self-centered, who falls in love with another man's woman and commits suicide. W H

Auden has said that the book made Goethe the first writer or artist to become a public celebrity. *Sturm und Drang*. ' . . . Not a tragic love story, but . . . a masterly and devastating portrait of a complete egoist . . . incapable of love because he cares for nobody and nothing but himself and having his way at whatever cost to others.'

Goethe's novel is said to have inspired more than a few suicides among fashionable youths of the time, similar perhaps to the way that some contemporary musical death-worshippers have loaned their lives to similar existential exhibitions, direct or indirect: James Dean, Jim Morrison, Curt Cobain, Jimmi Hendrix, Janice Joplin, and others.

If Young Werther killed himself in frustration over being unable to have his Lotte –

> 'Adieu! I see no end to this misery except in the grave . . . To lift the curtain and step behind it. That is all! And why with fear and trembling? Because no one knows what one may see there? Or because one cannot return? Or because it is, after all, a peculiarity of our mind to apprehend that confusion and darkness exist in places of which we know nothing definite?'

– Kierkegaard's Johannes sets about with incisive determination to have his Cordelia, and he *does* have her via ' . . . my pact with the aesthetic (which) makes me strong, that I always have the idea on my side. This is a secret like Samson's hair which no Delilah shall wrest from me'.

Clearly this is *not* Kierkegaard's philosophy – who spoke of the greater sins of reason than passion – but the casual reader of the *Diary*, as the casual reader of *Werther*, might take it literally and *believe* Johannes's delusion that 'woman's essential being is being for an other' and 'man's courtship is a question, her choice only an answer to a question.'

Johannes stands on Bleacher's Green (now *Blegdamsvej*, also featured in von Trier's *The Kingdom*, just above the street lakes) and readies his attack: 'Now my soul is attuned like a bent bow, now my thoughts lie ready like arrows in my quiver, not poisoned and yet able to blend themselves with the blood.'

And when his labors are done, when he has had her, he leaves swiftly, done, with no sweet sorrow of parting: 'I will have no farewell with her, nothing is more disgusting to me than a woman's tears and a woman's prayers, which alter everything and yet really mean nothing. I have loved her, but from now on she can no longer engross my soul. If I were a god, I would do for her what Neptune did for a nymph, I would change her into a man.'

Kerrigan entertains a certainty that Kierkegaard's *Diary* is inter alia a response to Goethe's *Sorrows*. Even Goethe's use of that phrase 'fear and trembling' – although Goethe's original German phrase, '*Zaudern und Zagen*', translates more accurately as 'hesitation and fear', and the German translation of Kierkegaard's Danish title of *Fear and Trembling* (*Frygt og Bæven*) is translated into German as *Furcht und Zitten* – seems to echo the title Kierkegaard will choose for the great work he published later that same year, 1843, *Fear and Trembling*, under the pseudonym Johannes De Silentio. The book was written in less than two months in Berlin after Kierkegaard had left Copenhagen, breaking his engagement with the woman he loved, Regine Olsen, for reasons that he himself does not quite understand:

'But insofar as I was what, alas, I was, I had to say that I could be happier in my unhappiness without her than with her . . . I had to hide such a tremendous amount from her, had to base the whole thing on something untrue.'

He sent back the ring, fabricated the appearance that it was she who broke off the engagement but she refused to go along with that lie explaining that if she could bear the rejection she could bear the disgrace as well. Kierkegaard was miserable but he hid his misery from the world, behaved as usual. His brother who heard him weeping all night wanted to go to Regine's family and tell them, to prove he was not a scoundrel, but Kierkegaard told him, 'If you do, I will put a bullet through your head.'

In his journal, on 24 August 1849 – seven years later – he wrote, 'I went to Berlin. I suffered greatly. I thought of her every day.'

In Berlin he worked on *Either/Or*, completed it in about eleven months.

There he would write, 'My grief is my castle.'

And, 'The essence of pleasure does not lie in the thing enjoyed but in the accompanying consciousness.'

And, 'The sun shines into my room bright and beautiful, the window is open in the next room; on the street all is quiet, it is a Sunday afternoon . . . I think of my youth and of my first love when the longing of desire was strong. Now I long only for my first longing. What is youth? A dream. What is love? The substance of a dream.'

If the cynical Johannes in *Either/Or is* in a sense a response to Goethe's foolish, self-absorbed Werther, and in another sense an expression of Kierkegaard's own emotional and spiritual struggles over his engagement. Kierkegaard's model for Johannes according to the novel by Henrik Stangerup, published in 1985 as *It is Hard to Die in Dieppe*, was Peder Ludvig Møller (1814-1865). The English version of Stangerup's novel appeared in 1990, translated by Sean Martin, with the superior title *The Seducer*, along with a preface to the English edition explaining the 'true' history of the main character.

Although something of Kierkegaard's behavior toward Regine Olsen might be deduced or intuited in his depiction of Johannes the Seducer – particularly if one compares some of his journal entries with the novel within *Either/Or*, the primary model for Johannes, according to Stangerup, was Kierkegaard's literary enemy, the above-named P L Møller.

Møller was secretly associated with an anonymously published literary review, *Corsaren* or *Corsair*, which means *pirate* in French, and was named from Byron's long poem, 'The Corsair'. The journal was published and edited by Meir Aron Goldschmidt (1819-1887) who would later have great success as a novelist, making his debut in 1845 with *The Jew*, even now said to be as fresh and contemporary as Malamud or Philip Roth. 55 years later, in 1900, the then 15-year-old Karen Blixen, aka Isak Dinesen, would be reading Goldschmidt avidly, inspired by his literary craftsmanship.

But in 1840, Goldschmidt founded *Corsair*, a satirical journal of liberal, radical, republican ideas, which came out every Sunday and is said to have played a part in the downfall of the absolute monarchy. Goldschmidt's journal was an economic success, and among his first purchases with the proceeds was a fine coat which Søren Kierkegaard, meeting him on *Østergade*, East Street, the first day he had it on, advised him not to wear it, emphasizing that he should dress as others do. Goldschmidt was embarrassed, for he had felt uneasy about the coat to start with; apparently he was most wounded that Kierkegaard should have thought he was proud of the coat. In fact, he had been uneasy about its fineness and uncertain whether it appeared affected. He sent the coat back to the tailor to be altered, having the fur collar and breast decoration removed.

Shortly thereafter began a series of attacks on Kierkegaard in *Corsair*, not so much literary attacks as satirical comments on the way he carried his bent figure along the street, about the need for anyone walking with him to keep switching sides as the philosopher veered back and forth across the pavement, about the cut of his trousers, a suggestion that the legs were of different lengths.

Søren Kierkegaard's work had originally been acclaimed in the journal, but he expressed disdain for it and announced that he would have preferred to be ridiculed in those pages. However, perhaps he did not anticipate personal ridicule. Perhaps he was being repaid in kind for his possibly well intentioned or at least not malign private comment on Goldschmidt's coat.

Or perhaps, as asserted in Stangerup's fictional account, it was only Møller who launched the series of anonymous attacks in 1845. Perhaps the anger smouldering since 1843 when Kierkegaard's *Seducer* appeared blazed out at last as Møller began to win respect and gain confidence with his literary annual *Gaea*. The attacks on Kierkegaard were as vigorous as they were venemous, stung the philosopher perhaps as cruelly as his own Cordelia portrait stung Regine Olsen, and they were answered in kind by the philosopher.

In any event, the invitation to be ridiculed was extended and accepted, and the philosopher received a more than due degree of publicly expressed personal scorn, including caricatures of his tilted physique by the *Corsair* cartoonist Peter Klæstrup who, even if he meant them in fun, hurt the philosopher.

Wounded, Kierkegaard felt deprived of the pleasure of his cherished strolls in the streets of Copenhagen, for now any group of students would titter as he passed, and he moved to the east side of the city to escape the laughter and the stink of water in the gutters of inner Copenhagen. He had enjoyed his commerce with the diversity of people on the streets, including the poorer classes – perhaps, however, in a manner akin to that expressed by the unexamined consciousness of Goethes' foolish Werther about 'the poor folk':

> 'I know quite well that we are not and cannot ever be equal; but I am convinced that anyone who thinks it necessary to keep his distance from the so-called mob in order to gain its respect is as much to blame as the coward who hides from his enemy because he fears to be defeated.'

Werther indeed will later be defeated by his own prideful, egotistical and counterfeit egalitarian attitude when he purposefully crashes a party of aristocrats and is unable to weather the resulting scandal – which, as much as his professed adoration of Lotte, impels him toward his own self-inflicted death.

Neither could Søren Kierkegaard weather the response to his overweeningly prideful invitation to be scorned. When the scorn came, he retaliated and withdrew.

As H C Andersen – whom Kierkegaard had called 'a sniveller' – portrayed him in 'The Snail and the Rose', he spat at the world and crawled back into his shell. But before he did so, he struck back at that other anonymous figure behind *Corsair*, P L Møller.

Kierkegaard had lived extravagantly, a generous tipper, attended by his servant, Anders, who he described as 'his body', and he died broke, with just enough to pay for his burial.

Kierkegaard and Møller were both ardent anti-Hegellians, but as Henrik Stangerup put it, they were like 'two bears sharing the same territory.' They diverged in literary method, however – Kierkegaard favoring subjectivity, Møller realism. Møller was a distinguished literary critic during the so-called Golden Age in Denmark. He had been among the first to recognize the gems of Hans Christian Andersen – although Andersen also was subject to the piratical barbs of the *Corsair*: his journals tell how one night he went to dinner with the Ørsteds to seek comfort from the pain of a Corsairian sting; Ørsted offered no comfort. Andersen returned home to his rooms at the Hotel du Nord on *Kongens Nytorv*, the King's New Square – now the department store Magasin du Nord, across from the Royal Theater. Late that night there came a knocking at his door. Ørsted had hurried from his home on *Studiestræde*, Study Street, to say that his wife had reprimanded him for ignorning Andersen's unhappiness. He explained that he had been deep in thought about a scientific problem and never noticed, but now he had come to assure him of his great affection, his deep belief. The world was wrong. 'You will be one of the world's recognized poets.' He put his arms around Andersen and kissed his forehead, and Andersen was so encouraged and moved, he reports in his journals, that he threw himself upon the sofa and sobbed.

But not all the Corsairian attacks ended such. The feud between Møller and Kierkegaard was so great that Goldschmidt in 1846 moved to Germany to flee the heat, leaving *Corsair* in the hands of Møller. Kierkegaard dealt with Møller in two strokes, separated by half a decade. First he took him as his model for Johannes the Seducer – as apparently Møller was indeed a shameless skirt-chaser or 'woman adorer' in the more understanding Danish phrase – but then, even more lethally, he revealed the fact that Møller was involved in the dreaded *Corsair*.

The result of the latter move, as Stangerup puts it, was that, Møller, the handsome critic with the famous wolfish smile, eternally handicapped by his proletarian background and constant poverty, had lost any chance of getting a permanent position at the University of Copenhagen. (A fate feared by many an academic to this day – permanent denial of the only tenure in town.)

With no hope of a future in his own Denmark, Møller fled to Paris in 1850, at the age of 36. Møller would outlive Kierkegaard by ten years. The philosopher died at 42 in 1855; Møller at 51 in 1865. But while Kierkegaard left behind him an oeuvre that would influence the world in the century to follow, Møller in his fifteen years of exile supported himself writing anti-German propaganda for the Danish State and newspaper articles while making plans for a great study of Danish literature and of French literature. In 1857, he won the university prize for his comparative study of French and Danish comedy, but his dedication to the flesh and to drink obstructed him. Already as a young man in Copenhagen he frequented the rat-infested pubs of Christianshavn, where his decine was already underway in 1847, in the company of failed drunken academics, writers, painters, theologians and medical students. He had a ground floor room at *Nørregade* 46, later another above a snaps distiller at *Store Kongensgade* 272.

Stangerup quotes Møller as having written in 1851, the year he left Denmark: 'One can nibble here and there in life – touching, hinting, arranging, and taking one's bearings on the elements that the brief human span allows us to embrace; that's all we can do, all we want to do, all we can hope to achieve with the powers granted us.'

In Paris he supported himself, barely, as a gigolo. In Normandy, Stangerup tells us, Møller collected tales, including the tale of the shepherd who curses the sun and is in turn cursed by the sun so that his wife and children die. He moves elsewhere to find a new wife in a poorhouse and have more children and that wife and those children die too, and again and again, he moves round and his wives die, and his name is Syphilis, the disease Møller ultimately died of in a lunatic asylum in Normandy.

Møller survives as little more than a footnote in Danish literary history and – once again – as a character in Stangerup's novel, *The Seducer: It Is Hard to Die in Dieppe*.

Ironically, Stangerup notes, among his writings is a single work of fiction, *Janus*, a novella about a seducer tormented by guilt and self-hatred who takes his own life.

Stangerup quotes Karen Blixen as occasionally asking, 'Whatever happened to that man Møller?'

Well she might ask, for he shared with her the affliction of syphilis – as did Nietzsche, Baudelaire, and Maupassant – although Blixen did not die miserably as he did; she even survived to note that she received her syphilis from the same man who gave her the title of Baronness and that, on balance, it was worth it. Somewhat perhaps akin to what Nietzsche wrote: 'As for my sickness, do I not owe it indescribably more than I owe to my health.'

In his autobiography, William Carlos Williams reports that the German sculptor and poet Baroness Else von Freytag-Loringhoven in New York once offered to sleep with Williams so that he could be infected with her syphilis and free himself to realize more fully his true genius. Williams declined.

Another chapter in the story of Søren Kierkegaard and Regine Olsen would yet appear as a *Regine Olsens Diary*, in which it is purported that Kierkegaard did not offer to take the onus of their break-up upon himself, but rather that it was *she* who would be free of him and *he* that begged her to say that he had called it off. The authenticity of the book is questionable, but most people interested in Kierkegaard and his time seem to be enjoying it thoroughly.

Contemplating these ironies on his bench on the bank of Peblinge Lake where Andersen once wept, Kerrigan watches a swan drift past like a question mark. He feels the presence of all this history, all this hurt and hurting, this love and rejection, weeping, sickness, pride, haughtiness, death.

He thinks about the assertion that the fall of man was the fall into language and thinks about Hemingway's 'Big Two Hearted River' and chuckles: I like language. It's a good language.

And he does not, will not think of what he saw when he peered out from his hiding place beneath his son's bed, his own mother, naked, speckled with blood, a pistol in her hand, crooning, 'Terry! Oh Ter-ry!'

No.

He is not unhappy. He has no reason to be unhappy here on the bank of Peblinge Lake where the teenaged Andersen wept into his fingers.

In the buildings behind where he now sits on *Nørre Søgade*, North Lake Street, on the right side of the third floor is the building where Ben Webster lived from 1965 until he died on tour in Amsterdam in 1973. There he would sit, as Bent Kauling tells it, by the window with the superintendent of the building, drinking beer and staring out the window across the lake. The superintendent, Olsen, could not speak English – he called Webster 'Wesper' – and Webster spoke virtually no Danish so they sat in silence, saying no more than *Skål*, and drank their beer, enjoying what Webster called, 'The world's luckiest conversation'.

Two silent men drinking beer, watching the lake.

And Dale Smith, the American bluesman who lives in Copenhagen, supplementing his musical income as a social worker, tells the story of helping an intoxicated Webster home after a gig once, only to have him phone next morning and demand, 'Where's my wallet?!' Dale told him he had placed it under his pillow before he put him to bed, and Webster went to check, came back and said, 'There's a whole lot of money in it!' Dale said, 'You got paid last night.'

Dale also tells of Webster getting fed up one night in the Club Montmartre with the tootling of some very progressive jazzmen and barking, 'Practice at home, motherfuckers!'

Kerrigan has a record he bought in the Jazz Cellar on Copenhagen's *Gråbrødretorv*, Grey Friars Square, recorded in Los Angeles in 1959: Ben Webster on tenor sax, Gerry Mulligan on baritone, playing Billy Strayhorn's 'Chelsea Bridge', seven minutes and twenty seconds of a black man and a white man fingerfucking heaven. Kerrigan knows of no cut as beautiful and moving unless perhaps it is Stan Getz blowing his tenor in alto range on Strayhorn's 'Blood Count', recorded at the Montmartre club in Copenhagen on 6 July 1987, when Getz was dying of cancer. Strayhorn himself wrote the number twenty years before when he was in the hospital riding his own cancer to its end.

Strayhorn wrote it for Duke Ellington to play in Carnegie Hall in 1967. It was the last piece Strayhorn ever wrote. He was Duke Ellington's right hand and Ben Webster had been lead solo in Ellington's orchestra at its best, Billy Holiday's favorite soloist. He came to Copenhagen to live, the only city in the world where he could go out without his knife, and he died in Amsterdam, his home still here, in 1973. Webster about whom, on the day of Kerrigan's birth, 18 September 1943, Jack Kerouac had written: 'Caught Ben Webster at the Three Deuces on 52nd. No one can beat his tone; he breathes out his notes.'

Webster, Getz, Strayhorn, Holiday, Ellington, Mulligan, Kerouac, all gone now. And Chet Baker, too, who fell or was pushed to his death out the window of the Hotel Prince Hendrick on Prince Hendrickstraat in Amsterdam on 18 May 1988. All gone.

But still Kerrigan can hear in his mind, clear as if he were hearing a CD, Webster's horn blowing 'Chelsea Bridge', cut into wax with Mulligan's baritone 8,000 miles from here, 40 years ago, fingerfucking heaven.

A wind is rising on the water, and laughing in his heart he quotes foolish Werther without moving his lips: 'And may I say it? Why not, Wilhelm? She would have been happier with me than with him.' It occurs to him that his cornblue-eyed Associate might have another man and wonders why he should be worrying about that, whether he cares.

He rises from the bench, feels the now swiftly moving air across his face, sees it chopping on the silver surface of the lake, alive in the ever-changing light of Copenhagen, and he has successfully banished the memory of his mother who successfully terminally murdered for him any possibility of horror, for no horror can exist beyond the horror she created in his life.

Silver speckles glit glit glitter on the lake, take me to you, away, toward, on, under, but do not make me drink that briney lake I love. And the beggar swans float in like questions, one another yet two more, cruel of beak and sharp of eye, I do not fear them any more.

A purple-necked duck waddles up onto the bank to see if Kerrigan has bread for him. The dirty lake water rolls in harmless beads like oil down its back and Kerrigan experiences the great joy and optimism of hunger and thirst, looking once over his shoulder to be certain no one can hear, amuses himself saying aloud, 'Adieu! I see no end to this misery except in the grave.'

The duck sees he has no bread and waddles away laughing.

Kerrigan laughs. 'Can I stand you a round?' he says and sets off at a brisk pace toward the opposite end of the lake, entertaining himself with the thought that in the dead of one November night in 1970, the East German authorities in great secrecy removed the remains of Goethe from the ducal crypt in Weimar where they had lain alongside those of the poet Edward Schiller since 1832,138 years before. The flesh remaining on his bones was macerated and the bones themselves strengthened. The laurel crown affixed to his skull was removed, cleaned and reaffixed, and then he was – still secretly – returned to his crypt, though they forgot to return his shroud and did not dare or bother to reopen the crypt to do so.

No doubt some official hung it on his social realist beaureacratic wall.

All this was discovered from records released in March 1999. The records also showed that among other things, the interior of the poet's skull had been examined, and it was recorded that found inside was 'a small quantity of grey dust'.

Kerrigan pictures the official pilfering the dust, preserving it in a little draw-string pouch, carrying it about in his pocket for luck, perhaps dropping it on a bar someplace as the gold miners used to drop a pouch of gold dust: 'Gi' me a shot a red eye!' Or, as that line delivered by the 'Duke', John Wayne, was once translated in a French subtitle: '*Un apéritif, s'il vous plaît.*'

12

The French Café *(Den Franske Café)*

Den Franske Café
Sortedams Dosseringen *(Black Dam Bank)* **101**
2100 København Ø

Dust particles carry on the wind that rolls across the lake, whirlpooling on the dirt walkway, smacking Kerrigan's face as he walks forward at a slant through it. At the far end of the lake, he takes a table outside *Den Franske Café*, The French Café, a literal stone's throw from where Kierkegaard's 1850 residence would still have been standing had it not been torn down to make way for *Willemoesgade*, Willemoes Street, which runs between the two twin towers erected there between 1892 and 1894.

His table is behind the concrete planters where he hunches against the wind to get a small Sumatra lit, then waits, smoking, with the sunlight in his face, for the tall young white-aproned waitress to bring his food – a platter of herring, crab salad, a wedge of brie which he plans to pepper liberally. When he opened his mouth to say, 'And a club soda,' it said instead, 'And a large draft Tuborg.' Startled by these unanticipated words, he paused, and then his mouth called after her, 'And a double Red Ålborg snaps if you have it!'

She smiled over her shoulder at him, one eye squinted shut against the sun, her white-swathed rump nothing short of magnificent, her breasts in a white tee-shirt truly mighty, and she said, 'We have it.'

And there it is again: Kerrigan in love. His blood rising with remembered words, Tim Seibles poem 'Bonobo':

> ' . . . let's get with the kisses –
> And let there be lots of fucking – proud, vigorous,
> variously paced, delirious, jubiliant . . .'

But he is not Tim Seibles, a six-foot black poet, former quarterback for the SMU football team, whose first collection of poems was entitled *Body Moves*.

Could try indirection:

You make me think of Bonobo.

What's Bonobo? she might ask pleasantly, perhaps twinkling.

It's a poem by a friend of mine about Bonobo apes, a non-violent species of ape who employ sex as their primary mode of social interaction. All kinds of sex:

> ' . . . Let thighs be questions
> and other thighs be answers . . .
> Let's take this one chance and be terribly
> kind to each other . . .
> Let's dress up
> in sweat only. Leave the money to the morticians
> and their cadavers.'

But he is not Tim Seibles so he just smiles politely to the cute-faced waitress's polite smile as she places the fish and drink before him, and as he eats, he watches swans and ducks, joggers, and then a single heron walking slow and precise as a Tai Chi practitioner along the bank of the lake (reminding him of a statement by a visiting fiction writer, Steve Heller, at Vermont College as he crossed the Green for breakfast and a wiry fellow was practising this art: 'If he can't move any faster than that even I can kick his ass.'), while the wind stipples the water into glittering spires of silver and black, and Kerrigan feels the beer chasing the snaps through his blood; the snaps makes a clean break for the shelter of the brain, but the beer plows right on after it.

He likes it here so very much, feasting his eyes on the whipping branches of the chestnuts, the potted yellow lillies framing the path line, the multi-spiring water and the imperturbable heron. He takes out his little pad and his Montblanc, swallows more beer and thinks of Tom Kristensen's Ole Jastrau who drank himself to the dogs. He thinks of Stan Getz's three years in Copenhagen at the end of the 50s when he came here to find serenity, freedom from drugs and drink, played his beautiful tenor four days a week on *Store Regnegade* in the old club Montmartre, owned by Anders Dyrup, the jazz-loving son of a wealthy paint manufacturer whose name is everywhere on Danish paint shops.

Getz played with bassist Oscar Pettiford, one of the great early be-boppers – half Choctau, part Cherokee, part black, married to a white woman – who came to Denmark to find a more tolerant social climate for his children. And he jammed at Montmartre with the musicians who came through – Art Blakey, Lee Konitz, Kenny Clark, Gerry Mulligan. Picture Stan on baritone and Mulligan on tenor, switch-hitting, with Jim Hall on guitar playing for four or five hours in the wee hours on Great Rain Street.

But within two years, Pettiford was dead, at 37, of a fluke disease, and one night after dinner Getz went outside the beautiful house where he lived with his wife and children and threw a brick through every window. Then he came back in and with a poker from the fireplace, smashed every plate in a collection of priceless Royal Copenhagen China which the landlord owned.

The doctor put him on antabus – a medication which causes violent illness if combined with drink – but Getz didn't take it because, he reasoned, he was not an alcoholic.

On another occasion he kicked his dog unmercifully, beat his daughter, cursing her for trying to stop him. He even put a loaded gun to his wife's head.

Too tortured to live with peace of mind, he returned to the states after not quite three years, though he came back frequently to Denmark. *Standinavia* was the title of one of his albums.

Kerrigan heard him play at Montmartre once in 1977, the new Montmartre which had moved to *Nørregade*, North Street, that runs from North Port, *Nørreport*, down toward *Vor Frue Kirke*, The Church of Our Lady, Copenhagen's cathedral, though it bears no resemblance to the bombastic cathedrals of southern Europe or their imitations elsewhere. He thinks now what it must have been like to be able to go hear Getz play four nights a week. He regrets that he missed the last concerts in '87 and '91.

Four CDs were made from the performances, *Anniversary* and *Serenity* from 1987, and *People Time*, a double, from '91, the year he died, at 64. (That would give me eight or nine more years, Kerrigan thinks.)

The *Anniversary* album concludes with Billy Strayhorn's 'Blood Count', the piece Strayhorn wrote for Ellington in '67 when he was dying, and Getz was dying when he played it in '87, and he said; 'I think about Strayhorn when I play the song. You can hear him dying. When it's in a minor key, you can hear the man talking to God.'

Kerrigan contemplates the fact that a man who could play such profoundly beautiful music, lines that search into the bottom of your soul and lift it up through an agony of pleading to an angelic plain, could be so helpless against the demons that had him terrorize his family.

He thinks again of Kristensen's Ole Jastrau, 'Jazz' in the novel *Havoc*, written 30 years before Getz's stay in Copenhagen. Jastrau lashes out to destroy a life that is destroying him as an artist, as a poet. He drives away his wife and child, smashes up their bourgeois apartment, exposes himself to syphilis, performs a wild awkward dance to the jazz of a wind-up gramophone, all the while accompanied by a younger man, Steffan Steffensen, a poet who shamelessly, scornfully uses him, abuses his hospitality, a young man fleeing from wealthy parents who are both infected with syphilis, as he is, as is the girl he has with him – a servant from his house whom he himself has infected.

Suddenly Kerrigan understands the difference between Kristensen the creator and Jastrau his creation. For just as Steffan Steffensen is Jastrau's alter ego, so is Jastrau, Kristensen's. What kept Kristensen from the dogs perhaps was his pen. He wrote it. Jastrau only lived it and even then not in the world but in the word, while Kristensen was his god, his creator; through Jastrau he both lived *and* uttered it. Getz had only the music, and beautiful as it was, as it is, it did not give him the power he needed over his demons. He only played it, interpreted it; he did not create it. But no, no, of course Getz created it, his breath shaped the notes, his being improvised the turns, the leaps.

So Kerrigan takes up his Montblanc pen, pleasingly hefty in his hand, and casts into words the spirit of the water suddenly subjected to the wind, flinging sand in the faces of the people at the café tables around him. One by one, they gather up their cakes and coffees and liquers and hurry indoors, hair dancing in the wind, blinking against the dust, smiling self-consciously, self-depractorily at their soon-solved predicament, but Kerrigan stays where he is, eyes squinted into the wind that cannot blow the ink from his page.

Grinning, he lifts his glass and drinks beer, swallowing the dust the wind has flung into it, letting the grit of it against his teeth be pleasure, and practises one of his favorite hobbies, the memorization and juxtaposition of dates:

In 1987 when Stan Getz was doing his penultimate appearance in Copenhagen's Montmartre club, dying, playing 'Blood Count' that Billy Strayhorn wrote in 1967 when he was dying, the great hornman Dexter Gordon who lived in Copenhagen from 1962 to 1976 was, incredibly, competing against Paul Newman for an academy award for best actor for his performance in the film *Round Midnight*, a composite portrayal of American jazzmen in Europe. Newman won. But Long Dexter Gordon, the soft spoken six and a half footer was described by the critic Alexander Walker in this way:

> 'Like many big men who move with a child's gentleness, Gordon has also an unsettling tension – you feel this big barrel might have gunpowder in him. His voice is like a great vintage full-bodied wine, glug-glugging into the vessel of silence he seems to occupy. Gordon always looks like he's listening to sounds we cannot hear.'

And in 1966, the same year Frank O'Hara died in his car accident on Fire Island, Gordon was arrested in Paris. The crime reported in the Paris edition of the *International Herald Tribune* was that he had trafficked in drugs in the student quarter; the *New York Herald Tribune* put a finer point on it, reporting on the 'American Negro jazzman', and 'a Danish blond' being arrested – crime enough right there to lock *him* up and shave *her* head. The Danish Home Office tried to revoke his visa to return to Copenhagen, but the Danish people rebelled. A rally in the Town Hall Square at the center of Copenhagen inspired the Home Office to renege. Dexter returned and lived eight more years in Copenhagen, before going back to America in 1974, twelve years before Kerrigan's mother did her thing.

In 1943, Kerrigan was born to an Irish father and Icelandic mother, exactly 100 years after the birth of Henry James and the publication of Edgar Allen Poe's 'The Black Cat'.

In 1831 Darwin sailed on the Beagle, 168 years before five states in the US would eradicate his discoveries from the teaching curricula of their schools (along with the Big Bang Theory), and in 1821, John Keats died at the age of 26, the same year Dostoyevski and Flaubert were born, two years after the birth of Melville and Whitman in 1819 which was six years after the birth of Kierkegaard in 1813, the year the Danish State went bankrupt, and five years after the birth in 1814 of Peder Ludvig Møller who would become Kierkegaard's enemy and serve as his model in *The Seducer's Diary* written in 1843 while Darwin was writing *The Origin of the Species*. Darwin's study would later be translated into Danish by J P Jacobsen, whom James Joyce in 1901 would call 'a great innovator', and Kierkegaard's fictional model of the critic Møller was stalking the innocent young fictional Cordelia along the banks of this lake where Kerrigan sits in 1999 savoring the taste of dust, glimpsing the beautiful willowy apron-wrapped hips of the waitress who brings him yet another large draft and another lovely smile.

He wonders what would happen if he kissed her. Just like that – jump up and steal a kiss from those lips, too quick for her to get away. He remembers Rumi:

'I would love to kiss you.
The price of kissing is your life.
Now my desire runs toward my life
Shouting, What a bargain! Let's buy it!'

Instead, he chances to speak to her as she gathers his soiled dishes and uneaten crusts, to quote the conclusion of Steen Steensen Blicher's *Diary of a Parish Clerk*, written in 1824, when Keats was three years dead, a depiction of the famous tragic love affair between a beautiful young Jutland aristocratic woman, Marie Grubbe (1643-1718) and her game warden, which ends in squalor and poverty in Copenhagen and is, still later, depicted by J P Jacobsen in a full-length novel:

'As for man,' quoth Kerrigan from Blicher, himself quoting scripture, to the girl, 'his days are as grass . . . For the wind passeth over it and it is gone; and the place thereof shall know it no more. But the mercy of the Lord is from everlasting to everlasting.'

The girl's smile is wise as Buddha's: 'Can I get you something else, sir?'

13

Café Rhythm Hans *(Café Rytme Hans)*

Café Rytme Hans
Østerbrogade *(East Bridge Street)* **35**
2100 København Ø

14

Red Light Café *(Café Røde Lygte)*

Café Røde Lygte
Trianglen *(The Triangle)*
2100 København Ø

Moved by another hunger now, less specific than the hunger for food or drink, he strolls up *Østerbrogade*, East Bridge Street, crosses *Trianglen*, the triangular joining of three avenues, pausing to look at the goddamned 7-Eleven shop where once stood a guest house and restaurant in which 200 years before, Peter the Great, Czar of Russia, slept.

He passes *Café Røde Lygte*, on the west of the three angles, the Red Light Café, whose red door lamps are innocent of prurience – a soccer bar which opened in 1886, the year after the birth of Ezra Pound in the U S and Francois Mauriac in France, seven years before the birth of Tom Kristensen who was born a year before Dorothy Parker in 1894, fifteen years before the birth, in 1909, of Kerrigan's father, who would migrate back from Brooklyn to Ireland in 1929 to meet his Icelandic wife-to-be.

He crosses past Café Rytme Hans, Café Rhythm Hans – where he can remember long ago sitting across a late-night table gazing into the brown eyes of a dark-haired girl wearing black pedal-pushers. She lived nearby, and he ended in her bed, and he could still remember the pleasure of seeing her naked and how she gasped when he touched her nipples, but he cannot remember her name or the circumstances of their meeting or precisely where she lived. Here somewhere it was, and his eyes sweep across the faces of the buildings on either side of the two-way street, avenue really, but he can only remember her room, her bed, not where it was, and he is reminded of a story by Dylan Thomas, 'One Warm Saturday', in *Portrait of the Artist as a Young Dog* – written in 1938 when Kerrigan was but a glint in his father and mother's eye – about a young man who goes to a fair and drinks and falls in with some people and meets a girl who likes him, and they go back to her place in some tenement flats. There is no toilet and he has to go out, down to the back alleys to find one, and when he's done, he cannot remember just where her flat was in this great maze of buildings. He looks and looks and knocks on doors. Someone who answers complains he has wakened their baby, and he asks where 'Lou's flat' is, says he doesn't know her 'other name', and all he can remember is her whispering to him, when he left, to return to her. He sits on the stairs for a time, but there is no love to wait for and no bed but his own too many miles away to lie in.

Kerrigan thinks of Thomas dying in the White Horse Tavern in Greenwich Village in 1953 at the age of 39 after 30-some whiskies. No, he died in St Vincent's Hospital in West Greenwich Village. Fatal glass of whiskey. Though the new theory is he died of something else entirely. And when someone came to identify the body, it is said, the forensic administrator asked what the deceased's occupation had been and, told he was a poet, asked, 'What's a poet?'

Part of the myth no doubt – like Kenneth Rexroth's accusation of the United States in general for the poet's death:

> 'You killed him!
> You killed him!
> In your goddamned Brooks Brothers suit,
> You son of a bitch!'

Kerrigan continues up East Bridge Street, past Café Oluf at the mouth of *Olufsvej*, McGrath's and the Park Café, Theodor's, St Jacques, Thygge's Inn on Viborg Street, down Århus Street past *Århuskroen*, the Århus Inn, the Café X-presen, offering three unspecified finger-sandwiches for a song, past *Café Åstedet*, the Stream Place Café, and thinks of the story by the Orkney writer, George McKay Brown, 'The Whaler's Return', about Andrew Flaws who returns from months at sea to be married, and between the port and the house of his betrothed in the next town are 50 ale-houses waiting to take from him his wages from the long whaling journey.

He stops here and there, buys rounds, ends in the field spying on a tinker wedding, is discovered, thrashed, and loses more money there. Finally, in the morning, muddy and tired, he finds his way up the lane of his betrothed's house, and he tells her he has just enough left of his money for the first six months' rent, while they see to the seeding and the harvest. She tells him they are also in debt for a shrouding fee and for the digging of the grave of her father who was killed by a horse while the whaler was away. But he says he already saw to that on his way in, and his betrothed replies, 'There are 34 ale houses in the town of Hamnavoe and sixteen ale-houses on the road between Hamnavoe and Borsay. Some men from the ships are a long time getting home . . .That was a good thing you did, Andrew Flaws.'

Kerrigan was once in contact with George McKay Brown. After reading the man's stories, he had wanted to visit the Orkneys to interview him, and they made plans for it by post, but Kerrigan never got there, and his last letters to Brown in 1995 went unanswered.

Then one afternoon only a few months before in Edinburgh, at a bookshop on Princes Street, he picked up a new anthology of Scottish verse which included a lovely poem by George Mackay Brown, an account of an outing, of Folster's lipstick wounds, of Greve's sweet fog on a stick, of Crusack's three rounds with a Negro, of Johnston's mouth full of dying fires, and in the bio notes, he learned that George had died in 1996.

Kerrigan had gone on to Milne's on Rose Street where 40 per cent larger spirits are served, and the Abbortsford, for pints of black Orkney where George had drunk with Hugh MacDiarmid and Dylan Thomas and W H Auden. He thought about the fact that the Orkney Islands had been Danish until 1468. He thought of the wild Danish-Scottish islands he had never seen, although he might have, the fine writer he had never met, although he might have done that, too.

He thought about the gaudy monument to Walter Scott on Princes Street and the modest plaque to Robert Louis Stevenson in Princes Street Gardens, of William Drummond of Hawthornden Castle where Kerrigan once was given shelter by an 85-year-old woman named Drue Heinz, heiress to the 57 varieties of ketchup fortune, and he thought about riding a mountain bike up and down the hilly roads of Lasswade where, at the entry to the motorway, there stands a sign: *Pedestrians, Cyclists, Horse-drawn Vehicles and Animals Prohibited*, and he looked about in vain for bespectacled four-legged creatures who might be capable of receiving that instruction.

15

Park Café *(Park Café)*

Park Café
Østerbrogade *(East Bridge Street)* **79**
2100 København Ø

He doubles back and across the street from the gateway to the stadium, pauses to gaze through the arched port at the tall silhouetted sculpture of the archer there, bow drawn, arrow aimed south.

Above the archway Albert Boucher's three runners at the goal, frozen in green bronze, strive to be first over the line, each reaching for individual victory.

He crosses, turns south, back to the Park Café with its crystal chandeliers and art deco sculptures, walls hung with large shadowy paintings. He gazes at one, a woman baring her breast and holding a knife at her heart. Must be a story there.

Up the stairs past a madonna and child to the terrace bar that looks over the sports stadium, where he orders a draft beer from the bar.

'How does it feel to work surrounded by all this art?' he asks the barmaid.

'What?'

'This art.'

She looks at the sculpture flanking the door, turns back to her work at the tap with a shrug. He carries his beer to a table beside a bronze girl on a pedestal holding a lamp against a sunny stone wall. He lifts his glass to her. 'I love you,' he whispers.

16

Le Saint Jacques

Le Saint Jacques
Sankt Jakobs Plads *(Saint Jacob's Place)* **1**
2100 København Ø

On the other side of *Østerbrogade*, East Bridge Avenue, from Sankt Jakobs Kirke, his leather-shod feet lead him to Le Saint Jacques. This was once Sankt Jacob's Bodega, a bucket of blood bar, but now in the hands of a French owner it serves excellent cuisine and boasts a magnificent icon collection – a whole beautiful wall of them behind glass, madonnas with child, saints with fingers raised in benediction.

He circles the bar and into the gent's to make room for more beer. He prays the ritual prayer it is his custom to pray while he awaits the water: *Glory be to God for dappled things*. A line of Gerald Manley Hopkins, which came to him one day in Dublin as he leaked in the Newman House men's room which used to be Hopkins chamber.

Now, however, he gazes up to find himself faced with a handsomely framed Picasso print mounted over the zinc trough. A line drawing of naked women dancing together, graceful interweaving lines, signed and dated 13-2-54, 45 years ago. Not more than that. How old was Picasso then? Born in 1881 (a year before Joyce). Would've been 73 and still another nineteen years to live: 73 and still finding new ways to depict women. Kerrigan remembers Picasso's *Les Demoisselles d'Avignon,* which he goes to look at whenever he is in New York – at the Museum of Modern Art. Painted in 1907, it depicts five women said to be from a brothel on Avignon Street. It is one of the earliest pictures in the development of cubism, but what interests Kerrigan more about it is the fact that two of the faces are unmistakably influenced by African sculpture. They might have been African ceremonial or fetish masks. It fascinates Kerrigan that 92 years previously Picasso would have thought to place faces of those masks upon the bodies of the women he was painting.

Kerrigan regrets that he had not known enough to have made a pilgrimage to visit Picasso while the man was still alive. He might have. Kerrigan was 30 when the master died. He hopes still to make a study of Picasso's many depictions of women – the cubist agony of *The Weeping Woman* (1937), the women of *Guernica* that same year (painted in Paris at 7, *Rue des Grand Augustins*, same place where Balzac wrote 'The Unknown Masterpiece' – how those walls must whisper, he thinks) and the horrifying *Woman in Pain*, a study not used in the final of *Guernica*. His *Bather Seated by the Sea* with her crab-like face from 1930, the strangely beautiful *Three Dames* of 1925, and his *Seated Woman* of 1959, a cubist melding of woman and chair, yet with clear naturalistic tufts of hair in the armpits.

On his way out, he orders a draft at the bar, a little bag of peanuts, then takes a wicker seat in the ebbing sunlight. He munches the peanuts from the tiny cellophane bag on which is printed *Please remember that small children can choke on nuts*. Here, kids, have some nuts. He dusts salt from his palms and fires up a Christian long cigarillo. Dry tobacco. Agreeably bitter in the mouth, smoke floating blue then grey up into the late-afternoon sun that glints white on the surface of the green-lacquered table top and glows amber in the beer.

Music lilts from inside the café and he recognizes Billie Holiday's voice, Ben Webster's tenor. He also recognizes the song, a lyric by Dorothy Parker:

'I wished on the moon for something I never knew
A sweeter rose, a softer sky, an April day
That would not dance away . . .'

Billie's voice so sweet and wistful, lilting and strong; when she says 'April day' Kerrigan's heart is filled with the accepted sadness of its retreating dance, and Webster's tenor softens it all with a reedy mellow cool nod. Kerrigan happens to know this was recorded in Los Angeles in June 1957 when he was still thirteen years old. The Chevy was a work of art that year. But two and a half years later, Lady Day would be dead. He thinks of Frank O'Hara's poem, 'The Day Lady Died'.

He loves the voice, the tenor, the lyric, the poem, by four dead people, but what bothers him is that the day Lady Day died, two days after Bastille Day in 1959, he didn't even know about it because he didn't even know about her – he was pushing sixteen then, and even if he was living in the city she died in, the city O'Hara describes in his poem, where he buys the *New York Post* and sees her fateful picture which Kerrigan knew nothing about from the other side of the East River where he lived with his 44 year-old mother who was gathering some of the experiences that would hatch the seed of the madness that bloomed later on the Palouse, same age as the Lady when she died and when he still didn't even know anything about her or about Frank O'Hara either who died in 1966 at the age of 40 in a Fire-Island car accident that Kerrigan vaguely recalls hearing about when he was 23 and lived on East 3rd Street between Avenues A and B, Alphabet City, where a young homosexual man impersonating the singer Paul Simon invited him to lunch and tried to seduce him by sensually tearing the meat from a fried chicken with his teeth and Kerrigan fled, just as he vaguely recalls hearing when he was 24 of the death of Dorothy Parker in 1967: An April day that will not dance away . . .

He sips his amber beer and wonders who might be dying today that he had never even or only vaguely heard of just as a silver-bearded man wearing a Copenagen-Jazz-Festival tee-shirt at the next table holds out a newspaper for him to see. It is the

Copenhagen daily tabloid *Ekstra Bladet*, boulevard press, open to the infamous page nine, which always reserves space for a picture of a young naked woman.

The man nods.

Kerrigan nods.

On the page is a three-column black-and-white photo of a woman wearing nothing but a string of pearls around the narrow waist above her pudgy hips.

'Mette from Valby is eighteen,' says the man, reading the caption aloud for Kerrigan's benefit.

Kerrigan nods.

'Tell you what', the man says. Kerrigan notices the man is drinking a strong, gold-labelled beer and a bitter and is thankful that he himself is not doing so. 'I pay 8.50 per day, every day, 11.50 on Sunday, just mainly to have a look at who's on page 9.'

Kerrigan nods, firms his lips to indicate seriousness of reaction.

'Don't get me wrong,' the man says. 'It's not porn. I hate porn. Degrading. To everyone concerned. But *this*. These *girls* are like, you know, *real*, right?' He says 'right' as the Danes do, in a negative form, *ikke?* Pronounced '*ik'* with a short 'i'.

'*Jo*,' says Kerrigan because that is what you reply when someone poses a negative question, even a rhetorical one that politeness requires you agree with. Not the usual affirmative *ja*, but *jo*. Pronounced *yo*. And if in agreement, it is exclaimed; if with reservation, drawled.

'*Jo*!' exclaims Kerrigan.

'Mette from Valby,' says the man in the Jazz-Festival tee-shirt. 'That's a real girl and she's so . . .' He studies the picture for a moment, still holding it at such an angle that both he and Kerrigan can see. '*Real*. I mean, look at her. *Ik?*'

Kerrigan nods. '*Jo*!'

'Mette from Valby. Helle from Albertslund. Maj is 23 years old and from Århus. Linda is seventeen and from Greve. I got a wall full of them. I look at them.' He touches his palm to his chest. 'And I feel happy. I look at them, and I got a reason, you know what I mean, like Joe Cocker. *Ik?*'

'*Jo*!'

'You give me reason to live, *ik?* I mean not *you*, but *her*, *ik?*'

Kerrigan nods, says, '*Jo!*'

The man lifts his bitter. 'Mette from Valby and a little taste of the "good old",' he says, nodding at the black snaps in his glass – *Gammel Dansk* – Old Danish – 'the Good Old'.

'*Skål*,' he says.

'*Skål*,' says Kerrigan and lifts his beer.

'It's good to chat once in a while, ik?' says the man sets down his empty glass, rises, nods, folds Mette from Valby beneath his arm and lists off across Sankt Jakobs Place toward the north harbor. Kerrigan wonders what the man's room is like. Pictures it, plastered with black-and-white newsprint photos of young Danish women, amateur models who pick up 500 crowns if their photo is selected to run on page nine, extra few thousand if you're the pick of the month. Smile and show how they look beneath their threads. I'll show you mine for 500 crowns.

Ik?

Jo!

He thinks again of Picasso's women, remembers the story about the man on a train who recognizes Picasso seated across from him.

'You! You're Picasso!' the man exclaims.

Picasso nods.

'I have to tell you,' says the man. 'The women you paint. They're not women. Women don't look like that.' The man pulls out his wallet and opens it to show a photograph. 'That's my wife,' he says. '*That's* a woman!'

'That's your wife?' Picasso says.

The man nods proudly.

'She's rather small and two-dimensional, isn't she?'

The sun has slid away from the Le Saint Jacques tables, slants across the other side of the little square.

17

Theodor's Café and Restaurant

Theodor's Café and Restaurant
Østerbrogade *(East Bridge Street)* **106**
2100 København Ø

Kerrigan drains his beer, crosses Sankt Jakobs Place to the sunny side. The tables are all taken, but anyway he sees what the pattern of his day will be: He already has to pee again. Good day to sit closer to the loo than to the bar. Inside the black and chrome interior, he finds the gent's, repeats the fate of the exasperated spirit, from urinal to urinal, proceeding to yet another urinal, unzips his fly, fishes out the little mouse and observes a curious phenomenon. There are two urinals, side by side, tucked within a bracket of walls, small, white, belly-high fixtures above which, fixed into the wall, is a strip of mirror wherein he sees reflected the little sparrowhead of his manhood. Further, he notes, if there were another patron at the urinal alongside, both their birdheads would be reflected to mutual view in the mirror strip. *Extraordinary*! Like advertising the bottom line of your tax return! Is this a gay café? No. Then why? Such a detail could not be inadvertent. A joke perhaps? Hardly feasible. Very odd indeed. He is grateful to be alone and zipped by the time another man enters. The new fellow goes to the toilet stall. Maybe everyone knows about this.

He did not wish to view his own circumsized little helmet and concentrates on the washing of his knobby fingers to be free of the image. Fresh air from an open window mingles with the smell of hand soap in which he has a stubborn faith. He tears paper towels from the dispenser with which to clap his hands dry, remembers as he pushes through the door again a line of Ferlinghetti: *Women's underwear is designed to hold things up/Men's to keep things down* . . . and is outside at the tables again, seeking a place to sit.

He approaches an empty chair beside a young woman reading a newspaper.

'May I?'

She nods with a contraction of her lips.

He sits, orders, lights a Christian. He holds the match before his eyes. The air is now so still that the flame seems not to move at all, seems perfectly still yet vibrant, eating the wood of the matchstick, violent yet stable – structured in a perfect symmetrical spire, at one and the same moment beautiful, fearsome, mysterious. He wants to call the attention of the young woman to this tiny amazement, to invite her to share this marvel. She turns a page in the newspaper, reads. The matchflame nips his fingers and he shakes it out. A glass of coke stands on the table before her, two fingers of cola in the slush of cubes. She folds the newspaper open, places it beneath the ashtray so it won't blow away, checks her wrist-watch, swallows the rest of her cola – Kerrigan watches her long white throat moving with the liquid. Then she sets the empty glass down with a clack, rises, departs.

When she is out of sight, he slides the ashtray closer, takes up the newspaper. It is the Copenhagen section of *The Jutland Post*, *Jyllandsposten*, folded open to an article about a hundred year old telephone kiosk which is about to be auctioned off on the King's New Square. The starting bid is 60,000 dollars. It is the first of a number of telephone kiosks designed by Fritz Koch in 1886, roomy and richly appointed with wood and copper and glass. There are only a handful of them left. That they survive out on the streets without being vandalized is a tribute to Danish civilization. It occurs to Kerrigan to buy it, live in it, or maybe use it for an office.

Sit there in his oversized telephone box on the King's New Square surrounded by a wide circle of elegant buildings, the Royal Theater with its great seated sculptures of Ludvig Holberg, considered the Danish Moliere, and Adam Oehlenschläger, the early nineteenth-century romantic poet whose little sister Sofie married H C Ørsted's older brother and was loved by many poets, including Jens Baggesen, and by H C Ørsted, too, for he called his own daughter Sofie, one of the women for whom H C Andersen yearned so tragically.

To sit in his elegant telephone box and write and watch the world of the elegant core of Copenhagen through 360 degrees of window all for a mere 60,000 dollars. An idiotic idea. Where would he get the money? Nowhere. He could take out a new mortgage on his apartment. He can not put it out of his mind.

You could just go look at it at least.

Ik?

Jo!

On the King's New Square, he sees his kiosk. The shutters are raised and a small truck is parked outside from which a waiter carries a tray into the door of the little pavillion, beneath its green copper spire. Inside, is just room enough for a white-clothed table at which a young blond couple sit, a feast spread before them, candles burning in crystal sticks, polished silver on white linen.

The waiter pours wine into a sparkling goblet and waits while the young man tastes it, contemplates, rolling it on his tongue, nods. The waiter withdraws to the truck.

'I thought this was up for auction,' says Kerrigan.

'Was,' the waiter tells him, readying the next course from the back of the truck. 'Went to the hammer yesterday. 700,000 crowns, 100,000 dollars at current exchange.'

Kerrigan looks at the newspaper he has carried beneath his arm. It is dated two weeks back. So much for synchronicity. He pitches it into a trash receptacle, trudges off across the square which is in fact a circle, yet finds himself stopping to look back at the kiosk.

The candles are tiny yellow spires in the windows and the faces of the young couple gaze upon one another silently and the wine sparkles red in their crystal goblets as they raise them to their lips, and he thinks of his own plan to sit in there by himself writing, watching the world move about outside.

18

Hviids Wine Room *(Hviids Vinstue)*

Hviids Vinstue
Kongens Nytorv *(The King's New Square)* **19**
1050 København K

– again

He looks across to the 275-year-old wine room beneath where the Blue Note and Grand Café used to be and where Jens August Schade wrote about

'The Finnish girl who just for me
in secret pulled her dress
so lovely up above her breasts
She was no awful floozie
she was just a little flute
with holes and breath to play
a little twilight melody
of love's enchanted spell . . .'

Inside the cave-like room, he goes straight for the pay phone with beer in hand and sifts through his wallet for the number of his cornblue-eyed Associate. He longs for her little book of starfish and sea anemones. Even as he dials the number, he wonders if his voice will slur, if she will be home at all on a late Saturday afternoon, if she has a man, if she will find him out of order, foolish, and the telephone line sends its little burring sound into his ear as he waits breathlessly, convinced she is already out somewhere with someone else and not walking barefoot around her apartment painting pictures from a palette of oils.

Then her voice is in his ear, and he is thrilled that she recognizes his at once, from the single syllable of his greeting.

'And how did you spend the day on your own without your Associate?' she asks.

'Miserably,' he says. 'I'm no good without you and your little book. I wandered around the lakes and thought morbid thoughts.'

'I had an aunt who lived there,' she says. 'In an apartment right above the French Café . . .'

'I was there today!'

' . . . She was a baronness. Really. Her third husband was a baron. Her fourth husband was a clerk. She was always married and always alone. She was so much fun. I spent so much time with her. She read me the funnies in bed, and we dressed up in costumes and laughed and laughed. She took her own life. She was 39, and I was thirteen, and my parents would not allow me to go to the funeral. My mother worried because I looked like her.'

Kerrigan is silent. He peers into the foam of his lager and lines up coins on the shelf beneath the phone and looks at a small cardboard sign propped on a table – a drawing of this place where three men in old-fashioned suits stand at the bar with a naked woman. He wonders if the woman is supposed to be an hallucination. He thinks of the Finnish girl Schade wrote about in 1962, wondering if his Associate's aunt were still alive then, and he considers the fact that his own mother did not have the decency to take her life after taking everyone else's. Or before.

'What was her name?' he asks.

'Why?'

He does not know how to respond, says nothing long enough that she asks, 'And what is Mr Kerrigan calling for at this blue hour?'

He knows she knows what he is calling for, but he tells it in another way. 'I'm on my way up to Long John's. To hear some happy jazz.'

'Happy jazz?'

'Right. That's what they call it. Dixieland, I guess. I thought you might care to join me.'

Her chuckle is complex. 'Oh, you did, did you? Well you know it's time and a half after six. Come to think of it, double time on weekends.'

'Oh, well, I meant, you know, like, personally.'

'You mean you meant you want me to do what I do for free?'

'I thought perhaps you might care to join me for dinner.'

'I think Mr Kerrigan is the Prince of Cups this evening.'

'I'm sorry, I didn't mean to . . .'

'Besides I've already eaten,' she says. 'I had a lovely pineapple sandwich.'

Mr Kerrigan, he thinks, is going to be sick. 'Are you painting?' he asks. 'Are you barefoot?' How he wished she would invite him over for a coffee.

'So many questions. Oh! there's the doorbell, got to run . . .'

So who needs her, thinks Kerrigan, and takes a seat at the little table near the door where he can survey the bar and the entries to the first two cave-like rooms. He drinks a pint of lager with a double Finlandia vodka in a snaps glass in honor of Finnish girls and Finland.

He raises his vodka and says, '*Multatuli*,' snaps it down, chases it with cold beer, says, 'Perkele!' and 'Earth, fire, I have suffered greatly, I haf just hod an orgasm.' The bartender in white shirt and black vest glances over. Kerrigan has committed a Danish sin: *at gøre sig bemæreket* – to call attention to oneself. He raises his vodka again, but the glass is empty.

'Once more, please,' he says and when the bartender brings the bottle to refill his glass, he says, 'I'm not mad. Even if I seem to be.' And nods formally. This time he keeps his toast to himself, thinks, Earth, fire, suffering, come, and snaps down the vodka.

He yearns back in memory for the Swedish girl who once fed him *svartsuppa*, black soup.

She fed me
goose blood soup
the Swedish girl
who looked like the virgin
Santa Lucia herself
radiant as a crown of candles.
'It is an old tradition,' she said,
in the way Swedish girls talk
sweet no-nonsense music
'It is made of the blood of the goose
you will eat tonight.
We do not waste. Eat your soup now,'
and her teeth gleamed in the candlelight
her face so pale
and eyes so very very blue.

A tear rolls down Kerrigan's boozy cheek for he is thinking now of Santa Lucia and the Scandinavian celebration each mid-December where the young virgins dress in white, wearing crowns of candles in their hair and march in a procession singing in angelic voices about Santa Lucia whose eyes were put out in her defense of her purity.

Another large iced vodka to keep company with his beer and make room for a return to his Finnish thoughts. He drinks to Keith Bosley:

'The ice in the vodka
swivels
and we are heading
north-east, not on pilgrimmage
but on safari, though this
is Europe still, to an extremity
a hand extended to the cold.'

Kerrigan drinks to Alexis Kivi (1834-1872) and to Johan Ludwig Runeberg (1804-1877) and Elias Lönnrot (1802-1884) and to Jean Sibelius who composed *Finlandia*, the name of the vodka he drinks now, and he drinks to Rautavaara and his contemporary encounters with the angels, and he drinks to all the Finnish girls who sing to him:

Terrence, she sings,
I am Edith.
Behold my fruit, my sea, my soul.
You are disappointed.

No, Edith,
without your fruit,
I was pressed into a book.
Without your sea,
I was drowned.
Without your soul,
I was never free.

Terrence, she sings,
I am Kirsi.
My locks slither,
But my blood has wings.
Do you think your will can know me?
Do you even hear me sing?
Your eyes askance, your ears are plugged,
You watch me in a shield.
I can shatter your craft,
Make you stone,
Fling you from the edge of dread,
For we two, we are one,
Yet still you shiver in the vestibule
as time trickles.

Terrence, she sings,
I am Aila.
I saw you naked rape the sphinx
Even as I sang.
Done is done.
It is not I who holds the grudge.
You brood alone.
Your seed was cold.
Something lies broken
far below
And you cannot find your tongue.

Terrence, she sings,
I am Eeva.
You do not see the future,
Just a path that curves away
into the green dark.
Your mind is full of thought
Your lung is full of breath
Your open mouth sculpts sound.
The words that fill your mouth
Are mine you know.
It is for me to choose your song
or go.

Terrence, she sings,
I am Satu.
I come from the wood.
Turn from the glass.
Forget the griefs of mouths
that scream and gasp.
Forget the better folk.
Speak slowly. Look.
I will teach you to kill.
See my claws?
I have them of my mother.

See my teeth?
Smell me.
Taste.
Growl in joy
For you have learned
For now we die.

Terrence, she sings,
Listen.

He listens. And hears only the chill echo of his Associate's voice on the phone telling him, go away, go away.

19

The Rosen Court Bodega *(Rosengårdens Bodega)*

Rosengårdens Bodega
Rosengården 11
1174 København K

Kerrigan perambulates. Up *Gothersgade*, Gothers Street, past *Kongens Have*, the King's Gardens, hooks left at *Nørrevoldgade*, North Rampart Street, down *Fiolstræde*, Violin Street, pauses at the mouth of a slanted dash of a street, *Rosengården*, the Rosen Court, that runs down to *Kultorvet*, the Coal Square.

He enters the door of a place so unremarkable it seems designed to be ignored, *Rosengårdens Bodega*, the Rosen Court Bodega. Smoke-darkened paintings with cracked oils hang on the yellow walls, an old-fashioned claustrophobic telephone booth with a tiny 'o' of a window in the door and an old waterpump mounted above it. A single customer nurses a beer at one of the tables.

Kerrigan takes a stool at the bar, orders a large draft lager, running a rough tally of how many he has had so far today. Half a dozen perhaps. More? A mere drop in the national bucket considering that on average every Dane drinks 104.6 liters of beer per annum. And that includes the ones who do not drink at all. And how many snaps and vodkas?

He still can see the reflection of himself in the mirror strip over Theodor's urinal, thinks, What a strange idea.

He can feel the beer, but not badly, and he's been walking a lot, too. His legs are tired and that is good. It helps keep him from thinking about whether he feels more foolish or forlorn.

The white-haired ruddy-faced bartender has a stool behind the taps. Kerrigan offers a drink and asks how old the place is.

'Buildings been here since 1850,' the man says, tapping himself a Carl Special. 'Before that this street was one of the oldest for street-walkers, after the church lost some of its power, and the people who lived here were not considered good enough to rub elbows with the orderly folk. This was where the garbagemen lived, the chimney sweeps, rag pickers, guards, cops, even the executioner lived here. And the guys who used to empty the shit-buckets – nightmen they called them – came around on their "chocolate wagons" to collect the shit. But when the prostitutes came, the orderly folk started coming, too, and the area was a bucket of blood. Fights, murders. But eventually the orderly people squeezed the others out. And then I guess they forgot what they came for in the first place. This place was built for a snaps distiller named Cadovius.'

Kerrigan lifts his glass. 'Here's to old Cadovius then.'

The bartender follows suit. 'N P Cadovius.'

They drink.

'Funny story,' the bartender says, putting down his beer stein. 'Or maybe not so funny.' He removes a stack of books from a low shelf on the wall behind the bar and points to a hole in the wall. 'That's from a bullet,' he says. 'From a liquidation during the war. There was an informer they called the Horse Merchant, *Hestehandleren*, came in here one day, and the resistance heard he was sitting here and sent three guys over to take care of him. They came on bicycles. One stayed outside to watch the bikes weren't pinched – this was during the war, things were scarce – and two of them come in and they shot him in the head. Say he squealed like a pig, big as he was, but everyone sitting here just looked the other way. No one saw a thing. Say when the two come running out again and jumped on their bikes, they were so jittery they crashed into each other, knocked themselves to the street. But they got away.'

The bartender falls silent then, and Kerrigan isn't much in the mood to talk. He sits, looking at the bullet hole, and thinking about the German occupation, the use of force, one people subjugating another, the very idea of weapons, pistols, projectiles designed to penetate and kill the body, like the opposite of a dick, firing pellets not of impregnation but of death. Wonder if the person who invented the first arrow, the first spear, the first knife to stab someone with, got the idea by watching his own dick penetrate a woman's cunt?

He thinks about the people who once lived here, the misery of their lives, the prostitutes, the executioner, the nightmen who went around and emptied other people's shit from the outhouses. What karma leads to that? Bad karma. Or is it karma at all? Maybe just chance turnings of fate. Could be me, could be you. But the Horse Merchant chose his path. Go with the oppressor, turn on your own. Who is *my* own?

He swallowed his beer, put a five-crown coin on the bar – 'Thanks for the stories!' – and was out into the late afternoon again.

20

The White Lamb *(Det Hvide Lam)*

Det Hvide Lam
Kultorvet *(The Coal Square)* **5**
1175 København K

A hundred meters toward *Kultorvet*, Coal Square, on the corner of the square, Kierkegaard, in 1838, had an apartment in number 11 where *Klaptræet*, Clapboard – a film café – is now. This is not far from *Krystalgade*, Crystal Street, previously called *Skidenstræde*, Filthy Lane, cousin to Magstræde, Toilet Lane. Danes rarely pull a linguistic punch; words are facts, said Plato. In *Krystalgade 24*, the philosopher F C Sibbern lived from 1832 to 1836, and Kierkegaard often visited there when he was a student.

Kerrigan looks up at the corner building where Kierkegaard lived 161 years before, pictures him there, his slanted body hunched over a book. This would have been five years prior to the publication of his first great work, *Either/Or*, prior to his public humiliation by the *Corsair*, when he still felt at ease roaming the streets, taking a coffee and a pastry, perhaps a liqueur, in one of the *konditoris* around the city – down just across from Hviids Wine Room, on the corner where the Italian restaurant Stephan A Porta is now; or up on *Strøget*, Walking Street, on Amager Square, across the street from the Dubliners Pub.

From Kierkegaard's window here, he would have been able to see the White Lamb serving house at *Kultorvet* 5, established in 1807, the year of the English bombardment which destroyed much of Copenhagen and killed some 1,600 civilians. The building the White Lamb is in was hit, too – the top of the building was blown off, but the newly opened serving house in the cellar survived intact. The building is from 1754 so it survived not only the British bombardment, but also two of the three great fires of 1728, 1792, and 1795.

Some believe that the force of the British attacks on Copenhagen was motivated not only to avoid the possibility of a strategic Franco-Russian adantage in Danish and Norwegian water and ports, but also by an old grudge at the way Caroline Mathilde, the young daughter of the Prince of Wales was treated in Copenhagen.

In 1766, the fifteen-year-old British noble, Caroline Mathilde, was married to Christian VII of Denmark. From the start the marriage was an unhappy one. Christian did not even deign to attend his own wedding, but had an emissary represent him on the altar, and after Caroline Mathilde had borne him a son, the half-mad king proceeded to neglect her completely.

At that time, the court physician, a German named Friedrich Struensee, made use of his intimacy with the royal family to obtain appointment to the post of cabinet secretary which put him in charge of all documents pertaining to the kingdoms of Denmark and Norway, the twin kingdoms over which Christian VII ruled. In the course of his machinations, while the king grew sicker, the young handsome Struensee entered into a love affair with Caroline, who was still hardly more than an adolescent.

By now, the king had been manipulated into signing an order that required Struensee's signature be placed on all legislation before it could go into effect. Struensee was governing Denmark, Norway, and Holstein – to the south, now part of Germany – as well as tending to the queen. When she gave birth to a second child, a girl, the infant bore such an undeniable resemblance to Struensee that the country was scandalized.

The language of the Danish court at the time was German. The former leading politician had been German, and some of the administration was conducted in German. Struensee decreed that *all* Danish legislation should henceforth be in German. He was enacting laws at a rapid pace, including one which established the national holiday known, still today, as *Storbededag* or Great Prayer Day, the consolidation of the formerly numerous religious days of observance into a single day – to increase the country's productivity.

He also began dismissing superfluous civil servants and had himself named Count. His governance of the kingdoms is generally considered fair and reasonably wise. Nor did he use his influence to plunder the treasury or acquire extensive holdings for himself, as he might; he lived modestly in two rooms. But he did help himself to the queen.

Such a love affair, if managed discretely, might have been possible in the royal courts of the time, but Caroline was young and in love and full of exhuberance after the years of neglect by her husband. She boasted of her affair to her chambermaids, carried on at great balls, lived openly with Struensee at the summer residence, is even said, on more than one occasion, to have proudly displayed her rumpled condition after Count Struensee had visited her chambers.

Finally, apartments were set up for each of them, one floor above the other, but connected by a secret staircase which was the talk of Copenhagen.

One night in 1772, after a masked ball, a group of conspirators broke into the sick king's bedroom and forced him to sign an arrest order for Struensee and Caroline.

The two were seized and an enquiry commenced. The queen denied it all, but Struensee – who apparently was not a physically brave man – confessed and was sentenced to death in a particularly brutal fashion. His right hand was chopped off before he was beheaded; his body was broken on the wheel and quartered. Caroline, at the request of her brother George III of England, was repatriated, her marriage to Christian VII having been annulled.

But the English didn't really want this fallen noble woman around either, not in London, so she was sent to Hannover, then under

English rule. She died only three years later of smallpox, 24 years old, deprived of the company of her two children, Frederick and Louise Augusta, whom she had been forced to leave behind in Denmark.

Thus, when the British bombarded Copenhagen, 32 years later, the memory of the poor child queen, Caroline Mathilde, might have further fuelled their cannon. Still, Kerrigan cannot help but find it cowardly – to bomb a nation from a safe distance, risking nothing for whatever noble or ignoble cause, perhaps not unlike the work of Messrs Bush, Clinton and Blair in Iraq and Serbia.

Ultimately Denmark aligned with Napoleon in retaliation, which wound up costing them Norway – a penalty awarded to Sweden.

Anyway, he thinks, after the bombardment, when they rebuilt, they incorporated the idea of Chamfered – angled or rounded – street corners which really improves the atmosphere of inner Copenhagen and turns every intersection into a small square.

Kerrigan can hear music from the White Lamb. He climbs down to the half submerged green door. Inside Asger Rosenberg is making faces and spanking his bass, a picture of a screaming mouth mounted on the wall just above his head. He sings George Shearing's 'Lullaby of Birdland'. To his right, a few people sit around a billiard table shrouded with a plastic cloth, and at the bar, one more step down, the regulars sit raffling and complaining loudly about the music.

Kerrigan orders a beer and sits against the wall while Asger goes over to 'The Girl from Ipanema', and a man so drunk he looks as though he is walking under water wanders back and forth, the antithesis of the dark, tall, tan, and lovely girl from Ipanema. One of the regulars, a broad-jawed, short-haired blond woman steps outside for a smoke, pointedly refusing to close the door behind her, and a young man comes in carrying a yellow plastic bag from the mouth of which protrudes the bell of a trumpet.

It is 8.45, and Asger speaks into the mike. 'We will now take a short but intense break following which we will be replaced by . . .'

Kerrigan misses the name of the replacement group, but recognizes that the platinum-haired woman in black by the door will be singing next. She is smoking a cigarette, and her neckline is low and skirt well above the knee, and Kerrigan realizes he is buzzed, watching the white face of the clock that says 8.45 on the wall between two windows that look out on the still light square while the sweet young barmaid puts on some pause music: Gerry Mulligan and Chet Baker blowing 'Bernie's Tune' that he happens to know was recorded on 16 August 1952 in Los Angeles, with Bobby Whitlock on bass and Chico Hamilton on drums, same day they recorded 'Lullabye of the Leaves', which comes on next.

Three and a half decades later, on 18 May 1988, Chet Baker would take his fatal fall out an Amsterdam window to die on the pavement.

Mulligan's baritone on 'Lullabye of the Leaves' reaches into Kerrigan's heart while Baker's scales lift it into an agreeable melancholy. A very old woman in a large hat sits at the covered pool table with a glass of beer and a bitter dram in a little stem glass which she lifts in Kerrigan's direction, tendering a smile. He raises his near empty pint to her, and a fellow at his side says with admiration bordering on awe in his voice, 'That's Lotte. She used to be an executive secretary. She's 86 years old.' Hearing her name mentioned, Lotte smiles again.

'What's the secret?' Kerrigan asks. She nods, smiling, and the stem glass is her answer, hovering at her very old lips, her handsome square face.

Jesus, he thinks, please let me be like her, live till I die.

Chet Baker is singing now, another 50s LA number: *Let's get lost . . . lost in each other's arms...* his voice, Fennelli-weird in its whiteness. A tenor sax and black bag lies on the covered pool table, a little candle-holder with two candles nearly burnt out. Asger's bass stands face into a corner like Man Ray's 75-year-old *Violin of Ingres*, painted on the back of a naked woman by Ray who was born in 1880, two years before James Joyce and Henry Miller.

Kerrigan goes in to piss, staring into a broken Tuborg mirror on a grafittied orange wall. When he comes out again, a tenor saxman is blowing his eyes out beneath a white lamp, and it is still light on the square outside the window, but Kerrigan's mind is still full of that strange white voice of Baker's: *Lost in each other's arms . . .*

He nods to the platinum-haired woman who is getting ready to sing and climbs up out of the White Lamb to the square, makes a right, away from Kierkegaard's apartment, and another right, down *Købmagergade*, Butcher Street.

21

Long John's

Long John's
Købmagergade *(Butcher Street)* **48**
København K

Heading for Long John's, he thinks about the fact that Henry Miller and James Joyce both were born in 1882, the same year that Nietzsche proclaimed the death of God and Heineken beer received the *Diplôme d'Honneur d'Amsterdam*, eight years before the birth of Adolph Hitler, when Queen Victoria was 63 and Sigmund Freud 26. In the last decade of the nineteenth century, one of Henry Miller's earliest literary heroes was Hans Christian Andersen; if Lotte was 86, that means she was born in 1913, when Joyce and Miller were young rogues of 31, both in Paris or headed there; in fact, Kerrigan had once met the Danish multi-artist named Jens Jørgen Thorsen in Charles de Gaulle airport and introduced himself, saying how much he had enjoyed Thorsen's film version of Miller's *Quiet Days in Clichy*, but at the same time advising him that his Irish grandmother despised him for his plan to make a film about the sex life of Jesus Christ.

'Well, that's okay, isn't it?' Thorsen said with a smile, and Kerrigan had to laugh, even if he was not beguiled by Thorsen's painting of Christ on the cross with an erection – an enormous work which had adorned a wall facing the platform of Hellerup station on the Danish railroad – one of the more conservative of Copenhagen's inner suburbs. In fact, the Cabinet Minister for Agriculture at the time had successfully manipulated to have the wall painting removed, a fact that brings a smile to Kerrigan's lips. Such a series of events could never occur outside of northern Europe – perhaps nowhere else other than in Copenhagen and Amsterdam for that matter, although in Amsterdam the picture would probably not have been removed. Thorsen did eventually make his film about Christ, too.

He wonders why the tumescent Christ on the cross bothers him. It seems gratuitous perhaps. Or is it? The Catholic Church worked so very hard for so many years to further the sexual frustration of the western world – so why not take a poke at their hero? Or perhaps it was not so much a poke at Christ as a poke at the false image of Christ fostered by the blue-noses.

He stops outside of *Rundetårn*, the Round Tower, the oldest observatory still standing in Europe, a five-year construction project, started in 1637, completed in 1642, built by King Christian IV (1588-1648). On a tall pedestal alongside the Tower is a bust of the astronomer Tycho Brahe, though he did his work in his own observatory on the island of Hven, off the coast of Zealand (where Kerrigan once made love with a beautiful blond Danish woman who reminds him of his Associate whom he cannot remove from his consciousness), and left Denmark in 1597 after a disagreement with Christian IV.

Not wise to disagree with kings, Kerrigan thinks.

There is a full sculpture of Brahe, illustrating his pride and temper, cut in 1859 by Hermann Wilhelm Bissen, on *Øster Voldgade*, East Rampart Street, but Kerrigan particularly admires this head, decorated with the royal elephant.

Brahe's student, Christen Sørensen Longomantanus, organised this observatory. The Brits bombed it in 1807, but failed to damage it seriously. In 1716, Peter the Great of Russia rode his horse up the inner spiralling ramp, 35 meters to the top, and his wife Catherine did the same in her carriage, while in 1902, an automobile drove up the ramp to the top and back down again, and recently there was a skateboard race from top to bottom.

Kerrigan notes that Brahe's bust is complete with nose despite the fact that, according to Kerrigan's sources, the quick-tempered scientist's proboscus had been sliced off in a duel so he had to be fitted with a metal replacement. On the moon is a crater named for Tycho, who discovered it, and one of Kerrigan's oldest friends, Barry Brent, now a researcher in the theory of numbers in Minnesotta, once wrote a never-to-be published novel entitled *The Summits around Tycho* in which he likened the contour of the crater's edge to medieval icons with fingers raised in benediction. The Tycho crater is also mentioned in Stanley Kubrick and Arthur C Clarke's *2001: A Spacy Odyssey* (1969) as the place in which the mystical monolith is found buried in moon dust – a tribute no doubt by Clarke to his Danish predecessor. Kerrigan would also like to entertain the thought that the fact that the 2001 computer, H.A.L. 9000, is programmed to sing 'A Bicycle Built for Two,' with its refrain of 'Daisy, Daisy' relates to the fact that this is the song the British coal miners sang to the Danish queen, Margarethe II – Daisy being her family nickname – when she visited in the 70s, but he knows this is highly unlikely because *2001* was made a couple of years before she even ascended to the throne. But the mention of Tycho is no coincidence.

Tycho Brahe is said to have died as a result of internal injuries incurred from a ruptured bladder suffered because he was too polite to excuse himself from the royal table to urinate when he was a dinner guest of some king.

Kerrigan sits on a stone slab in the tiny square beside the tower, contemplating Tycho's crater, his nose, his pride, his bladder, but his thoughts all float on a background of Chet Baker's eerie white voice: *Let's get lost, Lost in each other's arms* – and he starts wondering how he himself will die since his own mother's bullets did not do the job.

There is bird shit on Tycho's bust, and over to his left, Kerrigan regards a monument with large medallion portraits depicting the eighteenth-century poets Johannes Ewald and Johan Herman

Wessel. The monument is topped with the sculptures of two protective cherubs that someone has crowned with a broken-down blue bicycle, which is what drew his attention in the first place – perhaps this had been the vandal's intention.

Kerrigan lights a cigarillo with a matchbook he has picked up somewhere. On the cover it says in English, *Old men should stick to hitting on old women*, and he thinks again of Lotte the 86-year-old executive secretary, wondering if she has ever read Ewald or Hessel, both of whom were born in the 1740s and died in the 1780s, who lived in the time of Struensee, middle-aged lover of the teenage Queen Caroline Mathilde, and who were *Sturm und drung* contemporaries of Goethe, whose skull was found to contain a small quantity of grey dust by East German bureaucrats one dark November night in 1970.

He considers the overview of history he labors to gather in his own skull and its ultimate fate. Grey dust that no one will even bother to peek in through his eye sockets for. But just to see it *once*, almost clearly, before then.

Ewald (1743-1781) is said to be one of Denmark's greatest poets, but Kerrigan knows only a few lines of his forgotten 'Ode to the Soul':

'Confess, you fallen, weak, wretched
Brother of angels!
Say why you spread unfeathered wings?'

Confess *what* precisely? he thinks, knowing only that the question is addressed to the fallen soul of mankind – confess why you spread unfeathered wings?

Wessel (1742-1785) was born in Norway, moved to Copenhagen as a teenager and produced a small body of comic-parodic anti-illusionist drama: 'I sing of – well, no, not really, I'm not singing, I'm actually *telling* about it, quite directly . . .'

His eyes wander to a plaque on the opposite wall, the Student's Café. The plaque pronounces that this was the home of the Student Union from 1820 to 1824, and Kerrigan tries to remember if this was where Jens Peter Jacobsen took his meager lunches in his youth when he would rise at noon, wander the city, eat an inexpensive meal at the Student Club, and then return to his spartan one-room lodging to write and translate until nine in the evening when he would go out again, wearing his top hat, to make merry in the cafés before returning to his room again to read *The Sagas*, *The Edda*, *The Tain* ('We followed the rump of a misguiding woman.'), Hans Christian Andersen, Søren Kierkegaard, Charles Dickens, Shakespeare, Tennyson, Edgar Alan Poe . . .

But since Jacobsen was born in 1847, a mere 35 years before Henry Miller and James Joyce, Kerrigan realizes he must have eaten his meager lunch at the *new* student's club up near the Town Hall Square.

Kerrigan is determined to obtain an overview of these facts while the grey matter in his skull is still sufficiently elastic to contain it.

J P Jacobsen lived a short life. He died in 1885, at the age of 38, three years after the birth of Joyce and Miller, and his fiction was lavishly praised by Sigmund Freud, Thomas Mann, Herman Hesse, Georg Brandes, James Joyce, and most of all by Rainer Maria Rilke, who called him 'that great, great writer'. How odd, Kerrigan thinks, that this Dane who was so admired by such outstanding artists should be all but forgotten now outside Denmark and perhaps a few other countries, at least in the English-speaking world. Other than the recent translation by Tiina Nunnally, published by the small house Fjord Press that specializes in Scandinavian literature, Kerrigan knows of no other English edition of the writer in print.

What Kerrigan remembers most of Jacobsen's writings is his story 'Mrs Fønss':

> 'She held the belief that there are sorrows which should lie in secret and should not be allowed to scream forth in words . . .because the one who uttered them will hear them still whispering in the other's mind . . .'

And the letter that Mrs Fønss wrote on her deathbed to the

children she had abandoned for love of a man not their father. The children, in turn, will hear nothing of her, but her letter is aimed to persuade them to receive, after her death, the man who has been so good to her.

> 'Dear Children . . . When people love . . . the one who loves most must humble himself . . . to be remembered is the only part of the human world that will be mine from now on. Simply to be remembered, nothing more . . . I have never doubted your love, I fully understand that it was your great love that provoked your great anger . . .'

Kerrigan drops the stub of his cigar and grinds it out beneath his shoe and experiences a moment of synchronicity. Remembering that Jacobsen also was the one who translated Darwin into Danish, he notices that the ragged half pillars and columns of stone near the bench on which he sits are sculpted with animal figures, a glowering owl, a toad, a bird of prey with open wings seizing a mouse in its talons.

He realizes that he is drunk, yet at the eye of his drunkeness is a sphere of startling clarity. He rises, concentrates on walking evenly along the ancient pavement to the red-clothed empty tables outside Long John's where a short, thick, square-headed woman with a bullet-shaped face approaches him. He sees her from a distance and words leap unbidden to his mind: *Ugly fucking bitch*.

'Please help me,' she says. 'I am so unhappy.'

And the ugliness of the words that had erupted in his mind draw pain from his heart. *Please*, he thinks, *don't let me hate*, and wonders who he is beseeching. 'Can hardly help myself,' he says, hoping it will sound humorous and soothing and hears the slur of his own words.

'The drummer inside,' she said. 'I know he loves me, but he pretends he never even saw me before.'

Kerrigan shakes his head, helpless, sorry, wishing he had the power of a medieval icon to raise his fingers in benediction over her, to gaze down from the moon and heal her, as he passes through the door without another word to where the notes of a raunchy honking sax fill the smokey air.

He orders a pint of lager and carries it to the tables in the rear, takes one all to himself and lights a cigar, and the difficulty of doing so informs him once again that he is drunk and moreover drunk in public, exposed, and has to deal with a sudden flash of terror of this exposure.

Am I a fucking alcoholic? Where the fuck is she? Why wouldn't she come when I called her?

At the end of the bar he sees a blurry saxman blowing a blurred red tenor, playing 'Oh Babe!' Happy jazz. Then Dorsey's 'So Rare', and the clapping of hands reminds him of the exploding of caps in a toy pistol which floats up images he long ago decided never again to countenance. The smoking pistol, naked mother: *Terry! Oh, Ter-ry!* Mama Kali. Mrs Rangda.Widow's tongue devouring the world. The cunt giveth and the cunt taketh away. Sacred images carry the power of life and death both because what gives life takes it back again and where we come from in the fogged past we return to one day in the dim future with the song of the Aged mother which shook the heavens with wrath echoing in the ear.

He looks at his cold cigar in the ashtray alongside a slender white vase of carnations which in Denmark do not have the pungent fragrance he remembers from carnations of his childhood, pinned to his lapel for first communion, baptism, dyed green for St Patrick's Day, pink carnation for the prom, but he does not want to remember that anyway, so it is just as well they do not have that pungent fragrance.

An empty pack of cigarettes lie on the table, Prince Extra Ultralights, and his beer is half empty. He raises his face to a pair of lamps in pink shades mounted on the wall. Their two-ness touches his one-ness and blurs into the 'So Rare' sax solo, Jazz's Jesus moving to him like a gentle hand to a whore where he sits without his Associate; without information he sits in this anonymous meaningless bar.

When was it built? What is the history of this fucking place?

He has to piss again, hoists himself up carefully and walks a wavery line back to the gent's, pushes through the door and stands regarding a glowing white urinal which vaguely reminds him of a story he once read by John Updike with whom he once chanced to eat breakfast during the course of which Mr Updike maintained distance by addressing him as Mr Kerrigan and marvelled that Kerrigan had chosen to expatriate to Denmark, asking numerous questions about bodies of water surrounding Denmark and the sorts of birds to be found in a Danish autumnal countryside for a book he was writing. The story Kerrigan remembers now was about a man in Manhattan who desperately had to piss but could not find a bathroom and when, after much searching, he finally stands before a toilet, in wonder, he sees it glowing like the purest, most utilitarian, most beautiful object he has ever beheld – the moment charged as it was with his great need – a work of art like Duchamp's *Fountain* urinal, found art from 1917.

Then Kerrigan's blurry vision catches a sharp detail on the wall above the urinal: a handle, which can only be meant for a drunken man to hold onto while he pisses. Laughter barks out his throat. He looks around for someone to share this marvellous moment with, but there is no one, he is alone there – as, thank god, he was at the mirrored urinal in Theodor's – standing in the middle of the Long John's gent's room barking like a dog, like a duck.

He gathers himself lest the laughter turn to puke, talking to God on the big white telephone. He unzips and takes out what the Theodor mirror has shown him to be the unimpressive little mouse that he thinks of as his manhood, directs it with his left while with his right he grabs the wall handle and sways there, pissing, as the notes of the raunchy sax seep in under the door, and he improvises a little dance, hanging by his left, directing with his right,'This is a pissy dance on the edge of monsieur's sword,' he sings, and the laughter erupts again violently. Then he catches himself doing this and is vastly grateful no one is in there to witness, just as the door opens behind him, and he gathers himself in, drops his hand from the wall handle, clears his throat and goes to the sink to meticulously wash his hands. He can smell the lemony aroma of the soap rising on the steam of the hot water, then dries his fingers beneath a nozzle of hot air from a machine, which he sniggers to realize bears the label *World Dryer*.

Dry this fucking wet old world then, sir! Having a merry time in his wet old cups. The Prince of Cups is in his cups! Get thee to a heel and key bar!

Outside, he sways, wondering if he is in possession of sufficient motor skills to negotiate a path to the bar and convince the bartender that he can be entrusted with another pint of lager. *Fug it all anyway. Cast your fate to it.*

Blurrily he sees a woman with a coarse nose sitting by herself nursing a small glass of beer two tables from his own.

'Hel-lo,' says Kerrigan.

'Hello, then,' she says. 'I like your Italian jeans. Can see the label. Not that I was looking at your bottom or anything.' Her accent is British, reminds him of the accent of a woman he once met in one of the bars on Pilestræde – Café Rex perhaps, formerly known as Hexerex, and he now remembers she was from the Isle of Mann and spoke like Basil Fawlty's wife in *Fawlty Towers*: '*I kno-ow, I kno-ow.*'

She had told him she lived on Kronprinsessesgade, just around the corner, and Kerrigan said 'Please let me follow you down,' thinking of an old Bob Dylan song, which, to his great surprise, worked. She lived in a tiny apartment with a huge grand piano and told him she would not have sex with him, but did allow him to undress her from the waist down to her white garter belt and manipulate her to a yelping orgasm which, in retrospect, perhaps lends credence to Clinton's definitions of 'having sex'.

In honor of that memory, Kerrigan now says to this British woman with coarse nose, 'Please let me follow you down,' and she says, 'Aren't you the sweet talker?'

Then his gaze skitters upward to a detail:

One of the lamps on the wall above his table is dead. He sits with a thump and watches: One lamp lit, one lamp dead. 'Just need forty finks,' he hears himself murmur, and as his head lolls forward, his glasses hit the hard wood surface and skitter to the checkered floor. He knows more than hears the sound of a lens cracking, and without shame or care, recognizes a new depth in his day, in his life perhaps, as his arms form a cushion on the table for his lowering face.

All I need's a paper fucking hat, he thinks, farting loudly three times in succession to his chagrin, as he gives himself to this void he has spent the day purchasing.

He should never have opened the window for the breath through it scattered many papers as he drooled on the table wetting his wrist and in the lecture hall driven by the undeniable need to shit he turned his back and saw the bare porcelain toilet affixed to the wall beneath the green blackboard, dropped his pants and made use of the opportunity only to find he had trapped himself: there was no paper and if he rose now all the others in the room would see his soiled backside . . .

And Christ did it smell!

The nudging hand that shoves him back to consciousness is about to invoke his rage, but he looks up to see the blurred image of cornblue eyes.

'Mr Kerrigan,' she says. '30 dollars an hour is hardly enough to babysit a baby of your proportions.'

'I can't quite see you,' he says.

'No wonder. You broke your glasses. I put them in your shirt pocket. Only one lens left.'

'Better than no lengs, *lens*, at all.'

'Think so?'

'It was I who placed them there on the table for him,' says the British woman with the coarse nose, still seated over her small glass of beer.

'Good for you,' says his Associate in charming English. And to Kerrigan adds, 'So. *Pjanking* in the sofa corners, too?'

'Sorry?'

'*At pjanke*. To flirt. As in the old Danish proverb, *No pjanking in the sofa corners.*'

'Are you jealous?'

Her eyes flash. 'What's it to you?'

'Are you his Mrs, then?' asks the British woman.

'Something of the sort,' she says, without looking from Kerrigan.

'Jesus,' he says. 'I love you.'

'Please. Spare me your bullshit. Sit up and buy me a drink, and I'll tell you about this place. Better yet, just give me some money, and I'll buy the drink myself.'

'Me, too. Vodka Collins.'

'You can have a Danish water.'

'How the hell'd you find me?' he asks and she takes a 50-crown note bearing the portrait of Karen Blixen from the little pile of money on the table, glancing harshly over at the British woman as if to say, Don't even think about it, honey.

The British woman huffs and picks up her glass, retires to a table further toward the front. Kerrigan is sorry to see her go, thinking how nice it might have been to share a bed with both his Associate and the coarse-nosed Brit.

'How *did* you find me?' he asks.

'Easy,' she tells him. 'You told me when you called where you would be.'

'Well I might have changed my plans. After your harsh rejectal of me.'

'Then I wouldn't have found you maybe.'

'Well you said you weren't gonna come.'

'I got bored.'

'Ha! You were thinking about me. You missed me.'

'Shall I leave again?'

'No! *Please.*'

He rallies a bit when she sets a small beer before him, and he lights a cigar. The band has either packed it in or paused, and he is wondering what time it is as a deaf and dumb man makes the rounds of the sparsely populated tables, laying a toy and explanatory note on each. The toy, he sees, holding it close to his myopic face, is a keychain attached to a little plastic bowl containing a tiny plastic gold fish afloat in some manner of fluid. The explanatory note, he knows, because he has seen it before, requests a donation of 30 crowns. His Associate is rummaging in her bag.

'The guys wants five bucks for that goddamn thing,' Kerrigan says.

She glares at him. 'And so what?' She digs coins from her change purse as Kerrigan lifts his glass, says, '*Skål*,' and 'Bowl,' and '*Kipis*,' and '*Nostrovja*,' and '*Slanté*,' and '*Salud*,' and '*Santé*,' and '*Tjerviseks*,' and 'To your very good health,' and '*Multatuli*,' and 'Earth, fire, suffering, and ejaculation'.

The effort wears him out. 'Now,' he says, 'We will take a short but very intense pause,' and lowers his face once again to the cradle of his arms, too blitzed for shame. 'Occupational blizzard,' he mutters and is gone, though he hears in the distance sniffing sounds and her voice asking, What is that *smell*?'

DAY THREE

Dax!

'It's only me, it's only me, it's only me!'

– Dan Turrell

22

BOPA Café

BOPA Café
Løgstørgade 8
2100 København Ø

The very high white ceiling to which he opens his eyes is not familiar. Two blurred, myopic flies move lazily in circles around its faintly crackled surface, the distance to which he tries, blearily and in vain, to determine.

He is in bed. A radio is playing in the next room. Gauzy curtains drift at a tall open window. Beneath an eiderdown, he is naked. And the history of his recent past is obscure. Vague clots of memory tease him from behind a dark curtain.

A door at the corner of the room is ajar and now swings in toward him so he sees his blurred Associate standing there in black jeans and a black tank top.

'He lives,' says she.

He listens, uneasy, with interest, to the words that form on his breath. 'I had a very unpleasant dream.'

'It was no dream.'

He fancies that in the blur of her mouth he can see a mixed expression of amusement, chagrin, incredulity, and sadism. He says,'No, I mean, I dreamt I . . . soiled my . . .'

'It was no dream.'

'You mean I really broke my glasses.'

'Among other things.'

'You didn't really . . .?'

She nods.

'Jesus.' His face is hot. 'How much do I owe you?'

'If I start taking money for something like that, I shall have to begin to vonder vhat my profession really is.'

Kerrigan's face is so hot he feels sweat on his brow.

'At least,' she says, 'You have the decency to blush.'

She leaves him to his shame, and he buries his mortified head beneath the pillow. The thought of it. Her *seeing* him like that. *Cleaning* him like a baby, or a doddering old man.

He recalls once at a family gathering years ago an aunt had an epileptic fit after dinner – she fell to the floor and began to vomit her entire dinner, it spread like a sea across the hardwood floor. The quantity was awesome. The men present held back in disgust and uncertainty while the women went to work instantly to clean her and the mess. Women could do that. *Would* do that.

And what his own mother had done.

In washed and ironed drawers, clean shirt, sponged and ironed trousers that had been hung in the tall open window to air, reborn from a long steaming shower, he brushes his teeth at great length with a throwaway toothbrush, spits in the sink and studies his pearly whites, which are less than pearly thanks to his increasing cigar appetite. He recalls dear old 'Uncle' Bud the lawyer with his boater hat who always palmed the then young Kerrigan a dollar when he visited and whose laughing cigar teeth always struck Kerrigan as wildly benevolent. Is this how we form our images of what is desirable? he wonders, considering that those kind palmed bucks may have been the root cause of the browning of Kerrigan's teeth. He remembers 'Uncle' Bud flirting with his mother, telling his father, 'Here's a gal I would wrestle you for, you lucky old S O B,' and Kerrigan recalls his mother's strained expression, not flattered, offended.

The OTC codeine pain killers his Associate has given him have killed not only his pain but a good bit of his shame as well, and he fairly dances into her enormous plank-floor living room with its three-meter ceiling. Some jazz music on the stereo has him feeling spry-footed, 30s raggy stuff, and he recognizes the voice of Leo Mathiesen:

> 'Take it easy, boy, boy
> Go to your home
> Smoke a ceegar.
> Let the others do the hard work for you.'

'Dexter Gordon loved old Leo M,' says Kerrigan.

'Who's Dexter Gordon?'

In the sunlight from the window, he can see her age, but she is a trim dancing fay of a girl nonetheless. He wonders if he could get her into bed with him. Always randy with a hangover. Hangover horns. He turns her once across the floor, delighted that she dances along, light as a feather on her feet, in his arms.

'Only one of the greatest tenor and soprano saxmen of all times,' he replies. 'Didn't you see the film *Round Midnight*? Won an Oscar for best film score for Herbie Hancock in 1987, I think. Gordon himself was nominated for best actor. Lost to Paul Newman in some shitty film. Gordon lived in Denmark on and off for years, one of *the* great hornmen. Someone played a Leo Mathiesen record for him once, and Gordon said, "Hey that's terrific," and the guy says, "You like that jazz, huh?" and Gordon tells him, "Jazz? That's not jazz. But I like it." Where are we by the way?' he asks, endeavoring to slip the question in nonchalantly in hopes it will not be noticed sufficiently to spotlight the fact he was too drunk yesterday to remember being transported here.

'East Side,' she says. 'The near-East. Holsteinsgade and Strandboulevard. And I'm not surprised you don't remember.'

'Know it well,' he says briskly. 'Home of Holsteins Bodega where I once went to hear jazz that turned out to be rhythm and blues. Good rhythm and blues. American black guy, great big guy named Dale Smith who also had a role in Jens Jørgen Thorsen's film about Christ. I walked in, and all along the bar sat a flank of very large men wearing very short hair and blue tattoos up and down their arms and necks. One of them looks in the bar mirror at me – I think I was wearing a silk tie and a cashmere topcoat – and he says, "Oh. The fine folk are here." I walked back to where the band was set up, ordered a beer and sat down to listen to Dale singing, *Wearin' those dresses/Sun come shinin' through/Can't believe my eye/That all belong to you*, and the guy from the bar comes after me. Stands there with a smirk, looking into my face, which is about all the warning a Dane gives before he clocks you, and he asks in Danish, "So how you like the music?" I tell him, using the Danish idiom, "*Den er skide god,*" It's *shit* good . . .' (That word again, thinks Kerrigan.) ' . . . and he smiles, pats my cheek sweet as can be, "Enjoy it," he says and leaves me in peace. Later I bought a round for the band – five men drinking strong drink – cost a song, like ten bucks!'

'I know the place,' she says. 'And I know Dale Smith.'

'Oh?'

'He's a friend. Lives a few houses from here. He makes his living as a social worker, and Jens Jørgen Thorsen is a friend of his.'

'He's a friend of yours?' says Kerrigan.

Her smile endears him, a mix of emotions that say none of your business, but I'll tell you because I like you. 'Yes,' she says. 'He's a friend.'

Kerrigan smiles happily back at her in thanks for this little reassurance and the fact that it was not given gushingly but with respectable begrudgement. Then he starts to wonder what he's up to. Showing jealousy tantamount to professing love. These hangover horns driving him toward her, desire.

Her smile is sweetly teasing, and Leo is singing: *To be/Or not to be/That's the question/But not for me . . .*

'I'm hungry,' says Kerrigan.

'You must have *some* constitution, Mr Kerrigan. I know a good place for brunch.' She gives him a look. 'No more accidents, though, huh?'

'You,' he says, blushing, 'are not a gentleman.'

She blinks. 'My ambitions have never been that low,' she says sternly and waits for the effect before adding. 'And how sweetly you blush. You know the old Danish proverb, A blush is the color of virtue.'

They sit in the sun over a plate of scrambled eggs and spiced sausage, cheese and fruit, watching the bocci players cast their glistening balls. He orders a bottle of cold Chardonnay, while a man and woman in dark clothes dance a tango on the concrete square.

With her left hand, his Associate holds the starfish and anemone notebook open on the table while eating with her right. He notices she occasionally chews with her mouth open so he can see the yellow eggs tumblng round on her pink tongue.

He says, 'Don't chew with your mouth open, honey,' and she pats her mouth with a paper napkin. '*Tak for sidst*, ey?' she says. Danish for 'Thanks for the last time we met', but also a euphemism for revenge.

'Right. You can have it from the same dresser drawer,' he says, using another Danish euphemism for tit-for-tat evening up.

'This was the headquarters of one of the main resistance headquarters during the second world war,' she tells him. 'BOPA is an acronym for the Danish *Borgernes Parti*, The Citizen's Party.' She daubs again at her pretty lips with the napkin, chews sausage, swallows, sips coffee. 'Leo Mathiesen, in fact, played various places during the war. He was Danish but he wrote and sang in English. English was forbidden by the German occupation forces so he just sang gibberish versions of the words.'

'Scat.'

'Yes, darling,' she says with a twinkle, for *skat* with a 'k' is a term of endearment in Danish.'Dr Werner Best was the German commandant under the occupation. He picked the best house in Copenhagen, a mansion just up the coast, actually right outside the city. Your Ambassador has it as his residence now.'

'I know, I've been there.'

'Oh! May I touch you?'

'I was a guest at the July Fourth celebration there once. Hot dogs, corn on the cob, and lots of drinks. Seems to me the Ambassador's name was Sandburg, Or maybe he was the DCM. I couldn't help but wonder if he was a relative of Carl Sandburg. Terrifying to think of Dr Best there. You know the recently unearthed diary of Eichmann? They want to use it to rebut the lying fools who claim there was no holocaust. In it Eichmann says, "When I see the images before my eyes it all comes back to me. Corpses, corpses, corpses. Shot, gassed, decaying corpses, a delirium of blood". Do you remember the war?'

As she butters a slice of Grahams bread, she gives him a rundown on the occupation in Denmark.

On 9 April 1940, the Germans marched in over the southern border of Jutland. There was a little bit of fighting and an air assault as well, but the Danes decided not to commit heroic suicide. Unlike Norway, where the resistance had the mountains to hide in and fight from, Denmark is completely flat. There were no natural barriers. Also unlike the Norwegian king, the Danish king, Christian X, stayed in his capital and rode on horseback through Copenhagen every day, as was his custom, all by himself. It is said that on 1 October 1943, when the Gestapo ordered the Jews in Denmark to begin wearing yellow armbands, Christian put one on his own sleeve for his ride through town next day. He rode through alone, no guards, no escort.

The Danish Ambassador in Washington, D C, was astute enough to place Greenland, Iceland, and the Faroe Islands under the protection of the allied forces so the Germans were unable to make strategic use of them, which could have been a catastrophe.

Germany plundered the Danish agriculture to feed its troops under the pretense that they would pay back. Some people, of course, *did* make money. There was also clandestine ferrying of Jews and communists across the sound every night to Malmø, to the safety of Swedish neutrality. The Swedes were very helpful. They also made a lot of money. Being neutral they could help everyone.

She lays a slice of medium old cheese on her buttered sour bread, bites, chews with closed lips, sips coffee, and he imagines how interesting her kiss would be, tasting of old cheese and the nice bitter aroma of coffee with cream.

In 1943, things started getting hotter. By August, there was a general strike, shooting in the streets. Hostages were taken. The Danes scuttled their own navy in the harbor, and in September, the Freedom Council was set up. In January 1944, the gestapo, accompanied by Danish police, liquidated the outspoken poet/priest Kai Munk (1898-1944), dragged him from his home and put a bullet in the back of his neck and left him in a ditch. You can still see a plaque over the doorway of *Larslejsstræde 1* here in Copenhagen, over near *Pisseranden*, where Munk lived from 1919 to 1921 as a student, 23 years before the gestapo murdered him.

'In the US,' he tells her, 'the Lutherans observe 5 January as the feast day of Munch, on par with Martin Luther King's Day.'

She lifts her eyebrows. 'He was hardly as great as King, but still . . .'

Throughout that year, she continues, there was sabotage and countersabotage. It was nowhere near what happened elsewhere in Europe, but it was bad enough. Nocturnal arrests, liquidations, random terror by the occupying forces. The lawful police were replaced by a makeshift police department set up by the Germans – the *hilfspolizei* – called *Hipo* for short or, more often, *Hipo svin*, Hipo swine – made up mainly of exconvicts and criminals. That's the kind of thing that can happen in a weakened society – as Kubrick and Anthony Burgess showed in *Clockwork Orange* when the juvenile delinquents grow up to be cops.

Meanwhile, in Denmark, thousands upon thousands of German refugees were streaming north from Germany, 200,000 in all, starved, filthy, lice-infested. It was clear Germany was losing the war; the question for the Danes was whether Denmark would be the last battlefield. But on 4 May 1945, the Germans capitulated, and Belgium, the Netherlands, Denmark, and Norway were liberated next day.

Copenhagen was filled with fleeing German officers and Nazis speeding for the border in their jeeps. There was some shooting in the streets, and candles burned in all the windows of the towns and cities – all the candles that Danes always kept in ready because the Germans frequently would cut off the power supply. It was a spontaneous display. The streets of Copenhagen glowed with thousands of candles in the windows. To this day, more than half a century later, there are still people who light a candle in the window on 5 May in remembrance of the end of the five-year occupation by the German 'cousins'.

On *Nikolaj Plads* in Copenhagen, near Nikolaj *Kirke* and the Café Nick, there is a corner basement shop known as the Art Library, *Kunstbiblioteket* in Danish, run by a very tall broad-chested man named Knud Pedersen and his wife, Bodil Ryskær. Knud Pedersen is now in his 70s. He initiated the Art Library, where anyone who wishes to become a member, for a nominal monthly charge, can rent original works of art to hang on their walls for a time.

Knud Pedersen was also one of the handful of teenage boys who started one of the very first organized resistance groups against the German occupation forces in Denmark. He and his brother and friends started the so-called Churchill Club, a sabotage group, and as a result, Knud was arrested at the age of sixteen and sentenced to three years in a concentration camp.

Kerrigan lifts the Chardonnay from the ice-bucket, refills their glasses. 'I've met him,' he says.

His Associate is clearly startled. 'You know all this already?'

'Only a little bit of it. But I did meet Knud. He started an on-line publishing venture and published one of my novels that I couldn't get out anywhere else. Eventually it was published in the States, but clearly this is a man who does not accept difficult conditions passively. And he's full of life and laughter. Funny thing is, his son is Klaus Ryskær Pedersen, the yuppie former member of the European Parliament who is under constant attack for allegedly mishandling funds. I guess the son has his own way of being proactive. Now he owns a net engine called Cybercity. I had an email subscription there once which I cancelled for various reasons, and the owner himself was on the phone to me next day to ask if he could do something to make it right again. A dedicated manager. 'You know,' he says, 'There have been a lot of interpretations of Denmark's role during the occupation – that it was noble, exemplary in the way you helped the Jews and communists escape to Sweden, that it was mercenary, that you made money and collaborated, that you took the only sensible and nonsuicidal course, refusing to die heroically. But you know the statue on *Genforeningspladsen* – Reunification Place, by *Hulgårdsvej*, on the northwest side of Copenhagen? It was sculpted in 1944 by Johannes C Bjerg, entitled *Denmark During the Occupation.* It's a sculpture of a muscular young man, a powerful body in a posture of doubt, his hands out, palms empty. *What can I do?* he seems to say. Hamlet perhaps. How to act when whatever you do means death all around you?'

'Well something *was* rotten in the state of Denmark,' she says.

'Thank God for the European Union,' Kerrigan says. 'All the fighting that has torn Europe apart over the years. Germany against France. France against England. Germany and Italy against Europe. You name it. All now finally annulled by a treaty tying their fates all together. The United States of Europe. You know many years ago on a train to Munich, I met a young German and when he heard I had chosen to live in Denmark, he apologized profusely to me for what the generation of Germans before him had done to Denmark, to all of Europe. I was touched and offered him a bottle of beer from the sixpack I had in my bag. "Ah!" he said. "Danish beer, yes, iss goot. But the Cherman beer iss de best in de vorlt!" '

She laughs so her blue eyes sparkle and instead of singing her praises, he sings the praise of her land.

'Shakespeare picked the right country, the right climate, for his melancholy Dane, although I admit I've grown to love the extremes of Danish seasons and light – the dark winters suit me. And the white nights of summer suit me even better. There is nothing, nothing like those white nights. The long late sunsets, the yellow skies – hell *every* colour! And the birds singing at three in the morning. You know the Belgian painter Magritte? His painting *Empire of Light*? It purports to show a paradox, as most of Magritte's paintings do – a dark city street beneath a bright sky. But to me that is a realistic portrait of a Danish summer night. You know, you're at a party that runs to half-past two and step out in the garden for air and the sky is light, the birds are singing, even if the world around you is still dark it's sun-rise. Deep winter, too. In some ways, deep winter is even better. I remember standing on *Langebro* once – Long Bridge – you know the one that connects Copenhagen with the island of Amager . . . A short bridge really. Why do they call it Long?'

'Back when it was built it probably was the longest they'd seen yet.'

'Right. Well I remember standing on it once in mid-winter, and there was snow on the ground, and the sky was white as the snow, and everything else, the water, the bridge, the ships in the water, the smoke rising from their stacks, was shades of white and grey and black. It was a pure and perfect black-and-white world. But as I stood there watching, suddenly my eye began to pick out little blots of color – the red of a robin's breast, a woman's long wool coat the blue of your eyes . . .'

'You should have been a painter.'

'Can't draw a straight line.'

'A straight line is rarely needed unless you're Kandinsky or Mark Rothko.'

'I think I'm starting to like you,' he says. 'You're quite good-looking, you know.'

'In the words of Odin, He who flatters gets?'

Kerrigan laughs and shoves his empty plate aside. To his surprise, not only does he feel wonderful, he has also got over his embarrassment about what his Associate did for him the night before when he was unconscious. Reborn again. His shame flares up for an instant, burns out again. He pours the last of the Chardonnay into their glasses and lights a cigar, looks into her cornblue eyes and asks, 'Did you know that just down the street here, on *Randersgade*, there's a cellar-club where people go to couple openly and watch others couple? Where couples couple with other couples, and men amuse themselves watching their mates couple with strangers and women are enjoyed simultaneously by two and more men?'

Her eyes watch his mouth. 'And you have been there?'

'No.'

'Is this too much even for *you*, then?'

'It's not that. It's just, you can't get a drink there. What's love without wine?' He trims his cigar, smiles, can see she is titillated and loves it. He's flying on gentle lust.'What now, my love?'

'What now, my *what*?'

'Excuse me. It's a song title. What now?'

'You say you like jazz?'

23

The Bicycle Stall Bar and Restaurant *(Cykelstalden)*

Cykelstalden
Østerport Station
Oslo Plads *(Oslo Place)* **6**
2100 København Ø

On *Østerbrogade*, East Bridge Street, they cross *Trianglen*, pass the eastern edge of Black Dam Lake, cross *Lille Triangle*, Little Triangle, and walk along *Dag Hammerskjölds Allé*, named for the Swedish UN Secretary General killed in an air crash in 1961 on his way to negotiate over the Congo Crisis – for which he was posthumously awarded the Nobel Peace Prize that year. Past Olaf Palme's Street, named for the Swedish Social Democratic Prime Minister assassinated in the 1980s as he and his wife walked home from the movies, never solved, thought by some to have been engineered by his own social democratic party, past the elegant old villas which have been purchased for embassies by the British and Russians and the ugly concrete box built by the Americans for theirs. The Americans seem always to have the ugliest embassies – Copenhagen, Oslo, Amsterdam . . .

As they wait for the light to change so they can cross Railroad Street, *Jerbanegade*, a wobbling white-bearded man totters out against the red, seat of his jeans hanging like a hiphopper's down to the back of his knees. Traffic honks, and he mutters 'Bah!' and sticks out his tongue at every vehicle that is forced to stop for him, red-faced drivers fisting their horns.

They are headed for *Cykelstalden* where normally there is jazz only on Wednesdays from five to seven, but this season the owner, Mogens, has decided to add a single Saturday.

Kerrigan grows meditative as they walk. He knows this bar from many years ago. He was in Denmark on business, before he had begun to take his writing seriously. He ate lunch at *Cykelstalden* one day and looked up to see the Danish poet Dan Turrell sitting at a nearby table over a bitter. Kerrigan was perhaps 30 at the time, and he knew Turrell's writing, knew him as a great fan of the American beats. Kerrigan was wearing a suit and tie because he was on his way to the embassy for some reason, an interview.

Turrell, whose fingernails were painted black, saw that Kerrigan recognized him and nodded, and Kerrigan wished to show him he was more than a suit and tie, wanted to open his mouth and howl out Ginsberg: *I saw the best minds of my generation destroyed by madness, starving hysterical naked, dragging themselves through the negro streets at dawn, looking for an angry fix, angelheaded hipsters burning for the ancient heavenly connection to the starry dynamo in the machinery of the night . . .*

Kerrigan wanted to stand up and chant: *Unscrew the locks from the doors!/Unscrew the doors themselves from their jambs!*

He was eating a bowl of vegetable soup with bread and butter and a glass of water because he was hungover and trying to get ready for his interview, and he wanted to send a beer and a bitter over to Turrell, Uncle Danny they called him or he called himself when he would stand up at a reading and say, *Det er kun mig, det er kun mig, det er kun mig. Onkel Danny – It's only me, It's only me, It's only me, Uncle Danny . . .*

He wanted to howl out some Rexroth:

> 'You killed him!
> You killed him!
> In your goddamned Brooks Brothers suit,
> You son of a bitch!'

Or Ferlinghetti:

> 'The upper middle class ideal is for the birds,
> but the birds have no use for it
> having their own kind of pecking order
> based upon birdsong . . .
> High society is low society
> I am a social climber climbing downward
> and the descent is difficult . . .'

He wanted this man to know that even if he had not yet published anything, even if he made his living as a glorified clerk, he was more than a suit and tie and bowl of alphabet soup. But he said nothing. He sat there spooning soup and the noodles of the alphabet into his mouth and eating bread and butter, and Dan Turrell finished his bitter and paid and left, a tall, slender, bearded man in dark clothes with fingernails painted black, and Kerrigan's path never crossed his again, although he did see him once again, more than a dozen years later in the Betty Nansen Theater when Uncle Danny introduced a reading by William Burroughs.

Turrell went on to publish a hundred books in his 47 years, and when he was dying, he made a CD of a dozen poems with jazz background synthesized by an electronic genius named Halfdan E. The next to last poem on the album is entitled 'Last City Walk' and it is in a sense reminiscent of J P Jacobsen's Mrs Fønss's last letter to her children.

But in this case, it is a last letter to a city, a reminiscence of a lifetime in a city, a last visit to a last bar for a last bitter, a last rummaging through the second-hand bookshops, a last look at the mothers hanging out their kitchen windows calling in their shouting children for dinner, stopping here and there to watch or to shake the city from his coat as a dog shakes water from his fur, all of it so fluid, so swiftly passing, and all through the city he walks in the company of all his friends that only he can see, and without being sentimental, they say goodbye to it all in silent conversation, and finally down by the King's New Square, they disappear, and then Uncle Danny does, too, and there is one less shadow in the street.

Turrell was dead shortly after.

Perhaps it is the remnant of his hangover that causes the sound in Kerrigan's throat, but his Associate glances at him and asks, 'Are you all right?'

He nods, not trusting himself to speak, thinking, The lesson here is when you see someone in a café you want to say hello to, whether you know them or not, say hello and don't be afraid to.

As they come to Østerport Station, the jazzmen are already setting up on the street outside Cykelstalden, and she is conferring with her starfish/anemone book as they walk. She tells him that the station has been in function since 1897, that the square *Oslo Plads* has its name not for the city of Oslo, which was at that time still named Christiania, for the Danish king Christian IX, when Norway was still under Denmark, but for the Nordic god *Oss*. The suffix *lo* is an old Norse form for 'light'. So it is the 'light of Oss', that the name celebrates.

Cykelstalden is a railway authority restaurant but has been managed in a special way. For about 25 years, up to last year, it was run by a fellow named Jeppe. But Jeppe died, only 52 years old. He was very well known in this quarter, and all sorts of people frequented his serving house. Jeppe was also the one who started the jazz here.

'I remember him as a slim young man waiting on tables in his wooden shoes,' says Kerrigan's Associate. 'With the years he put on a good deal of weight, and he seemed to live in another dimension, but he still loved to charm the women. *Hej skat*, he always said to me. *Hello, treasure. Hello, darling*. If you want to see, there's a fine portrait of him in the back bar here. Painted on his fiftieth birthday, two years before he died."

'Were you in love with him?' Kerrigan asks.

'I never saw him with a woman,' she says, and they sit at a table with a blue and white checked cloth, edges lifting in the sunny breeze. Kerrigan remembers then he was here one other time, a dozen years ago with the American fiction writer Gladys Swan and a friend of hers from France, a Jungian analyst named Monique Salzmann. It was the last day of their visit to Copenhagen, and the three of them sat in the sun, gazing out toward *Marmorkirken*, the Marble Church, drinking iced aquavit, snaps, and Gladys and Monique looked at him, and one of them said suddenly, 'We have been talking about you, and we have decided that you have to kill your angel.'

Kerrigan had no idea what they meant, and they never explained themselves, but the statement evoked an immediate image in Kerrigan's mind of an angel cowering in a basement awaiting execution. That image grew to a story entitled 'Murphy's Angel', for which he won a Pushcart Prize in 1990, under one of his pseudonyms.

He would like to share this memory with his Associate but fears she will think him a braggart so he keeps it to himself.

She greets the waiter by name, and touches his arm as they order. From where they sit, they can see the new manager, Mogens, tending the taps beneath the Tuborg umbrella, over his left shoulder the green dome of the Marble Church. The waiter, wearing red suspenders, relaxes in the sun for a moment, and a strikingly pretty blond waitress named Trine expertly carries a tray with half a dozen golden pints through the corridor of tables. The cold beer down Kerrigan's throat is golden, a liquid field of wheat, and a curly-haired man comes over and kisses his Associate on her lips.

'*Hej*, Peter!' she says cheerily, and touches his face, and the shadow of a bird drifts across the table. They chat while Kerrigan, unintroduced, studies the poster announcing the Stolle and Svarre Jazz Quartet featuring Jørgen Svarre on sax, Ole Stolle on trumpet, Mikkel Finn on drums, Søren Christiansen on piano, and Ole 'Skipper' Moesgård on bass. They play here every Wednesday and at the Tivoli Gardens every Monday in season.

Peter and Kerrigan's Associate are still chatting and Kerrigan studies a metal sign on the wall which directs customers to park their bicycles on the bike rack, cautioning that they will otherwise be removed 'without responsibility'. Kerrigan recalls the charming sign he spotted in the Central Station: *It is forbidden on these premises to drink beer, wine or spirits*. Not to put too fine a point on it.

He notices then a stout man in hat and checkered jacket standing in the shadows beside the clarinette player. He seems about to draw something from his pocket and fear touches Kerrigan, but passes again as the hand comes away empty. Kerrigan does not wish to explore the source of the anxiety he felt.

His beer is already more than half empty and touches another fear, and the musicians are milling about, not yet playing. He wishes that Peter would go away, even though he likes the man's face and manner, and perhaps communicates that wish for suddenly the handsome, curly-haired man kisses her again on the mouth, nods to Kerrigan, and withdraws, saying, 'I have a family to go home to.'

'Who's he?' Kerrigan asks, feeling foolish.

'Peter.'

'I gathered. Is he your lover?'

'Vouldn't you like to know.'

The piano player starts in then, and Ole Stolle begins to sing 'Blueberry Hill' and Kerrigan gazes off to the cupola of the Marble Church, blurred as an impressionistic painting to his uncorrected eyes, facing toward the harbor, and he finds himself thinking of Admiral Nelson and the Battle of Copenhagen in 1801.

Nelson with one detachment of ships was firing upon the city. The Danes were responding valiantly, and the other British Admiral, Parker, signalled Nelson to cease firing. The losses were too great. Nelson kept firing, and his first officer called the cease-fire signal to his attention. The one-eyed Nelson took out his telescope, but put it to his blind eye. 'I see no signal,' he said and kept the cannons going. Then he sent word to the city that he would set fire to the Danish floating batteries he had captured, with the crews still in them if they did not surrender.

Olfert Fischer, the Danish Admiral, carried out the Crown Prince's order to cease fire, a surrender.

Kerrigan despises Nelson for this, thinks how terrible a man to hail as a hero, pictures him atop the 56m tall pillar at the center of

Trafalgar Square in London, a monument to his victory over the French-Spanish fleet in 1805, and ponders with bitter satisfaction the fact that in 1966 the IRA blew up the Nelson Pillar in Dublin. He experiences an intense hatred for the British bastard, although he at least partially realizes that his anger stems from annoyance that the curly-haired Peter kissed his Associate, twice, on her pretty lips, and is further annoyed that he should be annoyed at that, even as the blonde Trine so young and pretty to gaze upon walks past and smiles right into his eyes. No reason for annoyance. And little sense to hate Nelson for someting he did nearly 200 years ago, but what good was history if one insisted upon putting the monocle to the blind eye? Which, of course, he realizes is precisely what he does constantly.

How lovely is the cupola of the Marble Church over Mogens's shoulder, a stone's throw from *Adelsgade,* Nobility Street, known in the nineteenth century as 'the headquarters of thieves and handlers', according to High Court Justice Engelhart writing in 1815 in the daily newspaper *Berlingske* (for which his Associate briefly worked). Engelhart referred to 'Jews and other people' who dealt in stolen goods in those days when after eleven at night the streets were full of thieves and burglars and the populace was protected by watchmen armed with mace-headed spears who would look the other way for a coin.

The death penalty for theft was abolished in 1771, but in 1815, there was a cry to reinstate it for burglary. The 'new' law of 1789 was described by a leading lawyer in 1809 as a 'beautiful specimen of humanity and wisdom'. It provided for two months to two years in the House of Chastisement for a first theft conviction; three to five years for a second offence; and life for a third offence – a nearly 200-year-old law which resembles America's today.

In 1815, the prisoners rioted against the food; cooked in a copper kettle, it was served coated with a green membrane, which was poisonous. The response was sympathetic but a third riot, in 1817, evoked a decision to execute every tenth prisoner by lottery until a forceful protest by public attorney A S Ørsted (brother of the discoverer of electromagnetism) resulted in the procedure's being dropped.

Ørsted was a strong force for the enactment of a more just penal system, but only in 1837 was the inquisition method of interrogation by rope and cat-o'-nine-tails abolished.

Kerrigan's beer is empty, and he attempts, unsuccessfully, to signal the waiter or, better yet, the waitress, Trine, for a fresh one, which embarrasses and annoys him further.

'Are you sulking?' his Associate asks.

'Yes.'

'Why?'

'Wouldn't you like to know?'

'See there,' she says. 'The fellow with the beard three tables down. That's our Minister of Defense.'

Kerrigan laughs.

'Oh, now you're in a good mood again.'

'It just reminded me of Mogens Glistrup. Remember when he ran for office and said he would abolish the Danish defense system and replace it with a recorded announcement in English, German, and Russian that kept saying over and over, *We surrender, we surrender, we surrender . . .*'

She laughs, too, now, but says, 'His party has led to a xenophobic one that has gained seats in the parliament, you know. Some would call it almost fascist.' She glances at the waiter, smiling in the sun, who nods and brings a new round.

'*Is* he?' Kerrigan asks.

'Is who what?'

'Peter your lover?'

'Sometimes you remind me of Hans Christian Andersen with all those feelings you have,' she says, and pokes him in the chest with her fingertip. He almost responds to the quick pinprick of indignation this evokes in him, but before opening his mouth realizes that she is teasing and says instead, 'Well, you are the perfect Sofie Oehlenschläger, aren't you? Collecting poets.'

She only smiles, and Stolle & Svarre are now going very cool on 'Moonlight in Vermont', and he is not afraid of anything with another fresh golden pint on the table before him, sparkling in the sunlight. He lights a cigar and wants very much to make love to her or at least to kiss her neck or even just the palm of her delicate hand or the arch of her sweet little trotter. He remembers his Swedish friend Morten Gideon in the Casino in Divonne Les Baines once, years ago, sitting with a beautiful Turkish woman he was trying unsuccessfully to seduce, and suddenly, in an unexpected moment of silence, Gideon's voice was heard to rise clearly out across the entire casino, 'I vant to kess your feet!'

Kerrigan is focused on his Associate's hands and her slender bare arms, thinking how good the life of the senses is, recalling the pleasure M Meursault derived from drying his hands on a fresh towel and his displeasure at the end of his work day to find the towel soggy from use. This is an insignificant detail, his employer tells him when he complains. But such details are seen to in the life of Copenhagen and are, perhaps, in their sum not insignificant. As Marx said, 'Quantitative change becomes qualitative change.'

After a pause, the quintet opens again with a dixie version of 'Toot Toot Tootsie, Goodbye', and Kerrigan says, 'God, when I was a kid that song terrified me.'

She looks curiously at him.

He says, 'It was the lyrics, you know that line about, *If you don't get a letter/Then you'll know I'm in jail . . .*'

'Why did that terrify you?'

'I don't know. Somehow it made me think of, or fear, someone I loved going to jail. I think it had something to do with a Dan Daily film I saw once where this guy has to go to jail, and he didn't really do anything very bad, nothing violent or anything. It was like some minor fraud or something, grifter type thing. It really scared me, like gave me an idea how unrelenting the law could be. Like fuck up even just a little bit and you're fucked. I don't think there's anything in the world that scares me as much as the thought of going to jail.'

She is still watching him. Then she turns away to light a Prince with an elegant silver lighter. 'My father,' she says. 'He went to jail once. For writing a bad check. In those days they didn't have these automatic credit provisions. He got six months. No probation. No one told me about it. I was ten, and they sent me to my grandmother's for a weekend when he had to be taken away. You had to ferry over there, and my father brought me to the ferry landing to see me off on the Friday. He had a little present for me – a coloring book. He was so loving and gentle, I didn't understand but it was so sweet. Then on Sunday afternoon when I got back he wasn't there at the landing. My mother was there, and when I asked where he was, she just said he had to go away for a while. No one would tell me where he was until one day in school – we were in a fine middle-class school, we lived well – one of the other girls asked me if it was true my father was in jail. I just laughed at her. And after school that day told my mother, expecting her to say how ridiculous, but as soon as I saw her face I knew. That's how I found out.'

Kerrigan put his hand on hers. 'Jesus.'

'Everyone has a sad story,' she says. 'Tell me yours.'

'Let's leave my family out of this.'

'Why?'

He just shakes his head, takes his hand from hers.

The musicians are finishing their last set with 'Love Me or Leave Me', and the sky has clouded over with a white-grey ceiling.

'Damn', says Kerrigan. 'I want some more jazz.'

'I know a place,' she tells him. 'It's small and dark and the jazz is on CD but it's good. Just over on *Classensgade*, Classens Street. But it does not open until four. There is another place, though, that will be perfect until then.'

'Well this one was wonderful,' says Kerrigan.

'Yes. Pity that in two years time most of it will be gone, taken over by the Danish railroad administration offices. Only the back bar will remain. There will be no more jazz, no more food, no more outdoor tables or restaurant, only the back bar and Mogens and the painting of Jeppe and the memories of what a vonderful place it has been.'

'Does your little book predict the future, too?'

'No, I follow the city planning journals.'

'How very sad,' says Kerrigan.

'Still the backbar is a good one. Nicely hidden. Mogens will have a success. And there are many good paintings there, too.'

They walk back past the ugly concrete box of the American Embassy, Kerrigan thinking he could as well hate Custer as Nelson, although putting everything into perspective one could as well sing the praises of any leader who, as Lincoln put it, at least sometimes 'listens to the angels of his better nature'. What right does a man have to complain and carp about a system that he only passively enjoys, without contributing a fart himself?

And as if ordained by God Almighty, at Little Triangle, a young man asks if they can spare some coins. Kerrigan doesn't like the look of him and decides it's wiser to buy him off with a two-crown piece, but his Associate asks, 'What do you want the money for?'

'A human being needs smoke and drink,' he says. His eyes are weak in a hard, weathered face, and Kerrigan wants to be away from him, but she persists. 'Don't you have a job?'

'I'm homeless.'

'Don't you get welfare then?'

'You can't get welfare without an address. It's true! No one cares about you if you don't have a home.'

'What do you do when you work?' Kerrigan asks against his better judgement.

'I'm a musician.'

'So why not play music on the street. Pick up some coin that way.'

'Man, those people are not worth my music. I could just as well blow them up. I want to, you know? Not you. You care enough to give me something, to talk to me. But the other bastards. Man, they don't care. I could watch them burn. I could just as well put a fucking bomb in the central station.'

'Don't do it,' Kerrigan says. 'You'll just end up in jail.' He wants very much to get away from the guy because he is torn between the desire to give him more money and start a fight with him, and he doesn't want to do either, and he is thinking about his Associate's father doing six months for a bad check and about his mother and where she ended up and her children and his wife whose family he doesn't even dare to visit here. The light changes, giving them an excuse to cross the street and get away, and she says, 'Maybe you just saved some lives,' as they hear the young man behind them stopping someone else to ask for coins.

'Cheap enough for two crowns,' he says.

They nip in through an iron gate, and Kerrigan sees they are in a graveyard.

'This is Garnison's Cemetery,' she tells him. 'We can take a short-cut back toward Christianiagade.'

It is a peaceful place of well-tended graves. Near the far gate on a large stone encircled by small trees, the engraving reports that beneath it lie the remains of 226 warriors who died under the Danish flag in 1864, on whose grave grows honor for they gave all for the fatherland.

Kerrigan pictures their 226 bodies all tangled together in the earth, bare-boned now, skulls grinning at skulls, warriors who died in the last battle Denmark ever fought, the war they lost to Germany, following which the country was never again a world power.

He notes that the stones are cut not only with the name and dates of birth and death of the extinguished lives beneath them, but also with the positions they held in this mortal coil, trades, titles, rank – as though they are all doomed to continue playing in eternity the roles they played within their mortal spans.

There lies Colonel Vilhelm de Fine Licht, 1821-1885, and housewife Anna; Baronesse Ellen Schaffalitzky and Lieutenant Colonel Ludvig Bernhard Maximilian aka Baron Schaffalitzky de Muckadell. Kerrigan tries the name on, pictures himself at a conference, offering his hand out to his Associate for a shake: 'Hi there, Muckadell here. Denmark. Good to see ya. Call me Schaffalitzky if you like.'

'It is a very fine Danish name,' she tells him as they pass the remains of Staff Sergeant N F Petersen and many others – a generaless (apparently the wife of a general), a mason, Customs Inspector Simonsen, a pharmacist, editor-in-chief, a civil engineer, journalist, priest, actor, grocer, taxicab owner, wine merchant, pilot. There is one Ludvig Fock, profession unidentified, and one Brigadier Percy Hansen.

'With a name like Percy he would have to be a fighter,' says Kerrigan and hears in his own statement the false manliness of his native land. 'Reframing,' he says, 'We've got a whole society here, seal off the gates and you've got a complete city of ghosts. See them all on dusty planks performing their functions. But it really is a lovely place. It would be good to lie here.' And he thinks of Dylan Thomas's Grandfather travelling about Wales furiously in a little pony trap looking for a good place to be buried. 'There's no sense in lyin' *here*,' he says. 'Ya can't twitch your toes without puttin' 'em in the sea.'

'But you're not dead yet, Dy Thomas. How can you be buried then? Come on home. There's strong beer for tea. And cake.'

But the grandfather only looks off at the sea without speaking, 'like a prophet who has no doubt'.

Kerrigan turns to his Associate. 'If your last dance is not already taken, would you consider lying here beside me?'

'It would be too late for much fun then,' she says with a glint in her blue eyes that fires his pulse and leaves him speechless.

24

Langelinie Bridge Danish Lunch Restaurant
(Langeliniebroen Dansk Frokostrestaurant)

Langelinie Bridge Danish Lunch Restaurant
Fridtjof Nansens Plads 2
2100 København Ø

The Langelinie Bridge Danish Lunch Restaurant lies all by itself in the tip of a triangular corner at the foot of the bridge that leads over to the Little Mermaid and other scenic wonders. The restaurant is itself a long, narrow triangle, the tip of which is a fenced-in outdoor area containing half a dozen tables. It is here they sit, and the proprietor emerges – a bright-faced young man who beams at Kerrigan's Associate.

'Hej, Allan!' she exclaims, and Kerrigan notes they touch one another as she orders their drinks.

'Shall we have a bite,' she asks Kerrigan.

'What do you plan to bite?' he asks.

'I was thinking of a smoked eel with scrambled egg on dark rye bread, all covered with fresh chopped chives and new ground pepper.'

'And a snaps?'

'And a snaps. An eel must swim, my treasure,' she says in Danish, and that word, *skat*, can be sincere or ironic or ironic covering a first border of sincerity which he wonders and hopes is the case just now.

He reads the menu like a little book of haiku, and somehow the misspellings of the English translations beneath the Danish seem to lend authenticity – *marinate heering, 3 pice open sandwich, fry egg, old Danish cheese with dripping* . . .

The tables are filling up now as Allan delivers their eel and beer, pours their iced snaps in double measures and in such a way that the liquor is convex atop the stem glass. They have to sink their mouths to the glasses lest precious icy drops be lost on the starched white table cloth.

The eel and egg and chives, dusted with black pepper, shoot to his brain, and Kerrigan watches the world around him, eyes lidded with pleasure. His lovely Associate, the jolly Danes, plates heaped from the ample buffet inside of many kinds of fishes and meats. He can see why Allan is so slender. He dances nimbly among the tables serving, while his wife Jeannette works the kitchen and the taps inside.

A stout moustached fellow who has excused himself from his lunch mates returns with the tail of his shirt showing through his flies. A slender blond woman at the table says in Danish, 'Would you try and close that peeport?'

'Oh,' he says, 'Out doing research again, are you?'

Everyone laughs; the sun is beaming down on them and a new couple come in to the sunny open triangle with a sheepdog on a lead and a puppy in the arms of the female half. All the women at all the other tables utter sounds of heartbreaking tenderness with lips and throats while the puppy trembles in its owner's arms, beholding with frightened brown eyes the brave new world of the Langelinie café.

To his surprise Kerrigan observes the cool control of his Associate's face dissolve in maternal yearning.

'Do you like animals?' he asks.

'Anyone who does not is a sad case,' says she.

'Birth itself is sadness,' says Kerrigan, and her blue eyes turn to him with an empathy that frightens him – it is as though she can see into his history. 'What does your little book say about this place?' he asks.

Slowly she turns the eyes that see away from him, down into her starfish book, and she recites the meager history there: Built in 1934 by the first owner who called it the TRIA café – tria for Triangle, the triangular crossing a few blocks over that was the center of the area, though reflected in this small triangle here. It was for years a sailors' bar where beer was purchased by the case with an opener thrown in. In those days there was only warm beer, a preference some still harbor. Today in a bar in Copenhagen if you prefer a room temperature beer you ask for it 'from the case' – *fra kassen*.

'So it was a sailors' bar.'

'Yes,' she says with private thoughts sparkling in her blue eyes. 'And where there are sailors there are girls.'

'Are you telling me . . .?'

' . . . that when the boys are at sea they grow weary of twisting asparagus.'

'Of *what*!'

Her smile falters and he feels a long-forgotten bluenose assert itself. He is startled, first by her bluntness, then by his own lack of humor. 'We call it spanking the monkey,' he says and is delighted to see her startled comprehension give way to bawdy laughter. Instantly she collects herself. 'Well, well,' she says. 'Enough of that. In 1996 it changed hands and became the Café Langelinie Bridge, then shortly after that Antonio's Italian restaurant, and now finally Allan and Jeannette's. They restored it to its original style with old pictures and lamps.'

They dawdle over coffee, unspeaking, leaning back in their chairs, sun in their faces. Then a mass of dark cloud moves slowly over the roof of the building across the street and they are sitting in dim light.

'Just in time to find an indoor place,' she says. 'And some jazz.'

25

The Fiver ***(Femmeren)***

Femmeren
Classensgade ***(Classens Street)*** **5**
2100 København Ø

Looking up at the street sign on the corner, Kerrigan exclaims, 'Jesus, this is *Classensgade*, Classens Street! This is where C Blomme lived!'

She glances obliquely at him.'And who is C Blomme?'

'The high school teacher who was poisoned in 1940. One of his students slipped poison into the tin of hard candies he was always sucking on. He lived at *Classensgade* 44.'

'This sounds familiar.'

'It's a Danish novel. By Hans Scherfig (1905 –1989). The novel is from 1939 and was translated into English by Frank Hugus – in 1980, I think.'

'*Stolen Spring*,' she says. 'Did you read that?'

'Well, I read Hugus's translation of it.'

'Scherfig was a painter, too.'

'I know. I have one of his rhinos. He was a kind of twentieth century communist Rousseau. Naive but moving. I love his elephants.'

'And here's our bar,' she says.

Like most Danish bars, it is utterly unremarkable to look at, narrow-fronted, tucked in between a narrow Persian restaurant and the blue barndoor entry of an apartment-building courtyard. A door beneath the numeral five beneath a lintel sign that says *Vinstue Bar*, Wine Room Bar, the two words punctuated by the face of a die showing five, and a white-curtained platewindow on which is lettered the word *Femmeren*, the Fiver.

Inside, a handful of regulars at the bar fall silent at the entry of Kerrigan and his Associate. It is a small dark room with vintage posters and advertisements on the walls – one of a strutting old-fashioned sailor advertising Tuborg, another advertising *Stjerne Øl*, Star Beer, a billboard reproduction of a Brecht-Weil play in German. Behind the bar, a woman in her 50s, not unattractive, but with whom Kerrigan would not like to tangle.

They sit at a round table in the corner, and the woman comes from the bar to serve them.

'That's Ruth, the owner. She opened this place in 1967.'

Then, simultaneously, it occurs to Kerrigan that he is sitting just around the corner from Søren Kierkegaard's 1850 residence and that the music playing on the sound system is Cannonball Adderly's *Somethin' Else*, which he happens to know was recorded in Hackensack, New Jersey, on 9 March 1958. The number playing is 'Autumn Leaves', perhaps the best variations he has ever heard played on this theme, with Adderly on alto sax, Miles Davis on trumpet, Hank Jones on piano, Sam Jones on bass, and Art Blakey on the skins.

He looks up at the backs of the heads of the regulars sitting around the half square bar. They have now resumed their talk. Kerrigan says, 'If I owned this place, I think I'd call it the Five Spot.'

The aural acuity of Danes often surprises him. He thought he had spoken softly, but all the way at the end of the bar, Ruth hears. 'No,' she says. 'That's not how you play the piano in Denmark. The Five Spot is the Five Spot. Or was. This here is *Femmeren*, The Fiver. It's not an imitation. For what it's worth, it's what it is. The original.'

'Gotcha,' says Kerrigan, lifting his beer. 'Great sounds by the way.'

A grey-haired, blue-eyed, bearded man at the bar nods at Kerrigan's Associate. She returns the greeting, tells Kerrigan, 'That is Ib Schierbeck who has owned and managed many bookstores in Copenhagen. He now runs the Paludan book café on *Fiolstræde*.' Schierbeck nods at Kerrigan. A slender black and white dog with white paws rises from beneath a nearby table and stands shivering by his Associate who scratches the dog's ears. 'Hello, Toto, little treasure,' she says and the dog's owner, a tall man wearing a Borselino, blinks affectionately in their direction.

'That's a 500 dollar hat,' Kerrigan mutters to his Associate, but she has now turned her attention elsewhere. She is gazing at a little one-man table in the corner beneath the Tuborg sailor where a lone bottle of beer stands in shadow.

'So lonely,' she says.

'The bottle?'

She nods, just as a woman comes up from the basement loo and sits to the lonely bottle.

'What's your name?' his Associate calls across.

'Jette,' says the woman, and soon they are in conversation. Jette is 40 years old, lives with her mother, is looking for an apartment. A librarian by education, she is currently on welfare. She is neither pretty nor homely, neither heavy nor slender. Her hair is brown, shortish, her eyes slate grey, and Kerrigan understands now that his Associate saw something in the aura of that bottle because this is a sadly lonely woman of 40 sitting alone in a dark bar, easy prey for dishonorable men, though no doubt protected by the family of regulars here.

Yet what were they to do? Offer false hope? A moment's respite? Jette and his Associate are now reading one another's palms, tracing one another's palm lines with blue ballpoint, and Kerrigan realizes that his Associate is pretty high.

Another CD is playing now. *Jazz Masters 25*, Verve label, Getz and Gillespie blowing 'Dark Eyes' from '56. The mere thought of the year fills Kerrigan with wonder.1956! He can remember the Chevies that year clear as day – the way the tail fins had begun to lift a little from the angular line of the '55, softly curving up, but not yet the sharp fins of the '57. In '56 the classic rock was just emerging – Chuck Berry, Bo Diddley, Jerry Lee Lewis, Buddy Holly, who would die three years later in a plane crash on 3 February 1959, when Kerrigan was still only fifteen. In 1956, Elvis Presley was still good, and Kerrigan was thirteen, just stepping into puberty. School dances at St Joan's and the impossible loveliness of Mary Ella Delahanty and Patsie O'Sullivan. He remembers Mary Ella's smile and Patsie's blue eyes and still can feel the sweet, pure yearning.

Another figure emerges from the basement now. Up the back stairway. A bearded smiling man wearing a great fool's cap – a blue and pale blue and white crown of spikes and bells. He poses before an advertisement for orange soda, looking pleased, perhaps a little bit tipsy, a row of bottles on the shelf above his shoulder.

Ruth says, 'That's Ole. My relief bartender,' and chuckles.

Kerrigan's Associate says, 'He's the one who first told me about *Somethin' Else*' and another man approaches their table, a smiling kind-faced man with spaces between his teeth and a wispy moustache. He says very quietly, 'Want to hear some jazz?' And goes behind the bar – apparently half the people in the place are bartenders – to put on a Danish Radio Big Band tribute to Duke Ellington, recorded in honor of what would have been the Duke's hundredth birthday that year. It begins with 'Take the A Train'.

'Billy Strayhorn,' says Kerrigan.

'Niels Jørgen Steen,' says the man with the wispy moustache. His name is Hans.

It occurs to Kerrigan as he replenishes their drinks, winning a smile from Ruth, that this place is a true Bohemian bar. Nothing trendy. Just a good old low-down neighborhood joint where people who like jazz and reasonably-priced drinks and friendly company can come and listen to Adderley and Davis and try to decipher the German on a Brecht poster, raffle for drinks, swap stories, play guessing games.

Gazing at the Brecht poster, Kerrigan experiences a deep longing to hear poor dead Bobby Darin sing 'Mack the Knife'. He asks Ruth if she has that among her CDs, and she pinches her nose by way of reply, but his Associate says, 'I have that. On an LP.'

'You *do*?'

She nods, and Kerrigan experiences a fit of shyness. Should I ask to borrow it?

'*Giver du så en natcap*?' he asks in Danish. 'Will you invite me for a nightcap then?'

She blows a thin stream of grey cigarette smoke through pursed smiling lips and assents with a nod.

'It was that girl,' she says as they walk down *Classensgade*, following the route that C Blomme followed while sucking his poisoned malt drop. 'That girl Jette. So lonely. So lonely. She reminded me of a girlfriend I knew when I was about twelve.' Then she begins to chuckle. 'We were in the country for a weekend, at a farm. And there was a horse in the pasture. A stallion.' She holds her palms out, facing each other, a foot and a half apart. 'He was enormous, and we couldn't quite figure out what it was so we tried to ask the farmer, and he said, "The horse? He's called Dax." We got hysterical laughing, and then all day, for weeks after that, all we had to do to break up laughing was one of us would say *Dax!*'

They are laughing together now as they walk through what, to Kerrigan's weak eyes, is the impressionistic night.

In her apartment again as Darin sings about Lotte Lenya, Mack the Knife, and old Lucy Brown, she lights candles, puts out ice and glasses, a bottle of Chivas, and they undress one another on the sofa.

'You are radiant,' he whispers, his eyes full of her lovely shoulders and breasts that look much bigger uncovered, tipped with nipples the size and color and texture of berries.

'He who flatters, gets,' she says.

Then he whispers, 'Dax!' and she laughs, but the laughter quickly turns to something else that draws them from self-consciousness and absorbs them in their senses.

The night is full of amazements. Kerrigan had heard the term multiple orgasms before, but never witnessed it. He listens in awe as she cries out again and again, lulls, begins anew, until finally he reaches his own single height and drops into exhaustion on the rumpled sheets.

Then she is weeping in his arms, and he strokes her hair. 'There, there,' he whispers, watching a silver triangle of moonlight on the tall white wall. 'What is it?'

'So hopeless,' she says. Her face is unattractive weeping, and his immediate thoughts are of escape, but he says, '*What*'s so hopeless?'

'Me. All of it.' She reaches to the bedstand for a Kleenex and blows her nose. 'I'm 57 years old . . . no, I lied, I'm 58 . . . and still mourning over lost chances and stupid choices. I've wasted all my life.'

'Hey, it's not too late. It's never too late.'

'I'll never be able to make up for all this lost time,' she says. 'I have never learned.' She draws back to look into his eyes. 'I have something in me,' she says. 'I *do*. But I have never been able to express it.'

He pulls her close and says, 'You will. You will if you don't give up,' and his thoughts are torn between escape and desire. All this emotion unnerves him. The fullness of her breasts against his chest, the fear of this, and the thought then that after coitus all animals are sad except for women and roosters.

'Cock a doodle,' he whispers into her shapely back, forking his thighs around hers, and 'You came five times to my one. Ms Five-to-One.' Or perhaps he only thinks it for he is already drifting away.

DAY FOUR

The Green Peril

'We drank absinthe – as light green
as the woods, as little frogs . . .'

– Jens August Schade (*In Hviid's Wine Room*)

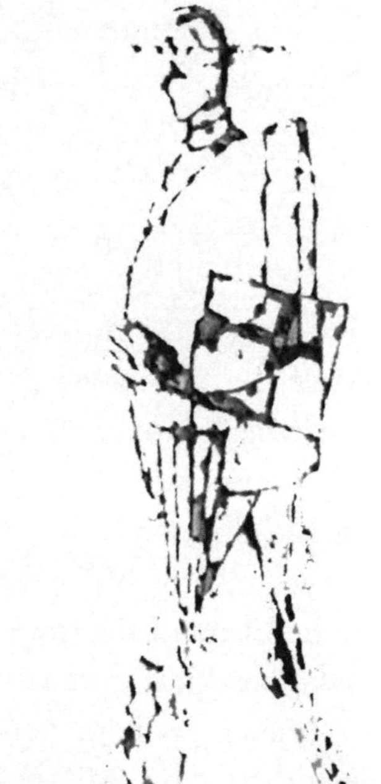

26

Øbro Eating House & Bar *(Øbro Spisehuse & Bar)*

Øbro Spisehuse & Bar
Øster Farimagsgade *(East Farimags Street)* **16A**
2100 København Ø

His first conscious thought when he opens his eyes and smells coffee is enthusiastic: to continue his tavernological studies, the exhilaration of sexual meeting . . . But then he remembers her tears in the dark, and the memory of the image of that silver triangle of moonlight on the tall shadowy white wall seems to speak ineffable things about the gloomy future.

He rises, slips into the shower, bathes his head with water, finds a brand new blue toothbrush in the medicine chest, tears off the cellophane wondering if it was purchased specifically for him – or for whoever. *Whatsoelse*, as his Associate is wont to say.

As he steps out again, towelling himself, she is in the bedroom door wearing red jeans and tee-shirt. Her eyes take in his naked body, and the sight of her doing that raises him behind the towel. 'Coffee's soon ready,' she says. 'I didn't make breakfast because I thought you might like to survey another brunch spot for your book. Brunch is very big in east Copenhagen these days. My treat this time.'

'Great,' he says, 'But you don't have to.'

'I know. But I want to. I insist.'

And as she moves back to the kitchen, she sings, *Livet er ikke den værste man har Og om lidt er kaffeen klar . . .* – a ditty by the contemporary poet Benny Andersen about the joy of everyday life, almost untranslatable, something like, *Living is not the worst thing to do/And soon the coffee's brewed . . .*

Kerrigan wanders about the living room as he waits, runs his fingers along the spines of books on a shelf: Kahlil Gibran, *Dreams*, *Women Who Run With Wolves*, *The Ninth Prophecy*, a leatherbound works of Jack London in four volumes in Danish, Ovid's *Art of Love*. He tips out the latter, leafs through to two places marked with tiny red feathers:

> 'Don't let the light in your bedroom be too bright: there are many things about a woman that are best seen in the dimness of twilight . . .
> Women who are getting on in years have experience . . . With them pleasure comes naturally, without provocation, the pleasure which is sweeter than all, the pleasure which is shared equally by the man and the woman.'

Amongst her CDs he finds a Coltrane, 'My Favorite Things'. He puts it on and stands by the tall window listening, staring out to the vast weed-sprung empty lot across the avenue, hearing the familiar melody devolve, spiralling away from the harmonies, becoming stronger then, when his sax seems to reach a place of pure formless sound, working slowly back down and into the melody again. He looks at the back of the CD and reads liner notes by the composer Lamont Young: 'If you believe that the universe is composed of vibrations, Coltrane's music is the beginning of an understanding of universal structure.'

The hair lifts on Kerrigan's arms as he hears the alto move back again out of the harmonies, breaking free of one structure to find a purer one, music without harmony, the supreme structure of the unstructured, pure sound, world without word . . .

The thought is so heady he has to turn from the window, and

his eye falls on a strip of orange wall between white-lacquered woodwork. Down the strip of wall are mounted half a dozen oil paintings, unframed, pinned to the plaster. Tiny pieces, miniatures.

He has to stand close to see without his glasses. The first is identifiable, a red frog on an abstract green and orange background. The next seems to be something, a purple on purple oval. At first he thinks it is an antique portrait, but on closer inspection, he sees it is an abstraction. There is a title, *Girl in a Swing*, and he can almost but not quite identify the subject of the title. Those that follow are by turn more and more abstract, figures from a dream, blue, red, white, black. All are painted on a heavy backing which feels between his thumb and finger more like cotton than paper, a very coarse cotton.

He lights a cigar just as she comes in with coffee pot and cups on an oval tray.

'These are amazing,' he says. 'Did you do them?'

'No need to humor me,' she says and arranges the coffee on a butcher block table.

'I'm not. I wouldn't. It's against my principles. They're fucking good.'

She smirks. '*Fucking* good,' and an odd, inexplicable rage takes him; he seizes her arms and squeezes, snarling into her startled face, 'I *said* they're fucking good!' He releases her at once. 'Oh, god,' he says, 'I'm sorry, I don't know . . .'

'It's all right,' she whispers, studying the backs of her arms where he has squeezed them. 'I'll be bruised. I bruise so easily.'

'I'm really sorry. I don't know what came over me. No, that's not true. I was mad because these paintings are excellent, and you won't admit it. Do you *want* to be unhappy?'

She is looking up at him now in a curious, naked expression he would never have expected to see on her face, and he remembers suddenly how she looked beneath him as they made love, eyes wide, brilliant with pleasure, a surprised smile as she came again and again . . .

'Do you really mean it?'

'*Yes*.'

'It's not because of my, last night . . .'

'*No.*'

Now she looks up at the pictures herself as though she has never seen them before. 'How could they be good? I painted them all in one weekend. Two days ago. The day I came for you at Long John's. I was desperate. I was in despair. It all seemed so hopeless, working as a secretary and playing at being an artist on the weekends.'

'You *are* an artist.'

'What makes you so sure?'

'I have a good eye. I can see it. It's right there.' He gestures up the strip of wall. 'Trust me. These pictures are fucking good.'

'*Fucking* good,' she teases. 'Maybe it's just because you fucked me. Maybe you're just cunt struck.'

'You're pissing me off again,' he says and glowers at her. 'Better watch it.'

Her eyes brighten. 'I like you that way,' she says. 'Do you 'ave a leetle Franshman inside you?'

'Dax!' he says, shoving his face toward hers, and they laugh together. 'Now we have to choose – is it breakfast or something else?'

'Why either/or? Why not both/and?' First the one. Then the other.

Øbro Spisehus & Bar, Øbro Eating House & Bar, on *Øster Farimagsgade*, a narrow deep place with its front window open in honor of the unseasonably warm late morning sun. *Spisehus* means literally 'eating house', and this is more of a restaurant than a bar, though fully licensed. The breakfast is a cross between brunch and continental and the wine is good and they don't get confused if you speak Danish, as they sometimes do across the street at *O's*, where they nonetheless serve succulent ribs.

'The food at Øbro is excellent,' she reads from her starfish book, 'and the brunch is well worth a try, though you won't always be able to get a champagne to go with it. The house white is good, though, and as for bloody mary's, they have the makings, if you can explain how to combine them. On a winter Sunday morning sit by the window and you can see the snow fall on Black Dam Lake just up Wiedewelts Street.'

'How long has it been here?'

'Not long.'

They order the brunch and a bottle of not very chill Alsatian champenoise, which Kerrigan, for fun, calls, 'Champ Noise'.

'And do you have *wienerbrød*?' he asks the pretty, dark-haired waitress with the Asian face. She smiles in apology. 'But you are welcome to bring some in from the bakery a few doors down.'

'Are you a *slik-mund*?' asks his Associate.

He smiles suggestively. 'You ought to know.' *Slik-mund* is the Danish expression for a sweet-tooth, *slik* meaning candy, *mund* meaning mouth, but *slik* also means 'lick', and he cannot hear the term without thinking of that.

She laughs.

'Did you know,' he asks, 'that what you Danes call Vienna Bread, *Wienerbrød*, the Americans call Danish pastry?'

'Yes, that is because there was a baker's strike in Copenhagen in the last century, and some imported Viennese bakers taught us to like the very delicate, layered pastry we call Vienna bread. American Danish is so heavy and syrupy.'

'You're not a *slik-mund*, I take it?'

'Most are either to spice or sweets, not both. I am to spice.'

'Well I would dearly like to spice you right now. And sweet you too.'

Her smile dizzies him with its open loveliness, and the sun is calming on their arms and faces, a blessed late April day, even if the *Politiken* he leafed through earlier predicted snow and what the Danes call *Aprilsvejr*, April Weather, which runs the full spectrum of the four seasons in constant flux, practically from second to second.

Then they are served scrambled eggs and spiced cold sausage in slices, medium old cheese and melon with fresh sourdough and homebaked rye. The wine makes him remember the pleasures of their bodies, and he smiles dreamily at her.

'Did you really like them?' she asks. 'The paintings?'

'No. I lied. They're terrible. And you're lousy in the sack, too.'

'Couldn't be worse than you. And your prick is much too big by the way.'

'So're your tits.'

'Dax!'

They titillate themselves by scanning the personal page of *Politiken*, reading the ads for housefriends, lonely transvestites, sadomasochists looking for a long-term relationship, exhibitionists seeking voyeurs. Then they take up the tabloid, *Ekstra Bladet*, and turn to the massage ads: *Pussyclub kinky hot superbitch Susi, supersexed blond with big tits and a piquant butt carries out your special wishes. Everything in rubber, leather and plastic. Hot nude stripshow, gentle tingling bondage, pee cocktails, slave rearing, nurse sex, baby treatment, analblockage, long-term bondage, public humiliation, weights clips thumbtacks pins and handsmacking with a ruler!*

'Here's one,' she says, '*Suzette offers devil-bizarre sheep herding.*'

'*Sheep* herding?!'

'That's what it says. And, *Sissi, genuine red cunt hair and double D cups.*'

'Yeah,' he says, 'but how big's the rest?'

'How's this? *Kiss my foot while your wife watches!*'

'That's original.'

'I'm getting excited,' she says.

'Why? Would you like to kiss my foot while your wife watches?'

Her eyes blaze at him. '*Yes!*'

'Maybe we should just nip up to my place around the corner,' he suggests.

She nods toward the back. 'I just have to . . .'

'No playing with it now,' he says.

As he waits he gazes the whole length of *Wiedeweltsgade* to the glinting surface of the lake and refuses to worry about whether or not there is some responsibility issue involved here. They are both adults. You don't have to fall in love. There is no rule about that. He pours the last of the Alsatian bubbly into their glasses, pours a drop, lets it foam off, then fills the rest of the glass. The wine sparkles in the sunlight as a bank of silver, dark-bellied clouds glides in across the sky over the lake and rowhouses.

The waitress is there. 'I have to close the front,' she says. 'It's going to rain in.' Kerrigan sees a few round wet patches on the pavement as the day closes its caressing hand.

The light darkens and inside the restaurant he can hear the music of the sound system. Getz and Gilberto doing Antonio Carlos Jobim's *Corcovado*. He is still standing and she comes up from behind and embraces him. Something in him wants to tense, but he receives it, melts into it, into the moment, into the joy of a woman wanting to embrace him like this from behind, rejects worry about later. Until later.

27

Krut's Carport *(Kruts Karport)*

Kruts Karport
Øster Farimagsgade 12
2100 Kobenhavn Ø

God, I *love* it here,' she says afterwards, standing naked at the front windows of his apartment, gazing out onto the rippling silver lake beneath the young green of the chestnut trees. He watches her from behind where he still lies naked on the foam mattress they threw down there. His bed is too narrow for love. He watches her from behind, studies her objectively, wonders if the flaws actually matter – at their age. What would she see if I were at the window with my naked backside to her?

He is thinking about those strange advertisements they read in the tabloid to titillate themselves, and the present in which he exists seems suddenly like some weird science-fiction picture of the future in which the world is organized in a strange manner with certain people as an underbreed in which they are manipulated by economics to sell their bodies to others who live in another sphere where the repression of their carnality is required as an imagined requisite for social order. This carnal suppression, however, calls forth strange desires that they must use the money their asexual occupations accrue for them to buy satisfaction amidst the underbreed. He has a vision of some rich fat-cat executive who pays a large sum of cash to a street woman to piss on him. The thought is too weird for him to pursue just now.

He stretches luxuriously to free his mind of it. 'What shall we drink now?'

'There's jazz at Krut's,' she says and looks at her watch – the only thing she is wearing. 'Starts in about an hour.'

'Tick tick tick,' he says, remembering the magpie that woke him that morning about a hundred years ago. He hasn't been reading his *Finnegan*, despite his promises to himself that this time he really would. 'Just think,' he says. 'If a person's not careful, he could die without ever having finished *Finnegans Wake*. What can you tell me about Krut's?'

'It is a vonderful little place. They have one of the biggest selections of whiskies in Copenhagen, and the whiskey menu has a map so you can see exactly where what you're drinking is from. They also serve chile which you can eat if you're hungry enough. But if you really wish a vonderful meal, eat in *Brasseriet* just a few doors from Kruts. Delicious food!'

Wearing his spare glasses, he leads the way back across the Potato Rows to the café beneath the sign in blue neon script, *Krut's Karport*, where there is a warm-up group setting up already – banjo, drums and bass. Lettered across the skin of the bass drum are the words *Stevadore Stompers*. She tells him it is very unusual to have a warm-up group here. 'Perhaps they are celebrating something.'

'Perhaps they are celebrating *Frøken* Five-to-One. Miss Multi-O. You give new meaning to the *multi* in *multatuli*.'

Her smile is a piquant cross of annoyance and pleasure and sensual pride.

On one wall hangs a framed green and yellow poster-size reproduction of an absinthe label – Krut's Karport's own brand of the 68 per cent spirit – 136 proof. The label shows a man in a dented blue top hat, chin in hand at a table, a glass of the green spirits before him while a red-haired woman standing behind the table studies the bottle against a green-yellow impressionist wall.

Kerrigan asks a passing waiter, 'Isn't absinthe illegal?'

'This is the only place you can get it in Copenhagen,' he says. 'We have a special permit.'

'What does your starfish book have to say about absinthe?' he asks her.

'Say my name, and I shall tell you,' she says, her pouting lower lip provoking him gently.

'Your name? Seems I did hear. Think I have it somewhere on the papers from the employment bureau.'

'You bastard.'

He smiles. They are both enjoying this. 'Münter, I think, wasn't it? Isn't that German by the way? With an umlaut? Is it your own name or your husband's?'

'Why not ask if it is my father's name? In fact, it is my mother's name. After my father died, I took my mother's name.'

'Which presumably was *her* father's name?'

'No, she carried her mother's name, too. Beyond this, I do not know. It is not German. It is from Alsace.'

'I have an Alsatian connection, too.'

'So perhaps we are cousins. But you still have not said my first name. I vant to hear it on your breath.'

'Annelise,' he says and enjoys the naked pleasure of the smile with which she rewards him. 'Very good,' she says, opening her starfish book. 'Now I shall tell you about absinthe.'

'Yes.'

'Originally absinthe was 72 per cent alcohol, more of a demon than a spirit,' she tells him. It created considerable social misery in the nineteenth century in France. Edgar Degas's famous painting *L'Absinthe* – a woman seated at a rough café table at the Parisian *Café Nouvelle Athènes* in *Place Pigalle* with a glass of the drink in front of her, her eyes vacuous – is a kind of portrait of late nineteenth-century French alcoholism.

'Absinthe is believed to have been concocted by a Swiss woman, Madame Henriod, in the late eighteenth century. It was distilled on a base of wormwood (*artemisia absinthium*) and anise (*pimpinella anisum*) – spices which are known to date back to ancient Egypt, Greece and Arabia. In the middle ages, these spices were used to cure flatulence and also as an aphrodisiac.'

'Liquor is still quicker,' says Kerrigan.

'Madame Henriod's formula was sold to an itinerant doctor who dispensed it as a cure for bad stomachs. From him, the formula was sold to a Swiss military man, Major Dubied, who set up the first absinthe distillery with the assistance of his son-in-law, Henri-Louis Pernod. In 1805, they began production in France. Originally it was drunk by French foreign legionnaires in North Africa, both as a water purifier, but also a cure for weak intestines and of course for entertainment. Then they brought the habit home with them, and it caught on.

During the so-called *belle epoque* of *fin de siècle* France, it was drunk by pouring it over sugar cubes in a perforated spoon balanced on the mouth of the glass. One brand of absinthe – with the ironic name *Terminus* – was advertised by the great actress Sarah Bernhardt – perhaps in an attempt to recoup a bit of the entire fortune she lost in a Monaco casino, then failing to kill herself. And the President of the Republic – Sadi Carnot – actually allowed his name to be used in advertising another brand.'

'Boy that has got to be the nadir in political uncorrectness.'

'It was referred to as *la fée verte*, the green fairy, by the French poet Paul Verlaine (1844-1896) – who is also known for having shot Arthur Rimbaud, the anti-authoritarian young poet (1854-1891), in the wrist in a lover's quarrel in 1873, the year Rimbaud wrote his most famous work, *A Season in Hell*. He was only nineteen when he wrote that.'

Zola, Baudelaire, and Van Gogh drank it as well. Van Gogh is said to have been under its spell when he sliced off his ear. It is said Van Gogh was gone on absinthe when he sliced off his ear.

The French working classes also used absinthe to 'disarray their senses', but more to escape the harsh conditions of their lives than to court the muse. There would have been many natural subjects for Degas to choose for his famous painting, but it was in fact posed, by the model and actress Ellen Andrée – she was also used as a model by Manet and Renoir. The man beside her in the painting is another painter of the time, Marcellin Desboutin. It is not recorded whether Mlle Andrée spiced her performance with a taste of the green fairy.

A contemporary and friend of the impressionists, Emile Zola (1840-1902) also portrayed the sorrows of absinthe, but more as a symptom of the social misery behind it. His 1877 novel *L'Assommoir* (translated by A Symons in 1928 as *Drunkard*) portrays the dissolution of a family in the Paris slums.

As a result of works such as Degas's and Zola's, soon the green fairy acquired a new nickname – *le péril vert*, the green peril. By 1915, it was banned, but the law that banned it did not forbid other anise drinks which were free of wormwood. In 1922, a new law allowed the production of anise liquors of no more than 40 per cent; in 1938, this was raised to 45 per cent – ninety proof.

Here the current French national drink, *pastis*, entered the scene – not green, but yellow in color, and when diluted with water (five to one) it turns a milky hue. Similar in taste to the Greek ouzo, Spanish anesone and aquardiente, Italian anisette and sambucca, and the arak and raki of the Levan and Turkey; pastis is however stronger and less sweet than any of those. The French drink pastis as an *apéritif* or as an afternoon or evening café refreshment.

There are numerous brands of pastis – Berger, Casanis, Duval and other less known though sometimes superior varieties, even one known as *La Muse Verte* (The Green Muse) – but the two best known today are Ricard (of Marseille) and Pernod. In the 1970s, the two producers merged and now have 29 factories in France and 42 overseas. Pastis remains the French national drink: "*Un petit jaune, s'il vous plaît.*" A little yellow one, please.

Jake Barnes in Hemingway's *The Sun Also Rises* drinks absinthe straight, unsweetened, towards the end of that novel and describes the taste as 'pleasantly bitter', but the 'correct' way to drink it is by dripping water through a sugar cube into it. Some place ice over the sugar and when the ice has melted and dripped through the sugar into the liquor, it turns cloudy yellow with a brown film over the top. It has been known to cause hallucinations.

'Absinthe seems to be having something of a comeback in Spain, Portugal, the Czech Republic, and even England, but the wormwood used now is not *Artemisia absinthiun*, which is illegal, but *Artemisia vulgaris*, and the level of *thujune* – an hallucinogenic chemical – is very low. The alcohol content is still high, however,' she concluded.

'How in the name of God do you get all of that into that little notebook, Annelise?'

'My script is very fine,' she says and gazes sweetly at him. 'Terry,' she adds.

'Terrence, please.'

'To say a person's name is like a caress,' she says and touches his cheek. 'Terrence.'

'Shall we have a touch of the Green Peril?'

'I should prefer the Green Fairy.'

'Or the Green Muse.'

The drinks come in tiny measures, two centiliters. They taste it straight, but it is too bitter, so they dilute it with sugar and water. A woman at the table beside theirs enquires about it.

'Is that concentrated lime juice?' she asks.

'No,' says Kerrigan, 'it is the drink about which Oscar Wilde said the first makes you see things as you wish they were, the second as they are not, and the third as they really are, which is the most horrible thing in the world.'

'I don't know about that,' she says. They chat a bit and she tells them she just got back from a milieu project in Ethiopia where she got fleas in a hotel. 'I felt a tickle down below,' she says, 'and pulled up my night dress,' pantomiming how she did that, 'and there they were, I was filthy with them.'

She lays her palm flat on her nice flat tummy to indicate where they were, and Kerrigan says, 'Lucky fleas. Would you like a taste of the Green Peril?'

The woman declines, indicates her glass of what appears to be wine, but turns out to be grape juice. She drinks up and is gone.

'You scared her away,' says Annelise. 'Are you such a lech?'

'Yes.'

'You do have the leer of the sensualist about you.'

'Thank you. And let it be remembered that my subject is Celtic and my season spring.'

'She *was* cute,' says Annelise and their eyes meet as they smile, agreeing tacitly to say no more for now.

'One other thing about absinthe,' says Kerrigan. 'They drank it in Tom Kristensen's *Hærværk* in a variation known as the Blom cocktail, a kind of martini with four parts absinthe to one part gin. Must have kicked like a horse. I understand people were drinking absinthe here in Copenhagen right up to the 1950s when it was banned. And now it's back. To let you know. It can really shake it down.'

Kerrigan is about to begin singing 'Do You Love Me' by the Contours, but the Stevadore Stompers seem almost ready to play. Annelise, however, has more to tell him about Krut's. 'You know the man who owns this place, Peter Kjær, was shot down last winter in the park, over behind here, *Østre Anlæg* -East Park. He was walking his dog and some idiot came up and called it a faggot dog. They exchanged words and the man pulled out a gun and shot him in the stomach. Then he ran away and threw his pistol in the pond there, and it froze over so even though he turned himself in, the case could not be settled until the spring thaw.'

Kerrigan can feel the blood drain from his cheeks and can see it reflected in her face. 'It is okay,' she says. 'He survived. He is still recuperating, but he is okay.'

Excusing himself, Kerrigan retreats to the men's room, stands gazing at the open bowl, the tall darkened window behind it, the taste of anise on his tongue. Green peril and pistols in the park. He will not think of these things. He leans over the sink and douses his face with cold water, dries it with his handkerchief rather than try to shove his mug under the World Dryer. He hears the fingers of the Stevadore Stompers' banjo player begin to dance over the strings and focuses on that, feels himself returning to the present as he steps back out into the bar room, threading around the closely placed drum tables to his absinthe. He lifts the glass. '*Skål.*'

She returns the toast thoughtfully and touches the back of his hand.

The banjo player has long grey-yellow hair and a yellow-grey beard. In Danish he says, 'I'm prepared to sing our first number in German in case there are any German tourists present today.' The people at the tables snigger, the joke being that if any Germans *were* present they would be unable to understand what he was saying in Danish.

'I think we should take care of our German guests,' he goes on in Danish, 'since they took such good care of us a few years ago. For about five years I think, wasn't it? I was thinking about this just the other week – on 9 April in fact.'

'9 April was the date of the Nazi invasion in 1940,' Annelise whispers.

Kerrigan wonders if the man heard Annelise talking about Alsace, studies his face and guesses he would have been perhaps ten years old at the start of the German occupation in 1940, wonders what demons might live behind the mask of his light irony as the man strums the introduction to the song, saying 'This is written by a German, too – but after all it *is* pretty slow and boring,' and he begins to sing 'Just a Gigolo' in German.

The Stompers do a few numbers and are replaced by the regular group. The absinthe *is* vaguely psychedelic. Kerrigan orders another, though Annelise goes over to white wine. He leans back in his chair and gazes through the window behind Bjørn Holstein, the yellow-shirted drummer, at the long pale street. A child runs in the direction of the lake at the other end of the street beneath a few flurries of April snow. The snow turns to a slushy rain which ends almost as soon as it starts, and sunlight colors the grey buildings across the way.

With his glasses on, he feels pleasure in seeing every brick in the grey brown wall, and as Asger Rosenberg on bass behind Mogens Petersen on piano sings Benny Carter's 'When Lights Are Low', Kerrigan finds himself contemplating the bricks, thinking of the hands that laid brick on brick to construct the wall, the building, the entire city. Thinking of the hands that made the bricks themselves, the hands that drew the plans, the people who envisaged it all, led the work. Men driven by ambition, greed, passion, the desire to be part of the force that raised a block of dwellings, a street, a civlization.

And the soldiers who marched in under orders of a madman and seized it. About Peter Kjær, who got shot in East Park, and whoever the fool was who shot him and ran away after calling his dog a faggot.

Asger is now singing Frank Losser's 'I Wish I Didn't Love You So' – *I wish I didn't need your kiss/Why should your kiss torture me like this?*

Kerrigan is now into his third absinthe and his thoughts ride the music into their own flight of ideas, back to Annelise's Germany, his own Alsace, where his father's ancestor fled, driven from Ireland in the eighteenth century by the Penal Laws, which denied Catholics the rights of citizens. Kerrigan's ancestor fled with the Wild Geese, not a noble himself, but attached to a noble family, and ended in Baden Baden where *his* son's son, Fred, in 1869, under pressure of conscription in the Franco-Prussian Wars returned to Ireland and ended in Brooklyn in 1880, the year Maupassant (1850-1893) published his first story, *Boule de Suif*, Ball of Fat, the first of his stories which his godfather, Gustav Flaubert, who would die one year later, permitted him, on his deathbed, to publish.

The story, which would make Maupassant famous, was about the Franco-Prussian War, about a French prostitute, a hypocritical group of well-off French citizens and a wasp-waisted German commander who marches his troops into Tôtes, making the pavement resound under their hard rhythmic step, driving the inhabitants into their rooms, experiencing the fatal sensation 'produced each time the established order of things is overturned, when security no longer exists and all that protect the laws of man and of nature find themselves at the mercy of unreasoning, ferocious brutality'. The detachments rap at doors and enter the houses and occupy the town.

A small group of people use their influence to obtain permission to leave in a large diligence to flee to Dieppe where they can find safety. In the coach are a variety of people representing much of a cross section of French society, from a count down to the simple woman mentioned in the title, the eponymous *Boule de Suif*, a butterball, a chubby woman with a sensual mouth; the implication being that she is little more than a prostitute.

At first the others in the carriage shun her, but when their journey through the snowy fields proves much more arduous than expected, and they have gone more than half a day without food and no prospect of getting any, they discover that she is the only one who has thought to bring provisions, a well-filled food hamper beneath her seat. Distracted by hunger, one by one they condescend to accept her humbly offered hospitality. They gorge themselves on the delicacies she has packed – chickens, pâté, glacéd fruit, sweetmeats, wine, savories. In a few hours they eat food that could have lasted three days.

They come finally to Tôtes where they are to spend the night, but find that it is occupied by Prussians. The commandant, a tall slim wasp-waisted man, examines their credentials before they go to their rooms, and he calls aside the *Boule de Suif*. Elizabeth Rousset. He wants to sleep with her, but she refuses vehemently, and in the morning, they find that the diligence does not have permission to travel on. When they enquire why, the commandant replies simply, 'Because I do not wish it.'

Each day, he sends a servant to ask Mlle Rousset if she has changed her mind and each day she assures him she will *never* do so.

At first, her travelling companions are outraged, but soon think it over and tacitly agree to try to convince her to give the man that which she has so freely given so many others. They conspire to convince her it is her patriotic duty to do so and when with extreme reluctance she does give in, they gather in the dining room and drink champagne to celebrate their impending deliverance. All but one of them, Cornudet, a beer-swilling democrat. The others grow intoxicated and bawdy, tittering over what is being perpetrated in the rooms above. Only Cornudet reprimands them for their infamy, but after he has stomped off to bed, another of them who has a habit of spying on 'the secrets of the corridors,' tells them that two nights before, Cornudet had unsuccessfully propositioned

Boule de Suif, and the others resume their merriment, content that Cornudet's outrage has nothing to do with honor or infamy but with mere jealousy.

When the couples retire to their chambers, it is with a charge of passion stimulated by the act of prostitution that is delivering them.

In the morning, however, when *Boule de Suif* appears at the carriage which the commandant has now released, they turn their backs on her. And as the carriage continues toward Dieppe, this time it seems that she is the only one who has not thought to bring along provisions. The others dine on their store and ignore her, letting her go hungry while they stuff themselves.

Finally the rage she feels at this injustice forces silent tears to roll down her face, and one of the good wives mutters that she weeps with shame, while Cornudet plops his feet on the seat across from him and over and over again, with an expression of disdain for his company, whistles *The Marseillaise*, and his song and the sobs of *Boule de Suif* echo between the two rows of people in the shadows.

Asger leans over the piano squinting at the sheet music, singing: *In your eyes I see such strange things, but your kiss denies it's true . . .* And Kerrigan is a thousand kilometers south in his thoughts, a thousand west to Ireland, ten thousand west to the place he will not visit where his mother wandered through the house calling softly, 'Terry! Oh Ter-ry!' amidst the bloody corpses of his wife and children and siblings and their mates and children. Most amazing is that this incident hardly even made the national news in a country where mass murder is commonplace.

How still he feels. Perhaps it is the absinthe. The room seems frozen as he views its small movements from within the deep stillness in which he is engulfed, while 10,000 km away, Asger sings: *Kiss me once and kiss me twice and kiss me then once more. It's been a long long time . . .*

Her fingernails are long and polished a deep green he notices now as they lift slowly to caress the back of his neck. His eyes turn toward her, and she says quietly, 'Hey. You're not alone, Terrence.'

WEEK THREE
DAY FIVE
As Sane as I am

'We have a huge barrel of wine, but no cups.
That's fine with us. Every morning
We glow, and in the evening we glow again.
They say there is no future for us. That's right.
Which is fine with us. '

– Rumi

'Drink *all* your passion
and be a disgrace.
Close both eyes
To see with the other eye.'

– Rumi

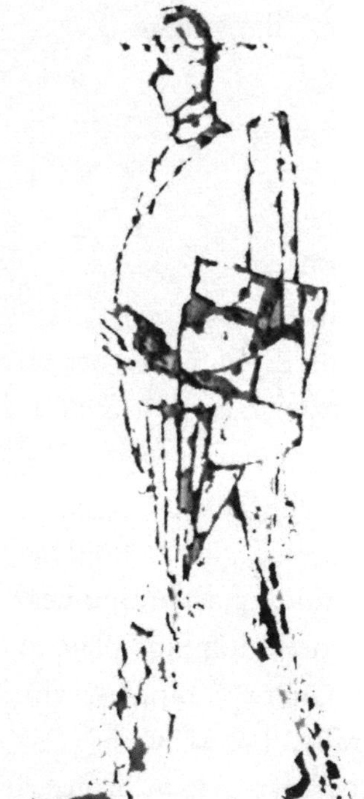

28

The Ditch *(Grøften)*

Grøften
Tivoli Gardens
Vesterbrogade *(West Bridge Street)* **3**
1630 København V

A long walk on a chillish spring morning chases demons. For a time. Unshaven but bathed, he hikes briskly, emerging from dreams of stolen gold and plundered churches, fleeing a fragment of memory that unnerves him. Away from the lakes towards *Strøget*, Walking Street, a mile-long pedestrian walk curving through the heart of Copenhagen.

At *Gammel Torv*, the old center, he pauses to consider *Caritas Springvand*, the Charity Fountain, Copenhagen's oldest surviving public monument, erected nearly four hundred years ago, between 1607 and 1609. A large round late-renaissance-style fountain, a pillar rising from the center on which stands Charity as the *Virgo Lactans* (in Danish *den diegivende jomfru*, literally the 'tit-giving virgin' – blessed be the paps you sucked!) Charity is holding a little child with a larger one beside, each holding a flaming heart, symbol of the love of God. At their feet, three dolphins play, and the fountain's water flows from the virgin Charity's nipples, which in Danish are known as *brystvorte* – literally, 'breast warts'.

This was cut in wood by Statius Otto, later cast in bronze by Peter Hoffmann of Elsinore.

Kerrigan thinks of a poem by the Irish poet Moya Cannon, 'Milk':

' . . . any stranger's baby
crying out loud in a street
can start the flow . . .
This is kindness
which in all our human time
has refused to learn propriety
which still knows nothing
but the depth of kinship
the depth of thirst.'

Kerrigan curses the tears the poem brings to his eyes, gazes upward at the overflowing nipples and remembers tasting his wife's sweet milk when his children were infants, all ended now as all stories. The thought whets the desire of his tongue for a drink of the Lethe waters known as beer.

He gazes across *Gammel Torv* to *Ny Torv* – old square to new square – toward the tall columns of the City Court (*Byretten*), built 1803-1816 by the architect C F Hansen. The building is tall and light, chiselled above the pillars in Danish are the words, *On Law a Land is Built* from the Danish Law of 1241. In the middle of the square is where executions used to be conducted, and off beyond the courthouse is *Slutterigade* (Prison Street) beneath the 'Bridge of Sighs', across which prisoners are led from jail to judgement.

At the end of *Slutterigade* is *Lavendelstræde* where Mozart's widow, Constanze, lived with her Danish husband, G N Nissen, from 1810 to 1821, marked with a plaque as such. Up the other way is Mojo Blues Bar at *Løngangsstræde* 21c, an excellent blues and dance club, but at this hour of day locked up tight. He heads down toward *Pilestræde*, Willow Street, to Charlie's Wine Room, but stands peering in through a locked front gate, not open till four. Some twenty years before, this was a bookshop owned by an Englishman named Charlie who was losing money on books so he turned it into a wine room which is still thriving, even after

Charlie's death, though its name and nature might be changed now that it is in new hands, recently purchased by another expatriate.

It is a narrow, deep cozy place where you can disappear at the back tables if you wish, or sit at the bar and find conversation. A favorite of expatriates – the Scottish artist, Martin Benson who has lived and worked for decades in Copenhagen, the British photographer, John Fowlie, the American David Grubb who once owned the Book Trader on *Skindergade* but left Copenhagen after the untimely death of his beautiful Danish-Norwegian partner, Bodil Bodkær Ness, a gifted textile artist, of whom Kerrigan has a striking photograph on a meter-long color strip tacked to his wall, the smiling barefoot weaver wearing a white nightdress. Kerrigan recalls once sitting beside her at the bar in Charlie's, ordering her a red wine and watching the elegant fingers of her hand take up the glass. 'You have beautiful hands, Bodil,' he said. 'Yes, I know,' she replied.

Kerrigan perfunctorily rattles the metal gate, turns away, up past the Bobi Bar at *Klareboderne* 14, where the literati drink, uncertain now what he wants. He doesn't want to drink with a bunch of writers, sitting and watching each other drink.

He thinks of Foley's Irish Pub at *Lille Kannikestræde* 3, owned by Mick Foley, an Irishman who used to tend bar in Woodside in Queens, New York, but if he goes into Foley's, he will be too tempted to have brunch, and he has a luncheon appointment in a short while with a Norwegian Valkyrie named Thea Ylajali and anyway is engaged now chasing demons.

He chases them out towards the King's Garden, enters the gate at *Brandes Plads*, with a nod to the bust of Georg Brandes, brother of Edvard who in 1885, having read the first 30-page fragment of Knut Hamsun's *Hunger*, correctly predicted for him a great literary future, though he could not know it would end in shame due to a combination of senility and nazi sentiments. He feels the blood pound furiously in his pumping legs. On a park bench someone has painted in white *St Fidelma Hear My Plea* across from the sculpture of *The Lion and the Horse* by Peter Husum from 1617, probably the second oldest surviving monument in Copenhagen.

It shows a lion sinking its teeth into the flank of a fallen horse trying ineffectually to bite the lion's mane. This was commissioned by King Christian IV who threatened to throw the sculptor in prison for taking so long on it. Christian IV had the emblem of a lion on his battle helmet, and the horse is meant to represent Duke Georg, whose helmet bore the emblem of a horse. Georg had apparently betrayed Christian during the Thirty Years War, even though he was Christian's nephew. Later, when Christian's son married Georg's daughter, Sophie Amalie, the statue stood outside the chapel where they were wed so that before and after the ceremony, she could glimpse this symbol of her husband's father felling this symbol of her own.

The discrete charm of Danish royalty.

Further on, Kerrigan passes Aksel Hansen's sculpture of *Echo* from 1888 – a realistic representation of the doomed nymph unable to express her love, able only to call out a repetition of the last word spoken to her. Her form is alert and distressed amidst the beech trees, and Kerrigan thinks of her vainly pursuing Narcissus himself doomed to love only his own reflection. Fleetingly he remembers the reflection of his mouse head in the mirror above Theodor's urinal, considers the fact that this ancient Greek myth is embodied here in this sculpture in a Danish public garden. Why? As a warning? Against being lost in oneself? He wonders if he will ever again open his heart to love. If he ever really has in the first place.

What is love really? Beyond passion, custom, tradition, social commitment? And with the question, a song ignites in his memory, Foreigner, 'I Want to Know What Love Is', which had been one of his dead wife's favorites. He can remember her face as she listened to it, the happy, dreamy longing of her eyes, and the emotion so terrifies him he feels he himself could be cast in stone by fear, trapped in it like Echo, like Narcissus, like a child hiding under a bed in terror of the unknown gods who drive the wind, the rain, hurl spears of lightning, rouse the boom of thunder.

His legs begin to tire, but he will not slow while the demons are after him. He leaves the park at a fast clip, cuts across the city and loops around *Dantesplads*, Dante's Place, named for the Italian poet, Dante Alighieri (1265-1321), on the occasion of the six-hundredth anniversary of his death 'so that the Danish people might strengthen their soul with Dante's spirit'.

From the center of the traffic island in the middle of H C Andersen's Boulevard rises *Dantesøjlen*, the Dante Pillar, sculpted by Einar Utzon-Frank. Atop the pillar stands not Dante Alighieri, but his beloved Beatrice, to whom he declared his love in the poem *Vita Nuova* (1292) and whom he sees again in paradise in *The Divine Comedy*. Beatrice Portinari, the wife of Simone de' Bardi (according to Boccacio; others say she was every pretty girl in Florence). Dante reports having first seen Beatrice when he was nine. Nine years later, she greeted him, and he was smitten with love for her, kept his love secret, and when she died, in 1290 at the age of 24, he turned for consolation to the *donna gentile* of philosophy.

In the paradise of *The Divine Comedy*, she guides him to the supreme bliss of contemplating God. Inscribed on the base of the pedestal are the words *Incipit Vita Nova*, here begins the new life, and on the ground a bronze medallion profile of Dante himself.

Kerrigan crosses to the opposite side of H C Andersens Boulevard, where a spotted yellow cat slinks through the wrought-iron bars of a fence, flank lean as all appetite and desire, and he wonders if he is lost in a dark wood of his life, far from the right road, wondering if his life will ever find a place for the true bliss of theological contemplation, if he even desires that. Where is he now in truth? Amidst the song of Augustine's cauldron of unholy loves in the Carthage of Copenhagen? Or in the proper place of mankind, the temporal joys of the carnal world, for the joy of the senses is wondrous indeed.

Perhaps, in truth, the mere desire for love, the yearning for God is all we can achieve on earth, the highest place. The question then is how to celebrate that desire, that yearning. Through rituals of blood and death and strife? Or through the enactment of ecstasy?

Passing the New Carlsberg Museum, *Glyptoteket*, he thinks of its beautiful indoor Winter Garden of palm trees and greenery, the central pool in the center of which reclines Kai Nielsen's marble sculpture *Vandmoderen*, the Water Mother – a beautiful naked woman acrawl with babies, one at each breast, others crawling up from the water onto her thighs, her belly, her flanks. He wishes to enter, to see her once again, but checks his watch -there is no time.

As he approaches the tall front ports of the Tivoli Gardens, he digs into his pocket to pay at the gate, pushes through the turnstile and releases his heart to the innocent worldly pleasures of this place.

Kerrigan flees to the Ditch, *Grøften*, and the company of his favorite headshrink, Thea Ylajali of Oslo, whom he met for the first time three years ago in Vigeland Park, strolling through the long sculpted esplanade of naked bronzes by Gustav Vigeland.

Now she sits across the table from him reading aloud the poetry of Constantine Cavafy (1863-1933) – specifically, a poem written 105 years before, 'The City': 'New places you shall never find, you'll not find other seas. The city shall follow you . . .'

Kerrigan responds with a quote of his own: 'Blessed are the paps which you have sucked.'

'Vhat is this?' she asks. 'Henry Miller?'

'It's Luke the Apostle. 9:27. *Blessed is the womb that bore you and the paps which you have sucked.*'

'Really? It says this in the Bible?'

'You bet!'

'Here's this,' she says, turning back to her book:

> 'When They Come Alive
> Try to keep them, poet,
> those erotic visions of yours . . .
> When they come alive in your mind
> at night or in the brightness of noon.'

It is bright noon, and Thea is six feet two inches tall, and she is in Copenhagen for only a few hours, a psychiatrist by profession.

He wishes to know whether she thinks he is mentally ill. He also wishes to know her carnally, to explore the heights and depths of her. She has the longest legs and shortest miniskirts he has ever witnessed, but there is no time for that now. She will board the boat back to Oslo in four hours and just as well.

He remembers an earlier adventure with her on the Oslo Boat, sailing across a storm-tossed Skagerrak back toward Copenhagen. They danced in the restaurant discotheque, gliding in a knot of people across the dance floor like some number choreographed by the pitching sea. It was to have been their night of carnal introduction – understood by the fact of their agreeing to share a cabin on the crossing. They danced slow, close, and a young drunken Norwegian kept tapping him on the shoulder to cut in, saying grandly, 'I vant to dance vith the voman,' so they retired to their sea-view cabin, but the pitching soon had them taking turns talking to God on the big white telephone on the wall above which was printed:

IT IS FORBIDDEN
TO THROW FOREIGN PARTICLES
IN THE WC BOWL

– as Kerrigan heaved into it everything he had inside him.

Somehow the crossing annulled all progress toward carnality in their friendship.

Now he only wants to talk to her, yet what he says is, 'Thea, have you ever considered the advantages of love with an older, shorter man?'

She blinks and smiles, unspeaking, over the edge of her modern Greek poetry and plate of smoked eel.

'Not a chance I guess,' he says.

'Do not be so sure of this,' she tells him, and the mouthful of smoked, peppered eel he chews goes straight to his brain with a jolt of optimisms. He lifts his glass, says, '*Multatuli*, Ylajali.'

'There is nothing wrong with you,' she tells him. 'You are . . . how shall I say it . . . groovy. Do they still say that? I could not bear a man who was not groovy.'

He has been telling her about his life, his project, his Associate, how last time they were together, following a hefty bout of love, clamped between her smooth sinewy legs, beneath her burning eyes and glinting teeth, he heard her whisper in the dark – or did he dream it? – 'God is a cunt.'

Kerrigan found himself not phoning again, or phoning with excuses (visitors, projects, business), fleeing in fear for his heart and other parts, but retreating to a perimeter from which he looked back, fearing the more he wants of the same.

God is a cunt, he thinks. *Shocking*. And wants nothing to do with anyone who would utter such an ungentille, offensive phrase. Although he is aware it might have emanated from the shadowy regions of his own mind. And he recognizes that the sentence can be read two ways – pejoratively or descriptively. Part of the new paradigm. The scepter replaced by the wheel of infinity. *Dio é una fica. Deus est kteis.*

'I wonder if we will become lovers today,' Thea says bemusedly, a forkful of eel hovering before her lips. Then she bites.

'Lovers?' he queries. 'I haven't even kissed your lovely arms yet.'

The sun shines through the branches of the overhanging trees across her lippy face, and he both desires and fears her, wondering if he should level with her there where they sit beneath an open-air display of miniature aviation balloons.

'This restaurant is groovy,' she tells him and flips a page in her book of poems.

'It used to be a hangout for the employees and musicians at the Pantomime Theater there next door,' he tells her.

In fact, built in 1874, it was originally known as the Theater Café. It is situated in a kind of ditch, just to the left past the peacock facade of the Pantomime Theater, on a slope which was, in fact, part of the original western moat protecting the city of Copenhagen. At first only a nickname, the Ditch stuck and displaced its original name. The balloon decor is in commemoration of the second manager of the Ditch, Lauritz Johansen, a famous balloon pilot. The restaurant is open all year, but is most lovely in the open air beneath the leaves on such a rare day of spring as this.

Kerrigan finishes the last heavenly morsel of his eel, convinced that it is nourishing mythological Celtic sectors of his soul as well as his body, and goes for the agéd cheese he has ordered, embellished with chopped onion, solidified meat drippings, radishes and a shot of Hansen's rum, a favorite among sailors. Cheese so old and strong it makes his gums ache.

'This requires a snaps,' he says and signals the waitress.

They toast with iced Norwegian Linje snaps (the 'e' pronounced as a long 'e' in English, the 'j' pronounced as an English 'y', the 'e' as an English 'a': Leenya). *Linje* is Scandinavian for equator; every drop of it is, by tradition, shipped across the equator in oak sherry kegs before bottling. It gives the aquavit a tawny tint and flavor at once spicey and mellow.

'*Skål*,' says Kerrigan and Thea reads,

> 'His chestnut eyes looking tired, dazed . . .
> he drifts aimlessly down the street,
> as though still hypnotized by the illicit pleasure,
> the very illicit pleasure that has just been his.
> . . . his blood – fresh and hot –
> is relished by sensual pleasure. His body is overcome
> by forbidden erotic ecstasy; and his young limbs
> give in to it completely. In this way a simple boy
> becomes something worth our looking at, for a moment
> the young sensualist, with blood fresh and hot.'

Kerrigan finds himself wondering whether she possesses sufficient knowledge of his background to make judgement on his mental state. Easy enough for her to pronounce him sane, knowing nothing of his day on the Palouse. And perhaps she herself is mad.

'Tell me your fantasies,' she says.

'I don't have to if I don't want.'

She laughs at his fear, producing in him a fantasy of himself naked and at her mercy as she prepares to devour his helpless flesh, laughing at his discomfiture. *God is a cunt. Dio é una fica.* You fica!

'I find it hard to relax,' he says.

'Relaxation is a wery much over-rated state,' she tells him and looks at her watch. 'By the way, a rhetorical question: how long does it take to get to your apartment from here?' she asks, smiling, blinking like a cat.

Afterwards he drifts in sweat-cooled sleep, her long naked body close beside him on his narrow electric bed, her voice hushed as she seeks to arouse him for yet another bout by telling him some of the fantasies reported to her by her patients.

'Isn't that unethical?' he asks.

'Not if I do not tell you the patient's name. Anonymous data.'

There is the dentist who dreams of being locked barefoot in an ankle stock, teasing female fingertips on the soles of his feet, at a time before public humilitation was frowned upon as inhumane; the circuit judge who sees himself on an operation table while half a dozen nuns confer around him about how to extract from him the sacred ambegris locked away inside his stones.

Kerrigan watches a red spider hanging in an invisible web on the other side of the window pane, twitching in the flow of air, limned in sunlight, and remains silent when Thea asks again about his own fantasties. He is thinking how it felt to have her sitting on him, her pillowy lips on his, his face between her thighs. What better fantasy than that? Smother me in your goddessness, three-personed cunt. Treble fica. Sweet female fig.

Her own favored fantasy, she tells him, is of sitting at her work table naked. It is very hot and she spreads her legs wide to air herself while unbeknownst to her a naked man creeps in the door on all fours, crawls silently across the room, beneath her desk . . .

Kerrigan's blood begins to stir. He goes to the refrigerator for a bottle of champagne, returns to her to drown his worry in it and her, thinking of Karen Blixen's advice to have a little bubbly with one's predicament.

At the gangway to the Oslo Boat, he kisses her. She has to lean down to his mouth. He says, 'My fantasy is to crawl up out of the water and climb the long blond legs of a beautiful blond giant Nordic woman . . .'

She laughs. 'You are as sane as I,' she tells him and is off up the sloping ramp, canvas overnighter on her shoulder, to return to her husband, a violin-maker who keeps two pet wolves.

'Aren't wolves dangerous?' he once asked her.

'So too are wiolins,' she replied.

At the top of the ramp she turns, waves, blows a kiss from her pillowy lips. *You are as sane as I*, he thinks. And *God is a cunt*. And, *IT IS FORBIDDEN TO THROW FOREIGN PARTICLES IN THE WC BOWL.*

29

Foley's Irish Pub

Foley's Irish Pub
Lille Kannikestræde *(Little Kannike Street)* **3**
1170 København K

Kerrigan stands in the center of the King's New Square, *Kongens Nytorv*, which is in fact a circle within a square, and wonders if he is pleased with himself. He thinks of Thea, tall and golden as the monolith of naked bodies at the heart of Vigeland Park in Oslo, the Wheel of Life, Gustav Vigeland's monument to existence. But his thoughts drift toward Gustav's brother, Emanuel Vigeland, and his monument to death, *Tomba Emanuelle*, at *Grimelundsveien* 8 in the *Slemdal* area of Oslo. Emanuel spent twenty years constructing his own mausoleum there, a vaulted churchlike structure, bricked-in windows, dark and echoing, black dimly illuminated walls painted with figures of copulating skeletons, women giving birth, skeletons giving birth, copulating sculptures barely visible in the dim corners.

He shivers.

Yet above the entry way is printed the Latin inscription: *Quicquid Deus creavit purum est.* All that God has created is pure. God who brings flowers and death. Sex and destruction.

At such a moment he might visit Sankt Ansgar's Church on

Bredgade, the Catholic cathedral in Copenhagen – a small and, Kerrigan thinks, holy place. But St Ansgar's, like most churches, is rarely open when he visits and when a man needs to visit a church he does not need to find a door that he cannot pull open.

Mick Foley's, however, is nearly always open when he visits.

To Foley's then, along the 750-year-old *Store Kannike Street*, past the residence of retired maidens, and into the sound-proofed bastion of contemporary Irish sound.

Stepping forth from the hindbar treads the eponymous Foley, Mick, short and gentle-faced, chin delicately bearded, wiping his mouth with two swipes of a folded handkerchief. Good Waterford man, not afraid to stand a round, once ran a raffle for two round-trip tickets to Dublin won by none other than Kerrigan himself at a Christmas shindig, proving the event was not fixed. Moral raffle.

He smiles in greeting, perhaps remembering Kerrigan as the guy who whenever he's in Dublin picks up the newest *Hot Press* for your man. Kerrigan happens to know a bit about Mick for it turned out one night when they were both into the Irish Mist boilermakers that Mick had lived for a time in Kerrigan's old hometown of Woodside, Queens, Long Island, New York – part of the barren wasteland mentioned by F Scott Fitzgerald in *The Great Gatsby* as Nick and Jay and Daisy motor past the billboard of eyes from West Egg toward Manhattan.

Many tales were exchanged that night, including one of Mick in his Woodside doorway while a black fellow held the snout of an automatic pistol to his temple and demanded his house keys.

'No fuckin' way,' said Mick, eyes downcast, gazing humbly at the floor, thumbs aligned with the creases of his casual slacks. 'But there is about 400 bob in the wallet in my hip pocket if you're in need of cash. Please leave me the ID if you would.'

'Shut the fuck up!' said the African-American robber while his colleague shifted from foot to foot, broad nostrils steaming uneasy Woodside winter air. They took the cash and flung the billfold back into Mick's face and didn't shoot him though they did leave him with a temple bone that twitches in response to atmospheric changes, right at the very spot where the pistol snout had touched it.

'How are ya?' enquires Mick who is not given to bandying people's names, perhaps for fear of getting it wrong, though he does remember that Kerrigan is a lager man. 'No mist today thanks,' says Kerrigan, unasked, by way of response, considering that he would rather not think about how he is, how Thea is, how his Associate is, how and who God is.

In the back room one Tom Donovan Goonery, sweating to die, climbs up against the not quite 200-year-old brick wall (circa 1814) and begins to slam his acoustic guitar, rendering one of his own compositions: 'The Thank You for Taking Care of My Morning Erection Blues.'

It seems to Kerrigan that Donovan puts all his life into his song; he hopes the man saves a bit for himself.

Mick Foley is drinking coke with a twist and, sensing perhaps that Kerrigan would rather listen than talk just now, tells him about the first establishment he ever managed, some 22 years before, when he was a lad of sixteen, hired by an uncle to help tend his family bar in Kilkee on the west coast, a clean and presentable place with music seven nights a week. The uncle, however, a farmer-auctioneer and part-time publican, had a habit of opening the till to count up the take under the customers' noses and pocketing handfuls of the receipts. One day he pocketed it all and disappeared, leaving behind a depleted, unpaid for stock.

Young Mick shot the troubles for him, struck a deal with the local beer alcoholics to clean the house each morning in return for the drink left over in glasses from the night before, reordered the stock COD with monthly payments on the outstanding debt. By the end of summer, the house was in order again, but Uncle Tom was back, counting cash in the till, and Mick left him to his fate. He took a job selling books for the *Messenger of the Sacred Heart*, run by the Jesuits on Leeson Street in Dublin, under one Jack Kennedy who promoted him from packing room to all-Ireland-save-Dublin representative of the *Heart*.

But the call of the publican's life had him. At the age of 21 he took a notion to up and cross the ocean to work construction and tend bar with his brother at McGovern's and Sallie O'Brien's in Woodside, both now alas defunct though thriving at the time. Young Mick banked a roll, happy 'till one of his best friends lost a game of Russian roulette in an after-hour's club.

At the back bar, Tom Donovan Goonery now is singing: 'That night in a house drinking Crowley's wine/The eyes of the old witch seek me . . .' while Mick tells how one night with a snootful of the Mist and a sack of White Castle hamburgers on his way home from a late shift and after-hours' session, beneath the Long Island Railroad trestle in Woodside, his Danish love told him she was in the family way and would be travelling home to Copenhagen to have the babe. Mick dropped his bag of burgers and thought of his own father who had left him with his mother at the age of six, and he knew he was going with her.

Tom Donovan sings, 'Dance to your Daddy/My little laddy/ Can you dance with the angels/That will teach you right from wrong . . .' and Kerrigan's pint is ready for replenishment as he listens to Goonery's music and refuses to think of his own gone progeny that he never dreamed he would outlive or of the Norwegian Valkyrie with whom he has just shared hot but unfulfilling love.

In Copenhagen, Mick was interviewed for a barman's spot by the Limerick woman who owned the Shamrock. Now a Waterford man tells the world what he can do while a Limerick woman is quiet by nature and suspicious of big talk. She took him on but as a temporary lounge boy, clearing empty glasses, no serving at the tables, please, you know?

Between that and a few other relocations and returns, New York again and Taillin in Estonia, a stint managing the Shamrock on his learned principles that what is required of a bar is that it be orderly and clean and well-supplied with stock and music, he opened the first Foley's where there once had been a bar named Ambrosia, now named Bloomsday on *Niels Hemmingsensgade*, just the other edge from here of Grey Friar's Square.

After two years at that location, Mick acquired with no little difficulty these premises and moved Foley's to this side of the Square.

Kerrigan is thinking of the principle of cleanliness, of the excellent Irish Ambassador Jim Sharkey who with his Asian wife once fed him a luncheon platter of the most succulent Irish lambchops, and of a Danish diplomat he met at a reception once who, on her way to a post in Dublin and mistaking Kerrigan's mid-Atlantic accent for British, bemoaned the fact that the Irish are dirty.

'But they do at least,' said Kerrigan to Ms Playplume, for that or something like that was her name, 'in contrast to the practice of Danish women from Gentofte . . .' (where she abided) ' . . . change their undergarments daily and wash with soap rather than scented waters.'

He deeply regretted the unfair and incorrect slur on Danish women who are as clean as the Danish summer day is long, but he could not resist the opportunity to enjoy the jagged music of Ms Playplume's startled giggle.

Goonery is now singing, 'Old brown shoes and carpet blues/and things you hide away . . .'

And Mick Foley built his house here in this building from 1862, itself constructed upon the ruin of a building bombed by the British in 1807, owned by various merchants, purveyors of cotton padding, wholesalers of thread, then an antique shop, and finally a public house, the Merry Rooster (*Den Muntrehane)*, owned by the Din family, who had acquired it via negotiations with the Lundeen Family, a member of whom took his own life in the upstairs rooms some quarter century before, possibly accounting for the moaning ghost reported to wander that floor on stormy nights.

'Never seen nor sensed him myself,' says Mick, 'though members of the staff tell me he is about and if he is there I believe he is concerned for the welfare of this building, so I welcome him, for we share a common cause.'

Here Foley's has been since December '96 through ups and downs, and with music most days by the best Irish musicians coming through Denmark and some fine Danish ones as well. The walls are of dark wood and the rooms are spacious, and at a table by the window, an amateur historian named Kristian Reich Wededge sits over a pint of the dark stuff thinking about the fates that bound his country of five million with the five million souls on the Irish isle.

Mick says, 'Why don't you come by Sunday night. We've some music and story telling as usual. We're soundproofed to 20 decibels so the retired ladies across the way can sleep in peace. I've given them my personal assurances.'

And into the bar walks Mick's Josephine, dark Irish woman from Derry, as Tom Donovan closes his set with Paddy Kavanagh's 'On Raglan Road':

> 'On a quiet street where old ghosts meet
> I see her walking now
> Away from me so hurriedly . . .'

And Kerrigan knows, as he tastes his third pint, that he must come up for a spell of air soon, and that air must be in Louis MacNeice's Dublin:

> 'Fort of the Dane
> Garrison of the Saxons
> Augustan Capital of a Gaelic Nation.'

30

Mansion Bar 4271 *(Palæ Bar 4271)*

Palæ Bar 4271
Ny Adelsgade *(New Nobility Street)* **5**
1104 København K

Out again from Foley's to wander, think.

Clouds drift overhead as he crosses *Kongens Nytorv*, green shadows on a damp afternoon in spring, and Kerrigan thinks about the fact that he has not washed away the remnants of the first two acts of love shared with Thea Ylajali. Coitus. Copulation. You are as sane as I, he thinks, wondering precisely how sane that might be, and enters the Palæ bar beneath the sign of the mermaid sipping a cocktail through a straw.

Years before, this was a bum-dive greasy-spoon coffee shop called Selandia – named for the island on which Copenhagen is situated. Since 1984, however, it has been a fine and noble establishment, worthy of the name of the street on which it stands, host to jazz and poetry readings by some of the best musicians and writers in Denmark. It also awards an annual prize of a not inconsiderable sum to a jazz artist who has distinguished him or herself by virtue of a contribution to the genre.

The bar has a subtitle as well – Palæ 4271 – which was the telephone number of the old Selandia in the days before automatic switchboards. You would dial 'Pa' and an operator would come on saying, 'Palae,' whereupon you would request the number.

The bar is already well-populated when Kerrigan enters. He orders a beer and finds an empty chair at a table facing the massive painting of a long, reclining nude – Goya-inspired or copied – which reminds him of Thea whose warm secreta has dried on him. It occurs to him that people carry many manner of secret around with them. And depression descends upon him as the voice of John Lennon warns him over the sound system that instant karma is going to slap him around the face if he doesn't join the human race.

This strikes him suddenly as funny, and his smile wanders toward the corner where a woman with a street-worn look sits over a basket of fresh roses. Instantly she rises, picks an amber rose from the bunch, and crosses to his table. He fumbles for some change, but she shoves his money hand away.

'It's because of your lovely smile,' she tells him, and tears spring to his eyes as he thanks her, breaks the stem from the rose and fits the bud into the lapel of his tweed jacket. The sweet scent fills his nostrils.

Now I am terrified of the earth, he thinks. It grows such sweet things out of such corruptions.

He thinks of Thea on the boat, thinks of laughing in the face of love, thinks of how incredibly sexy she looked naked and how incredibly sad he feels that he fucked her, wondering whether he is indeed insane. He wonders why the memory of her is more satisfying than the actual experience was. And he remembers that it was, in fact, Thea who introduced him to the principles of the Anal Triad, a psychotherapeutic index for the anal personality: excessive concern with money, with detail, with argument. Montblanc in hand he doodles on the paper coaster from beneath his beer:

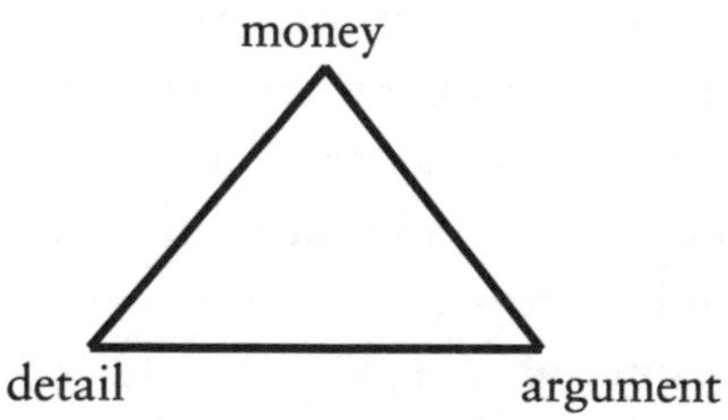

Gives it a subtitle: 'Anal Triad'.

Across the room from him sits a man who looks at your left pocket with his right eye, a description of the state of being cross-eyed that a Dutch friend once told him, and he smiles, but the smile goes sour. He is on his second pint and the bubbly buzz which had been settling begins to rise again into his stale mouth and takes the form of anger. Digging into his pocket for a coin he heads for the phone booth beside the door of the women's room, dials his Associate whose name, incredibly, he is unable to recall at this moment, even though her phone number is clear in his brain, a lapse which almost drives him to hang up in terror, but her voice is already in his ear, and he is already saying, 'Did you or did you not tell me that *God is a cunt*?'

'Easy boy,' she says, and he leans into the wall, knees buckling.

'Did you tell me that or not? It is important that I know.'

'Why?'

'Because.'

'Can't you take a joke?'

'No.' Then he adds, 'So you *did* say it? You have to understand. It is not the content that concerns me, only the fact of whether or not those words were spoken by you to me.'

'Come over and I'll tell you.'

'I can't. I have to go. But I need to know.'

'Where are you going?'

'Where? Why to the Velvet Room.'

'Vhat is that?'

'A kind of strip joint right up around the corner of New Nobility Street.'

'Mmmm. Take me vis you.'

'Why? So you can get a closer look at God?'

She laughs, and he does not know whether to be enraged or amused. 'Come on,' he pleads. 'Did you say it or not?'

'I can't remember. One says so many things. Have you ever been in the Welvet Room?'

'No,' he lies, remembering the time he was there with his Swedish millionaire friend, Morten Gideon, who sat with a bemused smile sipping very old malt whiskey while a very young angel-faced woman caressed his thigh and his neck, and the other time he went there all by himself, and another impossibly beautiful woman danced just for him, slowly undressing as she danced for him alone, then walked straight across the dance floor to where he sat and, with an abrupt flick of her head, whipped her long black hair across his cheek. Which almost cost him a thousand crowns for a bottle of champagne; the champagne only buys you the right to negotiate for what comes next at whatever further price is decided upon.

Gideon said, 'It's only fuckin' money, man,' but Kerrigan never paid for it in his life. Except that once when he couldn't even get it up. So he paid without even getting it. Which meant he could still brag that he never paid for it in his life.

A woman pushes past him to the toilet, and he sees a handful of familiar faces enter the bar, expatriates: an impecunious American who is an amateur mathemetician writing a book about the number '1', a Scottish painter whose specialty is abstract representations of burning forests, a moustached Brit who was once mistakenly arrested and incarcerated as the ringleader of a cocaine smuggling band, held in isolation for half a year until they discovered their mistake but, because he had been in possession of two joints, he could not take action. There are others as well, and Kerrigan can hear from the sound system that John Lennon is now singing 'Imagine' – a song that pisses him off: a billionaire doubting the general public's ability to imagine a situation where there is no money.

'Fucking fraud,' he says aloud.

'*What!*' His Associate asks into the phone.

'I wasn't talking to you.'

'Where are you? Who are you with?'

'I'm sorry, I have to go,' he says, observing with satisfaction all the sensory evocations that accompany taking the old-fashioned black plastic receiver from his ear and placing it with a click into the bifurcated cradle of the black pay phone. There is a click, a jangling of coins in a chute, even an aroma of chemical plastic and ear moisture. He removes the receiver again and holds it beneath his nostrils for another sniff. The woman's room door opens and the flower lady steps out, stopping for a moment to observe him.

'Are you smelling the phone?'

'Of course not.'

'I didn't think so.'

'You're as sane as I,' he says and tries to remember whether his Associate admitted to telling him God is a cunt. And another matter, it occurs to him, is whether or not the God she referred to began with a capital or lower case 'g'. If she said it, did she say it in English or Danish: *Gud er en kusse*. Or perhaps *Gud er en fisse*. The new Nordic feminists call themselves *Fisseflokken*. How to translate that? The Cunt Club? No. The Twat Pack? No. The Pussy Pack perhaps.

He lifts the receiver again, dials, hears her voice. He is sniffing at the plastic mouthpiece as he speaks into it. 'I really don't have time,' he says, 'I have to catch a plane so please tell me.'

'A plane to where?'

'Please!'

'I do not remember!'

Kerrigan hangs up and steps away from the telephone to allow a large round-headed man to use it while he watches a small automated doll with a curly black wig and gold jacket on a shelf above the front window play a toy saxophone as Gerry Mulligan on the sound system blows 'Lullaby of the Leaves' on his baritone, and Kerrigan hears the round-headed man on the phone order a taxi. 'For Olsen,' he says, as Kerrigan considers the fact that Mulligan on the sound system and the automated doll on the shelf are blowing a horn invented by the Belgian Antoine Sax, born 1814 (same year as P L Møller, model for Kierkegaard's *Seducer* one year after the Danish state went bankrupt and Kierkegaard himself was born), died 1894, whose portrait currently adorns the Belgian 200-franc note until it was to be abolished by the Euro.

A plan is taking form as he positions himself by the side bar glancing from the Hans Henrik Lerfeldt 'Chet Baker' with horn on the wall above a large early black-and-white portrait photo of Dexter Gordon with horn diagonally across from Sonny Rollins in red bent forward blowing his ax. Beside the front window is a 5ft wood sculpture of a sensuous woman bearing a bunch of wooden bananas and above her, from the ceiling, hangs an antique sousaphone. High on the wall opposite him is a green and black and grey and white abstract Lerfeldt nude and to the right a Billie Holiday and old tin signs announcing in Danish, 'Here are served all manner of beer and specialities, rolled sausage and meats minced and salted.' A very large orange kite in the form of a ray dangles from the ceiling, flanked by a tuba, and the plan is hatched. He lunges for the door.

DAYS SIX, SEVEN, EIGHT

INTERLUDE

A Foray into the Black Pool of Dubh Linn

'In this city aflood with beer and alive and aloud with festivity . . . from the aftermath of which one awakes disorientated and bleary-eyed and often unable to speak at all.'

– J P Donleavy, *The History of the Ginger Man*

'Whisky: It keepeth the reason from stifling.'

– Raphael Hollinshed, 1577

'It must always be remembered that his locale was Celtic and his season spring.'

– The Hon John M Woolsey, United States Vs. *Ulysses*

31

McDaid's

McDaid's
3 Harry Street *(off Grafton Street)*
Dublin 2, Ireland

It was the woman with the roses who created a distinct picture in his mind of Molly Malone, the 'Tart with the Cart', in her bronze infinity at the delta of Suffolk and Nassau and Grafton streets in Dublin, which made him know where he must go and no question in his mind.

He was even familiar with the flight schedule and saw by his watch there was just time, and a taxi idled on New Nobility Street as he stepped out of the Palæ Bar 4271. He opened its passenger door.

'Olsen?' the corpulent driver asked, turning in his seat.

'Yes. Kastrup, please. I've only 40 minutes to catch the last flight to Dublin. Can you make it?'

That everything meshed so perfectly was proof to him that this was meant to be – the taxi, the last flight, the fact that he had a 3,000-dollar credit line on his Diner's Club card, that huffing and puffing like a walrus, *kookookachoo!* he made it to the gate where a smiling green-clad Aer Lingus flight attendant who had been alerted from the ticket office and whose bewinged identity shield proclaimed her name to be Sheila Nageary, awaited him holding open the portal with both hands like a protective goddess above a church door, and said, 'You look like a man who needs a glass of champagne, Mr Kerrigan.'

Oh wonders of the business class!

The fact that a room was available at Trinity College, the very room he requested in Building 38 where J P Donleavy had had his rooms while studying science and conceiving *The Ginger Man* in the 1940s, then known under the title of *S D*, the initials of Sebastian Dangerfield, the eponymous *Ginger Man*, the fact that it was a balmy May evening, that McDaid's – established in 1779 – was not only open but that the outdoor tables were set up, and he sat there on Harry Street with a pint of the blackest black stuff contemplating the fact that in the story "Grace" in *Dubliners*, Joyce has the main character, Tom Kernan, fall down the stairs of this bar going down to the gent's, as a symbol of the fall from grace and a parody perhaps of Dante, although today the gent's is *up* a tricky couple of flights (especially tricky for a man in his cups) – *but!* in the fall, biting *off* a piece of his tongue so that he speaks indistinctly, thus falling not *into* but *from* language, in constrast to Joyce's theory of the fall from Grace being the development of language – all of this convinced him that God's plan, be God cunt or prick or something quite else, both perhaps, neither, whatever, that God's plan, small 'g' or large, was for him to be in Dublin at just this moment, and he felt certain the reason for this might reveal itself now or later or through some affiliation with an event of the past.

Considering the fact that he had read somewhere that Joyce's own father is said to have fallen down the stairs of this bar and bitten his tongue in the process, Kerrigan feels the sweat on his forehead, smells himself, and wonders what in the name of fuck he is doing here suddenly in a bar in a city on an island in the Atlantic when he is supposed to be in Copenhagen writing a book about *that* city's bars.

Yet he is by no means sorry to be in McDaid's at this very moment. Years ago, it is said, this bar was the city morgue, later converted to a chapel for the Moravian Brethren who were said to bury their dead standing up. The ceilings are high, he can see in through the door, the wood dark, the windows tall and gothic, and Kerrigan considering that Joyce's own father, John Stanislaus Joyce (1849-1931) was the person who in fact fell down the stairs here, contemplates how coincidental are the sources of our art, albeit touchingly so and considers how Joyce the son credits his father with an enormous amount of his material and ideas – the spit and image of *Ulysses*.

In the 1940s and 50s, this bar was a favorite haunt of Gainor Stephen Crist, American GI-bill expatriate from Ohio studying law at Trinity, to be driven to glory as the model of Sebastian Dangerfield in *The Ginger Man*, Donleavy's comic novel, although said Crist, broken by drink, would later wind up bad-mouthing the same Donleavy.

Brendan Behan, after his release from Borstal, drank and sang and roared here as, later, did Patrick Kavanagh, a segment of whose diary was featured in each issue of the 1950s Dublin literary journal *Envoy*, edited over the tables of McDaid's.

Could any of this explain his presence here? Yet there had already been other signs which he felt might decipher the reason. First of all, a postcard handed to him for no ostensible reason by a young woman with a stud on either side of her nose and black painted lips. Printed on the back of the card was:

> *Fierce talk*
> *Loose liquor*
> *Hard girls*
> *The Pre-HAM Social Transgressive Cabaret*
> *GRISTLE*
> *Entry £5*

On the obverse, however, the card said *Homo Action Movies for Butch Queers*, filling him in, so to speak, on the meaning of the acronym *HAM*, so he discarded, so to speak, the card.

Perhaps the meaning then is that you are in fact a homosexual butch queer faggot in disguise, he thought, but rather took comfort in his memory of the statement in some book by Norman Mailer, *The Prisoner of Sex* perhaps, that any man who proceeds to the fullness of adulthood with nary a homosexual interlude has earned the right without hesitation to describe himself as heterosexual.

Kerrigan remembers once, on safari in South Africa outside Kruger Park, a question over the campfire from the young ranger who had that very day saved his life, twice: once from a charging white rhino who the ranger and tracker frightened off with a combination of shouting, dancing and a well-aimed stone catapulted into the rhino's tender underbelly; and once from two slender and thus dangerously hungry young lions who crawled after them on their bellies out of the bush and the ranger got them away by organizing a full speed backward march. 'Never turn your back on 'em,' he whispered crisply over his shoulder, then added, 'But watch there's no hippos behind us in that dam!' That night in the mess tent over gin, the eyes of the jungle watching all around them, a black outline of an elephant walking quietly through the grass outside, the ranger said to Kerrigan, 'My name: Brendan? What do you know about it? I know that it is the name of an Irish poet because it was given me by an Irish nurse in the orphanage where I was born, but what I need to know is whether that Irish poet named Brendan was for women or was he for men? I've heard both stories and would like to know the fact of this.'

'Brendan Behan, no doubt,' said Kerrigan, since the ranger was born in 1964, the year of Behan's death. 'From what I have heard, he was a great man for the ladies,' said Kerrigan and refrained from mentioning the interview he once read that had been conducted by an American journalist who asked Behan pointblank, 'Are you bisexual?' 'Sir,' Behan replied, 'you are no gentleman.'

It seems to Kerrigan from a reading, for example, of Behan's story 'After the Wake', that the roaring poet covered both areas and perhaps easy enough to understand since he was imprisoned for revolutionary activities at the age of sixteen, and a sixteen-year-old in prison with men would likely by cunning and force be taught other manners of carnal interaction.

By which Kerrigan certainly means no slur upon the way of life of friends who love those of their own kind. It is said that Greeks and Arabs consider it most natural and certain monkies and rodents as well, though some animal psychologists describe it as a feature of the so-called 'behavioral sink' that results from urban overcrowding.

'Bollocks!' shouts a lad in the street speeding past on roller blades along Harry Street.

There were signs at Trinity College as well, one outside the main entrance said, *Cyclists Dismount.* And one in the shower, which Kerrigan had refrained from using, said, *After showering kindly remove hairs from the plumbing outlets.*

In the name of God's sacred teeth, Kerrigan thinks, did she or did she not utter that sentence, and if so, what quite did she mean, and why should it matter so?

Another sign in Trinity on the lead-netted window of the at-that-hour inaccessible doors of the Buttery breakfast room: *Notice: Video monitoring is in operation in this area. Pilferers will be severely dealt with.*

A smiling waitress steps out of the doorway of McDaid's and asks if he would be wishing another pint of the black stuff or any other thing.

'Do you think I ought?' he asks.

'A bird never flew on one wing,' she tells him.

'Another then,' he says and thinks, And yet another as a propeller on my tail, as he examines the ten-pound note with which he will pay. On its front is a green-toned portrait of James Joyce (1882-1941), jovial as C G Jung (1875-1961), whom in theory Kerrigan might have met until he was eighteen years old, who published a psychological analysis of *Ulysses*, by whom Joyce's wealthy American patronness Edith Rockefeller McCormick tried unsuccessfully to pay Joyce to be psychoanalyzed, and who unsuccessfully attempted to psychoanalyze Joyce's mentally ill daughter, Lucia (1907-1982).

Alongside Joyce's green portrait is a mountainous peninsula which, turned sideways, bears a striking resemblance to an erect phallus and powerful scrotum ('What did Molly have on her mind?' an Irish friend once asked, pointing this out to Kerrigan). On the obverse of the bill is a map of Dublin showing the Liffy and the face of Anna Livia and the first sentence of Joyce's *Finnegans Wake*: 'riverrun, past Eve and Adam's, from swerve of shore to bend of bay, brings us by a commodius vicus of recirculation back to Howth Castle and Environs.' *Central Bank of Ireland £10, Ten Pounds, © Central Bank of Ireland 1993.*

Kerrigan wonders if the Central Bank of Ireland has claimed copyright on Joyce even while he admires the irony of the fact that irish money depicts this great writer that was so hated here for so many years and did not set foot in Ireland for the last decades of his life.

Kerrigan is saddened to think, as he sits musing over the Joyce money, that in just over two years time, in accordance with international treaties, it will have become a collector's item, replaced along with the national currency of twelve other Member States of the European Union, by the nondescript 'Euro', whose notes would bear no writerly portraits.

The British ten-pound note, one of those not destined to give way to the Euro, depicts a yellow-tone Charles Dickens (1812-1870) and a cricket match scene from *The Pickwick Papers* (1836) (© *The Governor and Company of the Bank of England 1993*) with a portrait of Her Majesty Queen Elizabeth II on the front concerning whom a scandal recently erupted when the Governor of Australia was reported to have touched her royal back on a state visit.

The ten-pound Dickens, however, is about to be replaced by one bearing the portrait of Charles Darwin (1809-1882), dead the year Joyce was born, author of *The Origin of Species*, setting forth the theory of natural selection which is banned from being taught in five states of the American union.

Scottish five-pound notes, by turn, have depicted the authors Sir Walter Scott (1771-1832) and Robert Burns (1759-1796) with mouse in field on the obverse, commemorating his 1785 poem to a mouse from which John Steinbeck (1902-1968) took the title of his breakthrough novel: 'the best laid plans of mice and men/go oft awry'.

The 500-Finmark bill, which *will* give way to the Euro, depicts Elias Lönnrot (1802-1884), the Finnish physician-writer who was responsible for gathering the scatter of old epic fragments and lyric folk poems, wedding songs, magic incantations, and proverbial phrases, and welding them together with a few lines of his own into *The Kalevala*, the Finnish national epic. Lönnrot travelled to the far reaches of eastern Finland, especially Karelia (now part of Russia) to record and preserve the memorized words of the then still surviving oral poets. With Lönnrot's influence, Finnish was finally adopted as the second official language of Finland; previously, only Swedish had been recognized. Two parallel streets in central Helsinki are also named for Lönnrot and *The Kalevala*, and the Finnish national day is 28 February – the date in 1835 that Lönnrot put his signature to the foreword of *The Kalevala*. Finnish, of course, is now – thanks to Dr Lönnrot -the first language of Suomi, the Finnish name for Finland.

The Slovenian thousand-unit note portrays Francé Preseren (1800-1849), the first poet in the Slovenian tongue, as opposed to the prevailing German tongue. Like Joyce, Preseren was not admired by the state during his lifetime. He made the mistake of writing a 'wreath' of sonnets in honor of the upperclass woman he loved, identifying her by starting each line of one sonnet with a letter of her name, and he was rewarded by ostracism. But today he is celebrated as the Slovenian national poet and his poem,'A Toast', is the country's national anthem, the opening lines of which are engraved on the obverse of the 1000 denomination bill.

It interests Kerrigan to consider how poets have saved whole languages, helped them to emerge – Finnish, Slovenian – or preserved them – Danish – helped countries and peoples from being engulfed by the 'major' European languages, English, German, French, Spanish, Italian. Yet even French has only existed as a national language for a couple of hundred years, forced from above upon the many area dialects of the area now defined as France and protected by an Institute.

The Danish 50-crown bill depicts a purple-tone Karen Blixen aka Isak Dinesen, while the now discontinued Danish ten-crown bill bore the portrait of Hans Christian Andersen, and the so far still circulating French 50-franc bill depicts Antoine de Saint Exupéry along with a likeness of the Little Prince himself and the hat which is a snake that swallowed an elephant – all, alas, to be lost to the European treaty on monetary unity. Perhaps someday the faces of Henry Miller or Charles Bukowski or Nathaniel Hawthorne or Walt Whitman or Allen Ginsberg will grace American bank notes; now, however, they depict only presidents with the exception of Alexander Hamilton (1757-1804), who was Secretary of the Treasury, on the ten, and Benjamin Franklin (1706-1790), a man of many parts, on the 100 – whose annual *Poor Richard's Almanack* (1732-1758) had this to say about love: 'Where there is marriage without love, there will soon be love without marriage,' and this about cats: 'All cats are grey in the dark.' Granted Jefferson (1743-1826), Lincoln (1809-1865), and Franklin were also authors of note, but that seems not the reason that they adorn the twenty, five, and 100 respectively. George Washington (1732-99), on the single, owned 150 slaves, and Hamilton, on the 10, was an unsuccessful presidential candidate and died, like Ruskin, in a duel.

Ulysses S Grant (1822-1865), on the 50, was bankrupt and dying of mouth cancer when he wrote his memoirs – which were dictated and printed without revision, in hopes of generating income for his surviving family. That was in 1885, twenty years after the American Civil War he helped win for the north. His memoirs were highly praised by Gertrude Stein (1874-1946), though Gordon Weaver (b.1937) has said 'they would bore the balls off a brass monkey' and compares Stein's talent to that of Yoko Ono as founded upon 'groundless arrogance'.

Kerrigan has read only a few pages of Grant and likely will never read more, although he has read both of Lincoln's important addresses and was startled at his expression in the first of political indifference to slavery, although the Gettysburg Address brings tears to his eyes, as does Jefferson's magnificent 'Declaration of Independence'. He also greatly enjoyed Jefferson's take on the apparently dull, plodding and rancorous George Washington as well as his warm portrait of Benjamin Franklin.

Grant's real name was Hiram U Grant, but was changed accidentally at West Point. He was President from 1869 until 1877, his nickname was Lyss, and in 1885, dying, he met Mark Twain (1835-1910), who suggested – perhaps recognizing the shortness of time Grant had left – that he complete his memoirs by dictation, at which time, Kerrigan reflects, Joyce was three years old.

The waitress brings Kerrigan's stout and takes away his portrait of Joyce with its quote from *Finnegans Wake* which once again he realizes he is not succeeding in reading and no doubt never will, not least perhaps because there are so many obscure puns right from the first two words, 'river run', which play on the French '*reverons*' (let us dream) and '*riverain*' (one who lives by a river), facts he would likely never have discovered without a gloss.

Consider this Kerrigan: You will no doubt die never having read *Finnegans Wake*. Or *War and Peace*. Or Grant's *Memoirs*.

He sips his stout, thinks of all the things he will never be able to fit inside his head before it begins its process of decay and dessication, a skull full of dust. Skull-alone in a dark place.

32

Davy Byrnes

Davy Byrnes
No 21 Duke Street
Dublin 2, Ireland

Kerrigan's slow feet walk him down Harry to Grafton where yellow and white and red flowers fill the passage and a woman sits on a case awaiting customers. He steps over crunching matter on the pavement, left past Bewley's Oriental Café to Duke, right to the familiar wood and glass facade at No 21. Always changing color, it is currently painted gold, a licensed premise for 200 years, under its present name since 1889, Davy Byrne's Bar & Restaurant.

Here for the first time in the 1940s, J P (Mike) Donleavy met Brendan Behan, and because the American did not like what Behan called him, a narrowback (ie. one who has not worked with his body, living easy in the new world, although Kerrigan has also heard it defined as a reference to how narrow they had to be if they were to be crammed into the ships that carried them across the ocean), Donleavy offered either to thrash him in the bar or to do so outside on Duke Street. Duking it out on Duke Street, so to speak.

But outside, Behan – perhaps shrewdly recognizing that Donleavy was a skilled pugilist who had trained with a professional boxing coach – offered his hand in friendship instead: 'Ah, now why should the intelligent likes of us belt each other and fight just to please the bunch of them eegits back inside the pub who wouldn't have the guts to do it themselves.'

Kerrigan spent a few hours with Donleavy once, at his house in Mullingar, outside Dublin, a mansion which features in Joyce's *Stephen Hero*.

Donleavy was a gracious host, served a tray of bread and scones and cheeses and tea while feeding great hunks of peat into the pungent fire. The walls of the mansion were filled with Donleavy's art, the shelves of his library were filled with various editions of his books, the music rack of the grand piano displayed the sheet music for one of his own compositions. And Donleavy himself drove Kerrigan in a vintage automobile to the station to catch the last train back to Dublin and stood there to wave him off as the train pulled away.

Kerrigan does not like to think of the sadness that descended upon him in the train, for Donleavy was the great American literary hero of his early 20s, after he had come through Joyce and Camus and Dostoevski, and seeing Donleavy in the last year before his seventh decade, Kerrigan himself in the last year of his fifth, he felt that one of the great moments he had always dreamed about had been fulfilled, but none of the promise that had always seemed imminent in his life ever would be.

As unlike as he was to this legendary writer, he felt an intense kinship to him; yet how, he wondered, could Donleavy ever know of his own woes from the Palouse. And it did sadden him that Donleavy took such evident relish in singing tales of fisticuffs and broken jaws, jolly bar-room brawls, never mentioning the cracking of skull bones that occasionally results in partial, sometimes permanent, even total paralysis, toothlessness, and/or reduced vision or hearing. Kerrigan tended to blame this attitude on John Wayne who he believed to have been a secret *amant* of Rock Hudson. Ironic, it has always seemed to him, that the homosexual serial killer of many young American men in the state of Illinois was named John Wayne Garvey, while another man, castrated by his wife for abusing her, was John Wayne Bobbit, currently alleged to be making his living, with a reinstated organ, as an alphonse and sexual curiosity in the state of Nevada.

Donleavy did, however, express sorrow at the inadvertent punching out of the teeth of a woman in a brawl on the Isle of Man, an event later translated into an anecdote in *A Fairy Tale of New York* where the main character, Cornelius Christian, accidentally punches an eyeball out of the head of a woman in an east side New York bar-room brawl.

Kerrigan has a specific reason for thinking these thoughts at just this time in just this place, for years ago he had a friend named David (nicknamed Davie) Burnes, a classmate from St Bartholomew's School, sweet-natured and very strong, whose mother used to tie him naked to a pipe in the basement and lash him with a leather belt, and who one evening in his twenty-third year at the now defunct Friendly Tavern on Corona Avenue in Elmhurst, New York, in response to a young woman's refusal to allow him to buy her a drink, punched her in the nose, breaking it with an ugly cracking sound, a girl of seventeen.

Who could have known the history behind that action? The young man, with an Indian head tatoo on his 15-inch bicep, would find no sympathy at all in his predicament and no bubbly would help him out of it either, for all the drinks and all the drugs he would consume in the twenty or 25 years to follow would only lead him to an early, undistinguished grave.

Kerrigan still can see Davie's handsome face, his sandy hair, can hear his husky voice, can remember in December of the third grade how Sister Mary Alequoe had wrapped a cardboard box in chimney paper and cut a mail slot in the top and told the class they could use this as a postbox to send each other Christmas cards; next day Kerrigan came in with half a dozen cards of smiling Santas and thumpety-thump-thump footed snowmen to mail to his friends and to Cathy Cantwell with whom all the boys were tragically in love, and after he had deposited his Christmas letters in the cardboard slot, Davie Burnes approached to ask him, his grey eyes pleading, 'Was one of those for me. Please send me a card. I *have* to have at least one.'

Kerrigan sent him a Christmas card and continued to do so every year thereafter until the man died in his 40s, tortured in his dying as he had been through all his too few years of living, someone who never really wished ill on anyone but driven by demons from his mother's basement.

This Davy Byrnes at No 21, Duke Street has a bar patterned with the bottoms of many champagne bottles cemented there half a century ago. Champagne and fisticuffs seem so incongruous.

Kerrigan's own father, a man of song and lyric, admired those who were 'good with their dukes', but Kerrigan has never understood why men should wish to punch each other's faces. He had tried it a time or two himself, was moderately good at it as a lad, did enjoy the power that befell a boy unafraid to throw his clenched fist into the face of another boy, but when he was thirteen, after a particularly vicious fight one day with another boy named Vincent Teofilo, where the two of them rolled over desks, tore one another's hair, punched one another's lips and teeth and jaws and skulls and eyes, Kerrigan no longer wished to. He did not lose the fight, but he knew enough later to understand that Teofilo means *I love God*, and even if the will of God had embodied tooth and claw and the need for every living creature to ingest the tissue of other living creatures, animal or plant, he thought it was a bum rap, and he did not wish to cooperate unnecessarily with this system.

Maybe God *is* a cunt. In the pejorative sense. Or maybe God *should be* a cunt, instead of the *prick* He possibly is.

But what is the cunt but the entry to a hole within which life is nurtured and from which it emerges? And what is the breast if not the only human organ which can only nurture and can not be used to strike, or fire a projectile, or cause any manner of pain other than the sweet agony of longing?

And what is a prick? Model of the spear, arrow, club, gun, bullet, missile, penetrating projectile of life and death.

> 'It happens that I am tired of being a man
> I do not want to go on being a root in the dark,
> hesitating, stretched out, shivering with dreams . . .
> It would be beautiful
> to go through the streets with a green knife
> shouting until I died of cold.'

The words are Neruda's, but Kerrigan thinks of his mother's gun. David Burne's mother's belt. Recalls a sketch by Emanuel Vigeland of a naked woman with a skull between her thighs. The fangs and voracious tongue of Kali. The inscrutable smile of Sheelanagig, exposing the entry to her womb.

Kerrigan contemplates the pie-sized sculpted medallion he saw of Sheela in the window of a shop on South Great George's St. It depicted the mysterious Celtic exhibitionist goddess whose image is found hidden away in nooks and corners of certain Christian churches in Ireland and England. The stylized image of a woman holding apart her labia, her eyes and mouth bemused, almost moronic.

Within your stony nook you lurk
In acrobatic pose.
You leer, you watch, and open jerk
The petals of your rose.
Come in, you breathe, come into me.
My cunt is what you crave.
The little death is yours for free,
As is the cold, cold grave.

This is not always a pretty world, he thinks, and at the bar orders a pint of the lovely black stuff. On a shelf behind the bar stands a bottle of Irish vodka – Boru – named for the first king of a United Ireland, Brian Boru, who routed the Vikings in the eleventh century, whose father was Kennedy, and who was stabbed in the back by a Dane while praying during Holy Week, a sanctified death to which Hamlet refused to deliver his uncle, slayer of his father.

Beside him now a leather-jacketted man with a flowered necktie, squat-nosed, sits scowling over a pint of lager. And beside him, a tall businessman in dark suit, legs crossed, munches a sandwich and reads *The Irish Times*, open on his lap. A white-haired man at the drum table by the wall, ruddy-faced, burgundy-sweatered, lifts an empty pint glass silently above his head and jerks it toward the bar. *More!* Ignored. *More!*

Three middle-aged women in flowered dresses, seated on an upholstered bench at a table, eat plates of ham and mustard.

Kerrigan orders half a dozen rock oysters, and the barman says, 'Ah, I wouldn't eat the rock oysters.'

'They're usually brilliant,' says Kerrigan.

'They are that, yes, usually.'

'The salmon then.'

'Now I'm your honest barman. You wouldn't want the salmon at this hour.'

'The cheese platter?'

'The cheese platter would be agreeable,' he says and when he has served it, 'Enjoy it now, there's a good stilton,' and 'Thank you very much indeed.'

Kerrigan wonders if this red-haired barman would ever seek to punch his face should he be angered by him for some reason. He himself would never wish to punch that honest barman's freckled puss.

On the ceiling are art deco lamps shaped like tulip bulbs. A stained glass door the same colors as the painted flowers in the ceiling recesses. The white-haired man, cane between his knees, jerks his empty glass aloft again. *More!*

There is an air of people enjoying themselves, pleased to be there, even those sitting alone unsmiling. As if reading Kerrigan's thoughts, a woman at a table behind him says in Danish to her companion, 'I recognize something here. Maybe Denmark used to be like this. Maybe I recognize something here we've lost.'

Across the street, through the front window, Kerrigan can see The Baily at No's 2 and 3, from which Mr Leopold Bloom on 16 June 1904, in the Dublin of James Joyce's *Ulysses* retreated in disgust from the gobbling pub-grubbing faces to dine on burgundy and blue cheese which Kerrigan eats now, 95 years later:

> 'He entered Davy Byrne's. Moral pub. He doesn't chat. Stands a drink now and then. Cashed a cheque for me once. Davy Byrne came forward from the hindbar in tuck-stitched shirt-sleeves, cleaning his lips with two wipes of

> his napkin . . . Mr Bloom ate his strips of sandwich, fresh clean bread, with relish of disgust, pungent mustard, the feety savour of green cheese. Sips of his wine soothed his palate . . . Nice quiet bar. Nice piece of wood in that counter. Nicely planed. Like the way it curves there.'

On the walls, painted murals of smiling people in a dark wood over a bright beach behind a light mountain – painted, Kerrigan knows, by the father-in-law of Brendan Behan.

Joyce drank here, too. And across the street in the Duke where he and James Stephens had their first meeting. The Duke was then called Kennedy's, and Stephens invited Joyce in for a tailor of malt whereupon, according to Stephens, Joyce confided that he had read the two books Stephens at that time had published, pronouncing that Stephens did not know the difference between a semi-colon and a colon, that his knowledge of Irish life was non-Catholic and so non-existent, and that he should give up writing and take a good job like shoe-shining as a more promising profession.

Stephens claimed to have responded that he had never read a word of Joyce's and that, if Heaven preserved to him his protective wits, he never would read a word of his unless he was asked to review it destructively. Yet years later, in 1927, when Joyce was near despair over the negative critique of the bits of *Finnegans Wake* he had so far published under the title *Work in Progress*, he is said to have toyed with the idea of inviting Stephens to complete the book for him.

Stephens was born in 1882, the same year as James Joyce and Franklin Delano Roosevelt, seven years before Adolph Hitler, the year Charles Darwin died. Joyce died in 1941, FDR and Hitler in 1945, and Stephens in 1950, at the respective ages of 59, 63, 56, and 68; Hitler's life the shortest of the four. Stephens had been one of Kerrigan's father's favorite poets, especially the poem he had read aloud to young Terrence on frequent occasions about a rabbit caught in a snare whom the narrator of the poem can hear crying out in pain, but he can not find him even though he is searching everywhere. Rumi, the thirteenth-century Persian poet, his real name Jalâl al-Dîn (1207-73), born in north Afghanistan, wrote a similar poem about the helpers of the world who, ' . . . like Mercy itself . . . run toward the screaming . . .' because they hear helplessness.

Kerrigan smokes a cigar thinking of this and of the other poets and writers who congregated here in Davy Byrnes – Flann O'Brien aka Brian Nolan aka Myles na gCopaleen, Anthony Cronin, Brendan Behan, J P Donleavy, and Patrick Kavanagh, not to forget Michael Collins himself, 'the big fellow,' as Minister of Finance of the Irish government, throughout the War of Independence, which held regular meetings in the upstairs room.

The old man jerks his pint up once again. *More!*

This time the response is immediate. A fresh pint of Guinness before him, cane between his knees, he surveys the room like an Irish king.

Kerrigan nods with respect and moves out into the May night.

Through the gates of Trinity (*Cyclists Dismount*), he treads across the cobblestones to Building 38 where, watching himself in the mirrors brush his brownish pearly whites, he fears sleep, recognizing that he will die someday, that he may die in bed feeling sweaty and alone beneath an overwarm blanket, knowing he is going far away and not a friend in sight to understand this journey, the awareness of which we all block out as long as we can, an ending which, though known, comes always as a surprise we secretly believe we might be exempt from simply because of the very special nature of being one's own unconditionally self-beloved self.

If there were a phone in this room, he would call his Associate and berate her, make her pay for his unhappiness for no reason other than that he suspects she would allow him to do so because of her apparently great heart.

For a moment he thinks he loves her and will propose marriage, but quickly dismisses the thought, knowing that it would involve other people, too, her daughters, witnesses, officials. In any event, marriage will do nothing to alleviate this pinpoint of fear of death. It is all illusion, delusion, and the job of human beings is to maintain that delusion in order to enjoy themselves and accomplish their work upon this earth: to live and be happy and love the heady liquor of drinking the air.

Because he can not face the task of removing his hairs from the plumbing fixtures, he plops still unwashed onto the bed in his skivvies, considering how Thea's fragrance will still be there somewhere yet, probably stale now, and even as he reaches for himself, he is off in a land where drink is dust and meat is clay, and his father waves from a distant shore, smaller now, but glad of face as Kerrigan calls out, 'Dad! Dad! Come over for a pint!'

And this is the house where people sit in darkness; dust is their drink and clay their meat. They are clothed like birds with wings for covering, they see no light, they sit in darkness . . . the house of dust.

33

The Waterloo

The Waterloo
38 Upper Baggot Street
Dublin 2, Ireland

34

Searson's

Searson's
42-44 Upper Baggot Street
Dublin 2, Ireland

Ireland has a standing army of 5,000 poets, Patrick Kavanagh once said, though the Irish do not, he asserted, give a fart in their corduroys for culture.

And near as many pubs or more, Kerrigan cannot but think, setting off to visit some of Kavanagh's old haunts, having dreamt inter alia of his own father waving from across the river – his father who had read him Kavanagh's 'The Great Hunger' years before Kerrigan was capable of appreciating more than the wonder of its language: 'He was suspicious in youth as a rat near strange bread when women laughed.'

But first he visits St Andrew's Church to light candles for the dead, kneels in a pew to which is affixed a plaque that says, *Pray for the souls of John and Eliza D'Arcy.*

Instead of praying for the D'Arcys, Kerrigan finds himself, eyelids lowered, remembering a dream in which he rode in a wagon with J P Donleavy, tickling the hairy calf of a Dane who sat cross-legged drinking in a pub. Later, in the Buttery, someone touched Kerrigan's shoulder and he leapt to his feet to greet an eyeless ghost-faced man who said, 'I want you to speak at Natal.' Still later there was a tall red-headed man, a giant really, looking down on Kerrigan in his bed at Trinity; the giant said, 'How good to see you smiling again.' The man's torso was naked and pale as his face but atop his head was a patch of carrot-red hair. Kerrigan pointed up at him and said, 'You! I know you! I've seen you a thousand times in Copenhagen!'

But the man shook his head, smiling mystically. 'No,' he said. 'I'm a Celt.'

'Your people,' Kerrigan said, 'are all turning into animals.'

'Ah, yes, but then will come the angels,' the giant bare-chested redhead replied. 'Seven times seven of them!'

Kerrigan retreats from the church and stops at Sweny's Chemist shop, No 1 Lincoln Place, where he sniffs a bar of lemon-soap, thinking of Bloom buying one of these for Molly, even as he knew she was preparing to cheat on him with Blazes Boylon. He hands over another of his Joyce tens, receives a bar wrapped in tissue paper and stores it in his hip pocket in honor of Poldy, poor peaceful cuckold Jew.

'Is it for herself?' asks the sweet elderly lady with a twinkle behind the ancient wooden desk, and Kerrigan smiles, nods, steps out to note that what used to be called Kennedy's public house across the street, mentioned by name in Beckett and Joyce, is now called Fitzsimmons, the name of a New York policeman who used to plague him and his teenaged friends in the 50s. And down across from the Davenport Hotel, where Kerrigan once ate calf kidneys in a sauce of Irish whiskey, is a pub called The Ginger Man (which could not be very old), where he is briefly tempted by the shepherd's pie offered in chalk on a blackboard outside the door.

He strolls north a block toward Merrion Square, past the birthplace of Oscar Wilde at No 1, who died in 1900, same year Nietzche died and Thomas Wolfe was born, Joseph Conrad's *Lord Jim* appeared, and Joyce's first piece of writing, 'Ibsen's New

Drama,' was published, a review of Ibsen's last play, *When We Dead Awaken* (1899):

> 'We only see what we have missed
> When we dead awaken.
> And what then do we see?
> We see that we have never lived.'

Thinking of the Grand Café in Oslo where a corner table is perennielly set for Ibsen, of Ibsen's play, *An Enemy of the People*, published the same year Joyce was born, the quintessential modern play about the wilful poisoning of the environment for profit, he pauses to look at the door of No 82 where Yeats spent six years, No 84 where AE (George Russell) wrote *Voices from the Stone* that Kerrigan's father so loved:

> 'Uncover: bend the head
> And let the feet be bare;
> This air that thou breathest
> Is holy air
> Sin not against the breath . . .'

– Come back across the river, Dad! Just for a little!
– Can't, son! Can't!
– It's all right then, Dad.

And J P Donleavy reported receiving a letter signed AE in 1957 in which the letter writer suggested that *The Ginger Man* made men worse than brutes, poisoned the minds of children, dragged the Saviour's name in the mud. 'The Holy Name of Jesus,' he wrote, 'belongs to a Person who will judge you soon.'

Donleavy called it his first ever fan letter. Kerrigan ponders what narrowness of thought might lie behind the need to react with so many capital letters and is saddened. Yet gladdened again to remember his discovery that this AE of the 1957 blue-nosed fan letter could not be the AE his father so admired for that AE shuffled off the coil 23 years before, in 1934, at the age of 68, having repented of his initial dismissiveness of Joyce's *Ulysses*.

'And there's no use giving you my name,' the bogus AE declared, signing only with those two letters.

Sin not against the breath.

And what else is poetry but a struggle for breath, a column of breath, the spirit jet upon which the soul conveys its desire and its wisdom?

He mounts the steps at No 96 to gaze upward at the little top floor flat where he once visited Theo Dorgan and Paula Meehan, a fine young couple of poets who fed him good Irish whiskey in generous quantity and did their best to make him feel respected and admired as they seemed to have surmised he needed badly to feel that. Salt tears blur his vision, and he fears the whole world sees him as an ageing fool to be humored, a fear he refuses to entertain, marching on to Grand Canal to look at the door with the fox head knocker at 33 Haddington Road, one of Patrick Kavanagh's many south side residences, a poor place with a tiny broken door pane, and Kerrigan asks aloud, 'Who bent the coin of my destiny that it sticks in the slot?'

He almost expects an answer, but fears it would be a rude one – *You pampered sniveller!* – and lets his oxblood-shod feet trot him past Parson's Bookshop, now a sundries store, and down to the Waterloo and Searson's on Upper Baggot Street. Not certain which one to visit for a pint, he visits each for a glass, finds himself mumbling into the second, 'I don't care if you don't like me, Paddy. I like you all the same.' Which causes two persons at the bar to look with surreptitious deadpans his way. 'Of course, who's saying?' he adds. 'Maybe you do like me.' And I'm not the only one in Dublin talking to himself, thinks Kerrigan, who has seen several already in protracted conversation with themselves.

But takes his leave all the same and crosses to the Canal where he sits on the bench of Patrick Kavanagh, dead in '67 at 62:

'O commemorate me where there is water . . .
Where by a lock Niagriously roars
The falls for those who sit in the tremendous
silence . . .
A swan goes by head low with many apologies
Fantastic light looks through the eyes of bridges . . .'

Then he crosses the lock to the other side and sits on the bench of Percy French, dead in 1920 at the age of 66:

'Remember me is all I ask
and yet
If the remembrance proves a task
forget.'

Kerrigan's childhood was full of the words of Percy French, carried on his father's gravelly breath:

'But her beauty made us all too shy
Divil a man among us
Would look her in the eye
Boys, oh, boys!
And that's the reason why
We're mournin' for the Pride of Petroval.
Boys, oh, boys! Hear me when I say,
When you do your courtin'
Make no mistake
If you want them to come after you
Then look the other way . . .'

– Come back across the river, Dad! Just for an hour! Sing one of the old songs.

– Can't, son! Can't!

– It's all right then, Dad.

Then he thinks of Odin's wiser Danish words: 'Remember to praise the body of the radiant woman. He who praises, gets.'

He considers this philosophical disagreement between Percy French and Odin and chuckles and walks along the Canal to another bench, this one made of bronze and fitted with a long-legged, rumple-suited, life-sized bronze of Kavanagh himself, arms crossed, legs crossed, staring through his bronze glasses into the real water of the Canal, crumpled bronze hat on the bronze bench beside him.

Kerrigan sits and imitates the poet's stance, speaks from the corner of his mouth, 'Your poetry sustains me, Paddy.'

– You've taste enough.

'You know I was *almost* a poet myself, Paddy.'

– Have you ever got a fag.

Kerrigan places a Sumatra in the crook of the poet's crumpled hat and heads north again.

35

Toner's

Toner's
139 Lower Baggott Street (at Roger's Lane)
Dublin 2, Ireland

Stopping at Toner's on Lower Baggott to take a pee, he first establishes his presence with a drop of the *craythur* at the bar, a small potcheen.

'It's not the real stuff you know,' says the barman. 'If you want the real stuff you have to ask the Garda, they've confiscated itall.'

Up in the gent's a very small boy stands at the trough and says over his shoulder to a man at the sinks, 'I can't, Dad.'

'It's all right then,' says the boy's father. 'I'll lift you up.'

'I *can't*, Dad.'

'All right then, let's zip you and go wash your hands.'

Real or not the potcheen craythur, Bunratty by name, pleases him and he orders a glass downstairs and mulls over the story about Yeats in this very public house. Pubs were said to be the rage among poets at the time, as if they weren't always, and it is said that Yeats asked his friend Oliver St John Gogarty (1878-1957) to show him a pub. Gogarty took him to Toner's where Yeats ordered a sherry which he drank in silence, ignoring the noisy life around him, then said to Gogarty, 'I have seen a pub. Will you kindly take me home.'

But as Peter Costello points out, this story is more likely a slur by the envious – what Donleavy referred to as the Irish bedgrudgers with 'a smile on their lips but not in their hearts'. Or, as Kerrigan himself has noted: They are always telling jokes, but how often do you see them laugh. Costello mentions that Yeats was a frequenter of pubs in the 1890s and was by no means so delicate as that, had in fact been one of the first to experiment with mescalin, imported by Havelock Ellis from Mexico in 1894, when Joyce was twelve. Oscar Wilde, says Costello, was the one who avoided public houses. And Wilde is generally known as a lover of his own sex, less known as a husband and father of two sons, whose wife changed their names when Oscar was thrown in Reading Gaol for publicly expressing, with the encouragement of his time, the love that dare not say its name, and wound up in exile, dead, buried in Père Lachaise in Paris where many a writer lies, skull full of dust.

Kerrigan thinks about Yeats and the mescalin, 105 years before. Kerrigan never ate the organic stuff but did try its chemical synthetic a time or three, can recall standing on a cliff over the Pacific in Ocean Beach, San Diego, 33 years before, watching the sea crash on the sandstone in a wild splash of electric color, droplets of red and blue and violet flying up into the moonlit evening. He remembers lying on the floor of an adobe cottage with a young woman wearing jeans and nothing else, his fingers on the denim at the fork of her thighs projecting images upon the ceiling of writhing blissful bodies in embrace which in some mysterious way they *both* claimed to have witnessed. And he can remember convincing himself that, since his body was composed of atoms in movement and the door was composed of atoms in movement, if he would only move purposefully and with true belief, there was no need to open the door, for his atoms could slip right through the spaces between the door atoms. The trick was to do it quickly, not to get welded in there. And he did that.

His painful bloodied beak brought him back to earth fast and ended his psychopharmaceutical experiments forever.

One small Bunratty more has him thinking about Gogarty, after whom a pub is now named over near The Temple Bar. More than that was named for Gogarty – Goggins in *Stephen Hero* and Robert Hand in *Exiles*, and the opening figure of 'Stately plump Buck Mulligan' in *Ulysses* is another. A poet, physician and politician, his poetry is said to have been overrated, in his lifetime, by Yeats who gave him disproportionate space when editing *The Oxford Book of Modern Verse*. A friend of AE, he died, after eighteen years as an expatriate in the U S, at 79 in 1957, the year of the greatest of Chevies, the same year the bogus AE wrote his message of capital letters to Donleavy, promising him that he would soon be judged by the Saviour.

Of the many books Kerrigan has lugged around the world with him in three steamer chests, none but one contain anything of Gogarty's – and that one is an anthology of verse by physicians, published by the British Medical Association, in which two brief poems from the Yeats Oxford anthology are included, neither of much merit. And in his immense and comprehensive tome *Inventing Ireland*, Declan Kiberd has but a single reference to Gogarty, referring to the post-independence narrowing of freedom in 'a new campaign againt the heretic within':

> 'The red light districts of Dublin, so raucously celebrated in the writings of James Joyce and Oliver St John Gogarty, were closed down by religious campaigners.'

But those raucous celebrations seem nowhere to be found except perhaps in the form of the pub that bears the wit's name.

So Gogarty slips away while Joyce lives on.

Kerrigan once visited Joyce's grave in Fluntern Cemetery in Zurich, at the end of the line of the No 6 streetcar, high above Zürichsee, the Lake of Zurich, and the flowing Limmat River, alongside the Zoological Gardens. Joyce sits there in bronze, walking stick by his leg, smoking, looking up from a titleless book that dangles open in his right hand which rests on his left knee, as he gazes westward, across a strip of bush, toward the stone that marks the grave of Elias Canetti (1905-1994), who died half a century after Joyce.

The sculpture is by Milton Hebald, and in a frame of shrub before it is a granite block inscribed with the name and dates of James Joyce (1882-1941), his wife Nora Barnacle Joyce (1884-1951), their son Giorgio (1905-1976), and the latter's second wife, Dr Asta Jahnke-Osterwaldr Joyce (1917-1993). A plaque lies flat on the grass beside it, requesting in German and English, *Please do not walk on the grave.*

There was something oddly life-like about the bronze Joyce, and Kerrigan thought of the first line of a poem by the Danish writer Klaus Lynggaard: 'So, Jim, we meet at last . . .' Lynggaard wrote that poem at the burial site of Jim Morrison nearly twenty years before, before Morrison's bust was stolen from his grave in the Parisian cemetery Père Lachaise; no one is likely to steal the Joyce sculpture which is near life size and must weigh a ton, and no doubt Swiss police would appear to apprehend anyone committing such a crime.

It was a beautiful, peaceful place to lie, to sit, surrounded by tall pines, autumn yellow poplars, red maples and beech trees. A bird house was affixed to a tree branch a few feet above Joyce's head. Kerrigan rested on the stone bench provided and lit a Christian of Denmark mini, contemplating his many hours spent in the company of Joyce's prose, how *Portrait of the Artist as a Young Man*, decades before, saved him from the living death of Irish Roman Catholicism and American jingoism:

> 'I will not serve that in which I no longer believe, whether it call itself my home, my fatherland, or my church: And I will try to express myself in some mode of life or art as freely as I can and as wholly as I can, using for my defence the only arms I allow myself to use – silence, exile, and cunning.'

Kerrigan recognized the fact that in life, by most accounts, Joyce was less than pleasant company, but it makes no difference.

His contribution to the world, to Kerrigan's world, was enormous, the pleasure and enlightenment Joyce's work has given Kerrigan have abundantly enriched his life, and he has dedicated more than one 16 June to a meditation on the lives of Joyce and Nora as he followed the real path of the fictional Leopold Bloom strolling Dublin streets on his long day's journey back to Molly's now famous *Yes*.

In life, on 16 June 1904, Joyce took his first stroll with Nora Barnacle. 'Barnacle by name and barnacle by nature,' complained Joyce's father about his son's alliance with the uneducated hotel maid with whom he would spend the rest of his life. His choice of that date as the one upon which Leopold Bloom took his walk was a tribute to Joyce's love for Nora, whom Molly Bloom (And Anna Livia Plurabelle of *Finnegans Wake*) so closely resembles. Since 1924, many others have also commemorated that day and those characters, year after year, in many cities of the world, celebrating Bloomsday. In Copenhagen there is even a bar named Bloomsday.

Joyce and Nora lived in Zurich briefly in 1904 and again in 1915-19 when the First World War forced them from Trieste. During those four years, he wrote much of *Ulysses*, supporting himself on private language lessons and gifts of money. When the war ended, he left, but returned frequently to consult ophthalmologists for his failing eyes and psychiatrists regarding his daughter Lucia's declining mental condition.

In mid-December 1940, he again fled to Zurich, this time from France, to escape the Nazi invasion, and there he died just a few weeks later, on 13 January 1941. Nora remained, with their adult son Giorgio, a singer, until she died in April 1951 and was buried in Fluntern as well; fifteen years later their separate graves were united there, and in 1981 (the year Canetti won the Nobel Prize for literature), the Hebald sculpture of Joyce was raised where they lay. Canetti died and was buried in Fluntern in 1994.

The Zurich guidebook, which Kerrigan bought in a *buchhandel* in the old town below mentioned neither Joyce nor Canetti, Freud nor Jung, Giacometti nor Tinguely, although it did specify that there were 1,500 animals in the zoological gardens alongside the cemetery. It also provided the following statistics: 'Zurich owns the world's largest number of public fountains (around 1,300), telephones, computers, private floral decorations, and oriental carpets and also has the most Nobel Prize winners.' This could not include Joyce because he never won one (which says more about the prize than about Joyce); Canetti did, although he was Bulgarian-Austrian – his novel *Die Blendung* (1935, translated by C V Wedgwood, as *Auto da Fé* in 1946) is perhaps his most famous.

The only literary fact Kerrigan's guidebook contained was in its Zurich Chronology, alongside the eighteenth century: 'Johan Jakob Bodmer, who translated Homer brought Klopstock, Goethe, and Wieland to Zurich.' Although it did not further identify Klopstock (Friedrich Gottlieb Klopstock, 1724-1803, the German 'Christian' Homer) or Goethe (Johan Wolfgang van Goethe, 1749-1832, one of the world's greatest writers whose grey brain dust was removed from his dead skull in 1970 by East German bureaucrats), it does mention that Wieland (Christoph Martin Wieland, 1733-1813, German novelist and poet) 'translated Shakespeare as a foundation for German classics' as a result of which, apparently, Zurich became known as 'Athens by the Limmat.'

Limmat flow past Joyce and Nora.

The third to last fact in the book's Zurich chronology was: '1968: beginning of period of unrest among young people.' It did not stipulate whether the unrest ever ended, but it occurred to Kerrigan that in 1968, he was 25 years old and that was the first time he read Joyce's *Ulysses* and saw Joseph Strick's film version of it as well as listening to Siobhan McKenna and E G Marshall's excellent recording of the Molly and Leopold Bloom soliloquies.

That was also the year he sheltered a deserter from the Vietnam War in his apartment in New York, his single 'concrete' act of resistance against that war. He identifies that act with Joyce, with his declaration from the *Portrait* of what he would no longer give allegiance to, and with the hero of his *Ulysses*, who was not a warrior like its eponymous Greek hero, but the pacifist, mild, cuckolded, humanity-loving, passionate Jew, Leopold Bloom.

The power of Joyce's literary stance aided Kerrigan's escape from the jingoism that four years earlier had him, without reflection, wearing on his jacket in the chill autumn New York City streets, in the wake of the Gulf of Tonkin Resolution, a *Bomb Hanoi*-button! Why he wore that button, other than an unhealthy childhood diet of John Wayne and Senator Joseph McCarthy, he did not know; but as he sat on the stone bench in Fluntern, gazing at bronze Joyce gazing at stone Canetti, who wrote about the psychology of fascism, he could not help but feel gratitude to these great people who helped bring him through his own youthful unrest and who worked so hard to contribute intelligent visions of the world to the world.

Kerrigan has rarely met anyone who has read *Ulysses* other than university scholars and occasional obsessed laymen and liars, although he has met numerous people who have bragged of *not* having read it, even if it has been voted among the 100 most important books of the century in both the US and the UK (in the US it was number one, in the UK number 100). He had a student once, when he was teaching, a very bright young graduate student in literature who complained that Joyce revelled in experiment for experiment's sake and was unreadable and professed a preference for any book selected by Oprah Winfrey anyday to slogging through Joyce.

He has heard the statement often: Isn't one of the big problems in the decline of literature that contemporary fiction and poetry has become too obsessed with 'experiment' for experiment's sake? Can ordinary mortals hope to understand all this egghead stuff without an advanced degree in literature?

And Kerrigan has always responded that a successful artistic experiment is an innovation and leads to a new way of expressing and perceiving something of human existence. A novel like Joyce's *Ulysses*, for example, which is probably more discussed than read, is an innovatively complex fictional presentation of western culture which functions on many levels. If one takes Homer as the beginning, so to speak, of western literary history, embodying classical Greek metaphors, values and symbols upon which the culture builds, then Joyce's novel might be seen in many ways as the conclusion or counterbalance, two millennia later.

Joyce's *Ulysses* parallels the journey of Homer's *Ulysses* – from the Trojan War back to Ithaca where his wife, Penelope, holding off many suitors who think Ulysses dead, and his son Telemachus, await his return – with the story of a single day in 1904 in the life of a lower middle-class Dublin Jew, Leopold Bloom, who spends the day of 16 June 1904 walking around Dublin in the knowledge that his wife is at home committing adultery with a theater agent named Blazes Boylan.

The chapters of Joyce's *Ulysses* roughly parallel the episodes of Homer's epic, and the levels of meaning of the book are myriad. One of its aims is to celebrate the human body, so each chapter is also characterized by a body organ. For example, in one chapter, Bloom defecates while a church bell rings in the background, a brilliant literary response to the church's hypocritical suppression of human bodily joy. The fact that Bloom is a pacifist everyman, a non-macho, non-nationalist, humanist, as an emblem of modern twentieth-century society, contrasts in a number of ways with Homer's representation of Ulysses, a heroic warrior journeying home from battle to his faithful wife, and makes a profound and prophetic observation of our times – feminist, pacifist, anti-jingoist, contra-dogmatist.

Among the many other things that Joyce's novel does is to parody, chapter for chapter, various writing genres, styles, and techniques, and also introduces and develops William James's concept of stream of consciousness, via an interior monologue also employed and developed by others, most notably perhaps Virginia Woolf.

Kerrigan can only agree that some of the other 'experiments' in the book may fairly be viewed as boring and as largely incaccessible to anyone without critical guidance as to what Joyce is doing, but the interior monologues – most particularly those of Leopold and Molly Bloom – changed the face of the twentieth century even for those who have never read Joyce.

Kerrigan bases this on his own experience with the book. When he read the Bloom soliloquies for the first time, then heard them interpreted on record, he was instantly changed, brought into a profoundly more intimate contact with his own consciousness, recognized at once the possibility of accessing one's own deeper thought processes and the simultaneity of time as a feature of the make-up of human pscychology, not to mention the severe attempts by society to keep each human being skull-alone with his or her own secret thoughts, fearful of expressing anything but what is sanctioned by conventional concensus thought.

Nearly 80 years after *Ulysses* first publication in 1922, stream of consciousness is no longer considered avant garde or innovative; it is a standard feature of literary practice throughout the world.

This, he told his recalcitrant young student, is the kind of power that literary experiment can have. So even if some experimental fiction is a challenge to read and some readers may not wish to accept that challenge, it is nonetheless an important feature of our literature, of our culture, of our lives as human beings (as opposed, say, to our lives as zombies).

In any event, Kerrigan is convinced that not many readers with even a modicum of sensitivity – whether or not they are English majors – would fail to be moved by the Bloom soliloquies, most notably Molly's gorgeous celebration and affirmation of human life and sexuality on which the last hundred pages or so of the book flows, concluding with her resounding *Yes*.

Probably most people are afraid of Joyce, would have a block against even cracking the cover of *Ulysses*. Perhaps the problem is that our educational systems are not sufficiently vigorous in teaching people to be active readers. Borges identifies 'good readers (as) poets as singular, and as awesome, as great authors themselves'. A reader ideally recapitulates the work of the writer, performs a 'kindred art', follows the map of the text across the same terrain and perhaps sees what the author has described, perhaps other things as well, perhaps different things.

Thus Kerrigan's answer to the question about experiment is, *No*. He does not think that contemporary fiction is obsessed with experiment for experiment's sake. In fact, most fiction being published today is not at all experimental. A very great deal of it is doing the same old thing in the same old way, and that's how most commercial publishers want it; they don't want to wake the sleeping reader, they don't want her or him to want something new or other because then they will have to revise their program and risk losing money.

There was a brief great flourishing of interest in innovative fiction in the 1960s and 70s, in writers like Samuel Becket, Italo Calvino, Jorge Luis Borges, Gabriel Garcia Marquez, Robert Coover, Donald Barthelme, John Barth, John Hawkes, William H Gass, and others. For those few years, words like metafiction, self-reflexive fiction, surrealism, fabulism, etc, were not, as they are for the most today in the wake of the 'dirty-realist' steamroller, unwelcome.

Postmodernists need not apply.

It interests Kerrigan that the man who coined, or perhaps purloined, the phrase 'dirty-realism' as a catchy tag for a *Granta* anthology in the 1980s, followed up by a next issue tagged 'More Dirt' and prefaced it with a statement on fiction that seemed to belie a slender understanding of the art, later became fiction editor of *The New Yorker* – perhaps one should call it the *new New Yorker*, although Kerrigan is not convinced the man is interested in any manner of newism or neo-newism.

Any number of contemporary literary journals and small presses, however, provide a greatly needed forum for fictional innovation and otherness where virtually all the genres can live together in exciting peace and where the truth of Wallace Stevens statement, 'The vegation abounds with forms', is recognized.

To Kerrigan's mind, people who insist that all fiction must be 'realistic' have a problem seeing the difference between life and art. When René Magritte captioned his realistic painting of a pipe '*Ceci n'est pas une pipe*' (This is not a pipe), many people were baffled. 'If it is not a pipe, then what *is* it?'

The answer obviously is, 'A picture of a pipe.' Which some people find pedantic. But the pigments in the painting could as well have been used to form any number of other images – a tree, a boat, an abstract . . .

Funnily enough, probably a considerable majority of people

today would not dream of hanging on their wall a painting whose subject was clearly identifiable as a realistic object in our supposedly orderly existence, for that seems no longer the realm of painting, but of photography; however, when it comes to fiction, most readers want – to quote the late Raymond Carver –'the real things that really matter to real people'.

Coke's the real thing.

And as John Cheever put it, 'Literature is not a competitive sport', God rest his enormous soul.

Kerrigan takes a long walk past the Shelbourne where Kipling and Dickens once slept, past Stephen's Green where one bright noon, 22 years before, a tinker girl picked Kerrigan's pocket and damn near got away with an envelope containing a thousand pounds in 50s.

How did she know? He has wondered ever since. How did she know what I had in my pocket?

36

The Long Hall

The Long Hall
No 51 South Great George's Street
Dublin 2, Ireland

He circles round to the Long Hall on South Great George's Street, alongside Upper Stephen Street, whose curve is said to follow the edge of the *Dubh Linn*, the black pool for which Dublin is named and where the Vikings moored their longships in 838AD. Here it was that the Danes settled, founding this capital, older by two centuries than their own.

Kerrigan steps along the curving street and thinks of Black Dam Lake in Copenhagen, his home there, and of the red-headed giant who visited him in sleep last night and told him he was a Celt.

Inside he sits behind the sixteen taps, watching his face in a fish-eye mirror by the cash register. The taps offer Guinness, Guinness, Guinness X Cold, Guinness X Cold, Kilkenny, Smithwicks, Bulmers Vintage Cider, Carlsberg Lager, Harp, Heineken, Heineken, Budweiser, Murphy's Irish Stout, Budweiser, Miller Genuine Draft. He sits beneath crystal chandeliers, by a stained-glass bar partition. On the back bar shelf a brass little mermaid on a polished marble rock advertises Carlsberg's Continental Lager and a man-sized grandfather clock with one hand bears a sign announcing *Correct Time*.

Kerrigan swallows half a pint of half and half.

And wonders again how the tinker girl had guessed he had so much cash in his pocket that day. Had she read it on his face? The naked face of Terrence Einhorn Kerrigan.

37

The Hairy Lemon

The Hairy Lemon
Stephen & Drury Streets
Dublin 2, Ireland

Passing the Hairy Lemon on his way to Temple Bar, he thinks of the lemony soap in his pocket, takes it out for a sniff and decides he will wash his private parts with it, to lave away with fragrant suds the remnant of Vera's love.

Why he wishes to do this, he does not know, but thinking of that part of his person reminds him that he needs once again to pee, so he enters the Hairy Lemon.

Moving by the hind bar, he notes a backpacker, tall and thin with dark-browed narrow eyes, open the satchel on his pack to pull out his wallet and, in so doing, drop a thumb-sized brown hard lump on the floor.

Kerrigan stops. 'Excuse me, my friend, but I believe you dropped your lump.'

The young man's narrow-eyed face pales. 'Not mine,' he says, eyes full of white.

'I'm sure I saw it fall from your kit,' says Kerrigan, but the boy shakes his head and backs away. 'Not mine I tell ya.'

Kerrigan bounces the clump on his palm. 'You're sure?'

'*Told* ya, mister. Not mine.'

Kerrigan shrugs, pockets the lump and exits the back door without visiting the gents after all. His heart is beating. He steps into the doorway of a second-hand bookshop to see if he is followed. Then he regrets having taken the boy's stash. He should have left it on the floor, but now it is too late so he continues across Drury.

38

The Temple Bar

The Temple Bar
47-48 Temple Bar
Dublin 2, Ireland

Through Dame Court, across Dame Street, down Temple Lane, he enters the Temple Bar where he retires to the basement, closing himself into a stall to empty his bladder and study the brown lump procured from the Hairy Lemon. He smells it, licks it. Then worries that it might be shit. But he returns it to his pocket and goes up to order and carry his pint out into the sunny backyard where he takes a seat alongside a barrel and lights a cigar, contemplating the antique tin signs mounted on the walls advertising Power's Whiskey, Bagot's Hutton & Co. Fine Old Whiskey, Murphy's/From the Wood that's Good, Bulmer's: Nothing Added But Time, Crested Ten: John Jameson & Son, Murphy's Extra Stout: On Draught and In Bottle, Lady's Well Brewery-Cork, Cantwell's Café au Lait . . .

And he recalls Cathy Cantwell in his first grade class in St Bartholemew's School in Elmhurst whose sweet young Debbie Reynolds' face caused all the boy's to dream of sweet tender love.

A yellow crane can be seen up above the rooftops against the blue sky with its scatter of soft white clouds. A young man at the next barrel says to him, 'I like your green tie,' and reaches to take it between his fingers. Kerrigan nods, concealing his annoyance at this transgression of perimeters, and the young man's young woman says hoarsely, 'You are a luvlie man.'

Kerrigan remembers once in McDaid's then, years ago, he had come from some literary conference and inadvertently forgotten to remove his name-badge, which said, *Dr T Kerrigan.* A woman approached him and said, 'Now what would you be a doctor of?'

Kerrigan, taken aback, noticed his tag then and said, 'Oh, of uh literature actually.'

'I think you're a doctor of bullshit,' she said.

He laughed, thinking she could scarcely have known how closely that description fitted his disseration on verisimilitude, and the woman's husband appeared.

'And what are you drinking?' the husband asked.

'I was actually having a mineral water,' Kerrigan said. 'Fizzy.'

'You'll have a whiskey,' said the man, and as things progressed, in the morning, the three of them sailed on the choppy green water of Dublin Bay in the couple's ten-meter sloop. They parted swearing to stay in touch, but never did of course, and in honor of that memory, Kerrigan now goes to the bar to request a taste of potcheen. The bartender gives him half a tumbler for which he will accept no payment.

'Sure it's hardly a taste at all, and it is not the real stuff anyway. If you want the real stuff you'll have to go to the Garda. They confiscate it all to keep on hand for their celebrations.'

Apparently, thinks Kerrigan, the standard line.

'*Uisce beatha*,' he says, raising the glass of clear liquor. 'Whiskey. It keepeth the reason from stifling.' Wise words spoken 422 years before by the Chronicler, Raphael Hollinshed.

But in Donleavy's old room at Building 38 in Trinity (*Cyclists Dismount* and *Kindly remove the hairs from the plumbing fixtures after showering*), it is not reason that stifles Kerrigan as he bathes his private particulars in Bronnley lemon hand-soap, thinking gloomily that he has no faithful Penelope nor even an unfaithful lusty Molly to bring the soap to.

He sits on the edge of his bed gazing out the tall window to the green and quotes O'Keefe aloud:

> 'In this sad room
> In this sad gloom
> We live like beasts.'

Then he recalls a fact he acquired from an article in *Time* that he glanced over on the plane, that most heart attacks occur between 4 and 6pm on Mondays and Fridays. It is currently, he calculates, Friday, but the hour of 6pm is long past. His legs are tired, and he wanders to the sink which he leans over to spit out a mouthful of blood, red and clotty.

He studies it with fascination, not unwilling to die, should this be what this event signals, but not at this specific point in time because he still has a book to complete, and he will be damned if he will allow all this expensive research to lay fallow.

He rinses his mouth, releases another clotty mouthful, sees his face in the mirror over the sink, red teeth, red tongue, pouchy eyes. He looks at the eyes, thinks of George Seferis, Nobel Laureate from 1963, the year he and Dan Blicksilver suffered in the military, 'And if the soul is ever to know itself it must gaze into the soul', noting that the pouches are now more than incipient; they are in fact greenish of hue and definitely pouched.

'When we dream,' he says aloud, 'and when we couple, we embrace phantoms.'

And he lays sidewise naked on his bed to sleep, relishing the chill through the open window, curious to see if he will dream, curious to see if he will die, meanwhile singing songs of the Greek George Thémelis (1900-1976) in his mind to keep him company lest he die without an opportunity to observe himself doing so:

'I move my body and my soul moves,
I put it to sleep, it sleeps.
I love, and my soul loves,
It tastes my body and my blood.
I sniff the air, and my soul sniffs also.'

And

'Outside of us things die.
No matter where you walk at night you hear
Something like a whisper coming out
Of streets you have never walked on
Of houses you have never visited
Of windows you have never opened
Of rivers over which you have never stooped to drink
Of ships on which you have never sailed.'

And naked in the chilly dark, curved atop his knubbly bedspread, he fancies he can hear the streets outside his window, the river beyond the Trinity walls, the voices of strangers in the courtyard speaking softly, the sound of a runner's feet moving swiftly over the barbered grass.

39

The Anna Livia Lounge

The Anna Livia Lounge
Dublin Airport
Dublin, Ireland

'Drunks fear the police
But the police are drunk, too.'
– Rumi

Taxiing out to the airport, Kerrigan thinks about death while the driver complains about his wife.

'She's moody, y'know, and like I'm out last Sunday for Father's Day, and I come home, she asks me next day when did you come in? I says, How do I know when I come in? I was bleeding drunk. I don't know, I don't know. She's moody.'

Kerrigan nods, pays lip service. 'With the best of them it's hard.'

'And isn't it the truth? Been here on business?'

'Escape really.'

'Wife lets?'

'She's ah, I'm ah, divorced.'

'Ah I figured as much, y'know. No escape without. Like the French fella says, what's his name? No Exit. How you say that in Frenchie, y'know?'

'*Huis Clos*,' says Kerrigan.

'That's exactly right. And no excapin' it. She's moody.'

All my life, on and off, I've more or less wanted to die, thinks Kerrigan. And perhaps now I shall. For real.

Contrary to the rules and the specifications of a sign on the smoking-section table in the Anna Livia airport lounge, Kerrigan lights an Apostolado cigar, *Cigares Danois de Qualité Supèrieure*, manufactured by Nobel, purveyor to Her Majesty the Queen of Denmark's Household, in an aluminum screw tube bearing the leaping deer logo of Hirschsprung, whose collection is gathered in the Hirschsprung museum on Stockholm Street in Copenhagen, outside of which is a sculpture of a mounted barbarian with two severed heads affixed to his saddle.

What will we do without the barbarians?

Puffing his Apostolado, Kerrigan is not chided for this lapse of orderliness by the male lounge attendant, although he is gently reprimanded for requesting a Black and Tan.

'You don't want to say that in this country,' the young man cautions in lilting Irish English. 'You know what the Black and Tans were?'

Kerrigan apologizes in hopes he will be rewarded with peace. The Black and Tans were the 1920 British-appointed police in Ireland, so called for the colors of their uniforms, hooligans with badges, akin to the *Hipo Svin* of Denmark, appointed by the Germans during the Second-World-War occupation.

'Quite right,' he says. 'Let's call it a 'half and half' instead.'

'Brilliant,' says the attendant.

Nothing against calling a spade a shovel, Kerrigan sits relishing his Black and Tan. Had they served champagne in the lounge he would have ordered a Black Velvet, Guinness and champagne, rather than the Guinness and Heineken that stands in a classic pint glass before him. The Apostolado is brilliant, and he recalls that it was given him by his Research Associate, whose sweetness he longs to be in the nearness of right now.

He draws savoringly on the cigar, fearing each moment that he will be requested to extinguish it. The smoke is so pleasant that he even inhales a bit of it, thinking vaguely it might heal the bleeding wound in his mouth.

No dreams that he can recall visited him last night at Trinity. And no signs have directed or cautioned or threatened him – other than the one forbidding him to smoke cigars here in the Anna Livia Lounge, and he has ignored that one, considering it an order from the likes of the long ridiculous sculpture of Anna Livia on O'Connell Street in Dublin, which the locals have dubbed 'the Floozie in the Jacuzzi', it being a representation of a scantily clad woman in a kind of bathtub meant to represent the river Liffy flowing through Dublin as well as Anna Livia Plurabelle, the matriarchal main character of Joyce's *Finnegans Wake*: 'Anna' from an Irish word for 'river' and Livia for the Irish 'Liphe' (for the Liffey), *Plurabelle* being, of course, the Italian superlative, 'loveliest'. Anna Livia Plurabelle, A L P, as the river stands for birth and rebirth and renewal. But where are the fangs, where the bulging eyes, where the long tongue that consumes, where the skull between her thighs, the smoking pistol in the hand that dangles down along her naked blood-spattered thigh?

You are never meant to see your mother's cunt, Sheelanagig notwithstanding.

Instead of dreams, he takes a hardboiled egg from a basket on the counter, cracks the shell and salts the egg and bites and thinks about the Queen of Denmark, Margarethe II, representative of the oldest unbroken regal line in Europe. A woman who stands a good 6ft in height, married to a French vintner named Henrique whose Danish is not quite as good as Kerrigan's which is reasonably poor. The Queen herself smokes cigarettes. She has even been known to smoke in public, and at a recent press conference questioned by a journalist as to why she was smoking, explained, 'There was an ashtray here', which endears her to Kerrigan. A woman who will not knuckle under to what is ordained by the bluenoses and a worthy representative of a liberal social democratic kingdom. The Queen has also translated French literature into Danish, designed costumes for the Royal Theater, and paints pictures. One of her sons, the younger, is married to a Chinese woman from Hong Kong, and she is pregnant by this Danish Prince, a royal mixing of racial bloods. Her other son, the Crown Prince, Frederick, is something of a playboy and an officer in the Navy Seals, subject to much criticism, yet an interesting lad who will no doubt be a worthy king, like his grandfather, Christian X, a true man of the sea, whose body was adorned with numerous tattoos.

Kerrigan decides that he will not spit into the sink in the Anna Livia men's room to see if he is still bleeding from the mouth. He will let that wait until tonight, before bedtime, to enrich his dream life. It occurs to him that with an open sore in his mouth, if he kisses a woman with a venereal disease he is liable to contract it. Perhaps he is suffering from cancer of the mouth hole. What an unpleasant way to die. Mouth bleeding like a menstruating cunt. Broken egg of death. Like Hiram Grant, aka Ulysses S, aka 'Lysse' who wrote his memoirs while dying of mouth cancer, racing the disease to the finish.

How much more dignified if the cancer were someplace more discreet – the lower leg perhaps, walk with a silver-headed stick. Yet he draws solace from the fact of the 9mm Ruger pistol, fully loaded and shootable, in the rubber-banded shoe box atop his closet.

But he will not take his life yet. He is a man with a purpose. He has a book to complete. Research to finish. An Associate to . . . what?

He leafs through a Danish newspaper – the book section of the Danish weekly *Weekendavisen*, which once featured a full-page interview with him conducted by the extremely prolific young Danish poet-critic-fiction writer Bo Green Jensen in recognition of Kerrigan's services on behalf of Danish literature.

Kerrigan always thought this to be a misunderstanding. In truth, his services to Danish literature have been far from great, a few handfuls of poems and stories translated, a single volume of *New Danish Fiction* edited, two minor anthologies of assorted contemporary verse and prose.

Perhaps he should do more. He feels a debt to the country

which has taken him in, treated him well, given him an old and lovely city in which to abide. He has a cherished postcard sent him by the beautiful, brilliant Danish novelist Suzanne Brøgger in thanks for the anthology, which included a selection of her work. Depicted on the card is a tall gilt Venus from the *Museo Nazionale di Napoli*, naked, breasts and loins enhanced with gold leaf; she has one foot raised from the ground so that she can tend to her ankle, and to maintain her balance, one handless wrist rests on the head of a tiny man on a pedestal beside her, his tiny penis erect. He is not quite half her size, a wingless cherub perhaps, and Kerrigan, delighted with this card, could think of no suitable response, decided finally no response was necessary.

Brøgger has written wonderful witty sexy novels – fictionalized memoirs which earned the admiration, inter alia, of Henry Miller. Perhaps her greatest work is a thick novel entitled *Ja* – in which among other things the main character buries herself in the lawn outside her home, a metaphor Kerrigan has seen elsewhere in literature and which stems apparently from Yiddish folklore. The title of the novel, he is certain, was inspired by the *yes* of Molly Bloom that concludes *Ulysses*, recalling her first act of love:

> ' . . . how he kissed me under the Moorish wall and I
> thought well as well him as another and then I asked
> him with my eyes to ask again yes and then he asked
> me would I yes to say yes my mountain flower and
> first I put my arms around him yes and drew him down
> to me so he could feel my breasts all perfume yes and
> his heart was going like mad and yes I said yes I will Yes.'

Kerrigan himself once published an interview in *Weekendavisen* that he conducted with the Danish poet Pia Tafdrup who this very year won the Nordic Prize for Literature, referred to in Scandinavia as the Little Nobel. Only three Danes have ever won the Nobel Prize, Karl A Gjellerup and Henrik Pontoppidan who shared it in 1917, and Johannes V Jensen in 1944, all men whose work is largely forgotten by the world. Jensen won the prize in 1944, the year of Suzanne Brøgger's birth, when Kerrigan was but a year old, and Dr Werner Best, the German commandant, was still occupying the mansion which now serves as the home of the American ambassador to Denmark.

One of the greatest of Danish writers of the twentieth century, known in the US as Isak Dinesen and in Denmark as Karen Blixen, born in 1885, three years after Joyce who never won, and died in 1962, the year of the execution of Adolf Eichmann in Israel, the same year that Blixen met Marilyn Monroe in New York, the same year Marilyn Monroe died. Blixen might also have been expected to win the Nobel. In fact, she reported that Ernest Hemingway, when he won in 1954, told her that she should have had the prize. Kerrigan saw her tell this story on a documentary film and thought, even if true, it was sad that she did not keep it to herself.

His cigar is nearly finished as is his Black and Tan. He has the drink replenished under the deck-name of a half and half and lights another cigar – a Nobel Petit Corona, 100 per cent tobacco, extremely dangerous to the health, cause of cancer, made in Denmark. It too is good though not quite so good as the Apostolado and can boast on its black and gold box, 'by appointment to the Royal Danish Court'.

If I am dying, he thinks, and if there *is* an afterlife, I will perhaps have the opportunity there to meet Karen Blixen, Marilyn Monroe, Ernest Hemingway, and many another person whom I have admired. That is if, in the afterlife, there is not the same kind of ranking system as here upon this earth. No reason to suppose so, however. For that matter, no reason to suppose there is an afterlife at all. Or that even if there is, the egos that distinguished us while living will still be in function.

Such thoughts, he thinks, are significant to a dying man, and begins to read an article in *Weekendavisen* which is a destructive review of a book about Louise Rasmussen, born in 1815 to an unmarried mother, but who nonetheless, despite the greatness of that obstacle in that time, achieved great distinction in society, first as the mistress of the Danish publishing magnate Carl Berling, with whom she had a child, then as the lover of Crown Prince Frederik VII and, later, when he ascended to the crown, became his queen.

Apparently she maintained her relationship with Berling after she was married and it is unclear to Kerrigan what this three-way relationship consisted of. It seems that Louise Rasmussen used her influence on Frederik on behalf of the people in furtherance of democracy. It was Frederik VII who adopted the Danish Constitution in 1849. When she died, Louise Rasmussen, who was shunned by the Danish aristocracy, left her considerable fortune to a number of Danish social institutions.

The review is illustrated by an early twentieth-century painting by H P Lindeberg which portrays Louise Rasmussen standing naked before a billiard table flanked by Berling and Frederik, both fully clothed and adorned with all their decorations and orders. At first Kerrigan thinks it is a question of an actual menage-a-trois, but reading the piece concludes it is about a triangle. Still he is uncertain and the review seems somewhat venomous.

It occurs to him that one of the things he has always wished to do in his life was to make love to two women at once, to experience the joy of being naked with two women, of being free to celebrate their bodies and offer his to their celebration, singly and in pair, the three of them twined together like some sacred triad, blessed trinity of the flesh. The thought of doing this rouses in him a sense of purity, of grace, of the extreme beauty and desirability of desire, of sensuality, of the human body.

He sighs, draws on his cigar. A very tall man enters the lounge and stands in the middle of the floor staring off to the side so that Kerrigan views him in profile, framed between portraits of Beckett and Wilde with the Business Center between them. He is wearing a black tee-shirt and light-colored trousers, is dark-haired, has a benevolent face and looks vaguely familiar – the president of a professional organization perhaps, despite his casual dress. That, thinks Kerrigan, is what this world requires, leaders in tee-shirts.

His flight is announced, and he leaves the lounge for the departure gate, but stops in the men's room on the way to spit into the sink. There is blood in the sink, but not quite as red and clotted as last night. To be certain, he rinses again, more forcefully, and the expectorate is redder and more clotty this time.

And as he boards the plane he cannot rid his mind of the Lindeberg painting which roused those thoughts of yet another unfulfilled goal of his existence. And also of the fact that Danes, unlike Americans, are terrible snobs, terrible snobs, despite the black tee-shirted professional leader who is boarding the plane just in front of him and laughing happily over something he apparently is reading on the front page of the *International Herald Tribune*, and Kerrigan feels on the edge of death that he should do something to sing the praises of the great-heartedness of the American people.

WEEK FOUR

Pint of View, The Coal Square Carousal

'Here we go round the prickly pear
Prickly pear prickly pear
Here we go round the prickly pear
at five o'clock in the morning.'

– T. S. Eliot

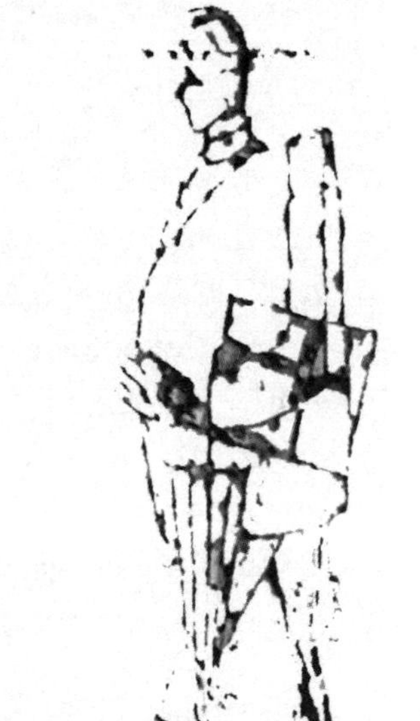

40

SAS

SAS
Drinks on Wheels on Wings
Boeing 737, in the air over Europe

The early flight from Dublin on Scandinavian is nearly empty in Business Class. Handful of suits scurrying home after doing business with the green tiger. Early, but not too early for a chill champagne with warm scrambled eggs and a single sausage, fried cherry tomato and a cantarelle mushroom. Which the young leader in the black tee-shirt, Kerrigan notes, is also amenable to four rows up on the aisle. How the stewardess smiles in this section. Smile fades when they go aft, through the curtain to the Economy Class where they dole out raw fish from a wicker basket.

'You know what Churchill said about champagne,' he says as the flight attendant beams and cracks the seal of the little bottle of Lanson's bubbly for him. She tilts her head obligingly, as if to say, *No, what?*

'Three prerequisites: It must be dry, it must be chill, it must be free.'

Oh you kid! She smiles and touches his arm. Maybe she genuinely likes me. *You're a luvlie man. God is a cunt. Can't you take a joke? You're as sane as I.*

Well suppose you tell me how sane is *that*, then, *hm*!?

He uses the tiny red plastic clothes-pin to attach his napkin to the lapel of his shirt and digs in. The eggs are runny, the champagne lukewarm. Luxurious problems. Mosquitoes in paradise. Reminds him, his Associate once told him about the ticks and chiggers out in the country where her family spent their summer holiday sometimes. Had to check one another's private particulars for the things, front, back and bottom:

– No! Really?

– Of course. It is very dangerous. You could become paralyzed if they enter your system. *Skovflåt*. Wood ticks.

– You mean like you look right into each other's, uh, apertures?

– Of course. It is perfectly natural. Do not be so prudish (*snerpet* in Danish).

Burn 'em out with a cigarette they used to say in the Army. Suck the venom out of a snake bite. And if you get bit on your privates, you find out who your buddies really are. There was a time for you. Kerrigan at Fort Dix in '61. Wanted to be a true American. Fantasies of action in Cuba. Jump the wall at Guantanamo, bayonette between the teeth, BAR beneath the arm, lobbing hand grenades. Medals and decorations for service above and beyond the call. What a sap! Him and Dan Blicksilver, the six-four wiry black-haired and bespectacled intellectual from Bard who was so good at absence.

– *Blicksilvah!* First Sergeant Robert M Coover used to bellow in his breathy bark. *Whar the hail is Blicksilvah!*

And where is Blicksilver today who had recommended Kerrigan to read the last hundred pages of *Ulysses* and find the blue parts. 'That,' said Blicksilver with a smile on his slightly wobbling face, 'is the reward that awaits you after plowing through the first few hundred pages.'

But the past is not a dimension it is wise to enter so he is grateful for the fact that some manner of hard thing irritating his hip brings him back to the here and now. He digs into his pocket to find a kind of dusty stone there which he drags out precariously, careful not to upset his fold-down table. He finds himself staring at a large brown lump resembling a petrified turd. Then, just as recognition finds its way to his consciousness, he senses a figure standing over him, looks to see the shining stewardess whose smile indicates she is fully aware, beneath her respectful gaze, of the nature of the thing in his fingers.

'Would you like to buy some duty-free goods, sir?' she asks, indicating the many sleek and shiny cellophaned packages in her trolly, but her smile says something quite else. And now a businessman in the seat across the aisle is also looking at the brown lump, though not smiling at all, and Kerrigan feels the blush ignite his face. He wonders what the fellow in the black tee-shirt would say.

'Hairy lemon,' blurts Kerrigan. 'Soap.'

'We do not have soap, sir. Just liquid soap in the lavatory.'

'No, no. This. Hairy lemon soap. Bought it at Sweny's Chemist. Featured in *Ulysses*. Joyce. You know, Leopold Bloom bought a bar for Molly on 16 June 1904. Poldy Bloom. Give us a touch, Poldy, Molly said. I'm dying for it. And he kissed her under the Moorish wall.'

Now she looks frightened, escapes with a wilted mouth as Kerrigan stuffs the lump back into his pocket. How to get rid of it? Cram it in the obsolete armrest ashtray. But they would know. Too large anyway. Already alerted perhaps. Witnessed. Their records show who sat here. Seat 7C, left two-seat aisle. Kerrigan, T E. Too old for this. Could go to jail. Smuggling. Mule. Alert the captain to have a SWAT team waiting at Kastrup. Swat him like a fly. Journalists, too. *Unknown Expatriate Writer Apprehended at Kastrup-Hash coup*. Held in isolation for thirteen days.

He sips bubbly with his predicament. Could bury it in the remains of his runny scrambled eggs. Not deep enough.

The businessman across the aisle is sneering openly at him. Kerrigan says, '*Tyv tror, hver mand stjæler.*' Old Danish proverb: Thieves think everyone steals. You have the leer of the sensualist about you. I am the proverbial *homme moyen sensuel*.

The man removes his gaze slowly. Very un-Danish to strike an attitude over another's vices. Must be a Swede. Or Norwegian.

You're as sane as I. Aren't wolves dangerous? So are wiolins. Luvlie man.

Kerrigan thinks of the sniffing dogs that patrol American airports, trained to nose out the goods, tries to remember if he has ever seen such a beast in Kastrup. See here, I hold an SAS Star Alliance Gold Card. Many, *many* air miles to my name. Entrée to the gold lounge where they serve complimentary champagne and Christian of Denmark cigarillos. Disposable toothbrushes in the loo and gratis newspapers in five languages. Bright row of bottles of strong spirit at your free disposal along with an ice bucket, tongs, sturdy drink glasses (no plastic cups there) and savory snacks. They even distribute free volumes of Scandinavian literature in the original Scandinavian with English translation, including Strindberg's *Alone*, Brandes *Thoughts on the Turn of the Century*, Hamsun's *Hunger, A Fragment*, Munch's *Notes of a Genius*, and Ibsen's *When We Dead Awaken*, which James Joyce reviewed at the age of seventeen, his very first published piece of writing.

'We only see what we have missed
When we dead awaken.
And what do we see?
We see that we have never lived.'

I know these things. I am the man and I was there and I will be there again, puffing a Christian, tippling bubbly in the company of great Nordic writing, and I may cause the lips of those who are asleep to speak. And I have a Press Card issued by the Danish Association of Magisters Joint Committee for Danish Press Organizations that entitles me to cross police lines, though subject to the provisions of the Ministry of Justice Circular No 211 of 20 December 1995. Freedom of the Press. I instruct you to let me pass. But it stipulates on the card that one is subject to obey instructions from the police at the site of the crime. Such as: *Please empty your pockets, sir, and assume the position.* Maybe one of those policewomen. Hurt me, please, so I at least get something out of this inconvenience.

Now you're fucked, Kerrigan. All these years of surfing only to wipe out over a stupid bit of greed. Robbing a frightened backpacker of his stash.

Unknown writer with tragic past held for questioning in Kastrup hash case.

Hashish (Arabic), n.(1598), the concentrated resin from the flowering tops of the female hemp plant (*cannabis sativa*) that is smoked, chewed or drunk for its intoxicating effect – also called *charas*.

Female hemp. Hash is a cunt.

Can't you take a joke?

Kerrigan thinks, Forgive, O Lord, my little jokes on Thee, and I'll forgive thy great big one on me. Old Robert Frost had a thought or two all right.

Everything will be all right. Optimism, said Voltaire, is a mania for insisting all is well when things are going badly. *Candide*. Fine novel that, published more than 300 years ago, and Voltaire had to run for it. Police after him for every manner of sin in print, against God, sexual propriety, king and country. To protect himself he had the book published simultaneously on the same day in Paris, Amsterdam, Berlin and London, and ran his bloody arse off to the little town of Ferney, just across the border from Geneva, where he built a chateau, convenient for a Swiss getaway, planted poplars along the entryway, and the town became known as Ferney-Voltaire and the townfolk called him '*Le Patron*'.

French cabdriver once when I insisted on being allowed to sit in the front seat bellowed at me, '*C'est moi qui est le patron, monsieur*!' Unlike the sweet waitress to whom I once said, '*Merci, madame*,' and she replied, '*C'est moi qui dit merci, monsieur*,' and slapped her ample rump as she passed me. Another missed opportunity that one remembers on the very lip of extinction.

Centuries after Voltaire, Bernie Cornfeld would flee from Geneva to Ferney-Voltaire when the Swiss kicked his investment firm out for questionable practices. He ran phone lines across the border in dead of night for there were at the time, in the late 1960s, no telephones there yet. Cornfeld was greatly beloved of the Ferney townfolk. Kerrigan had lived there for a time in the mid-70s and the town was awash in lovely young Swedish girls. Kerrigan remembers once eating too much foie gras and drinking too many cognacs and vomitting into the bidet in his little hotel on the *Grand Rue*. Grand rue it is, all right.

Cornfeld, also known as *Le Patron*, was arrested nonetheless in the early 70s, and one of Nixon's friends, Robert Vesco, was called in to take care of the 180 million dollars remaining in the company till. People's pensions. Dirty business. Vesco invested the remaining money in a private gunship and absconded to the waters of Panama. No doubt ended in jail himself, or dead, one or both of which will also be your fate, you fool.

Kerrigan clicks the telephone out from beneath the armrest, swipes in his plastic and dials her number. He wants just to hear her voice once before they lock him up. Ironic to be able to reach her like this, so near yet so far, years about to separate them. Time goes by so slowly and time can do so much. Long lonely nights.

She answers on the first ring. 'This is Annelise,' she says in the Danish manner. He only listens, the rush of the jet in his ears, as she says, 'Hello?' and he can think of nothing to say to her.

Then the pilot requests the passengers to fasten their seatbelts and place their seatbacks in an upright position, so Kerrigan feeling less than upright sits strapped in and upright, looking out the window at the shadow of the plane over the blue sea (not wine but sky), the green sea (not snot but jade), moving landward, alongside a sailboat, over the fields of Amager, over a bunch of cows in a field, a herd of horses, over miniature scale-model cars and roads and houses, finally larger, much larger than before, over the airfield where the great wheels bang down and roll along the tarmac.

He knows he must easily be subject to suspicion, a man without luggage, not even a cabin bag, in rumpled clothes, who has been sighted by a cabin attendant with a double thumb-sized lump of hashish – word *assassin* originally was *hashishin*, thugs who smoked hash and went out on a rampage of killing – in his hand yet he does not dare discard it for fear he is being watched. He recognizes that this is unreasonable yet his mind is awash with fleet fish-like thoughts of scientific methods by which they can test the fingers and pocket lining for hash residue and the fear that his fate will be harsher if he tries to escape it. At least he was honest. Owned up to his sins. So lock him up but keep the key handy.

He can think of no more horrific fate than jail, and he does not believe any angels will appear to give him a respite in the country. Supposedly the Danish penal system is much more humane than the American where, in the year of 1999, 1.8 million people are incarcerated, more than half for nonviolent offenses under the new, tough, mandatory minimum no-parole drug sentences (even when we know that Clinton blew pot and suspect that young Bush snorted coke and you can't snort without inhaling either), but Kerrigan doubts the Danish jails are all *that* humane, set up not to correct but to punish. Even the Danish Minister of Justice has been quoted as saying that no one ever became a better person by doing time. You are locked in a room, terrorized by brutal types who belong to secret societies and no escaping their rule unless you are like the Hell's Angel assassin who writes books about his philosophy of life, has a fax in his cell, and an arrangement whereby he is let out on leave to tour the lecture circuit. In fact, this same convicted murderer was once referred to in print by a journalist as a psychopath and he took her to court for offending his honor and won a penalty from her of 5,000 crowns for defamation of character – which in Denmark is known as 'an offense to honor'. Perhaps, he argued, he was a murderer and had cold-bloodedly assassinated the leader of the rival gang, the Bullshitters, but where was the medico-scientific evidence to support her claim that he was a psychopath? He had murdered not psychopathically, but with full reason and purpose. Therefore, whether or not he was evil, he was not mad, not psychopathic, he argued and was supported by the courts in his argument to the tune of 5,000 crowns.

Kerrigan knows that he will not do well in prison. If only he had his pistol with him, he could retire to a restroom and plug his brain. Keep his reason from stifling forever, unless of course he would end in hell or purgatory for such an act or, as the Buddhists were said to believe, would be immediately recycled as an insect: Oh, no you don't buddy! No exit for you. Go immediately to worse shit, do not pass go and collect nothing but more misery. Is there no way to end it all forever.

His pistol! If they apprehend him, search his premises, they will find it. Last exit closed. No excape, as his Dublin cab driver said. He remembers the expat Brit he knows in Copenhagen who was held for half a year in isolation, charged with a drug coup about which he knew nothing, but because he was in possession of two joints when they nabbed him, he had no recourse. Same story here. They could pin whatever they want on him. Yet isolation would be preferable to the society of criminals. God knows if the stories are true of what they do to each other, what they do to the weak, anal rape the classic method by which victorious soldiers demonstrate their power over the vanquished, even as James Dickie indicated in the climactic scene of his novel *Deliverance* as standard practice. There are even jokes about this on tv sitcoms, and it is not funny. It would hurt. Very much. Not even masochistically pleasing, just goddamn downright ugly brutal pain, tearing of the rectum. Humiliation and pain. Miserable society that allows such practices. Some people even applaud it.

Your honor, this man completely *forgot* he had hashish in his pocket. Therefore, I call for immediate dismissal, I think they call it.

On the other hand he knows another British fellow who was one of the hostages in Iran and who used his imaginative faculties to ward off ill-treatment – he fed his captors 'secrets' gleaned from the pages of a Tom Clancy novel. Perhaps the imagination can serve even there. Perhaps I could start a writers workshop, thus becoming a valued colleague of the other cons who would then refrain from bestial practices, come to me as a senior, request my guidance.

Kerrigan, in terror, confesses to himself that he is a physical coward.

The uniformed man at the passport control booth glances at Kerrigan's identity card and says in Danish, 'Ah, here's an American who has had to learn to master this horrible Danish language.'

'I try anyway,' says Kerrigan in Danish, and they both laugh.

'Welcome home,' says the Dane in Danish with a smile, and Kerrigan smiles, too, though he is wise to him: It's a test; they speak Danish to you cheerfully, but if you don't understand you reveal yourself as a possible thief of a national identity card for purposes of illegal entry into this social democratic kingdom.

No dogs on leashes are sniffing about the baggage area, and with a distinct sense of watching eyes all about him, his legs stiff and heavy, he strategically positions himself behind a black man and walks through customs unmolested while the black man in front of him is stopped and questioned.

Saved by Nordic racism!

The tall young professional fellow in the black tee-shirt comes out behind him, and as they pass through the automatic doors to freedom, he gives a side-wise smile and a wink. 'Hash and eggs, ey?' he says and is gone.

He leaves the train at Nørreport station, deliciously relieved. A free man. He will not be banged in the butt after all. Yet he cautions himself against optimism. *Ingen kender dagen før solen går ned*, he thinks. Danish proverb: No one knows the day before the sun has set. Like Sophocles, *Oedipus*: Count no man happy until he is laid in his grave.

Kind of coprophiliac double meaning there.

The sun is brilliant. Rare day of spring. Soon time for *en hivert*. Lovely Danish word, that, for a drink: A pull. Sounds better in the Viking tongue: *Hivert*.

– What'll it be, sir?

– A pull of whiskey, please.

A jogger bounces past on *Frederiksborg* Street, name of a bank on back of his shirt: *Unibank*. Unicorn logo. *Enhjørning*. Kerrigan's middle name there almost.

He crosses *Kultorvet*, The Coal Square, where the outdoor cafés are folded out to the late May sunlight. Down *Købmagergade*, Butcher Street, where the windows of Long John are folded open as well, Happy Jazz playing from within, singer and chorus: *I'm the sheik Of Araby, Your love belongs to me . . .*

On *Amagertorv*, he pauses to observe the tabloid headlines mounted on placards outside a newspaper kiosk, all apparently dealing with the same heinous crime, like some medievel ballad: *Baby Corpse Found in Stream* and *Baby Corpse Found in Plastic Bag* and *Baby Lived Two Hours in Bag in Stream . . .*

Why do we so relish this gore? A little girl outside a bakery window says in Danish to her mother, 'I want my cake *now*, mommy! I want it *now*!'

Kerrigan pauses and looks down at her. 'So do I,' he says, 'And I've been waiting *much* longer than you.'

The girl closes her mouth and gazes up at him with large blue eyes. The mother's mouth is mirthful. Kerrigan, the hero of the moment, smiles at mommy whose cleavage is lovely as the summer day. Known in Danish as a *kavalier gang*, the Cavalier passage. Such a beautiful thing, the passage between the breasts that bear the milk of human kindness.

Down this side street here Kerrigan once saw late at night a first-story window fly open and a bare-breasted young woman lean out to vomit into the street something that appeared to be red wine. The memory reminds him of what emptied from his own mouth into the sink at Trinity. Perhaps it was a dream.

– It's just a dream, Jimmy.

Terry! Oh Ter-ry!

A woman cycles past illegally on the walking street, but Kerrigan doesn't mind for she wears a middi-skirt and each pumping turn of the pedals flashes the peachy cream of inner thigh, visions of eternity, the immortality of humankind. She sees him looking and smiles. And that is another reason why he loves Denmark. Write an essay: 'Why I Love the Kingdom of Denmark,' by Terrence E. Kerrigan. Women don't mind if you take a discreet peek. *Yes, I'm beautiful*, her smile says. *Thank you for noticing. Did you enjoy the look? And you're a noble gent yourself, despite the rumpled clothes and cheek stubble – manly that. And I can tell your jeans must've cost. Hundred dollars I bet. Ceruttis, no? You're a luvlie man. Love your green tie.*

May I squeeze your butt?

Of course, madame, yes, and you are a vision in a dream of all the lovely weightless lightness that causes the heart to soar with poetry. Light as a bird, not as a feather.

A man slouches past with two rotweilers on leashes held short. His sleeveless muscular upper arms adorned with dark blue tattoos, bracelet-like. Viking designs perhaps. Or Celtic. It seems to Kerrigan this man must be very afraid in his heart and therefore perhaps dangerous.

A hand-lettered sign near the *Amagertorv* fountain proclaims that *Allah is the Only God* while a representative of the Association for the Advancement of Islam stands ready to field questions, and from further down the walking street, a group of marching fools appear bearing placards that pronounce:

No sex No cry! And *Families for Pure Love*! And *No More Free Sex*! And *Sex is Never Free!*

The Association of Families for Pure Love descend upon him like a flood, hollering, 'Yee-*ha*!'

Will you shut up! he thinks and remembers once in the movies when he was a kid, a woman turned to him and said just that, 'Will you shut up!' and he said, 'Yes!' and shut up, to the great merriment of his friends.

The Pure Lovers recede toward the King's New Square, and Kerrigan eyes a pregnant girl who bears her belly proudly. *Must* be triplets. Touch it for luck? You are so beautiful with your swollen nose and lips so all abloom and stuffed with the life you are growing. Oh how I would love to lay with you filled with most gently respectful affectionate touches upon your swollen body you beautiful humble life-giving goddess!

There a young man keeps a small beanbag of some sort

constantly in the air by the deft manipulations of his feet and knees, and two women walk past, one with a sleek midriff and crumpled up face.

O city of the hundred vices! Kerrigan sees a poster plasterd to a trash basket that says *La Petit Gaga* and another advertising a play by Hans Christian Andersen about a mother. *A boy's best friend is his mother.*

He reverses direction, heading back toward the Coal Square where a plan is hatching in his skull for an exercise in point of view.

He once had a professor of creative writing who complained about manuscripts that kept shifting point of view from character to character, saying, 'It's like going to the theater and being forced to change your seat every five minutes.' Professor Weaver it was, and what a strange web we weaver, as Paul Casey's brother Jim once remarked.

Kerrigan's plan is to drink a pint of beer in every café on the Coal Square, moving full circle around, clockwise perhaps for the sake of symmetry, to see what variety of wonders this exercise in point of view – pint of view rather – might reveal to him, changing his seat after every pint. And realizes that, in this circular square, clockwise is itself a point of view.

41

Vagn's Beef and Sausage Wagon
(Vagns Bøf og Pølsevogn)

Vagns Bøf og Pølsevogn
Kultorvet *(The Coal Square)*
1175 København K

He stops first at Vagn's Beef and Sausage Wagon to fortify his stomach from amongst the wares offered:

Wienerpølse	Vienna sausage
Knækpølse	Elbow sausage
Medisterpølse	Medister sausage
Hot dog	Hot Dog
Fransk hot dog	French hot dog
Ristet pølse	Fried sausage
Almindelig pølse	Boiled sausage

Settling on a Vienna sausage on a tiny bun, the ends hanging out on both sides, center piled high with mustard, ketchup and chopped raw onion, he digs in. A treat! His cholesterol sings marvellous hymns in his blood, and he munches happily as the sexy woman in the flower stall wraps a bunch of pink carnations in white paper for a smiling, snub-nosed woman who clearly intends to brighten her rooms somewhere while a wiry blond fellow in the fruit-stand alongside sings out, 'Hey ten delicious Danish plums for a tenner! Ten Danish plums for a tenner!'

Another bite, tangy mustard on the palate and onion sweetening the breath for an earthy kiss perhaps. Nibble those drooping ends with their little stubs of fried string. Yum. You are what you eat: Kerrigan has occasionally dreamed of being a hot dog consumed by a lovely young maiden! There's a fantasy for his giant Norwegian headshrink, who once called him mini-Terry, giving him an erection of irritation and humiliation. Aren't wolves dangerous?

Now the flower lady is calling out, 'Hey ten pretty roses for a tenner! Ten pretty roses for a tenner!'

Before starting his cycle of Coal Square cafés, he weaves through the benches at the southeast corner of the square where derelict Inuits lounge, drinking export beer with gold foil at the neck.

'Any surplus today, friend?' one of the Inuits asks, and Kerrigan tosses a two-crown coin into the man's hat.

He enters the *Biblioteksboghandel* – The Library Bookshop – so named because the business school alongside it used to be the main branch of the Copenhagen library. He drifts down to the basement and rummages among cut-rate offerings – novels, poetry, history, coffee table books about airplanes, war machines, madonnas, art, masks . . .

He leafs through the mask book, pauses to study a full-page color photograph of a long, white, slit-eyed mask from the Cameroon, glaring out at him from beneath curved horns. Among the words of the caption beneath, the phrase 'grimacing devil' catches his eye. He flips the page to see a mask of the furious widow Kali, tongue lolling to devour the world in her rage, her hair aflame, tusks curving from her jowls, black eyes bulging with rage. Kerrigan commands his eyes from the page, demands that his mind not remember his mother after his father's funeral, curly hair dyed fire red, her hyperthyroidic stare as she sat before the television each night out on the Palouse, peeling – as wrapping from a gift – the oiled rag in which his father's side-arm had been wrapped, then wrapping it up again.

'Please stop doing that, mother.'

'Don't be such a silly,' she said and stuck her tongue through her teeth. 'It's not even loaded.'

Kerrigan shuts the book, moves on.

There are how-tos and opera books, travel guides, a whole wall of cheap classics which he feels as though he has read and would not admit to not having done, though in truth he has barely ever more than scanned a good many of them. Read a few though, more than a few, yes. He takes down Lucretius, reads on the back what is said to be the only existing biography of Lucretius, by St Jerome:

> 'Titus Lucretius, the poet, born 94 B C. He was rendered insane by a love-philtre and, after writing, during intervals of lucidity, some books, which Cicero amended, he died by his own hand in the 43rd year of his life.'

Kerrigan buys the book, a ten-crown bargain, buck and a half, that fits into the rear pocket of his Italian jeans, and goes back out onto the Coal Square where a tall thin man with a sickly pale face and dented jaw approaches.

'Sir, can you help with a coin for a homeless man. And it's not junk, sir, you can check my arms,' he says, rolling up his sleeves. 'See? No tracks, sir. Not a one.'

Give the man some coins. Could be you. Out on your arches with your plastic bags. Kerrigan palms him a handful of metal, and the man moves on without so much as a thanks, stopping to speak to a woman at a café table.

'Miss, can you help a homeless man. And it's not junk, miss . . .'

42

Laura's Café

Laura's Café
Kultorvet
1175 København K

Still smacking his lips with the memory of his sausage, he starts his café carousal at Laura's, little tucked-in section of half a dozen tables with a slung-jaw Turk happy to provide him with a pint glass of amber lager.

Who can be happier than a man with a pint and a cigar at a table in the early afternoon sunlight with a book of pre-Christian Latin poetry, purchased for a pittance, on the table before him?

Here in this very café he once sat with the Danish novelist Lotte Inuk whose real name is Inuk Hoff Hansen, christened Inuk because by chance born in Greenland, and who increments her writing income by reading Tarot. She read Kerrigan's cards and the last card she turned down was of a man lying on his face with seven swords buried in his bleeding back.

'This is not an unalterable future,' she told him. 'And please remember that the swords are metaphors for devotion to quests for that which is base.' And Kerrigan wished to take her soft hand in both of his and kiss it gently though refrained from attempting to do so because she was so much younger than he and involved with a German fellow writing a doctoral thesis on Kafka.

And look over there at that guy in purple jogging bottoms playing pocket-pool I tellya! And oh so would I when I see that gal in rust-colored pants clinging just so to her big powerful butt! He gazes with devil-slit eyes upon it, imagines horns upon his own head, a love-philtre emptied in the beer that drenches his parched mouth. Let me die of love, then. Let me die of dedication to the beauty of the feminine species. Let me, as the Danish poet Karsten Kok Hansen once advised him, 'Love love love as though your life depended on it cause it does.' Or as the Frenchman gesturing to the fork of a woman's thighs once said, '*Rien sans lui.*'

From where he sits he can see diagonally across the square the opening into *Rosengårdens* street where the nightmen and executioner used to reside, thinks of the nightmen in their 'chocolate wagons', collecting the shit of the city in the days before sewers, right up to the early part of this century on whose outer edge he perches, imagining himself as a curiosity being studied by some citizen a hundred years hence, the year 2099. A brook too broad for leaping.

Please leave quietly said the sign on back of the door of one of the pubs he once visited in London, and Kerrigan responds now, belatedly, No sir, I will *not* leave quietly; I shall depart with much noise and stamping of feet and I shall let the door smack harshly shut behind me!

Yet Kerrigan now greets the eyes that read these words. Terrence Kerrigan greets all happy boys and happy girls glancing back to the past. Is *anyone*, in fact, reading this? Who are you? Are you free or slave? Do you have beliefs or is all belief long dead? Do you live in fear and shackles? Do you know the passionate joy of intellectual speculation? The beauty of the human body. Do you have a lover to carress? Do you know the golden pleasures of beer? Do you know, dear children of a future time, that love, sweet love, was once a crime?

You can see me, but I can't see you, and by the time you read this *if* you ever do, please remember that my blood was Celtic and the season spring, and Georg Brandes' *Thoughts at the Turn of the Century*, published in 1899, will seem a true antiquity, 200 years old, longer than any person can ever hope to survive unless medical science and the world economy make leaps not yet imagined possible.

Kerrigan will ask no questions of his reader a hundred years hence for he is aware he is ill-equipped to do so, just as Brandes was when he said in 1899, 'The pointed question of future European politics is this: In the twentieth century, will Russia or England becomes the world's greatest power?'

And the turn-of-the century world he describes in 1899 was one in which 'The large powers are dividing the globe between them. They strive to do it as peacefully as possible inasmuch as they want to avoid a world war. They still go about it quite inconsiderately. For the sake of their economic advantage, they victimize not only the unlucky nation, which they subject to fire, sword and full horror, but additionally all the surrounding smaller nations. These are swallowed up for the benefit of national unity, used as barter goods, or delivered to brutality so that peace can be preserved. That is how, with the consent of Christian Europe, the Sultan allowed 300,000 Armenians to be murdered.'

With but four fingers of beer remaining in his glass, Kerrigan's mood turns glum, considering the place that used to be called Yugoslavia, the bombs and missiles, slaughter, rape. He considers the fact that but eight years ago he was the happy editor of a small anthology of Yugoslavian literature, and none of the work he gathered for it seemed to focus anywhere but on the profound existential matters that go beyond national concerns. He thinks of Susan Schwartz Senstad's novel, *Music for the Third Ear*, which, under one of his pseudonyms, he had the privilege of introducing in a special issue of *The Literary Review* shortly before it found its British and American publishers – a book about the child produced by one of those rapes, by a woman raped repeatedly every day by a variety of men of another ethnic background than hers so that their seed would be carried in her body and so that none of them could be called the father because it might have been any one of a hundred, thus none of them bears responsibility for the child.

This is fiction, but the facts are true, and they are dated 1999.

The story ends with the rejected child hated by everyone, his mother, his father, all the people of Europe who do not wish to have to consider his existence or the way it came about, a skinny lad of four or five whose name is Zero (named that by a mother who cannot bear the thought of his existence and would have aborted him had her keepers not forced her to carry and deliver him), firing a toy cap pistol at the world. The unvoiced question, of course, is what manner of pistol will his hand hold fifteen or twenty years hence – in the year 2020, say?

The child Zero is akin to Kosinski's *Painted Bird*, Jewish child survivor of the anti-semitism of the twentieth century's third and fourth decades, but Kosinki's child had the option of Amerika (even if Kosinki's own fate there ended with an untimely bath and plastic bag over his head), while Senstad's Zero is already hated, cut adrift in western European host countries whose social democracy has worn thin as the paper of the *Magna Carta*.

Incongruously, as the mind's multi-clustered synapses function, Kerrigan recalls once in a bar politely requesting in Danish some matches (*tændstikker*), politely clarifying that it was *matches* he needed, and the barman, voluntarily bald and beefy, remarked politely, 'When you live here, sir, perhaps you should consider going and learning Danish.'

'I can say '*drikkepenge*', which in English is 'tip', which you shall not be receiving today.'

'Who needs it, sir?' asked the voluntarily bald and muscular barman, turning his back on Kerrigan, hurting his feelings and making him sad that he had responded as he had.

Go to the next café.

43

Nacho's Café & Tequila Bar

Nacho's Café & Tequila Bar
Kultorvet
1175 København K

He drains his beer, moves three meters south to a table at Nacho's Turkish Mexican Café & Tequila Bar, obtains a pint of green Tuborg at the counter and places himself at the outer perimeter of the tables. To his right, a bronze sculpture of a bench with a bronze elderly couple seated on it, a reresentation of the couple from Hans Christian Andersen's 'The Elder Tree Mother', first published in P L Møller's literary annual *GAEA* in 1845, long before Møller's syphilitic madness in Normandy, illustrated with a copper plate by Frølich, just prior to the intensification of the venomous exchange between Møller and Kierkegaard which would leave them both poisoned according to the Stangerup story.

Twenty meters across the square, the personnel at Jensen's Beef House Café are distributing free helium balloons to children who are jumping about like puppies or young goats. A lady bug lands on the back of Kerrigan's hand, alongside a pale age-spot. He speaks the ritual in his mind,

'Lady bug, lady bug, fly away!
Your house is on fire,
And your children will burn . . .'

and just for good measure adds the Danish ritual:

'Marie Marie Ma Høne
Flyv op til Vorherre
Og be' om godt vejr imørgen!'

Funny, thinks Kerrigan, that the Danish is so less gloomy. The ladybug in Danish is called a *mariehøne* – a Maria Hen – and the ritual chant is:

'Maria Maria My hen
Fly up to the Lord
And pray for good weather tomorrow.'

He blows her off his hand into the air with a fanning out of spotted wings. She lights up in the sun, and what could be more beautiful and full of hope than the new full pint of golden beer he hoists into the air to toast the unknown faces watching from the future?

Who *are* you, my friends? Singular really. For you can only read this on your own, one person and a book, I can only address one of you at a time, only one of you at a time can let me in.

If you have come this far, you could only be a friend. Let me tell you where I have buried my fortune, and if you hurry you can find it before anyone else gets there. I want to give you everything I have, paltry though it may be to you in your place of wealth and vantage in the future. 100 crowns, 100 years ago was a fortune. It would afford a month's rent and sustenance, a suit of clothing, a hat, a pair of shoes, many cigars and much strong drink. Today it hardly affords a decent bottle of wine or two, and a pack of cheap cigarillos, or 2.5 pints of beer. What will constitute a fortune 100 years hence? Perhaps it will have little or nothing to do with money. Perhaps it will have to do with a patch of grass, a tree, a tiny glimpse of a blue sky. Perhaps it will have to do with a plastic key card that gives entry to an account whose monetary units are replenished by hours of service at some authorized task. Perhaps it will have to do with the ability to decode black scratches which are symbols of the sounds we make with our mouths and allow any human being to transmit the secrets of his or her mind to the skull cages of others.

The Coal Square most likely still will be here, but housing what? Owned by whom? Dedicated to what pursuits? He looks across at the White Lamb café from 1807. Even the Duke of Wellington's entire fleet of barborous gunships did not succeed in undoing the Lamb, barely nicked its roof. Nelson and the Duke of Wellington are dead, and in 1966 the IRA blew away the pillar in Dublin commemorating Admiral Nelson, but the White Lamb's golden beer flows on nearly 200 years after Nelson and Wellington's attacks on this city, and perhaps will still serve its useful function 100 years from now at which time virtually all currently treading or crawling the earth will have dust for brains.

What else? That corner building with the Clapboard Café where Kierkegaard lived in 1838 – surely, yes. And these trees? How many of them? He sits up, rotating in his chair, and counts. Ten of them, spaced irregularly around the square. Larch trees and beech. How old are they? He cannot be sure. Some are large and old, some slight and green and new, witnesses to all this life and bustle of shoppers, mothers and fathers pushing baby carriages, Vagn selling sausages, a bookshop which for a mere ten crowns, a dollar and a half, gives me this slim back-pocket volume written two millennia past by a Latin poet driven so mad by a love potion that he took his own life at 43, a fact Kerrigan considers at 56. Yet managed to make use of his lucid moments to record words still read now, more than 2,000 years later.

In truth, how vast is the culture of this brave new world!

He shifts his chair and tips back his head to gaze upward at the spreading branches of the beech tree above him, the little fig-shaped leaves, branches overlapping to form a protective mosaic whose shadow drifts on the ground beneath – shelter from sun, from rain.

He thinks inevitably of Joyce Kilmer, 'Poems are made by fools like me/But only God can make a tree', and then remembers the potion which his Associate produced on the occasion of their last meeting when she whispered, or he imagined her doing so, that God is a cunt. She had a tiny phial concealed in her hand. Poppers. Amyl Nitrate. She shook it and sniffed, held it to his nostrils, and the sensations of his palms against her skin were charged, electric. For but a few seconds, their copulation was truly golden.

From behind him he hears two Turkish waiters chatting in Danish, can not quite catch the words. 'She knows we like . . .' He hears tramping in the distance, and the Pure Love Brigade comes marching across the square again chanting, 'No sex! No cry!' and 'Yee-*ha*!'

American bluenoses out on a spree, damned from here to eternity, Lord have mercy on such as ye. He promises himself that if they come again, he will by god, moon the blue-nosed fools with his hairy fat pimpled pink butt.

Yee-ha!

He can see a window open on Peder Hvitfeldts Street with bed covers hanging over the sill to air out all the sex and fuck germs. Just think of all the prick, cunt, asshole, armpit germs clinging to them. Then the breezes carry them away in the air, floating right over the heads of the marching prudes – Yee-*ha*! – take a shower of sex germs!

Free as the air. Over Kerrigan's head, too. They land on his scalp, remnants of love illicit and sacred, perversion, inversion, missionary couplings, and the partakings of oral joys. Love whippings, cock suckings, cunt lappings and humpings galore! Golden showers, secretory overflows. The germs dust down over his face and shoulders and his rod goes stiff. He breathes through his mouth ingesting sex pollen, washes it down on the golden beer and moves to the next café, Jensen's, slightly hunched to conceal his secret, thinking *God's sacred teeth, I'm half pissed already and I am so fucking horny still even at my advanced age so sweetening all lamentation!*

44

Jensen's Beef House Café *(Jensen's Bøfhus Café)*

Jensen's Bøfhus Café
Kultorvet
1175 København K

I'm pissed and I'm proud! he chants privately, crossing the few meters to Jensen's, noting that it says *UFF* on the storefront behind the café in yellow and black letters with black outline. *UFF.* And, *Quality used clothing.*

He settles with a beer delivered by the plump-wristed hand of a daughter of God whose taps are in a kiosk like the one on the King's New Square that he almost bid on in auction. Her smile as she hands over the frothy glass would change the mind of Gilgamesh.

Oh you gorgeous bitch! *Gawjus! Vidunderlige kælling!* Which translates literally as Wonderful Cow, the title of a Danish popular play of the 70s in which a couple of dozen well known Danish actors and actresses danced naked on the stage for the love of Eros. Gorgeous Bitch! Just another way of saying what Prince meant when he sang, *Sexy mother fucker shakin' that ass, shakin' that ass . . .*

The beautiful women are multiplying and their tits tell all, kid. Their men must neglect them or they would not be out parading their loveliness this way. Or perhaps they parade their loveliness because their men have made them mindful and proud of their magnificent forms.

Or maybe they are God, gods, the new gods, the goddesses of the new paradigm calling forth the most beautiful of desires, to gaze with joy and wonder upon the body, to create new life. Why don't you come up and see me some time, big boy? Join me in a prayer on behalf of the sacred body.

The sunlight through his beer gleams on the table before him, a glass of golden fire, cool and wonderful in his mouth as he swallows deeply, and deeply again, and again . . .

45

The Clapboard Café *(Klaptræet Café)*

Klaptræet Café
Kultorvet
1175 København K

On the back of his hand he tallies the pints with the strokes of his Montblanc, just to know, because one loses count so easily, and sees there are already four strokes as he takes his table at the Clapboard and surveys the square from this pint of view, taking inventory:

There are seven outdoor cafés, one sausage bar, four restaurants, a business college, a bookstore, one employment agency, a fucking 7-Eleven, one used clothing store (UFF), one unused clothing store, ten trees, a flower stall, a fruit stand, a travel agency named Albatross ('Upon my word I slayed the bird/That made the breeze to blow . . .'). The apartment that Sørgen Kierkegaard called home in 1838 and the White Lamb serving house that the Duke of Wellington's cannon failed to destroy in 1807, though it did dent the roof. The Duke was then known as Arthur Wellesley (1769-1852), born in Dublin and commemorated there in Phoenix Park by a 205-foot granite obelisk (1817) located just inside the park's main gate, on the eastern side and but a stone's throw from the feet of Finn MacCool, who like Holger Dansk, sleeps beneath Dublin, dreaming the history of the Irish race.

Finn's feet and God's teeth, and yellow leaves blow across his table. Jensen's personnel are still handing out complimentary helium balloons, two of which fly up into the blue and silver sky. The mother of one of the children ties a balloon string through the hole in the center of a five-crown coin so it cannot fly away; the weight of the coin holds it down, lingering in the air a foot or so above the pavement, and Kerrigan watches another mother bend to this task and would give an award to that rump if he were chairing a committee charged to do so. Happy the chair beneath her, said Leopold Bloom.

I love these women so, and look! There goes one eating a big green apple with her white teeth, how her lips compress over the tight green skin, and see, that infant there can hardly walk, tottering after the copulating pigeons who move on, hopping with a scurry of wings, foiled in the act by a tot: *Yee-ha!*

Get thee to a heel and key bar, sir! And you, there, sir, you stoop-shouldered fellow of grimacing visage, stand up straight! Walk like a man!

Now comes a party of roller bladers swooping through like maurauders, at the speed of frustration, as Lance Olsen put it in *Burnt*, and there up above the Niels Brock International Business College, Kerrigan remembers, on the fourth or fifth floor, are the offices of *Det Danske Selskab*, The Danish Cultural Institute, whose publication department once was run by a woman named Kate Hegelund whom everybody loved and who one day for unexplained reasons at a most untimely age was dead.

Her smiling face, her braided golden hair, her gentle ways never to see the new millennium.

46

Nico's Café

Nico's Café
Kultorvet
1175 København K

Now he runs a line across the four strokes on the back of his hand and buys a little bag of crisps to munch along with the green Tuborg draft purchased from the Nico alewife, remembering the books that Kate Hegelund gave him. He knows practically nothing about her, met her at some function, received her card, which he still has tucked away inside the cover of a book entitled *Songs from Denmark, A Collection of Danish Hymns, Songs and Ballads in English Translation*, edited by Peter Baslev-Clausen, the Danish Cultural Institute, 1988. And printed on the back of the book is her name, 'Kate'. She gave him *her* copy. Because he expressed interest in the book, and hers was the only one left, and that was how she was.

She would send him copies of the books produced by the Institute, at least one of which he had reviewed somewhere. Now he tried to remember something about Kate. He and Gordon Weaver and she at some function in Odense once, coming back on the train, waiting for the train at Odense station, perhaps a decade past, had stopped in the DSB Café for a snack of very old cheese and beer and snaps.

Yes, I can close my eyes and see her face, such a lovely gentle woman you would think only the most pure and reverent thoughts of her, wishing never to cause disappointment to appear on that bright round blue-eyed face of radiance, no, or were the eyes in truth brown, the hair commune yellow? Kate I hardly knew you, remember only that you had spent some time in Indochina, and I thank God I never got drunk enough in your presence to express unseemly desire, evoking disappointment in your eyes, the memory of which would now deeply sadden me . . . I think you had a child if I remember correctly. And that is all I knew yet I remember your face after all these years, your smile, your light and gentle manner that gave such brightness to everyone you spoke to.

And then you were dead. And no explanations. Was it something about a bicycle accident? A head injury?

I can still see in your hand a book of essays you handed me, shyly offering it, published on the occasion of what would have been the hundredth birthday of Isak Dinesen/Karen Blixen in 1985, titled *Out of Denmark: Danish Women Writers Today* – which, being 15 years ago, would now have to be called Danish Women Writers Yesterday.

There were essays on Karen Blixen, Kirsten Thorup, Suzanne Brøgger, Dorrit Willumsen, Elsa Gress, Inger Christensen, and Pia Tafdrup. And a companion volume by another publisher which contained original work by the women who were subject of the essays. That was titled *No Man's Land: An Anthology of Modern Danish Women's Literature*. Kerrigan reviewed the two books jointly in *Translation Review* under his pseudonym.

The title *No Man's Land* was the title of the essay by Suzanne Brøgger in which she discussed the new centre of society which lies on the periphery of 'the old phallocracy'. He remembers Brøgger saying, 'Woman do not wish to get on top. Our goals have never been that low.' Here too was an excerpt from Karen Blixen's *Letters from Africa*, translated by Anne Born, where she said, 'If it did not sound so beastly I might say that, the world being as it is, it was worth having syphilis in order to become a Baroness . . .' and 'My craving for money is partly due to the fact that for me material and physical and visual things, I think, more than for most people, are an expression of something spiritual.'

Kerrigan considers this, baffled that such a great writer could make such an idiotic, ego-trapped statement. But he recalls then in the essay about her in *Out of Denmark* by the Danish poet Thorkild Bjørnvig, born in 1918, who probably knew Blixen as well as anyone ever did, he explores the many facets of her identity – as an idea of nature, a marionette, a wild animal, a teller of tales, and a creature free of identity, relieved of and escaped from identity, in a state of 'permanent adventure and pleasure'. In the essay, Bjørnvig quotes a poem by Dinesen's favorite twentieth-century poet, Sophus Clausen:

> 'Are you wiser than the tree . . .
> Don't you think the forest saw you with its thousand
> silent branches,
> though you thought yourself alone . . .?'

The glass is empty, and Kerrigan's intoxication has ebbed with five strokes on the back of his hand as he glances from tree to tree around the square, their leaves trembling with the life of the air that touches them, wondering if their thousand silent branches sense his presence, immediately dismissing the thought as worthy only of his own ego cage, for it is the question of an ego, the least important part of his being.

47

The White Lamb Café *(Det Hvide Lam Café)*

Det Hvide Lam Café
Kultorvet
1175 København K

The outdoor tables administered by the White Lamb are few, a single row of four or five, and he strokes the back of his hand with the nib of his Montblanc, beginning the second set of five pints, his mood heavier than he would have expected it to be.

He is thinking about Thorkild Bjørnvig whom he has met a couple of times and corresponded with, a gentle gracious man who with the utmost delicacy once pointed out to Kerrigan an utterly idiotic mistake he had made in translating one of Bjørnvig's poems. A mistake that could only come about by carelessness. Bjørnvig understood, it seemed, that the mere fact of discovering the mistake would cause Kerrigan shame and so he did his utmost not to exacerbate that shame.

It was the kind of act which improves the world because it taught Kerrigan a lesson in humility and gentleness that left him eager to apply what he had learned in his own future dealings with members of the human race. Bjørnvig has been writing poems for many decades and in the most recent years has devoted his attention to ecology. The poems Kerrigan translated were delicate and beautiful observations of nature – a raven rising into the sky, swallow chicks on a rainy day, or the breath of the sea at Hebrides Bay.

Bjørnvig also has written a book about his friendship with Karen Blixen, *The Pact*. He and Blixen both were very taken up by the question of their identity and whether it is an historical or a cosmic question.

It occurs to Kerrigan as he swallows the first of his sixth pint and gazes up at the green leaves above his head that he has never even asked himself who he is. Perhaps I am just a drunkard. Perhaps, because I do not even ask, I doom myself to being no one, nothing.

'I'm nobody, who are you?'

Dickinson's words lift in his blood with the beer, and he thinks perhaps it is all right not to have asked that question. It is difficult enough work just to be, without having to know quite who it is you are being:

'How dreary – to be – Somebody!
How public – like a Frog –
To tell one's name – the junelong day –
To an admiring Bog!'

Just that I not occasion evil, he thinks. Or harm a child. If but my life be like Kate Hegelund's smile.

Halfway down the beer and his eyes are on the front of the building where Kate Hegelund worked. He lifts his glass to her, wishes her well in her eternal rest or eternal joy, surely the only two possibilities for such a person, and feels water in his eyes.

This day is not proceeding as the carefree carousal he anticipated. An image flashes in his mind of the slit-eyed devil grimace he saw earlier in the mask book, and he wonders if it hexed him. Then of the Kali he had commanded himself not to admit into consciousness. But then he remembers the Lucretius in his back pocket.

He swallows the rest of the Tuborg and leaves the White Lamb behind, crossing the center of the square.

48

The Coal Square Restaurant Café
(Kultorvet Restaurant Café)

Kultorvet Restaurant Café
Kultorvet
1175 København K

The bar of the last of the Coal Square's seven cafés is housed in a shack where Kerrigan marks the seventh stroke on the back of his hand as the waiter taps his beer. He sits in the sun with Lucretius in his hands, but he is thinking about Pia Tafdrup whose work he came to know through Kate.

No, he met her at a poetry festival in 1985 at the Betty Nansen Theater. She was billed between Ken Kesey and Ed Sanders. Pia is that rare creature, a full time poet in her mid-forties with nine collections in print, a few anthologies of contemporary Danish poetry, a play, a book setting forth her poetics.

Her poetry is intelligent and sensual. Though not postmodern, its direct concern with craft and language reflects a sensitivity to the postmodern era's concern with art as a means of, rather than a mere way to, identity.

And there it was again, that word, *identity*. The mirror in Pia Tafdrup's poems is contained as an object *within* the poetry, where 'larks cut the pages of the day' waking a sleeper from a dream about a reader in which books are mirrors.

It seems to Kerrigan her vision shows a hurt perhaps not unlike Sylvia Plath's but less at odds with existence. If Plath's work was an extended suicide note, Tafdrup's is a catalogue of beguilements, poetic moments with 'the dark language', the 'white fever', visions that bloom from the concrete (a butchered hare bleeding onto a newspaper, the wings of a bird frozen to a lake beating against the ice) as well as the concretization of visions (the cold 'a white hand that opens and closes in darkness', and the dead who 'cast shadows in the blood of those still living') in a place where 'the invisible makes everything more visible' for 'the glass clear seconds a song lasts'.

He remembers then a line from one of her poems about the butchering of a hare that ends,

> ' . . . each of us
> must die
> far from the words
> perhaps in the depth of sleep
> or in the hasty flight of dreams'.

He thinks of Kate again, and he thinks of himself now, perhaps dying from some wound in his mouth. It seems somehow a fitting end for a writer, through a wound in the mouth. The wound of the mouth. *Where you sin you shall be punished.* Old Spanish proverb. And the word was made blood. He can taste it now beneath the wheaty flavor of the beer, the metal taste of his own blood.

He closes his eyes. The day is hot now and humid, but with an occasional saving breeze. He is dying it seems, near an end he has hastened with his imprudent but most enjoyable behavior. And with his eyes closed or with his eyes opened, it is the same, for he is alone and that startles and unsettles him. At such a moment there ought to be a witness. A woman who loves him. A man who admires his work – a man whose own work he himself admires. A woman whose work makes him see. An artist perhaps, who once painted a picture for him of a red frog perhaps.

How public like a frog.

An image appears in his mind of the table beside his bed. It is as though he is lying in bed on a humid night, motionless, the hand of death closing ever so slowly, imperceptibly, around him, and on the bedside table is an 8.5 by 11inch white pad with pale blue lines the color of water too beautiful to be real. How lovely the pad is. If he could only reach it, he would caress it like a lover's back, a woman he knew whose back beneath his palm was joy, splendor.

Such words! But what others would suffice for her?

Who *was* it? Her again. The Associate. Will he never be free of thoughts of her?

You have not lived right, Terry-boy. I've lived the only way I could. You could have done better, been more prudent, careful, you would have lasted longer.

Who wants it?

He opens his eyes and realizes he is almost asleep there for a moment. He sees on the surface of the round metal table before him a half full pint of beer and a book. Lucretius. He opens the book at random, as the Romans used to do to find a sign, and he reads:

> 'O miserable minds of men! O blinded beasts! In what darkness of life and in how great dangers is passed this term of life whatever its duration! Not choose to see that nature craves for herself no more than this, that pain hold aloof from the body, and she in mind enjoy a feeling of pleasure exempt from care and fear?'

And

> 'Hot fevers do not sooner quit the body if you toss about on pictured tapestry and blushing purple than if you must lie under a poor man's blanket.'

And

> 'The sores of life are in no small measure fostered by the dread of death. For foul scorn and pinching want in every case are seen to be far removed from a life of pleasure and security and to be a loitering, so to say, before the gates of death. And while men driven on by an unreal dread wish to escape far away from these and keep them far from them, they amass wealth by civil bloodshed and greedily double their riches piling up murder on murder; cruelly triumph in the sad death of a brother and hate and fear the tables of kinsfolk. Often likewise from the same fear envy causes them to pine: they make moan that before their very eyes he is powerful, he attracts attention, who walks arrayed in gorgeous dignity while they are wallowing in darkness and dirt. Some wear themselves to death for the sake of statues and a name. And often to such a degree through dread of death does hate of life and of the sight of daylight seize upon mortals that they commit self-murder with a sorrowing heart, quite forgetting that this fear is the source of their cares, this fear which urges men to every sin . . . For even as children are flurried and dread all things in the thick darkness, thus we in the daylight fear at times things not a whit more to be dreaded than what children shudder at in the dark and fancy there to be. This terror therefore and darkness of mind must be dispelled . . .'

From inside the restaurant behind the café, Kerrigan hears music, John Lennon singing, 'Mother,' and deep inside his mind, the lilting voice, *Terry! Oh, Ter-ry!*

He shudders and closes the book, looks into his glass and does not think about the woman who killed all dread as the tramping of feet approaches up Butcher Street:

'*Yee! Ha!*'

The Pure Love Militants again.

Kerrigan remembers the promise he made to himself to moon them if they came back, but does not move.

A life is built on promises unkept.

It seems such an indifferent number of pen strokes to stop on. Seven. If seven pints in seven pubs should drink for seven years . . . If seven time seven angels should appear in a dream of animals . . . If seven pints of view . . . If much of a which of a wind . . .

The slung-jawed Turk at the tables in Laura's seems to be watching him with a smile as Kerrigan rises from his table here, tucks Lucretius back into his hip pocket and salutes in the name of Housman:

> 'For I have been to Ludlow Fair
> And left my necktie God knows where
> And carried halfway home or near
> Pints and quarts of Ludlow beer . . .
> And down in lovely muck I've lain
> Happy till I woke again.
> And then I saw the morning sky
> Heighho the tale was all a lie . . .
> And nothing then remained to do
> But begin the game anew . . .'

The Turk pulls back a chair for him as he approaches to begin a new circuit of the old square.

CHRISTIANSHAVN

Adventures in Urology

'And if your eye or ear offend you
Pluck it out, man, and be whole!
But play the man, stand up and end you,
If your sickness is your soul.'

– A E Housman

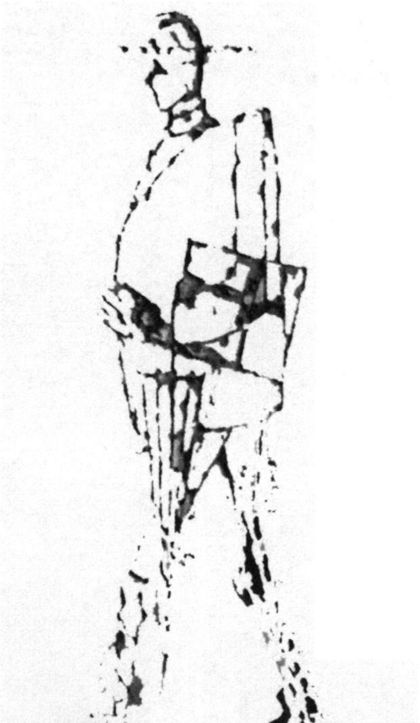

49

The Ferry Café *(Færge Caféen)*

Færge Caféen
Strandgade (*Strand Street*) 50
1401 København K

But instead of recycling the Coal Square, he walks, back down Butcher Street, east over Højbro Place, past the equestrian statue of Bishop Absalon, founder of Copenhagen, wielding the axe of battle and domesticity. Past *Holmens Kirke* where Queen Margarethe II married her French prince consort Henrik.

Kerrigan floats on easy feet over Knippels Bridge, spanning the slit of harbor between Zealand and Amager islands, to *Strandgade*, left to where *Strandgade* meets *Christianshavns Kanal* and the masts of small pleasure craft tip with the breeze on the lightly billowing water, mast fittings clanging agreeably. He stands on the wooden bridge for a moment, Wilders Bridge, watching the surface of the water change with the miniscule constant changes of the Danish afternoon light.

He gazes down *Strandgade* to *Christians Kirke* which was built in 1759, a few houses down from the former home of the famous sea captain, Tordenskjold, whose portrait and name appear for some reason on every little box of stick matches manufactured by H E Gosch & Co. and whose statue was sculpted by the

Norwegian, Gustav Vigeland. Born as Peter Wessel (1690-1720), the Danish-Norwegian sea hero was awarded the noble title Tordenskjold in 1716, four years before his death at the age of 30 in a duel. Tordenskjold is also commemorated in the Danish phrase, '*Tordenskjolds soldater*', which means Tordenskjold Soldiers, from a strategy he once employed when defending a fortification against a far greater force. He had his few men move about and show their faces again and again from different spots, creating the effect of having many more than in fact he had. The term today is used to indicate an undermanned enterprise in which the same people appear in many roles. And Tordenskjold's house today is the home of the Danish Writers Union of which Kerrigan is a silent member.

Past a stucco wall of ochre yellow, he enters through the door of the Ferry Café, with its porthole window. His mouth cannot room more beer just now, or his belly house it, so he orders a double *gammel dansk*. The woman behind the bar, red-grey haired, a face that has lived, serves him his bitter dram (dram being a measure for snaps originating from the Greek word *drakhem* – a weight unit equalling 4.25 grams, same root as the Greek currency unit, *drachma*, to be replaced by the European currency unit, foiling all future plans by Greek taxi drivers to pull the old 5,000/50,000 drachma note switcheroo), and answers his question that the café dates back to 1850. The walls are panelled with ship planks, and a ship's-wheel lamp hangs from the ceiling. Beside the bar, a brass ship's bell stands ready to be rung should some generous customer buy a round for the house, and a pool table shrouded with a sheet of green plastic.

He takes his drink on the canal side of the establishment, gazing across to Wilders Place and the tipping masts while a couple of bureaucrats from the Cultural Ministry across the street finish their lunches of liver and bacon and onions and mushrooms.

The black bitter liquid, he imagines, caulks the wound in his mouth.

You have to go to the doctor, he knows he will be advised if he reveals the fact of this wound to anyone.

Then he will have to try to explain why, like Bartleby the Scrivner, he should prefer not to. He had enough of medical intervention two years ago when he visited the Urology Department of a Danish hospital that will remain here unnamed. He was having an affair at the time with a lady physician who, listening through the bathroom door once when he peed, told him he should consult a urologist.

'Why?'

'Because you piss like an old man.'

'How does an old man piss?'

'Wery wery slowly. And gruntingly. You've got an obstruction. Could be your prostate. Someone should look at it. I'll make an appointment for you.'

Which she did and which he kept. Never guessing that he would be required to remove his pants and shorts and mount a table so that a pretty nurse could squirt anaesthetic down through the lips of his penis. He inhaled through his teeth, and she made sympathetic noises, but then proceeded to run some manner of wire down his prick to his bladder and another up the old kazoo. The one wire was attached to an electronic measuring device and the other to a plastic bladder of water, which she began to feed through into *his* bladder.

'As soon as you feel the urge to micturate, please do so into that butterfly pail which will measure the speed and completeness of your micturation.'

'Now,' he said almost immediately, for the wire in his organ was tickling unbearably. She removed the wire and waited. Nothing happened. She tapped her foot. He blushed. A blush is the color of virtue. Old Danish proverb.

'Shall I leave you to yourselv for a moment?'

'Yes, please.'

She did, but still nothing happened, which, when she returned and saw the empty pail, displeased her.

He was instructed to wait, and a team of health personnel entered to take a sound picture of his bladder.

'It is almost completely empty,' the head of this team told him. She was also a beauty, dark-haired and smiling down at him where he lay sans-culottes on the table.

'Is that bad?' he asked, somewhat tired of being naked before all these women.

'No. That is good, as far as I am concerned. But we will have to take more tests.'

A resident appeared, a very large man with very large fingers, who announced he would have to palpate Kerrigan's prostate for which process Kerrigan was requested to get up on his knees on the edge of the table, perched rather like a rabbit, when without prelude, warning, or lubrication, one of those large fingers, sheathed in plastic, shot to its mark.

Kerrigan yelled.

'That seems to be in order,' the young doctor pronounced, 'but we will want pictures.'

The next team was led by a Senior Resident, another very large man, assisted by three unidentified uniformed women. It occurred to Kerrigan that men of a certain bent might pay large sums of money to experience this for their psycho-sexual amusement, but he himself was not amused when the doctor, wielding a not slender wand-like photographic apparatus, smiled with many teeth and said down into Kerrigan's reclining face, 'Want to bet this is not going to be anywhere near as terrible as you fear?' and proceeded to shove the camera down his dick.

Kerrigan yelled.

'Please try to relax,' the doctor snapped.

Kerrigan yelled again. And he did not stop yelling until the camera crew withdrew its equipment and the young Senior Resident said, 'You may feel the urge to micturate now,' and Kerrigan filled the pail the nurse produced for him and had to request another. She guided him like a blinded, staggering Oedipus to his clothes and helped him dress, led him into another room where he sat on a stool beside a desk and waited.

The Senior Resident with the fat fingers appeared, and Kerrigan decided he would cooperate no further.

'Did you have a hard time of it?' the doctor asked.

'It was not fun,' said Kerrigan.

'Well your prostate is very slightly enlarged,' the doctor said.

'We can correct that surgically, which is the most effective way, or pharmaceutically.'

'I think pharmaceutically,' said Kerrigan.

'The surgical intervention is much more effective and certain,' said the physician as Kerrigan calculated whether he was being enlisted to allow some junior doctor to complete an empty square in his list of surgical training requirements. The physician continued, 'We just cut a tiny slice off the end of the prostrate.' He held his fat forefinger a centimer from his fat thumb to indicate how tiny this slice of prostate salami would be. 'And then you won't have to be getting up so often during the night to pee.'

'I never get up during the night to pee.'

The doctor looked at his file. 'Here it says that you do.'

'Well then someone has written the wrong thing there because no one asked me, and I didn't say it, because it is not so.'

'Are you afraid?'

'You bet I am.'

'It will not improve the situation to lie about it.'

'I came here because my girlfriend, who is a pathologist, told me I piss like an old man.'

'Exactly!' He wrote a prescription. 'Take these twice a day and you will piss like a young man again.'

Kerrigan took the pills for a week, found himself falling aseep at inappropriate moments, for example while discussing his pension fund with his bank advisor. He went to his GP with headaches and was told his blood pressure was dangerously low.

'Isn't it good to have low blood pressure?'

'Not when it is so low you are in danger of fainting and cracking your skull on the pavement or the edge of the bath tub.'

Informed about the urology pills, the GP phoned the hospital, spoke with the Senior Resident in question. Kerrigan heard the word '*forskning*', which is Danish for research. Then his GP put down the phone and said, 'Stop taking those pills. Eh, right away.'

So Kerrigan went down to *Vesterbro*, to a bar he knew, to visit a fellow he had once met researching an article about the drug culture in Copenhagen. From this fellow, for an exorbitant price, he purchased a nickle-plated 9mm Ruger pistol which he loaded and placed in a cigar box, wrapped around with two stout rubber bands, at the back of the highest shelf in his bedroom closet. This he was saving in the event of very serious illness.

His plan, should that day come before his health was so badly deteriorated that he could not, is to rent a pedal boat and pedal out into the middle of Black Dam Lake where he would place the barrel of the Ruger against some vulnerable part of his skull – the temple perhaps, or between the eyes – to save the Danish hospital system a fortune and himself a lengthy and painful humiliation. And to feed the ducks and swans and fishes as well, the delicacies of intracranial tidbits. Picture fragments of his consciousness flying about the lake in the gullets of seagulls and mallards, perhaps even the heron, or swimming deep in the murky waters amidst the ghosts of dead lovers and bankrupts who chose to end it in that ancient lake, thought by many to be artificial but in fact geologically natural and millions of years old.

With pleasure now, he goes into the men's room of the Ferry Café, unzips his pants, grunts a bit and pees freely, loudly, healthily into the white porcelain. What greater joy and luxury than that of well-functioning plumbing?

50

Eiffel Bar

Eiffel Bar
Wildersgade *(Wilders Street)* **58**
1408 København K

Two double bitters anaesthesize his mouth, and Kerrigan wanders off down the cobblestoned street of *Wildersgade*, named for an eighteenth-century shipbuilder, to the Eiffel Bar, over the door of which a red rectangular sign hangs bearing a likeness of the Eiffel tower. A price list for beers and liquors in the window of the gleaming facade announces prices that transport him back a dozen inflationary years.

The bartender, dressed like a French waiter in a snug black vest advertising Tuborg Classic beer on the back, greets Kerrigan when he enters. 'Good day,' he says. 'So pleased you could come.' A band-aid is stuck to his freckled bald front spot. Kerrigan orders a double cognac to put a knee on the content of his stomach. He knows that at this price it is not cognac, but brandy, two star no doubt, but welcomes the scratchy stimulation on his itching wound as he chats with an elderly man who, he learns, is the proprietor, owner since 1960 when he emigrated from the Netherlands. The building is from 1736 and the bar dates back to the 1930s, originally called Café Wilder, then Café Jakob finally the Eiffel Bar since 1960. At the end of the bar-room is an ornate spiral staircase that seems to lead nowhere – at the top of which he has heard, ladies of the night once held court, though he cannot ascertain if this is mere legend. Kerrigan peers up the spiral staircase anyway, thinking that prostitution in Denmark has in fact been legal since 17 March 1999 – a St Patrick's Day event, though Irish birth control would surely have ruled over eros that day: pour it down till you can't get it up.

The owner shows Kerrigan out to the backyard where there are tables and pots of herbs and spices – flowering chives, dill, cress, mint. The Dutchman points through a portway between two back buildings to a row of cozy old houses on the street outside. It might have been a canal street in Amsterdam, but the man says, 'Bogus. They were put up in the 60s. That was a level flat lot when I came here. Bogus.'

'Well at least they tried to harmonize with the architecture.'

'Bogus.'

Inside, a couple has just arrived and is greeted as Kerrigan was by the band-aided barman. 'So pleased you could come.'

'A beer for me,' says the man, 'and do you have any white wine?'

'Only by the half bottle,' says the barman.

'Give her the half bottle,' mutters a man hunched at the bar. 'She'll give you a good time for it.'

Kerrigan takes his cognac to one of the front tables, watches himself in the mirrored wall and considers the fact that he ought to be very drunk but isn't. Or perhaps he is so drunk he does not recognize that he is. Still he hears no slur in his voice, sees only one nose on the barman's face, one band-aid on his freckled head, and the cognac is not sliding tastelessly down his throat. If anything, he feels blank. Perhaps he has neutralized his consciousness. He takes out pen and notepaper and watches his steady hand write down keywords about the bar.

51

Strong Otter *(Stærkodder)*

Stærkodder
Overgaden Neden Vandet *(High Street at the Water)* **43**
1415 København K

Outside again on *Wildersgade*, his feet for which he is thankful follow the cobbles back to the Canal, turn him right to *Overgaden Neden Vandet* – High Street At the Water, and stroll him slowly past more tipping masts. Over the doorway at number 51B a plaque on the brick wall announces that the resistance group *Holger Danske* was founded and housed there during the German occupation, 1940-1945.

Holger Danske is a legendary viking hero who is said to have been sleeping for hundreds of years and who, it is told, awakens in time of Denmark's need to come to its aid. In the catacombs beneath *Helsingør Slot* – Elsinor Castle, where Hamlet is set, based on the Danish figure Aumlet – is a stone sculpture of the sleeping giant, seated, sword across his knee, head tipped in slumber. And his was the name taken by the Danish resistance group – the sleeping giant who woke to aid his country in need.

This legend is similar to that of the warrior giant who sleeps in the earth beneath Dublin, Joyce's Finn MacCool, dreaming Ireland's history. Finn's feet and Holger's sword and God's teeth.

At the corner with *Sankt Annæ Gade*,St Anna's Street, is the serving house *Stærkodder*, named for another mythological Viking figure, a giant of great strength, Strong Otter. The outside walls of the long bar are spattered with grafitti, including one that says, *Fuk Racism*, and a rumpled blond pink-faced man stands outside holding a bottle of gold beer; he says something Kerrigan cannot understand, repeats it, but Kerrigan still cannot understand. The man's lips are drawn back, but Kerrigan is uncertain whether he is smiling or grimacing. He shakes his head to indicate bewilderment and enters the bar. Wood-panelled walls mounted with a ship's wheel. Half a dozen men, sailors perhaps, or the descendants of sailors, sit scattered amongst the tables. There is no bar, but rather a folding counter.

Kerrigan drinks a beer amongst the silent men and halfway through becomes aware of himself sitting there as though he has awakened from sleep. He takes out a cigar, feels in his pockets for matches and finds the lump of lemon soap in one pocket, the hashish in the other, and thinks about hashishinating his consciousness.

In the breast pocket of his jacket, he finds his notepad, his Montblanc. He writes:

> The heron of forgetfulness
> Hovers over the ale-drinker.
> He steals men's wits.
> Thus spake the High One.

52

Christianhavn's Boat Rental & Café, Established 1898
(Christianhavns Bådudlejning & Café, Anno 1898)

Christianhavns Bådudlejning & Café, Anno 1898
Overgaden Neden Vandet *(High Street at the Water)*
1407 København K

He heads for Christiania, but something makes him stop first at Christianshavns Boat Rental & Café.

Here, on this 101-year-old platform mounted upon the canal, Kerrigan now sits again with a glass of beer, gazing upon the view beneath the bridge where covered boats bob on rippling water. A poster beside him celebrates Ernest Hemingway's hundredth birthday, an event Hemingway himself of course never got to see, having consigned his brains to a shower of shotgun pellets 37 years before when Kerrigan was but nineteen, reminding him of the beginning of a story by Robert Coover, 'Beginnings', which began something like, In order to get started he shot himself, and his blood, unable to resist a final joke, splattered the cabin wall in a pattern that read: It is important to begin when everything is already over.

Of all the people Kerrigan might have met, but never did, Hemingway for some reason does not worry him. The poster includes portraits of two leopards which Papa no doubt would gladly have blown away.

Kerrigan once stayed in the Swiss chateau of Hemingway's German publisher, Heinrich Maria Ledig-Rowohlt, who introduced paperback books to Germany. He was the German publisher not only of Hemingway, but also of Faulkner, Nabokov, Updike, Camus, Sartre, Henry Miller, and Harold Pinter. During his stay, Kerrigan was given the chateau library to write in for a fortnight, and among the books and papers there he came across a letter from Hemingway to Ledig-Rowohlt from the 1930s in which Hemingway reported being in hospital with an arm broken on a hunting trip. He noted however that before he injured the arm he had shot a big horn mountain sheep ram, two bears, and a bull elk and written 285 pages of his new novel. He mentioned that Dos Passos had been with him when the accident occurred, but was not hurt himself and did not shoot anything. He went on to complain about the German translation of the title of *A Farewell to Arms*, and with a threat to take his new novel to 'a big Jewish publisher' if he is not treated better in future, he closed the letter with warmest regards from himself and Mary, and then no doubt went out to pick a fight with Antoine de Sainte Exupéry.

Kerrigan enjoys the beer in his throat and the sunlight on his face, thinks of the time he was here with his friend Thomas McCarthy, an Anglo-Irish story writer and novelist who was supporting himself as an executive for an automobile tire company. How many years ago? It was in fact only his second meeting with McCarthy, who had published a few of Kerrigan's things in a journal he edited. The first meeting had been a quiet one, but this time the two of them wound up tipsy and dancing with bimbos in the Mojo Blues Club in the wee hours, confessing each to the other how relieved they were that their initial judgement of the other as being a strait-laced bore was incorrect. Come to think of it, he and Thomas had no doubt served as male bimbos that evening.

McCarthy used to edit the literary journal *Passport* which, like many another literary journal, had gone under after a dozen or so issues. McCarthy himself has published a good many fine short stories here and there over many years as well as a novel about the

IRA entitled *A Fine Country*, and Kerrigan thinks about how many people there are like that, writing and publishing their stories and poems in obscurity for little or no pay, for the sheer pleasure of doing so, of putting into language some deep inner thoughts and visions in order that the envelope of their solitude might be breached, that their inner landscape might be viewed by another in the interests of human communion.

He thinks of Calvino's observation in his essay on 'Quickness', quoting Gallileo:

> ' . . . above all stupdendous inventions, what eminence of mind was his who dreamed of finding means to communicate his deepest thoughts to any other person, no matter how far distant in place and time? Of speaking with those who are in India, of speaking with those who are not yet born for a thousand or ten thousand years? And with what facility? All by using the various arrangements of twenty little characters on a page!'

And in that way, thinks Kerrigan, the stories of Thomas McCarthy or of any other of the thousands, tens of thousands and more little known writers, might be stumbled upon in the years to come, beyond our lifetimes, a hundred years from now when Ernest Hemingway would have been 200 years old and long beyond shooting any animals or having imaginary punch-ups with other writers living or dead who threaten his manhood, some curious browser might find in a bin outside a used bookshop, or on the back shelf of some library, or in a mouldy carton in some basement or attic, a yellowed copy of *Passport* or *Cimarron Review*, *The Literary Review*, *Potpourri*, *Agni*, *Confrontation*, *Glimmer Train*, or novels published by tiny presses or big ones, novels written by people who were noticed and admired and celebrated but not made famous – like Duff Brenna or Gordon Weaver, W D Wetherell, Walter Cummins or Gladys Swan or thousands of others – or those written by people who were hardly noticed at all, but whose books survive with the same half-life as those more known, might take the copy away to sit somewhere and leaf through, reading at random the still recorded most private thoughts of men and women now long gone from the earth – find wonder in Brenna's marvellous books of America, in Weaver's books of language, Swan's carnival stories, Wetherell's fictions of the American spirit.

Kerrigan finishes his beer, climbs to the street, thinks about the alphabet and the word and the theory of James Joyce that the fall from grace was the fall into language. He thinks about his dreams which often seem to him about as prelingual as he can ever hope to get, down below the place of language, where consciousness is image first.

He thinks about the lump of hashish in his pocket, remembering those days long decades past when he smoked himself into a languageless trance, sublimely hashishinated.

He thinks of the Free State of Christiania, and fingering his pocket hash-stash, considers the old Danish proverb: '*Hvo der vil have kernen må knække nødden*', If you want the meat, you have to crack the nut.

53

Woodstock Café

Woodstock Café
Bådsmandsstræde *(Boatman's Alley)* **43**
Christiania
1407 København K

Across the Canal to *Prinsessegade* and left to Christiania – so-called *Fristaden*, the Free State. A former military fort, it was taken over by squatters in 1971. An area of about 750 acres with 150 buildings, woods and ramparts and moats, it is entered through a gateway over which hangs a sign: 'You are now leaving the European Union.'

The Danish population is split 50-50 over Denmark's membership in the, at this writing, fifteen-country Union, with ten others waiting to enter and three in special relationship with the Union. The Danish opposition fears that Danish life will become standardized, that the Danish language will be lost to the international English which is rapidly becoming the lingua franca of a political entity whose twelve languages are increasingly difficult to manage in administrative meetings. They also fear the common European currency, against which Denmark, Sweden, and the UK have taken a stand.

However, the value of the European Union slowly begins to suggest itself. The European Court recently and for the first time ever has levied a fine on a Member State of the Union for failure to comply with European law – Greece has been fined 15,000 dollars a day for every day that passes until it fulfills the requirements of an EU directive on the dumping of dangerous waste. While this may not seem a great amount, it is over a million dollars a year, and other cases are now about to be decided as well, against Greece and France, and the cumulative effect could be of concrete meaning for the future of European cooperation – for European civilization even. Not to mention the importance that binding these nations together legally can mean for the future of a continent torn by centuries of internal war.

The population is also no doubt equally split over whether the so-called Free State of Christiania should be allowed to continue to exist. In the beginning, the squatters who took it over paid neither taxes nor water nor electric bills. In 1973, the government decided to allow the squatters to run a free state there for three years as a social experiment, but five years later, a decision to level the area was supported by the Supreme Court. Some violent episodes, clashes between police and Christianiters, were followed by a law passed in the parliament to legalize the area. In 1996, it celebrated its twenty-fifth anniversary.

There was a drug problem for some time involving motorcycle gangs and hard narcotics, but the thousand inhabitants managed to rid the place of the violent elements and the hard drugs. Attempts to sell hard stuff there today are dealt with harshly – it is said that anyone caught trying is stripped, beaten, and turned out the front gate – but soft drugs are allowed, sold openly on a broad dirt pathway called Pusher Street, where varieties of hash, skunk, and pot are sold by weight.

Various other enterprises also flourish here – most notably the restaurant *Spiseloppen* , the Eating Flea – and the concert hall where, inter alia, Bob Dylan has sung. Many artists live there as well – painters, gold and silver smiths, sculptors, musicians, writers – and the living quarters and social establishments, kindergartens, nurseries, are originally and strikingly appointed. It is now possible to have a guided tour of the area for twenty crowns, about 2.5 dollars. But the only way for a new inhabitant to come in is by becoming the lover of someone who already lives there.

Kerrigan leaves the European Union through Christiania's front entrance and follows the rutted dirt roadway toward Pusher Street. There are no motor vehicles here, only bicycles, and many unleashed dogs wander about or lie in the dusty sunlight. Kerrigan tries to imagine what it must have been like when the bikers suddenly showed up one day and took over, what it must have been like for the people established here in their homes and studios with little or no possibility of police protection. Something like the little town in Marlon Brando's *The Wild One*, worse.

At one of the stalls in the shopping bazaar area, he buys a chillum from a man with one eye, and proceeds down Pusher Street to the Woodstock café where he and Paul Casey once spent an evening drinking and smoking weed in the company of an ageing three-fingered hippie who had lost the other two fingers working in a gherkin factory in the Netherlands. 'Somebody got a surprise in the pickle jar,' he said.

From the bar at the end of the long room inside, he orders a black bottle of gold-label beer which he carries to an outdoor table and sits in the sunlight.

Using his notepad as a workplace and the blade of his tiny Swiss army knife, he cuts a sliver of hash from the lump he has carried in his pocket all day, then segments the sliver and fills the bowl of the chillum, lights it with a stick match and draws the smoke into his lungs. Before exhaling, he releases it into his mouth and holds it there in case it has a healing effect. He draws three times on the pipe, then lets it go out, tucks it into his shirt pocket and moistens his palate with strong beer.

Across from where he sits, at a broad outdoor café, a woman on a bench piles her long hair upon her head, elbows raised. The sun sparkles in the yellow locks. He smiles. How do they know how that makes us long for them?

Two Africans sitting three tables away make him think for a moment he is in the Third World.

'Such a step is not without being controversial,' he hears one of them say to the other, who laughs warmly.

At another table, an elderly man is cleaning his nails with a penknife. The woman across from him says quietly in Danish, 'That is rather undelicious.' He glares indignantly at her. 'I *have* to. I have a fungus under my nails!'

Kerrigan changes his seat so that they are behind him. He finds himself staring at the earth, which is very interesting to look at. The texture of the dirt is fascinating and several tiny ants wander about, tiny reddish-brown marvels. His mouth is agreeably dry and the chill glass of the beer bottle against his fingertips wonderfully pleasant.

It occurs to him that one strategy might be to throw his wallet into the moat on the other side of the dirt ramparts, and then to die here where no one knows who he is. He might never be identified. This seems an interesting strategy.

An Inuit woman approaches him to ask if he would like to buy a genuine Inuit sketch. She holds out a drawing of a rooster. He thanks her no, wondering what it is like to be a rooster, remembers the old adage that after sex all animals are sad except for women and roosters.

Then he thinks of his Associate again, how she would look with her elbows in the air piling her hair up upon her head, and the thought of his Associate reminds him that if he obliterates himself here in Christiania, he will never complete his book about Copenhagen, and that would be a sloppy way to die.

The sun on the skin of his face and hands and the tips of his ears is marvellous as he floats down Pusher Street past the stalls and scales and roaming dusty dogs, the bearded tatooed men and nose-jewelled women. Out of the sun and into the shade again on the wheel-rutted earth. Kerrigan experiences himself as very very far away in this strange place, re-enters the EU through the wooden archway and floats up Prinsessegade towards Torvegade, where he waits for a taxi across from Elephant's Bastion.

No taxi comes. Then he remembers a place just up the road he has passed a thousand times on his way out to the airport and has always meant to visit but never yet has.

54

Ravelinen Summer Restaurant

Ravelinen Summer Restaurant
Torvegade *(Torve Street)* **79**
1400 København K

A *raveline* is a triangular defence work standing in a moat between two bastions, the two outer faces of the raveline protected by ramparts. The restaurant Raveline is built upon the site a raveline lay outside of the defensive gate of the island of Amager, a so-called Zone of Servitude, where until 1909 building was limited in order to keep a free field of fire and deny cover to any enemy approaching the city.

The Restaurant Ravelinen stands where the old fortification used to be. The old yellow sentry building, which dates back to 1728, is now the restaurant's kitchen. The restaurant consists of two roofed-in sections built of strips of brown wood and an open gravel yard of outdoor tables that look out onto the old city moat and embankment.

This is where Kerrigan sits with a very tall glass of lager staring down to the gravel that crunches beneath the soles of his shoes.

The gravel reminds him of something very sad, so sad he does not wish to think of it for his stomach seems to be falling toward its own bottomless center as the not yet recognized memory rises to the surface of his thought. He sits there a long time staring at the gravel. Then he looks up at the wall beside the kitchen doorway across the gravel yard and the ancient yellow sentry post where he sees an advertisement for a *Pinse Frokost*, a Whitsun Lunch, celebrating Pentecost, Monday, 25 May, and he remembers then what the gravel reminds him of.

He had been at another restaurant with his Associate – M G Petersens Family Garden in Frederiksberg, established in 1799, at Pileallé 16, on the west edge of Copenhagen. They sat outside with a drink, and she had gazed down at the gravel, a distant look in her eye. When he asked what she was thinking, she told how she and her first husband's family used to have a traditional Whitsun celebration each year. They would eat an enormous Danish *smørrebrød* lunch on the Saturday. *Smørrebrød* means literally 'butter-bread', but such a lunch consists not only of three or four different kinds of bread with butter and swine fat, but also a couple of dozen courses on the table, three or four kinds of herring – pickled, fried, curried, sherried – smoked eel with scrambled egg and chives, caviar, cod roe, smoked salmon with parsley and pepper, fried plaice filets, smoked halibut, fresh calf liver paste, wild boar paté, pickled beef, country ham, lamb meatballs, calf meatballs, pork meatballs, half a dozen Danish cheeses . . . They would drink bottled beer and iced snaps, would *skål* and sing drinking songs in honor of the women, in honor of the company, in honor of the papa eel which would never come home to his eel family again. They would party all night and on the Sunday morning, at sunrise they would move over to Hansen's Family Garden 'to see the Whitsun sun dance' as they ate breakfast with strong coffee and morning snaps and many kinds of bread and cheese and sausage and pastry. There was music and dancing to happy jazz and people wore old-fashioned straw hats.

A celebration of this sort requires a certain sense of pace regarding the drink, and this pace was something that her first husband had never mastered. As in many other places, it is customary at Danish gatherings for wives and husbands not to sit together. Thus she and her husband were at separate tables. At one point she saw him down on the ground, swimming in the gravel. He swam from his table through the gravel over to her and reached up to pinch her very hard on the inside of her thigh.

'Did you enjoy dancing with Martin?' he hissed and then swam back to his own table. Martin was the man on her left with whom she had just danced. Everybody was dancing with everybody. But her husband never danced. He only watched her dance, and sometimes he pinched her afterwards if he didn't like the way she danced or who she danced with. Or he would tap the tabletop in front of him with his index finger until she stopped dancing and came to sit beside him. If she didn't stop dancing, she knew what was in store for her later.

On this occasion, however, one pinch had been sufficient. She rose and went off by herself into the Frederiksberg gardens, through the hedge maze and the stone-path pond. She looked at her leg. There was a red-black spot where he had pinched her. Then she decided not to return to the party. She walked all the way home to their apartment on the other side of the city and went to bed.

Later in the morning the doorbell rang. She knew he had no key, but she did not know what would happen if she let him in. So she waited on the other side of the door without making a sound. He rang again and again. Then the ringing stopped. She looked out through the mailslot and saw him sleeping on the doormat. Fearing the neighbors would see him, she opened the door and dragged him in, all the way to the bathroom. He was unconscious. There was vomit on his shirt, and the lining of his necktie was torn out, hanging down below his knees. His pant leg was smeared with mud.

Fearing he might be in a coma, she did what she had always seen done in the movies in such cases. She filled a bucket with cold water and splashed it into his face.

He awoke instantly in a growling rage and lunged at her. She ran. He chased her around the nine rooms of their apartment. Every so often he would catch her by her long blond hair and yank with all his might so a handful of hair would tear out of her scalp in his fingers. He kicked her in the back of her knee and when she fell down, he sat on her and slapped and punched her.

Then he put his fingers round her throat and began to choke her. She tried to tear his arms away but he was too strong. She began to see spots buzzing in front of her eyes. She decided she would allow him to kill her, she stopped resisting.

He stopped, too. He got off her and collapsed on the floor, curled up into a fetal position, whimpering. She packed a bag very quickly and called a taxi, went to her parent's house and asked if she could sleep in her old bed for a little while.

When she woke, two men were there with a stretcher. Her father had decided she would be better off having a rest in the hospital, in the psychiatric ward.

'*You*!?' Kerrigan said.

She nodded. 'I had no fight in me. Everytime I tried to speak I sobbed. I couldn't catch my breath. Perhaps my father thought I had broken down in hysteria. He got me all the way to the hospital, but the psychiatrist who spoke to me there said nothing was wrong with me. He told me to go back home and send my husband in for treatment.'

That had been the beginning of the end of their marriage. Two months later she was alone with their three daughters in a two-room apartment. Her husband had cleverly registered everything they had in the name of his parent's company so she had no claim on it, wanted no claim on it. She wanted only not to be pinched and punched and accused of things of which she was not guilty. She wanted her daughters not to be slapped and shouted at. She wanted to be free of living with a man who became someone else when he was drunk which was nearly every evening.

Kerrigan stares at the gravel, grey and black and white pebbles that slide beneath his shoe as he shifts his feet on it. The sound saddens him immensely. It makes a sound that somehow calls up the word *children*. He pictures his Associate's husband swimming in the pebbles, reaching up with a crazed face to pinch her leg, then swimming away again. Kerrigan is sad for the man, that he lost such a beautiful wife, the mother of his daughters, because his ego was so weak it required her subjugation to it. Madness.

It occurs to him the entire world is full of madmen, that there is no such thing as civilization, that it is all just a behavioral veneer. Or rather that we live in an illusion of normalcy, of normal, reasonable behavior.

Close to the surface of his consciousness are images he wishes not to see. Faces so far away. How do you survive that? You survive. On the flow of time. You get over it. One day you tell yourself, get over it, and you get over it. Even if you never do. His 12-year-old marriage was in a stale season at the time and perhaps that was even worse. His boys just kids still, little kids – Roger a chunky crew-cut 11-year-old, Billy slim and blond and sweet, the two of them running from grandma. He heard them plead, and she said, 'All right, boys, it's all right,' and shot. The three of them dead before he could get to them, and the others, too, so he hid, like a kid himself, first beneath the bed and then in a closet, and she called, 'Terry! Oh Ter-ry!'

No surprise somehow. You saw it in her eyes for years. Her moods. The sudden coldness. The time she sat at the kitchen table making a scissors dance into the wood around his hands, saying, 'Hold them still now or who knows?' It wasn't even evil. Chemicals. A drop too much or too little of this or that, too much this combined with too little that. Who can hate powder, atoms, fluid? It merely is. Unimpeachable as grass and trees, a microbe, the earth that mulches the bodies of the dead into succulent fruits and gorgeous flowers.

But you did see it long before. Those crazy staring eyes. And you were helpless, numb to tell the crooked rose it was breeding a mad winter fever. And what breeding now in the hospital on the Palouse? Do you think about me, mother? Do you dream about the boy who got away? And still in truth you feel nothing. You gaze upon these memories with a blank heart, arid eyes. Dear Mother, you gave me life and slew my heart for me. Thank you. Your loving son, Terrence.

His mouth is dry again and he has not touched his beer. He drinks off half the glass in one long succession of swallows, working it down his throat, cold and delicious.

He wants very much to comfort her at this moment, his

Associate, to make her believe in comfort, for it seems to him if he can make her believe then it will be true. And he wants very much to go and sit alone by his front windows and watch the sun set over the lake, to watch the light – pale red, pale blue – ripple on the water while silhouettes of men and women and children and dogs and joggers move past beneath the silhouetted trees like a picture in some forgotten childhood book.

Outside on the grassy ramparts beneath the shelter of trees, he smokes another pipe of hash, slowly, meditatively, watching the sun move lower in the sky and marvelling at the thousand colors of light on the water, stippled like an oil painting, and he feels the ellipse of the universe on its slow elliptical course around him and around that the mysterious darkness.

When he gets back to the apartment, opening the door, he has the sense that someone else is there. He stands very still at the door, which he has not yet clicked all the way shut behind him and listens. There is nothing to hear. He switches on the hall light and steps into the living room, reaches for the wall contact, but something makes him pause – as surely as if someone has whispered to him not to turn the light on.

Then he sees someone is sitting in the shadows on the sofa, and his heart clenches up tight against his ribs. He tries to speak but his throat is too thick and dry.

Someone is at his desk as well, the shadow of another person, sitting sideways on the chair, shoulders hunched in the shadows. He begins to wet his pants but manages to stop before more than a few drops have spurted out.

As he considers whether he is in possession of the strength and speed to run, he glimpses yet a third shadow by the bookshelves, where the African fetish stands, and he knows he is doomed. The figure lifts the fetish, a small ebony carving of a woman. *The woman*, he recalls his youngest boy calling it decades ago. Before. On the wall beside the shelf hangs the medallion likeness of Sheelanagig, the exhibitionist goddess, staring, idiot-mouthed, holding open her vulva – whispering, *My cunt is what you crave. The little death is yours for free, as is the cold, cold grave.*

He tries to reason, to understand what might be happening. Does it have to do with the hash? Has someone followed him from Christiania? What can it mean?

His body is heavy and light at the same time. He feels as though he is suspended in water, in film. Each step is labor, the lifting of the foot, the bending of the knee. A dance under water. He decides to pretend he notices nothing, allows his hand to complete the motion it began, moving toward the switch for the overhead lamp, and clicks it on.

Light leaps into the room, but his eyes continue to gaze only directly in front of him, seeing nothing but his work table, the window, the lake outside, silent figures jogging past on the dusky lake bank. He pictures himself down there – a Hitchcock film – looking up at the window here where an unseen horror is about to unfold.

But he is not down there. He is here. His legs find power to carry him resolutely across the floor to the dining table where all his writing materials lay spread out.

He sits, hunches over his work, but notices his pen trembling as the three figures move in silently behind him. From the corner of his eye, he sees a hand come to rest on the surface of the table. Its fingers are dark, olive, Mediterranean shadows. Kerrigan's breath labors heavily from his lungs. He begins to weep into his palm.

Without a sound they draw chairs up around him and he feels one lean close in, can feel breath on his neck as words whisper into his ear, and he realizes then that they mean him no harm.

He begins to write.

WEEK THE LAST

Phantoms

When we dream and when we couple,
we embrace phantoms. The libertine turns
everything into a phantom, and he himself
becomes a shade among shades.'
– Octavio Paz

'But now my desire and my will
were revolved like a wheel which
is moved evenly by the love which
moves the sun and other stars . . .
And I believed myself transported
to a higher salvation with my
lady.'
– Dante Alighieri, *The Comedy*

'I have seen the door that is not there
still open.'
– Tim Seibles

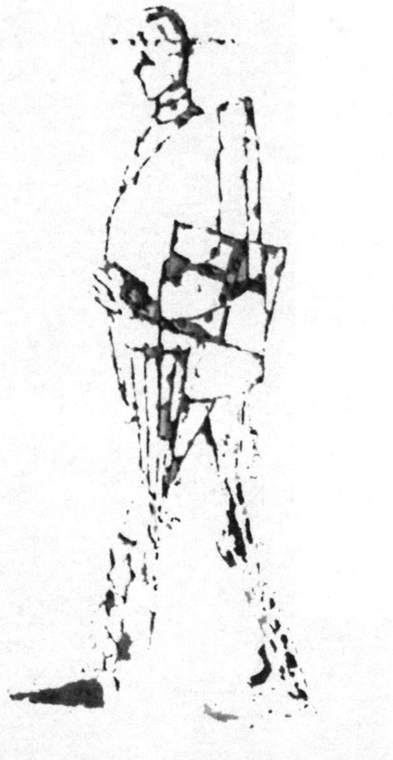

55

Zach's Café

Zach's Café
Istedgade *(Isted Street)* **128**
1650 København V

From a dream in which his wife is chiding him for not having properly divided the fruit in an enormous bowl and offering it around, he wakes with a jolt realizing that the telephone has been ringing for some time.

A voice with a Swedish accent speaks from the other end. 'Terrence! Kerrigan! Are you all fugged up or what?'

'Give me time,' he mutters hoarsely, and the laughter is familiar. It is the laughter of Morten Gideon who visits him from time to time when he is in from Stockholm to find peace to smoke cigars and drink alcohol, to converse and fulfill secret assignations with his many women.

Kerrigan met Gideon years ago at the Casino Divonne Les Bains, first noted him there rather by the loud and clear pronunciation of his Swedish voice addressing a ravishing blond Turkish baccarat tablemate in these words: 'I vish to kees your feet!'

To which the Turkish beauty – an occupational health physician by profession Kerrington would later learn – replied, 'Yes, yes, doctor. Down boy.'

Kerrigan spied Gideon again next morning at the breakfast buffet where he sat nursing a Fernet Branca and boiled egg and could not resist extending his compliments and enquiring whether Gideon's proposal had brought him into contact with the lovely Turkish trotters.

'It is all a dream in the dark,' said Gideon and invited Kerrigan to join him in a Branca, the beginning of an extended friendship.

'What the fuck you doin'?' Gideon demands now.

'I'm writing.'

'You're so fulla shit I can smell it! Listen. Meet me. Let me invite you out to dinner. I want you to meet this woman and tell me what you think. Meet me at the Café Petersborg. I'm staying next door at the Hotel Esplanaden. My plane will touch down in half an hour. Meet me there at three.'

'I have no idea what time it is.'

'Well look at a fuckin' clock! Find out! Get with the program! You gotta meet this girl. She is really sweet. I want you to tell me what you think. Be there! Three o'clock. Come on, give me a life sign, I got to go. See you at three.'

Cautiously he fills his mouth with water, gargles, decides not to look, spits, looks. The water is only pink. He gargles again and the water comes out clear. He tries to look at the roof of his mouth in the mirror over the sink, but can see nothing. He decides to purchase an oral mirror, like in the dentist's, to get a look.

Gideon. Gideon is the chairman of half a dozen different international companies. With kinky blond hair and thick lips, big dark-framed eyeglasses and black suits and big glossy black golf shoes, he rules whatever he puts his hand to. To Gideon every woman is a challenge, but he is not content to look. He wants the comfort of their bodies, of their acquiesence.

'Hey,' he says, 'I'm a passionate guy. I need love.'

His third wife has just left him. He has seven children by various women. He is an intellectual businessman and has excellent taste in cigars with a budget to keep it busy.

Kerrigan splashes several palmfuls of cold water into his face, leans on the sink for a while, assessing how he feels.

Slowly it dawns on him that he feels reasonably well. He gargles once more and wishes he hadn't when it comes away pink again, darker pink. He thinks about saying, 'Gideon. You'll never believe it, but I'm dying.'

'Fuck you, bullshit, you're not dying. If it's your prick that's worrying you then try some fuckin' Viagra!'

Kerrigan moves on pigeon toes to his dining table, sees a fat stack of freshly written yellow pages, does not dare to read them. He peeks. First sentence looks good. Second, third, fourth, too.

Cheered, he decides not to read further just now, wonders if he could get his blood changed somewhere, whether that would help, a complete change of blood, but realizes that this would place him in the hands of health personnel again.

He argues with himself, recalling all the times that doctors and nurses have helped him: the time he tore a muscle in his leg, the time he got a four inch splinter in his knee, the time a mysterious painful lump appeared on his finger and a GP anaesthetized it and gingerly removed from the heart of the lump a sliver of green glass that he recognized as coming from one of the Alsatian wine glasses he had broken while washing it, the time he was crippled with pain in his leg and three simple injections cured it, the lump that was cut painlessly from his back, the doctor friend who removed stitches with a fingernail clipper using gin both to sterilize and anaesthetize, the senior medical official with whom he has travelled often and on repeated occasions in many cities shared great quantities of strong drink with and who has outquoted him everytime in Shakespeare-quoting competitions.

His head is light so he switches on the radio to the classical channel, hears Johan Strauss II (1825-1899), 'Little Woman of the Danube', and the swaying rhythms of the waltz soothe his mind. His gaze rests on the smooth lake, paddling ducks, bobbing joggers. A couple stroll beneath the green chestnut and a woman passes pushing a stroller as memories carry on the strings of the Vienna Philharmonic – the New Years Day brunch his wife always prepared for the four of them to dine on as they watched the Vienna Concert on television – 'Tales of the Vienna Woods', 'The Blue Danube', 'On the Beautiful Blue Danube'.

They ate scrambled eggs and drank champagne, even the boys got a glass of the bubbly, right from when they were five or six, and the year which had just begun could not have begun more elegantly. None of the petty cares of daily life mattered then, no quibbles, grievances, petty jealousies, nothing. There were only the Strausses, I and II, the hundred, 150-year-old music, the bubbly, the winter sun through the living room's plate window, the food on the smoked glass coffee table – yellow eggs on a blue china platter, smoked eel in grey-white strips on a bone-white plate ready for the chives and pepper, delicate sausage slices, black pudding, cheese, fresh fruit, juices, toast, apricot jams and marmelade. And on the color screen of the TV the beautiful young Austrian women in their beautiful gowns, the young cavaliers in their waistcoats and colored butterflies and cumerbunds, waltzing with such fluent grace.

And Kerrigan with a good cigar, one only (perhaps two for it was only once a year), Cohiba perhaps, Esplendido or Robusto, gifts from the generous Gideon, better by far than a Bible, or a Davidoff Tubo No 2, handrolled in the Dominican Republic. A cigar that might have burnt for an eternity, its thick, redolent smoke coiling up into the motes of icy sunlight through the frosted window, a single candle in the Irish crystal stick he gave her for Christmas, his wife seeing to them, replenishing their plates and cups because this was her New Year gift to her family, and if the gowns of the Austrian women were a tad gaudy, if their blue gazes were a tad vacuous, it did not matter for these were moments of supreme success and there was no happiness like theirs then.

On the floor, the children's Christmas gifts, toy cars of bright metal, troops of innocent soldiers on parade who would never fire a shot in anger, yet unread books of gleaming freshness, and out the window their cherished lawn now white with snow beneath a freezing perfect blue sky, the magnolia's winter-bare black bones dusted with snow, a mere few years before it all would be taken away – the meaning of existence, of family, a net of human beings joined by blood and marriage, a tiny clan devoted to one another despite the occasional argument or jealousy, despite trouble, always stronger in the long run than the puny threats to it, stronger than all but one – his mother, whose eyes were like the Danish sky, changing, always changing, from warmth to ice, or the Icelandic landscape, vast and grey and empty. Or bulging. And the blood that joined them all would be spilled and spattered over her living room out on the open Palouse – dead, gone, as all stories end, though this one ended leaving only the two of them, her with a reloaded pistol and him beneath the bed, watching her bare spattered feet step across the floor, a grown-up child stricken with fear: 'Terry! Oh, Ter-*ry*!'

He decides that what he needs is a haircut. Perhaps a manicure. A pedicure.

While his barber, Katrina, fusses with his hair and his ears and eyebrows and chats about the pleasures of motherhood and sorrows of being a wife, Kerrigan leafs through a magazine which proves to be a love comic called *Dentist Romance*. About a chairside assistant named Jacqueline who falls in love with dark, handsome Etienne Davignon, Doctor of Dental Science. He is older than she, grey-templed, black hair sheened purple, and explains to her about DNA while they view X-rays of gums and toothroots in his lab, while she sighs up into a thought-bubble, thinking, *If only he knew how I feel . . .*

At the end of the day, she accompanies him to his home on the coast to review a backlog of X-rays. He patiently explains to her the various spots on the film, but Kerrigan cannot stop considering the fact that the most often used word for *gums* in Danish is, *tandkød*, literally, *tooth meat.* Jacqueline's thought-bubbles are cloudy cushions of sighs. She and Etienne reach simultaneously for the light screen switch and his fingertips linger on the back of her delicate hand.

'Oh, darling!' her word-bubble blurts, and a gridwork of lines on her cheek indicates that she is blushing.

'You could be my daughter,' says Etienne's word-bubble.

'I am a woman,' replies hers. 'Or haven't you noticed?' Her eyes downcast, the straight lines of her lips suggesting a slight bitterness.

His thought-bubble contains an inner confession that he *has* noticed, and the smooth, full, perfect-lined curves of their lips meet. But he pulls away to stand at the window, facing out over his pool area and the sunset, his back to her, his wrists crossed at the small of his back, as though bound. 'I would grow old while you are still young,' says the word-bubble connected to his mouth by a sharp, pointed shaft. 'And while you are still in your prime, I would . . .' His face lifts to watch yellow leaves drift down from a tree silhouetted against the yellow sky. 'You would be alone.'

'Oh, darling,' says her word-bubble in a billowy cloud. 'The only thing I could not face is never to have known your . . .love.'

Kerrigan speculates over the meaning of the elliptical dots while Katrina trims the hair in his ear and asks, Danish fashion, 'What for a land-man are you?'

'American,' he says.

She appears startled and looks at his face in the mirror, touching his cheek lightly. 'Now I always just assumed you were Italian,' she says.

Kerrigan is not displeased and watches as she bends down to plug in the electric razor. *Clip me, darling!* his thought-bubble thinks and pictures them embracing romantically.

'It must be your dark coloring,' she says and goes for his sideburns with the electric razor while Kerrigan wonders what dark coloring she is referring to; his eyes are blue, his hair grey-beige, and his skin fair. The razor nibbles agreeably at the nape of his neck while he returns to Jacqueline and Etienne swimming together in his pool, an underwater view of them smiling, kissing, bubbles rising from their smiles and their kisses. Although it is left to the imagination, they could very well be swimming without suits. Kerrigan studies the frame carefully, alert for any sign of a suit on either of them; the body areas in question are in shadowy water, but there is definitely no trace of swimwear. Racy comic, he thinks.

Then a sunset scene with a bottle of champagne, both of them in robes, and his bubble says, 'The end of August already. A nip of September in the evening.' A harvest moon is round and bright in the now dark sky.

'Oh, Etienne,' her bubble whispers in tiny letters. 'We shall have many bottles of champagne together before November comes. We shall share a long December of love.'

Despite his puzzlement over her words, Kerrigan cannot but feel a stab of anguish at the impending pain of their separation by time, by age, by death. Poor sad doomed cartoons.

He says aloud to Katrina, who is dusting him with talc, 'Love is what makes us unhappy.'

'What?' she asks in Danish – which really sounds like a vintage New York Jewish '*wha . . .?*' '*Hvad*?'

'Love and connection are the culprits,' he says. 'All the clichés founded on truth.'

She removes the leopard-patterned sheet from him and shakes his grey-beige locks to the tile floor. Her smile is bewildered, although it also says she would like to follow his train of thought if it has a merry destination. He likes her mouth. Her gaze flicks from his eyes to his chest to his lower body, to the magazine, and she says, 'That's 135 crowns. Now you can surprise your wife with your nice trimmed curls.'

'Alas,' he says, 'I have no wife,' and she blurts out merry laughter, as though he has said something quite else, something merry and mildly flirtatious.

Champagne on his mind and nearly three hours BG – before Gideon, Kerrigan finds himself recalling the wise words of Karen Blixen: *It is always advisable to take a little bubbly with your worries. And your brunch.*

And there happens to be tucked away in his billfold two free drink chits from a new café that has just opened on the west side, on *Istedgade*, which happens to be the real street on which the fictional Ole 'Jazz' Jastrau lived in *Havoc*. What better choice of a place for scrambled eggs and crisp bacon, cheese and bread, juice and the bubbly?

So when he crosses Øster Farimags Street to access the opposite traffic lane, he can only conclude that the appearance of a taxi cab at just that moment, green taxi lamp glowing in the mild afternoon, means that the universe and all the laws of synchronicity salute and support his decision.

'I love this street,' the freeloading fictional poet Steffen Steffensen says to Ole Jazz in *Havoc*, looking down *Istedgade* from the block where it starts.

'Why?' Jazz asks, and Steffensen tells him, 'Because it's long.'

Words Kerrigan ponders while listening to a jolly Pakistani cabdriver tell him about a friend in Bangladesh who owned two things only: a shed and a coconut tree. From the sale of his coconuts, he earned enough to support himself in his shed for the entire year, and even had a surplus so that he could give something to the poor.

The cabdriver laughs merrily. 'He did not know, you see, that he himself was poor! And so he was wealthy!'

The story seeps into Kerrigan's consciousness, and he says softly to the driver, 'That's a beautiful story.'

'It *is* a beautiful story!' the driver shouts. 'I never forget this story!'

'And I never will either,' says Kerrigan as they cruise past *Jerbanescafeen*, turn right onto *Istedgade*.

'I hear from your accent you are from a country other than this,' the driver says. 'I am guessing you are from America, and I am guessing that I am right in my guess.'

'You *are* right,' says Kerrigan, thinking of the parable of the coconut tree and the poor man wishing to give something to somebody, wondering if the driver is angling for a tip.

'I think this is so,' the driver says. 'I love America. There they are sufficiently intellectual. There you have the beautiful desert with the beautiful great cactus. In my country, they are not intellectual enough. In my country they have the great desert but it is not beautiful because they have no great cactus. If they were more intellectual, they would plant such cactus and have a truly *lovely* desert!'

'Saguaro cactus,' says Kerrigan, thinking Auden:

'Welcome to my lovely desert
Where even dolls go a-whoring
Where cigarette ends become intimate friends
And it's always three in the morning . . .'

'What is it called, say this again,' the driver asks.

'Saguaro.'

'*Saguaro*,' the driver repeats happily. 'I am not forgetting this word now I finally have it. Thank you for it. Saguaro.'

Kerrigan watches porn shops zip past to left and right, drug addicts and hookers leaning in doorways, clustered on the street, and wonders where this parable-speaking driver is headed. *Driver where you takin' us?* Sings in his head as he watches the street numbers rise slowly.

'I think,' says the driver and looks at Kerrigan via the rearview mirror, 'that you once loved a tree. Very much. You loved that tree.'

Kerrigan tries to think of a way to calm the man, but picking through his mind, he remembers the peach tree. 'How did you know?' he asks.

'I know. What tree was it?'

'A peach tree. It was the only tree that grew in our yard in New York and every summer we picked the peaches, and they were so delicious. We had peaches for breakfast and for desert and for afternoon snacks. We had peach pie and peaches with cream and sugar. They were so delicious. I loved that tree. I did.'

'I know this.'

'Then there was a hurricane and it blew down. Our poor tree. I missed it so much.'

'I think,' says the driver, 'that everyone in the whole world should be required on their birthday to plant one tree. The tree is the cousin to the man, to the woman. I think you come from America and you have lost your tree, you must plant one tree in this country!'

Have you planted a tree here?'

'Yes!' the driver shouts, grinning wildly back over his shoulder.

'Many trees many trees! I have no land but I sneak like in the night and plant trees. Here, there. Someday come with me – no charge, nothing! I show you my family of trees I have planted all these many 30 years in this fine country!'

He pulls up alongside number 128, the long front of Zach's Café, and Kerrigan pays him, gives him a 20-crown coin extra.

'You give me too much.'

'That's for a tree,' says Kerrigan. 'Plant a tree. In commemoration of our conversation.'

The driver laughs wildly. 'I do that! I like you, mister. The trees are going to help you.'

The outdoor part of the café is not open so Kerrigan goes in and takes a table by the broad front window. The walls are adorned with oil-paintings of red, blue and green robot-like faces. One of the faces seems to be smiling, and Kerrigan sits there, thinking of the Pakistani driver and the parable of the coconuts, watching people walk past on the sidewalk. There are many brown faces, and he ponders the fact that his chance decision made him privy to the coconut tree story, which really *is* beautiful and made him remember his own beautiful peach tree and the fact that he has never planted a tree anywhere. It occurs to him that the driver was a saint. He wonders whether in fact the man is a secret tyrant in his own home, beats his family, but he chooses to dismiss the thought as an example of his own stilted view of the world: suspicion, cynicism. If you are poor but think you are rich, what in truth are you? And if you are affluent and live in cynical suspicion, what are you then?

A tall, lean, dark-haired man who looks vaguely like Jack Palance brings a menu, and Kerrigan enquires whether he might exchange both his free drink chits for a glass of the bubbly with which he intends to drink the health of his hairdresser, Etienne Davignon, DDS, and his chairside assistant, the Paki driver, and the rich-poor coconut tree owner, but the tall waiter apologizes that they have no champagne.

'Champenoise then? Sekt?'

'Sorry.' He smiles like Jack Palance.

'Is the owner here?'

'There are twenty owners. I'm one of them.'

Kerrigan begins to fear he is drunk and must drink himself sober again. 'Have you got a Stoli?'

'Of course.'

Kerrigan orders a double on the rocks with a full brunch, and the vodka is delivered quickly, sacred, clear, on pure ice in a stalwart tumbler, and he lights a Caminante cerut of the leaping deer, A M Hirschsprung & Sons, who owned the statue of the barbarian on horseback with two severed heads hanging from its saddle. This cigar factory was founded in 1826, a year notable for the fact that as far as Kerrigan knows, no author of great note was born during it. As he puffs his cerut and ponders this, wondering whether it is worth researching, a woman at the next table – perhaps his own age with lips painted the color of the Queen of Midnight Tulips which once grew on his front lawn, leans closer to ask, 'And *what* is a Stoli? If I may be so bold to enquire.'

He blows a pleasingly slender stream of harsh grey smoke from pursed lips and tells her, 'Stoli is, I guess you would say, a kind of Yuppie abbreviation for Stolichnaya, a Russian vodka which is the favorite of many a vodka drinker. Russian distilled and certainly one of the best I have ever tasted. When it comes to vodka, these distinctions are pretty subtle since vodka has virtually no taste, they say, but that is why the little taste that *is* there is so important. A little bit like the colors of a Danish landscape deep in winter – you have your greys, your whites, your blacks, your shades of grey smoke, white smoke white and grey sky and suddenly you perceive a little splash of color – a bird, say – and the senses go gaga. Anyway, Moskovskaya is also good, also Russian, while Absolut – Swedish – I drink only if it is the only thing available. What right have the Swedes to think they can make vodka? Although I do understand vodka has been sold under the name Absolut since 1879, and they are certainly good at snaps, so why not vodka? Finlandia – Finnish, of course – is not bad at all and very modestly priced; I suppose after all their years of dancing with the Russkies they learned a thing or two, and it is especially pleasant to drink chilled Finlandia vodka while listening to Sibelius's *Finlandia* symphony. The Finns, incidentally, say *kipis* when they drink. The Estonian stuff is not only very cheap but very perfectly drinkable. They drink it like the Russians in big glasses, very cold without ice, and when they drink they say *Tjerviseks*, which sounds rather provocative, but simply means to your very good health or something. The Irish make a vodka called Boru which is excellent, named for Brian Boru, the first king of a united Ireland – he drove the Vikings from the Emerald Isle in the eleventh century, though they did manage to murder him with a dirk in the back while he knelt to pray, and he was also the father of the first Kennedy – which means ugly-headed by the way – but was my father's mother's maiden name, a lovely woman. Or was he the *son* of the first Kennedy? It is so difficult to keep these facts in order. Anyway, there is also a Danish so-called vodka, Danza, but – please forgive me – I have never been able to stop laughing long enough to order it – again no doubt, an unfair prejudice when you consider the fine variety of Danish aquavite, even if the factory that makes them has now been purchased by Swedes. The American stuff is not bad by the way, filtered through mountains of charcoal as they say, and they – Smirnoff that is – also make a black-label stuff that is distilled and bottled in Russia which can perfectly well hold its own with any vodka – superior! One word of caution – do not partake of the Smirnoff blue label unless you are looking to get thoroughly bombed. Hundred-proof brain-cell burner. Stick with the red-label if you must drink American. I have heard it said that vodka was invented in Poland 500 years ago, though the word *vodka* is from the Russian *voda*, for water, and dates to 1803, so who can say for sure? A good Polish vodka is Belvedere – the Belvedere House by the way is the Polish equivalent of the White House in the US. Oh, but there are so many other varieties of spiced vodka as well – to be taken at room temperature for the taste – some of them fine in the way that a truly fine cognac or armagnac is, but personally I prefer the clearest sort. It is, as the novelist Gordon Weaver wrote, "Pure, cold, clear like pure water. Purity." '

'You're quite the lexicon, aren't you?' she says, and the glint in her eye kindles Kerrigan's blood. Think of it, he thinks, taking in the slight pursing of her Queen of Midnight lips, the matching nails, wonders if perhaps the toenails too are painted that shade, and perhaps her underpants and her bra would match as well, lacy stuff that her gaze would invite him to peel down to as they lay on the genuine Persian carpet of her flat somewhere while perhaps Ravel's *Bolero* egged them on. As he prepares to do and say as she might wish in order to be able to accept his invitation to the dance, block-lettered words rise abruptly in his mind: GOD IS A CUNT.

Again. Herself. Insinuating some right of a fidelity to which he is in no way bound. This would *not* constitute unfaithfulness. In *no* way. He thinks of raising his glass, saying *Multatuli*, the one toast he has forgotten to tell her about, but in the moment's hesitation, she drains the last residue of whatever she is drinking from a stem glass – Fernet Branca perhaps, or just plain Gammel Dansk – and stirs to rise in such a way that he can see into the top of her plum-colored satin blouse, a farewell glimpse inviting him to eat his clumsy heart out.

It is not too late, yet he does not speak, watches her sturdy thighs carry her away, and an unmistakable lightness of relief buoys his posture. Along the bar he walks then to the gent's to pray his afternoon prayer:

'When I have swallowed down my dreams
In thirty, forty mugs of beer, I turn
To satisfy a need I can't ignore
And like the Lord of Hyssop and Myrrh
I piss into the skies, a soaring stream
That consecrates a patch of flowering fern.'

Prayer complete he washes his fingers at the porcelain sink and sucks up a palmful of cold water, which he gargles and spits into the sink. Still pinkish.

Back at his table, the vodka is disappointing for it was champagne he wanted. A little bubbly with his predicament.

Staring out at the yellow afternoon, he is barely conscious of the fact that a small brown-complected man with crooked teeth is waving at him from the curb. Still semi-consciously, Kerrigan gives half a wave back, and the man approaches the plate window, presses his face to it, smiling. Kerrigan thinks he is surely smiling at someone else, but there is no one nearby. He thinks again of the man with the coconut tree who did not know he was poor as this snaggle-toothed fellow presses to the glass, gazing in and waving his fingers.

Kerrigan accidentally smiles back, then quickly nods dismissively, and the man moves toward the door. Now comes the touch no doubt, thinks Kerrigan, steeling himself, and the little brown man wobbles on splayed feet toward him, then leans disagreeably close to Kerrigan's face and utters some strange foreign words.

'The same to you, I'm sure, sir,' says Kerrigan dryly, withholding his eyes, and the man turns away, yet even as he withdraws, the foreign words ring clear of their heavy accent. What he had said in Danish was, 'I wish everything good for you in your life, and now I am going again.'

Kerrigan lunges to his feet, opens the door and steps out into the warm, yellow afternoon, but the little brown man is nowhere to be seen.

56

Café Petersborg

Café Petersborg
Bredgade *(Broad Street)* **76**
1260 København K

Champagne, he thinks, is an apt topic for the Café Petersborg. For it was here, one evening in 1845, that the light-music composer H C Lumbye (1810-1874), who lived nearby on *Toldbodgade*, heard a champagne cork pop and was inspired to compose his famous 'Champagne Gallop'.

Established in the mid-eighteenth century, Café Petersborg was named for the old imperial capital of Russia and in honor of the fact that the Russian Consulate was then housed in the same building; the Russian Orthodox Church still stands alongside of it. It was also here that Hillary Clinton ate lunch when visiting Copenhagen as First Lady of the US a year or two before.

And on the other side of the Café is Hotel Esplanaden where Morten Gideon will soon be checking in. Kerrigan drinks his first beer of the day, noting with satisfaction that it is already well into the afternoon, and thinks about the hotel next door.

Years ago, before it was renovated and engulfed by the Comfort Inn, he had an assignation there with another man's wife. He had slyly reserved the room one afternoon before a function he knew she would be attending. She came with her husband, a lawyer Kerrigan knew from one of the ministries that funded a project he was involved in. Kerrigan had been in Copenhagen on a visit. His own wife was still alive then, but all he could think of was the lovely Catherine.

Cheat.

The function was held in magnificent apartments over *Grønningen*, cattycorner from the hotel, what they call a Patrician apartment with vast rooms, high ceilings, tall windows. Kerrigan was seated across from Catherine in the enormous dining room and could not keep his gaze from her sparkling blue eyes, her dark blond curls, the smile she so generously served him.

A trio played after coffee, and he danced with her the quickstep and foxtrot he had learned as a boy in dance school. Dancing with another man's spouse in his presence is an exercise in civilization. You come close. You smile. Your bodies touch. A meeting of the eyes, the fingers, the breasts, the lower parts, rhythmic movement together, perhaps a tiny kiss. And then you part. Civilized.

Kerrigan had not been civilized that evening.

In the dance their eyes met as his hands took concealed liberties with her body. His thumbs moved onto her breasts, lingered there, found her nipples, his eyes fixed on hers. When the dance was over he kissed her hand so innocently. Two dances later she returned to him of her own volition, and his heart was glad.

They were amongst the last on the dance floor. Her husband left early with a kiss on her cheek – he had an eight o'clock meeting next day – and Kerrigan was dazzled by the discrete indiscretion of the Danish bourgeoisie.

At the end of the evening he said loudly, 'May I find you a cab home, madame?' and she offered her arm, both aware that everyone who could see and hear was aware and enjoying the discrete spectacle they were making of themselves.

Out on *Grønningen*, in the snowy midnight air, he told her he had a room across the street at the hotel.

Her smile was speculative. 'So you knew you would have *someone* tonight.'

'I hoped only for one person. You or no one. You dazzle me.'

'You're a liar, but I like it.'

'You or no one. I'm dying for you.' Give us a touch, love.

It was true. They rode the tiny grill-doored elevator up to the third floor. The room was narrow and deep with three-meter ceilings and red plush curtains, and they made love in the narrow bed.

By 2.30 he was dressing.

'You're not leaving,' she said.

'I have an early meeting,' he told her and saw in her face she knew it was the same meeting her husband was attending.

'You *bastard*.'

'Why is it when a woman says that to a man it always sounds like a cry of admiration?'

'Don't deceive yourself.'

'I will cherish this night always,' he told her, and he did, he does.

Cheat.

Yet he wonders now at the vivid memory of that dark narrow room, the tall plush red curtain, the ceiling high above their bodies, the pale lamplight on her sweated curls – all of it gone, twenty years behind: Catherine, his youth, even the room and the hotel are so utterly changed now that they might as well be gone, too.

What was that moment? Good? Bad? Both? Neither? Nothing? All of it like a dream behind him now, the embrace of a phantom.

'*Fuck* you anyway,' says Morten Gideon loudly entering the café. 'Hey, this place is pretty nice. Let's get outta here. I don't wanna run into Hillary. I misbehaved last time I saw her. Looked down her blouse and said, Take me to Cairo with you. Show me those beauteous pyramids.'

'Plagiarizer,' says Kerrigan. 'That was Hamilton Jordan's line to the wife of the Egyptian Ambassador in Carter's White House.'

'I know,' says Gideon. 'And so did Hillary. She said, "Try at least to be a little original, won't you, Dr Gideon?" '

57

The Custom House Bodega Bar & Restaurant
(Toldbod Bodega Bar & Restaurant)

Toldbod Bodega Bar & Restaurant
Esplanaden 4
1263 København K

Down the street they order black velvets at the Toldbod Bodega, choosing a table in the second of many rooms. Named for the Customs House where the Esplanade ends in Copenhagen Harbor, near the royal landing dock, the Bodega is some 200 years old. In this building, the same H C Lumbye lived and composed many of his works, completed the 'Champagne Gallop' he started at the Pedersborg.

Kerrigan contemplates the fact that even as Lumbye began to introduce the Viennese waltz and gallops and polkas to the emergingly affluent Copenhagen middle classes, a man named Ole Kollerød, awaiting his execution for having slit the throat of a coachman named Lars Petersen, was writing the story of his life as a vagrant and petty criminal in and out of jail, entitled, *My account of the unfortunate fate that has pursued me since my 6th year and until my 38th year, the age I have reached at the moment of writing*. He reported the time of writing his story as 'the best time of my life, because I have never known any pleasure or been allowed to do anything useful since I was stupid enough to commit the first offense for which I was punished'. At the age of six. In Denmark, the death penalty was only employed for murderers at that time, unlike England where theft was a hanging offense.

Hans Christian Andersen describes as a boy witnessing the hanging of the daughter of a rich farmer who had plotted with her sweetheart and a servant to kill her father. Andersen wrote, 'At the place of execution where they stood beside their coffins, they sang a hymn with the Vicar, the girl's voice ringing out above the others.' Andersen almost fainted.

Ole Kollerød was executed by decapitation in October 1840, just over a year after the first Straussian concert, held on 10 June 1839 in the D'Angleterre Hotel on *Kongens Nytorv*, bringing Copenhagen at last up to date with Vienna, Paris, Berlin, and London, where the waltz and gallop craze already was well underway in replacing the staid music of the past.

Following the Napoleonic Wars and the Danish bankruptcy of 1813, the spirit of the Danish society was subdued, but in the late 1830s, people were getting rich again and wanted to kick up their heels. The waltz was what they needed, considered so sensuous that only the strait-laced Germans could dance it without succumbing to its erotic charms.

H C Lumbye was a key person in the new lively music which, ironically, was seen to support the existing conservative order of absolute monarchy against the constitutionalists. People subscribed to the monthly publication of Lumbye's piano sheet music, and on 15 August 1843, the Tivoli Gardens opened, heralded by the music of Lumbye's Tivoli waltzes and polkas.

The *Corsair* – in the process of making a laughing stock of Kierkegaard – also complained about Tivoli's popularity at a time of censorship and other social ills. As to 'The Champagne Gallop', the *Corsair* commented that it was only for the rich and that Lumbye ought to compose a 'Beer & Snaps Gallop' for the people.

Kerrigan sips his porter and champagne mixture with 'The Champagne Gallop' riding in his head, thinking of Kollerød slitting Petersen's throat, and in turn having his own head chopped off, even as Lumbye's cork popped and the bourgeoisie galloped gaily across the D'Angleterre dance floor, contemplating what tableaux might be painted of contemporary Denmark and contemporary Europe as popular sentiments swing further and further right and nationalist affinities approach pre-Second World War levels, all while he listens to Gideon expound upon his new love, a woman half his age 'with skin like milk'. He repeats this phrase several times. 'Like *milk* I tell ya,' and 'Whatta body on this kid, let me tellya,' then concludes, 'She's a nice kid.'

They light cigars from Gideon's pocket humidor, Cohibas Exquisitos, and Kerrigan remembers the day he sat in Gideon's office in Gamla Stan in Stockholm smoking a corona while Gideon, with a young woman on his knee, spoke into the phone to the chairman of the ethics committee of one of his organizations, reprimanding him quietly for a confessed indiscretion with one of the professional staff.

'Bob, listen,' he said. 'It is not that I give a fuck but we can't be seen to do these things. You gotta get with the times.'

Bob had, according to his account, accidentally placed his open palm on the woman's breast while attempting to help her on with her coat; according to the account of the woman in question, the palm in question had been inside the lapel of her blouse and halfway down the cup of her bra.

'Bob, don't help them on with their coats.' He puffed his cigar and kissed the secretary on her lips; she was having difficulty stifling her laughter and Gideon rested his cigar hand on her slender, stockinged thigh. 'Let 'em put on their own fucking coats and no one can accuse you of things you didn't do.' Under the circumstances, Gideon had to request Bob to deliver a written apology, which he did, following which he was sued, the written apology serving as the prima facie evidence, and the matter was settled out of court for six American figures, although Bob still had to deal with his wife after that and with his own image of who he was. There it was again: identity.

'The old pig,' laughed the young woman on Gideon's knee when the phone call was completed.

'Gimme a fuckin' kiss, you're beautiful,' said Gideon.

'You know he wants to play *doctor* with me,' she said over her shoulder to Kerrigan, her slender arms laced around Gideon's neck.

'Hey, I *am* a fuckin' doctor,' said Gideon. 'I don't fuck around *playing* doctor. You got the real thing here, baby.'

'You dog you,' said Kerrigan. 'I'm a doctor, too.'

'Yeah, a doctor of bullshit. What was that word again?'

'Verisimilitude.'

'A doctor of fucking verisimilitude.'

'And you're the doctor of love, ey? Professor of desire. Set their souls on fire.'

Gideon, a man of many parts, surprised Kerrigan by flinging some Carlos Fuentes at him: 'Hey, love is doing nothing else. Love is forgetting spouses, parents, children, friends, enemies. Love is eliminating all calculations, all perceptions, all balancing of pros and cons. That's my fuckin' motto.'

'Order! Order!' said Kerrigan.

'Love has nothing to do with order, my friend Kerrigan! Columbanus: *Amor non tenet ordinem*. Get with the program.'

Trimming his cigar on the black plastic ashtray at Toldbod, Kerrigan wonders why Gideon wants him around.

'Why so morose?' Gideon asks.

'Touch of black dog, I guess. The ancient questions. Why do people do bad things? Why do bad things happen to good people? Is there no hope for divine perfection? Does perfection exist, and can the finite human mind know and attain it?'

'Ha!' barks Gideon. 'Ha! Why do bad things happen to good people? Read fuckin' Augustine. *Nemo bonus*. There *are* no fuckin's good people. None of us is without sin, not one. So sit back and enjoy the fuckin' ride, son!'

Kerrigan's smile is wan enough to draw Gideon's scrutinizing eye. The Swede leans forward, elbow on knee, and draws contemplatively on his Cohiba. 'Seriously. What the fuck is wrong?'

Without realizing he will say it, Kerrigan tells him, 'I am dying, Egypt, dying.'

'So what? We're all dying. And my name's not Egypt. Tell it to Hamilton Jordan.'

'No, I'm really dying.'

Gideon signals for another round and says, 'Gimme the skinny, slim,' and having heard, he produces a surgical flashlight – an aluminum-cased penlight – from his inner breast pocket and, grabbing a spoon from a utensil trolly to use as a tongue depressor, says, 'Open up and say *ah*!'

'Hey, gimme a break.'

'Gimme an *ah*. Come on. Let's get this diagnosed and out of the way so we can have some fun.'

Kerrigan gags on the spoon as Gideon peers into his mouth on the beam of the slender chrome flashlight. 'It's a fuckin' cyst. Almost healed. It's nothing.' He smirks. '*Dying*. Wash your mouth out with listerine. Better yet, have a double Stoli neat. Waiter, two iced Stolis.'

'How long since you practised?'

'Hey I read the fucking literature. *New England Journal of Medicine*. *JAMA*. *The Lancet*. *Current Medical Periodicals*. When everyone else is looking at skin mags on the jake, I read the literature. It's a fuckin' cyst. Relax and quit infecting the evening with your gloom.'

'You're sure?'

'Would I lie to ya?'

'Are you *sure*?!'

'Abso-fuckin'-lutely!'

'Well what would that be from?'

'You don't get enough fuckin' vitamins probably. Change your fuckin' diet. Eat more greens!'

'Jesus, if you're right that is good news.'

'Now you're fuckin' talkin'!'

58

D'Angleterre Bar

D'Angleterre Bar
Kongens Nytorv *(King's New Square)*
1050 København 34

59

The Dining Room Restaurent & Bar

The Dining Room Restaurant & Bar
Radisson SAS Scandinavian Hotel
Amager Boulevard 70
2300 Copenhagen S

In the bar of the nearly 250-year-old D'Angleterre Hotel, the original of which was consumed in the great fire of 1795, and where young society cavaliers and ladies found themselves unable to refrain from joyously moving their bodies to the waltzes of Vienna and Lumbye while Kollerød wrote the account of the fate sealed for him from his sixth year, Gideon introduces Kerrigan to a young British woman attached to the Embassy Trade Council and orders champagne at twenty dollars a glass and fresh cigars at 25 an Exquisito, his pocket humidor having been momentarily exhausted.

'Kerrigan is an author,' says Gideon, and the woman asks polite questions about his books. 'How did you wind up here then?' she asks. 'Is your wife Danish?'

Kerrigan nibbles from the munch bowl and sips champagne, and Gideon tells him, 'Save some appetite. I've reserved a table at *Restauranten*. It doesn't get better than that.'

Remembering a meal experienced at the top of the Scandinavian Hotel on Amager Boulevard, which he is certain matches or excels whatever Gideon might have planned, Kerrigan apologizes. 'I'm so sorry I can't join you,' he says because Gideon has asked him to say this on their way down *Store Kongensgade*, Great King Street.

'What!?' exclaims Gideon. 'You *got* to! I reserved for three. It's the best food in Copenhagen.'

'I'm really, truly sorry,' says Kerrigan, 'but I really can't. In fact . . .' He checks his watch. 'I'm late already.'

'Some goddamned friend,' says Gideon. 'I come all the way to Copenhagen to introduce you two and you run right off!'

Kerrigan can see from the British woman's cleavage that his departure will create no problems. He takes her hand. 'I really do apologize and hope that we will meet again.' And, as once advised by a Dutch lawyer is the polite thing to do, kisses not her hand but his own thumb upon her hand. It tastes like stale cigar.

Gideon follows him to the door where he furnishes him with another Cohiba. 'You got fuckin' talent,' he says. 'You deserve an Oscar, an Emmy, a Tony, and a Golden Palm.'

'I feel dirty,' says Kerrigan.

'Yeah but that's when it's best.'

Outside on *Kongens Nytorv*, Kerrigan looks across at the kiosk he wanted to buy and further across the square to the New Harbor with its long line of serving houses which he has not yet researched in depth. He cannot publish a book on Danish serving houses without the New Harbor where he has passed many an agreeable afternoon and evening and deep night with friends like Duff Brenna, Greg Herriges, Mike Lee, Paul Casey, Dennis Bormann, Gordon Weaver, David Poe, Jay Fisher, Pat Mulvihill, Jeff Freiert, Chad Stockton, Jim Durgin, Liam Jennings, roaring with pleasure and golden beer. He thinks of the Drop Inn with its portraits of Kafka and Dan Turrell where it is said that the poet Jørgen Gustava Brandt once threw a bottle of beer at the literary critic of one of the tabloids; Kongens Bar where Kerrigan once drank hot shots with two secretaries from a ministry who were wonderful to kiss; *Skindbuksen*, named for the leather overalls of the chauffeurs that used to frequent it, where his favorite Danish poet Schade composed songs to his sexy muses. He thinks of Sankt Hans Torv on the northside and all its cafés – Sebastopol, Værestedet, Pussy Galore, Café Funk, Trafik Café, Café Rust, Mexi Bar, of Café Rex and Pilegården, all the serving houses of the Grey Friar's Square, Frederiksberg, Vesterbro's famous *Barbar Bar*, Barbarian Bar, named for a bar in one of the most humorous Danish TV shows of all time – the *Sonny Soufflé Show* by the same two comedians who made the Søren *Kierkegaard Road Show* and the *Russian Pizza Blues*. There were still all the yet to research bars of the City center, Amager, Vesterbro. Husmann's Vinstue where Simon Spies shed his clothes with a bevy of whores and let the tabloids photograph the scene . . .

It is impossible. He can't go on. He goes on.

He wonders whether Gideon's diagnosis is correct or whether he was just trying to cheer him up for the role he was to play in his erotic comedy of the moment. *Nemo bonus.*

Cheat.

On the street outside the hotel, two bald, thick-set young men pass wearing *Blood & Honour* tee-shirts, sleeves sawed off at their hard shoulders. A third, wearing a shirt that says *Hang Nelson Mandella*, a smoldering cigarette dangling from his lip, eyes squinted against the smoke, sees Kerrigan looking and leers into his face. For an instant their noses are only a couple of inches apart. Kerrigan's heart lurches. The muzak from the D'Angleterre lobby plays a Strauss number, and the leering boy moves on, glancing back over his shoulder. Kerrigan looks away, then back in time to see the young man grind his cigarette out on the trunk of a young willow. Kerrigan moves to the tree, lays his fingers on the tender young bark. With his clean white handkerchief he brushes the ash away, touches the shallow burn-wound as though his fingers might help, as though the bark might feel, the slender branches above his head might see and take succor.

A uniformed doorman steps up and salutes. 'Taxi, sir?'

Kerrigan palms the man a twenty-crown coin and heads for the apartment on Strand Boulevard. He knows he should have phoned first but reasons it will be harder for her to turn him away at the door.

The street door buzzer rings without hesitation, and he wonders as he crosses the lobby what she will look like, whether she will be as lovely as he remembers. Barefoot. Fingers and smock spattered with oils.

She is already at the door as he turns down the hall.

'Are you drunk?' she asks.

'A little. Should I go?'

She opens the door wider. 'I've always had a soft spot for a man who drinks. You know what Caitlin Thomas said about that?'

'No. What?'

'"There is a brotherliness about a drinking person which is coldly lacking in the straight and narrow enemies of drink. The mere thought of going near a man who is not mellowly pickled, and whose breath reeks of his native fleshly self, is squeamishly impalatable to me." '

'Now *you're* memorizing too, ey?'

'I'm a quick study.'

Nonetheless she doesn't sit beside him on the sofa. She takes the chair instead. He regrets to see she has two noses and is about to develop a double row of eyes and eyebrows. This will never do. And he is trying desperately to overcome his amazement that she could quote Dylan Thomas's wife at such length. He knows the book she quoted from, *A Leftover Life to Kill*. It was not a beautiful book.

'To tell you the truth,' he says, 'I see no romance in Dylan Thomas's knocking back 30 shots in a row. It is not a beautiful act, and I don't believe there could be any real pleasure in it.'

She watches him, smiling, and he can see the meaning of her smile – it is meant as a mirror to show him himself.

'I know,' he says, 'but I am not an alcoholic.'

'Denial is the first sign.'

'Yeah. On the road to twelve step city. I'm not on that road. I would never drink 30 shots in a row. I drink to be happy. I drink to bring my unconscious up into the light of consciousness. The kind of drinking that Thomas wound up doing is just to obliterate consciousness altogether. Thomas killed himself with drink. Believe it or not I'm keeping myself alive with it.'

'I think you drink to strengthen the walls around you. Your grief is your castle. Take the walls down, Mr Kerrigan, let some air in.'

'What do you know about my grief?' he asks more harshly than he meant to. He feels lost, frightened by the closeness of her approach. The liberty she has taken to judge his behavior, an act of interest bordering perhaps on love and all the hated museum of love's presumptions.

'I'm sorry,' he says. 'But I have to say I don't love you.'

'I know. I don't love you either.'

'I mean I do *like* you.'

'I know,' she says. 'I don't like you either.'

The silence extends, dangerously close to the point of an estrangement that terrifies him. 'How have you been?' he asks.

'It's all been *røv og gulvsand.*'

'How's that?'

'Ass and floor sand. An idiom. I guess it means a bunch of crap.'

The words hearten and frighten him. 'Have you read Proust?' he asks.

'Is that why? Because I have not read Proust? Because I am not an academic? Not intellectual? Not *good* enough for you?'

'No. I'm talking about love. What Proust said about love. The impossibility which love comes up against. "We imagine that it has as its object a being that can be laid down in front of us, enclosed within a body . . ." But it is the extension of that being to all the points in space and time that it has occupied and will occupy. "If we do not possess its contact with this or that place, this or that hour, we do not possess that being. But we cannot touch all these points. If only they were indicated to us, we might perhaps contrive to reach out to them. But we grope for them without finding them." '

She says, 'You have a remarkable power of memory. Even when you are playing the Prince of Cups. Do you ever just live in the moment where you find yourself? Someone once said, *A writer? A writer is someone who watches himself live.* Maybe there is something wrong with you. Something that happened to you. Something that somebody did to you, or didn't do to you. Maybe you can't love anybody but yourself.'

'And maybe there is nothing wrong with me,' he says. 'Have you considered that? Maybe love is an illusion. Or impossible. Or simply non-existent. Look,' he says and wipes his mouth. 'Can I have a drink?' And watches her move to the book shelf that serves as her bar. He likes what he sees, especially her rump which he would follow gladly, wrong or right, guiding or misguiding, but he is reluctant to associate grandiose words or concepts with the beguiling powers of a backside. He remembers then his little quatrain about her backside: *My mind then squandered on a rump?/By those hips parenthesized?/Up from the chair two comely lumps/Over her shoulder her fetch-me smile.* He is about to recite it, but stops himself.

There is more to this, but they have both occupied too many distant points in space and time. He feels he knows so much about her, but how can she ever know him? How can she ever join him in that moment of obliteration: *Terry! Oh, Ter-ry!* He thinks about all the things she has told him and wonders how he will ever tell her what has happened to him. His fear and love. Kali. Sheela. The syphilitic men and women who shared their disease with one another. Life itself a venereal disease. The little death. The long goodbye. How can he begin?

I won't, he thinks. Nothing good could come of it.

With a deep Stoli on three ice cubes, he tells her, 'I have heard Americans apologize to the Indians and the Vietnamese, and the Germans apologize to the Jews. I have even heard Japan apologize to China, but I have never heard the Brits apologize to Ireland or to any of the other lands they savaged. If a Brit bumps into you on the street he'll gush. *I DO beg your pardon!* But if he occupies your country for five centuries, rapes your fields and your women and your language, he'll laugh in your face and call you Paddy. I even once heard a Brit chuckle about what Nelson did to Copenhagen.

"That was just a warning," he said. "So watch out!" Can you imagine that?'

She says, 'I saw on television a British official apologize to the South Africans once.'

'Right. I saw that, too. They apologized to the Boers for putting them in concentration camps. That was where concentration camps were invented. On the other hand, I suppose Denmark never apologized to Ireland either for what the Vikings did there, all the plunder and rape and the murder of Brian Boru with a knife in the back while he was praying. Of course the Danes also founded Dublin, but that's how the British excuse themselves too – saying if it wasn't for them there'd be no trains and hospitals and whatsoelse in South Africa and India and you name it. I don't know.' He realizes he is babbling, desperate for a subject.

'I was bombed by the British,' she says. 'On 21 March 1945. It was an accident. They were aiming at the building the Germans had taken over as their police headquarters but they hit the French school instead – the Jeanne d'Arc School – where I was in kindergarten. I was buried in the rubble for a whole day, speaking to the other children buried with me until I realized they were not answering me. They couldn't, you see. For they were all dead. I didn't speak again for nearly three months afterwards. Not a word. I was five.'

'I'm sorry. Really sorry.'

'It was an accident. The British bombers were doing their best. They liberated us. Montgomery was our hero. And all his men who risked their lives and gave their lives for Europe. English and Scots and Welsh and Irish, too. And of course the Americans.'

Kerrigan is ashamed of himself. 'I'm sorry,' he says.

She is drinking a glass of white wine. 'Why in the world are we talking about this?'

He shakes his head, realizing that it was a subconscious ploy on his part to get away from the subject of love, to warm with a blanket of anger the cold deadness his mother left inside him.

'What do you want?' she asks then with disturbing finality. 'Why did you come here?'

'I need you. To help me. Finish this book.' He sips his Stoli.'Will you?'

She nods. 'But not without a contract.'

'Look,' he says. 'By my calculation there are a total of 1,535 serving houses in Copenhagen. I have that figure from a report of Copenhagen County's Health Committee. They recently issued a plan to reduce alcohol consumption by 5 percent by closing 77 serving houses. The public laughed in their communal faces so they dropped the plan. There are still 1,535 serving houses, and that means if I am to complete my study, I have some 1,480 places left to research.'

'And new ones opening every day.'

'And older ones closing every other. No telling how long this will take,' he says. 'I cannot do it alone. Will you help me?'

'And what will you give to me?'

'What I will give you? I will give you a banquet, a feast the likes of which you have never known and which you will never forget while there is still an appetite in your blood.'

'Tell me more.'

'We will start with a flute of Peiper Heidsick and a preliminary appetizer of curry vanilla crème ice over scraps of *Østersø* salmon in estragon oil, followed by a tiny cup of the juice of melons and oranges spiced with ginger. Then a spoonful of avocado with anchovies, peppercorn, gelé and a mint leaf; another with the prime end of an octopus leg in chopped chives and shredded raddish with balsamico.

Only then does the meal itself begin. We'll start with a small, perfect, hollowed-out Southern Italian tomato stuffed with snails, a knuckle of marrow on the side, all resting on a sheen of balsamico and dusted over with the thinnest chips of roasted garlic and chili with a delicate roll of salted durum bread on the side.

With that course we shall drink a single glass of North Italian – *not* Alsatian – Gewürztraminer, Alvis Lageder, Alto Adige, 2000. Then, to clear the palate a tiny in-between of coconut sorbet sprinkled with pistacio nuts and bathed in pistacio oil, topped with fresh-plucked sorrel leaves.

Now we are ready for the main course – a long, slender slice of roasted duck breast, the skin crisply perfect, on a sauce of spiced licorice, alongside to the left a single, choice stalk of Romaine lettuce with estragon, beneath an apricot topped with a sprinkle of cold couscous and half a dozen tiny tender carrot slices; to the right, in a small bowl, a delicate carrot mousse topped with cold couscous atop a nest of roast duck scrapings, that which is otherwise lost, gathered for the delicacy it is. With the duck, a glass of '98 Chateau Simone Palette Provence. You would never drink this wine without such a plate and before we drink we will dip our long noses into the large bell of the glass to inhale the bouquet of French Provencal earth and grape, an aroma of deep earth. Nothing sweet here or mild. This is the heady smell of the earth that nourishes from its corruptions, the earth that is a woman's cunt.

And then, after a pause for two puffs of a cigarillo – or, in your case, a Prince extra ultralight, the cheese: a double wedge of Puligny Saint Pierre goat cheese over preserved dates – not candied mind you, but preserved, cooked a bit and tasting of date meat not sugar, with beetroot leaves, red-veined and agreeably bitter, leaving driblets of red juice on the cheese.

For the goat, a Bourgogne, a 2000 Mercurey *premièr cru* Les Puillets, Albert Sounit. Again the bouquet of earth tramped by goat's hooves.

Now we have a bit of the Mercurey remaining in our glasses and will get the last taste of the goat dancing from our tongues with three pre-dessert morsels: a spoonful of almond in cherry; a spoon of liquid bitter chocolate containing a morsel of kiwi and topped with shreds of leaf celerey; an eggcup of elder flower sorbet with rhubarb and a cube of homemade marshmallow dusted with sage crumbs.

And then we are ready for the noble rot – a glass of 2000 Latinia Nasco Vendeminia Tardiva, Agr. Santadi from Sardinia. This has the color of a perfect chunk of polished amber, tastes of raisin and apricot without being sweet and at 15 per cent alcohol content is at the border of being a fortified wine. What has been done to the grapes of this wine is the work of people who preserve the very concept of European civilization. The grapes are chilled to just below freezing so the water freezes but not the grape, and the mould that grows on it is the rot which gives the noble taste. With it we will eat a sweet almond meringue with raw vanilla crème, redwine syrup and fresh minced strawberries.'

'Please! No more!' she says though her eyes are bright.

'There is more – a double expresso with a tiny cup of white-chocolate mousse and a paper-thin biscuit of nut chocolate.'

'Have you taken to memorizing menus now, too?'

'As I told you, this is a meal you will be unable to forget.'

'And what then?'

'Then I will take you home to our bed and fuck you with all the love I have in me – I don't know how much love that is, but what is there is for you.' Now he has said it and his eyes are wide watching for her reply.

But what she says is, 'Not after such a heavy meal, please!'

'It is *not* heavy. It is peristaltically of perfect balance. Your bowells will wonder why you have suddenly decided to treat them with such kindness. You won't even feel moved to break the palest wind.'

She is amused as, he thinks, most women are regarding the functions of the body. 'And where would we partake of such a meal?'

'In the Dining Room.'

'*What* Dining Room?'

'*The* Dining Room, the one where Rasmus Grønbech plies his arts, 25 floors up above this city. In the Hotel Scandinavia, the heart of the city at your feet like a scale model. You'll see it all – the green copper towers and pastel stucco walls, cars and buses gliding through the streets, cyclists and joggers on the canal banks, international ferries and cruise ships steaming from the harbor into the open waters of *Øresund*. You'll see it all, and if you want you can reach down and pinch up a cathedral between your thumb and finger, lift a Mercedes from the boulevard below and peek into the windshield at the surprised little faces of the tiny people hurrying to find what they cannot find because they are going the wrong way. All this will I give to you.'

'Are you satan in the wilderness?'

'Are you the Holy Saviour?'

'I'm just a girl.'

'You're divine.'

She looks into his eyes. 'I still want a commitment.'

He reaches to his breast pocket, lifts out Gideon's Cohiba, unwraps the cellophane. 'Do you like music?' he asks. And hands her the paper ring from the cigar. 'Here's a whole band for you.'

She smirks but slips the paper ring over the pointed red nail and first knuckle of her slender little finger and stretches her hand out as if to admire a diamond.

'Maybe we should, like, plant a tree here or something,' he says and can barely hear his own voice.

'We could do that, Terrence.'

'Who knows what sorrow might await us?' he says.

'*Den tid, den sorg*,' she replies. 'Old Danish proverb: That time, that sorrow.'

He raises his Stoli to her, recites:

> ' "Wine comes in at the mouth
> Love comes in at the eye
> That's all we shall know for truth
> Until we grow old and die."

Old Irish bullshit. From Mr Yeats.'

'Why,' she asks then, 'Are you sitting all the way over there, Mr Kerrigan? All by yourself.'

He rises, crosses to her CD rack, hoping, finds just what he wants and puts it on. As the first lilting notes of 'Little Woman of the Danube' drift across her century-and-a-half old rooms, he bows beneath the three-meter ceiling, extends his arm. She accepts it, smiling, and his hand takes her slender waist as they dance, turning, across the broad plank floor, and the world spins dizzily with them.

BIBLIOGRAPHY

Acroyd, Peter, Dickens. New York: Harper Collins, 1990.

Agrelin, Ove (Ed.), Med en Gammeldansk i köket. Malmø: GammeldanskensVänners Forlag, 1998

Andersen, Benny, Cosmopolitan in Denmark & Other Poems About the Danes (tr. Cynthia La Touche Andersen). Copenhagen: Borgen, 1995

Andersen, Hans Christian, Forty-Two Stories (tr. M. R. James). London:Faber & Faber, 1930, 1968.

Arbaugh, George E. and George B., Kierkegaard's Authorship. London: George Allen & Unwin Ltd., 1968

Balslev-Clausen, Peter, Songs from Denmark. Copenhagen: The Danish Cultural Institute,1988

Berg, A. Scott, Max Perkins: Editor of Genius. New York: Washington Square Press, 1978

Bertmann, Annegrett (Ed.), No Man's Land, An Anthology of Modern Danish Women's Literature. Norwich: Norvik Press, 1987

Billeskov Jansen, F. J. and Mitchell, P. M., Anthology of Danish Literature, Vol I and II, Bilingual Edition. Carbondale, Il.: Southern Illinois University Press, 1972

Bjørnvig, Thorkild, The Pact: My Friendship with Isak Dinesen (tr. Ingvar Schousboe and William Jay Smith). Baton Rouge, La.: Louisiana State University Press, 1983; Souvenir Press, 1984

Bjørnvig, Thorkild, Three Poems (tr. Thomas E. Kennedy), in The Literary Review (Fairleigh Dickinson University), Vol. 39, No. 4, Summer 1996

Brandes, Georg, Tanker ved århundredskiftet / Thoughts on the Turn of the Century Introduction Jens Christian Grøndahl (tr. Martin A. David. Bilingual Edition. Forlaget Geelmuyden, Kiese, SAS

Borum, Poul, Danish Literature: A Short Critical Survey. Copenhagen: Det Danske Selskab, 1979

Borup, Morten (Ed.), Georg Brandes og Emil Petersen, En brevveksling. Copenhagen: Lademanns Forlag, 1980

Bosley, Keith. Skating on the Sea: Poetry from Finland. Newscastle & Helsinki: Bloodaxe, 1997.

Brandes, Georg, Kamma Rahbek, Bakkehusmuseet, 1990

Bretall, Robert, A Kierkegaard Anthology. New York: The Modern Library,1946

Britt, Stann, Dexter Gordon, A Musical Biography. New York: Da Capo Press,1989

Brown, George Mackay, "The Whaler's Return," in Winter's Tales 14 (ed. Kevin Crossley-Holland). New York: St. Martin's, London: Macmillan, 1968.

Cahill, Thomas. How the Irish Saved Civilization. New York: Doubleday, Nan Talese, 1995.

Calvino, Italo, Six Memos for the Next Millennium (tr. Patrick Creagh),Vintage, 1996

Cannon, Moya, 'Milk,' in The Literary Review, Small Gifts of Knowing: New Irish Prose and Poetry, Vol 40, No 4 (ed. Thomas E Kennedy), Madison, N J: Fairleigh Dickinson University, 1997

Carr, Ian et al, Jazz, The Rough Guide: The Essential Companion to Artists and Albums. London: The Rough Guides, 1995

Cavafy, C. P., Collected Poems, Revised Edition (tr. Edmund Keeley and Philip Sherrard), Ed George Savidis. Princeton, N.J.: Princeton University Press, 1992

Christensen, Peter Thorning (Ed.), The Fortifications of Copenhagen: A Guide to 900 Years of Fortification History (tr. Donald Bryant). Copenhagen: The National Forest & Nature Agency, The Ministry of the Environment & Energy, 1998

Coover, Robert, "Beginnings," in The Literary Review: Stories & Sources (ed. Thomas E Kennedy), Vol 42, No 1. Madison, N J: Fairleigh Dickinson University, 1998.

Copenhagen Jazz Festival, Program, 2-11 July 1999. Copenhagen: The Copenhagen Jazz Festival, 1999

Copenhagen This Week (April, May, June, July 1999). Copenhagen: Politikens Serviceselskab, 1999

Corbett, William, New York Literary Lights, Graywolf Press, 1998.

Costello, Peter, The Dublin Literary Pub Crawl. Dublin: A & A Farmer,1996

Daiches, David (Ed), The Penguin Companion to Literature, Britain and the Commonwealth. London: Penguin, 1971

Dal, Erik (Ed), Danish Ballads and Folk Songs (Tr Henry Meyer), Copenhagen: Rosenkilde & Bagger 1967

Dante Alghieri, The Divine Comedy (tr. Charles Eliot Norton), Great Books of the Western World, Encyclopaedia Britannica, 1952

Deane, Seamus, Introduction to James Joyce's Finnegans Wake, Penguin, 1991

Donleavy, J. P., The History of the Ginger Man, An Autobiography, Penguin,1995

Donovan, Tom, The Blue Planet and D. Band Live, Marsk Music,Farupkirkevej 27, 6760 Ribe, Denmark

Dungannon Charles E. (The Duke of St. Kilda), "Danish Brew" (tr. Thomas E. Kennedy), previously unpublished

Eliot, T S, Collected Poems, 1909-1962. faber and faber, 1963

Ensig, Kirsten, Turen Går til København. Politikens Forlag, 3.udgave, 1996

Erichsen, John, Et Andet København, Sociale Fotografier fra Århundredskiftet, København: Gyldendal, 1978

Fargnoli, A. Nicholas and Gillespie, Michael Patrick, James Joyce A to Z, London: Bloomsbury, 1995.

Ferlinghetti, Lawrence, A Coney Island of the Mind. San Francisco: City Lights Books,1958

Friar, Kimon (Ed & tr), Modern Greek Poetry. Athens: Efstathiadis Group,1982

Gilgamesh, The Epic of (Intro. N. K. Sandars), Penguin, 1977.

Ginsberg, Allen, Howl and Other Poems. San Francisco: City Lights Books, 1956

Goethe, Johann Wolfgang von, The Sorrows of Young Werther (tr. Elizabeth Mayer, Louise Bogan and W. H. Auden). New York: Vintage, 1990

Grant, Ulysses S., Memoirs & Selected Letters. The Library of America,1990.

Guldbrandsen, Alice Maud. Fra Adel til Lægestand. Copenhagen: Lægeforeningens Forlag, 1994.

Hansen, Ib Fischer et al (Eds), Litteratur Håndbogen, Vol 1 & 2, København: Gyldendal,1998

Hansen, Jesper Vang, Rundetårn, Rundetårns Forlag København (undated). ISBN 87-88714-10-1

Harsløf, Olav and Røssell, Anne, Kartoffelrækkerne. Copenhagen: Husejerforeningen ved Øster Farimagsgade, 1986

Hassø, Arthur G. (Ed.), Ti Dage i København og Nordsjælland i Frederik VI's Tid af en Ung Dames Rejsedagbog 1821. København: Høst & Sons 1940

Hendriksen, F., Kjøbenhavnske Billeder fra det Nittende Aarhundrede. København: Foreningen Fremtiden, 1927

Höm, Jesper, The Faces of Copenhagen, 1896-1996. Copenhagen: Forlaget Per Kofod, 1996

Hotellet fra Pjaltenborg til Palads. Københavns Bymuseum, 1999 (undated, no author)

Housman, A. E., A Shropshire Lad. New York: Illustrated Editions Co.,1932

Hugus, Frank, "The Ironic Inevitability of Death — Hans Christian Andersen's Lykke-Peer," in Hans Christian Andersen: A Poet in Time. Odense University Press, 1999

————, "Opera as Allegory in Hans Christian Andersen's Improvisatoren and Lykke-Peer," EDDA-Hefte 1. 1999

Ibsen, Henrik, When We Dead Awaken (tr James Walter McFarlane), Scandinavian Words 6. SAS/Forlaget Geelmuyden. Kiese. 1998

Igoe, Vivien, A Literary Guide to Dublin. London: Methuen, 1994

Jacobsen, Jens Peter, Mogens & Other Stories (tr Tiina Nunnally). Seattle: Fjord Press, 1994

Johansen, R. Broby, Gennem Det Gamle København. Copenhagen: Gyldendal, 1948

Joyce, James, A Portrait of the Artist as a Young Man (Intro. Anthony Burgess). London: Secker & Warburg, 1994

————, Finnegans Wake (Intro, Seamus Deane), Penguin, 1992

————, Ulysses (Intro Declan Kiberd), Penguin, 1992.

Kambor, Richard, On Camus. Wadsworth Philosophical Series. Belmont, California, 2002

Kartoflen, 6.årgang, nrr 4, 5, 6, 1999

Kaul, Flemming, Europas dysser og jættestuer. København:Lægeforeningens forlag, 1998

Kavanagh, Patrick, Collected Poems. New York, London: W. W. Norton,1964, 1973

Kennedy, Thomas E. and Hugus, Frank, New Danish Fiction, anthology issue of The Review of Contemporary Fiction. Normal, Il.: Dalkey Archives Press, 1995

—————, "The Secret Life of Kierkegaard's Lover," in The Literary Review (Fairleigh Dickinson University), Summer 2002

Kennedy, Thomas E., Contemporary Danish Poetry & Prose in Translation, in Cimarron Review (Oklahoma State University, Stillwater), No. 92, July 1990

—————, "A Mixed Gathering of Danish Women," in Translation Review (University of Texas, Dalles), Nos. 36 & 37, 1991, pp 52-3

—————, "The Exporting of Pia Tafdrup," Tordenskjold (publication of the Danish Literary Information Agency), 1989

—————, "An Interview with Pia Tafdrup" (in Danish), Weekend Avisen Bøger 27 Feb 1992

————— (Ed.), "Contemporary Nordic Writing" in Frank: An International Journal of Contemporary Writing & Art. Paris: No 6/7,Winter/Spring 1987, p. 63-116

Kiberd, Declan, Inventing Ireland. London: Jonathan Cape, 1995

Kierkegaard, Søren, Enten Eller (Either Or), Bind 1 & 2. København. Gyldendal, 1843, 1996

Kinsella, Thomas (Tr), The Tain (from the Irish Epic Táin Bó Cuailnge), Oxford University Press, 1969

Kirkenin, Heikki and Sihvo, Hannes, The Kalevala: An Epic of Finland (tr. M. Lauanne and A Bell). Helsinki: Finnish-American Cultural Institute, 1984

Kjærgaard, Thorkild, "Hovedpine og Gemenheder," a review of Pernille Arenfeldt and Pernille Frederikke Hasselsteen, Din hengivne Louise – Louise Rasmussens breve til Carl Berling og kronprins/Kong Frederik VII, 1844-1850. Københaven: Fremad, 1999, review in Weekendavisen Bøger, Nr. 29, 23-29 juli 1999, s. 1

Kristensen, Tom, Glimtvis Åbner Sig Nuet (poems). København: Glydendal, 1994

————, Hærværk (Havoc), Gyldendals Tranebøger, 1930 (reprint)

Lange, Bente, The Colours of Copenhagen. The Royal Danish Academy of Fine Arts School of Architecture Publishers, 1997

Larrington, Carolyne (tr), The Poetic Edda. New York: Oxford University Press, 1996

Lauring, Palle, A History of Denmark (tr David Hohnen). Copenhagen: Høst & Søn, 1973, 4th edition

Ljungkvist, Carsten and Meinke, Herbert, Jazzanekdotter. Århus: Forlaget Ildhuset, 1997.

Lönnrot, Elias, The Kalevala (tr Keith Bosley), Oxford University Press,1999.

Lucretius, On the Nature of Things (tr. H. A. J. Munro), Great Books of the Western World, Vol. 12, Encyclopædia Britannica, Inc. 1952.

Lundgreen-Nielsen, Flemming (Ed), København læst og påskrevet: Hovedstaden som litterær kulturby. Københavns Universitet: Museum Tusculanums,1997

Madsen, Hans Helge, Østerbros Herligheder — en bydels identitet. Københaven: Nationalmuseet,1986

Maggin, Donald L., Stan Getz, A Life in Jazz. New York: Quill/William Morrow, 1996

Mosey, Chris, "French Tipple," Scanorama magazine, Dec 96/Jan 97

Museumsbygningen Kunstauktioner Catalogue 9, 1999

Neruda, Pablo, Selected Poems (Ed N Tarn, tr A Kerrigan, W S Merwin, A reid,N Tarn), Penguin, 1982.

Nørregård-Nielsen, Hans Edvard, Kongens København, En guldaldermosaik., København: Gyldendal, 1994

Nygaard, Georg, H. C. Andersen & København. København: "Fremtiden",1938

Olsen, Jørgen Steen and Berning, Hugo, Tidens Pil gennem fem generationer. København: Forlaget Consensus, 1989

Olsen, Lance, Burnt. La Grande, Oregon: Wordcraft of Oregon, 1996.

Pedersen, Knud, Churchill-klubben. København: Borgen, 1991

————, Breve fra Fængslet, Churchill-klubben anden del. Københaven: Stig Vendelkærs Forlag, 1964

————Churchill-klubben, 3.del: Sidste krigsår. København: Samleren, 1977

————, Unoder Fra Churchill-klubben til Kunstbiglioteket. København: Børgen,1995

Petersen, Robert Storm, Storm P. Udvalgte Historier. Børgen: København, 1993

Preseren, Francé, Poems/Pesmi (tr Tom M S Priestley and Henry R Cooper Jr), Ljubljana Vienna: Hermagoras-Verlag, 1999.

Proust, Marcel. Rembrance of Things Past (tr C K Scott-Moncrieff and Terence Kilmartin), NY: Knopf, 1982

Raabyemagle, Hanne and Smidt, Claus M (Eds), Classicism in Denmark. Copenhagen: Gyldendal, 1998

Rasmussen, Peter Bak and Munk, Jens Peter, Skulpturer i København. København: Børgen, 1999

Rayfiel, Selma, Unpublished letter to Thomas E. Kennedy, September 24, 1998

Regine Olsens dagbog, udgivet af Erik Søndergaard Hansen med eferskrift ved Johns. Nørregaard Frandsen. Højbjerg, Denmark: Hovedland, 2001

Rimbaud, Arthur, Poems (selected by Peter Washington, tr Paul Scmidt). Everyman's Library. London: David Campbell Publishers, 1994

Rumi, The Essential Rumi (tr Coleman Barks with John Moyne). San Francisco: Harper, 1995

Scavenius, Bente, The Golden Age Revisited, Art & Culture in Denmark, 1800- 50. Copenhagen: Gyldendal, 1996 (tr .B Haveland and J Windskar-Nielsen)

Schade, Jens August, Schades Digte. København: Gyldendal, 1999 (The poems quoted here were translated by Thomas E Kennedy with the kind permission of Gydendal.)

Scherfig, Hans, Stolen Spring (tr. Frank Hugus). Seattle: Fjord Press, 1986

Schmidt, Lars, "Forslag: Færgefart på Søerne – igen," Østerbro Avis, Onsdag den 7.juni 2000, side 4

Seedorf, Hans Hærtvig (Ed), Bakkehusets Billedbog, Bakkehusmuseet, København, 1979

Seibles, Tim, "Bonobo," in Poems & Sources: The Literary Review (Fairleigh Dickinson University, New Jersey), Vol 44, No 1, Fall 2000, p. 71-2

Senstad, Susan Schwartz, Music for the Third Ear. London: Doubleday/Anchor; New York: Picador, 2000

Smidt, Claus M. and Winge, Mette, Strolls in the Golden Age City of Copenhagen (tr .W. Glyn Jones). Copenhagen: Gyldendal, 1996

Spink, Reginald, Hans Christian Andersen and His World. London: Thames & Hudson, 1972

Stangerup, Henrik, The Seducer: It is Hard to Die in Dieppe (tr. Sean Martin). London: Marion Boyers, 1990

Stephens, James, Songs from the Clay. New York: Macmillan, 1925

Storm P., 700 Danske Ordsprog. Sesam,1997

Strømstad, Kirsten and Poul, Rundt om søerne. København: Christian Ejlers Forlag, 1996

Strømstad, Poul, Residentsstaden Kjøbenhavn, Gader, Torve og Pladser Indenfor Voldene. Skandbergs Forlag, 1991

Tafdrup, Pia, Four Poems (tr. Thomas E. Kennedy, Monique Kennedy, Anne Born) in Colorado Review, New Series, Vol XV, No. 2, Fall/Winter 1988

————, Tusindfødt. København:Gyldendal, 1999

————, Hvid Feber. København: Bøgens, 1986

————, Dronningeporten. København: Gyldenal, 1998

Theisen, Torben, Billeder fra det nu forsvundne Østerbro. Lyngby, Denmark: Dansk Historisk Håndbogsforlag, 1984

Thomas, Caitlin, Left Over Life to Kill. Boston: Atlantic/Little Brown & Co.,1957

Thomas, Dylan, "One Warm Saturday" in Portrait of the Artist as a Young Dog. New York: New Directions, 1955

————, "A Visit to Grandpa's" in Quite Early One Morning. New York: New Directions,1955

Thomsen, Allan Mylius, De Ydmyge Steder (The Humble Establishments). Copenhagen: Dansk Hotel-Portier Forening with Copenhagen this Week, 1997

————, Sangerinden Uvæsenet: En nostalgisk odyssé gennem Københavns berygted sangerindeknejper i tiden 1820-1920. Forlaget Parlando 1996

Thorlby, Anthony (Ed),The Penguin Companion to Literature, Europe. London: Penguin, 1969, 1971

Thurman, Judith, Isak Dinesen, The Life of a Storyteller. New York: St. Martin's,1982

Tønnesen, Allan, Bakkehusets Historie, Frederiksberg gennem Tiderne XVII,1995

Travers, Martin, An Introduction to Modern European Literature from Romanticism to Postmodernism. New York: St. Martin's, 1998

Treo, Thomas, "Manden med Medicinen" (on John Lee Hooker), in Ekstra Bladet, lørdag, 29.maj 1999, s. 30-1

Turrell, Dan, and Halfdan E, "Gennem Byen Sidste Gang" in Pas På Pengene! Copenhagen: Mega Records (MRCD 3220) (undated)

Valore, Peter Braams, Sophie Ørsted og Digterne, Bakkehusmuseet, København, 1991

————, Hundeposten, Adam Oehlenschlägers breve til Kamma Rahbek. Bakkehusmuseet, København, 1999

Van Gogh, Vincent, The Letters of Vincent Van Gogh, selected and edited by Ronald de Leeuw (tr. Arnold Pomerans). London:Penguin,1996

Verlaine, Paul, Selected Poems (tr. Martin Sorrell). Oxford World Classics, Oxford University Press (undated)

Vesterberg, Henrik, "Spies Baglæns," Politiken,2.sektion, s. 6, Sønda g d.1.august 99

Vinding, Ole, "James Joyce in Copenhagen"
(tr Helge Irgens-Moller)

Vinther, Palle et al, Revue Verdenslitteraturen 1989, Århus, 1989

Voltaire, Candide and Other Stories,
London: Everyman's Library, 1990.

Wamburg, Bodil (Ed), Out of Denmark. Copenhagen:
Danish Cultural Institute,1985

Weaver, Gordon, 'Whiskey Whiskey, Gin Gin Gin," in Quarterly
West, No 17, Fall/Winter 1983-4. Salt Lake City, Utah:
University of Utah.

Wilson, Jason, "Absinthe-Minded Traveler," in Hemipsheres,
Feb 2000, p.114, 116

Yeats, W. B., The Collected Poems. New York: Macmillan, 1968